# SOUTHERN THUNDER

RONALD E. MORGAN

Triangle Books

*I would certainly like to thank my wife, Mary Ann, and my daughter Kathleen for their help and patience in the creation of this book.*

*Southern Thunder is dedicated to my ever-patient mother, Elizabeth Johnson-Morgan-Cole, whose family walked behind a covered wagon, leaving Indiana behind, bound for Missouri and the hope of greener pastures.*

*Mom is no longer with us but I am sure she is looking down from above, glad that I am keeping busy.*

Triangle Books are published by
Research Triangle Publishing, Inc.
PO Box 1223
Fuquay-Varina, NC 27526



Library of Congress Catalog Card Number: 95-72490

ISBN 1-884570-42-9

Printed in the United States of America
10 9 8 7 6 5 4 3 2 1

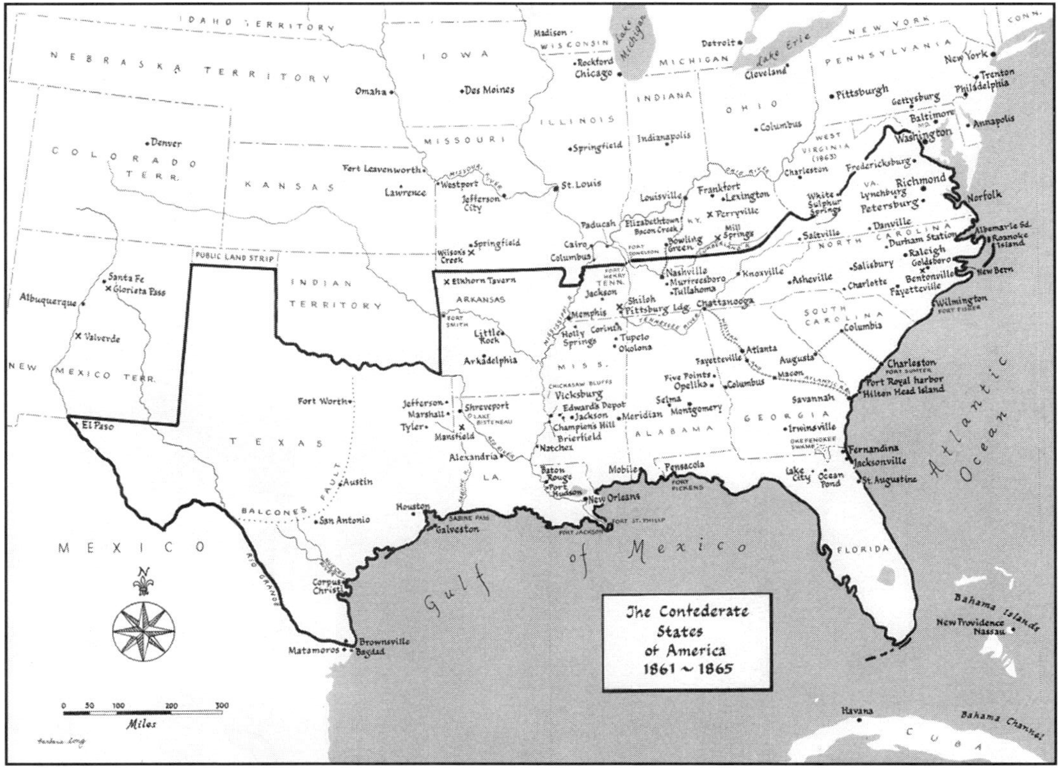
The Confederate States of America 1861 ~ 1865
IDAHO TERRITORY
NEBRASKA TERRITORY
COLORADO TERR.
Denver
KANSAS
Fort Leavenworth
Lawrence
Omaha
IOWA
Des Moines
MISSOURI
Westport
Jefferson City
Wilson's Creek
Springfield
St. Louis
WISCONSIN
Madison
Rockford
Chicago
Lake Michigan
ILLINOIS
Springfield
INDIANA
Indianapolis
MICHIGAN
Detroit
Lake Erie
OHIO
Cleveland
Columbus
NEW YORK
PENNSYLVANIA
Pittsburgh
Gettysburg
New York
Trenton
Philadelphia
Baltimore
MD.
Annapolis
Washington
WEST VIRGINIA (1863)
Charleston
White Sulphur Springs
Fredericksburg
VA.
Richmond
Lynchburg
Petersburg
Norfolk
CONN.
Louisville
Frankfort
Lexington
Perryville
Mill Springs
Paducah
Elizabethtown
Bacon Creek
K.Y.
Bowling Green
Cairo
Columbus
Fort Donelson
Fort Henry
TENN.
Jackson
Nashville
Murfreesboro
Tullahoma
Knoxville
Chattanooga
Shiloh
Pittsburg Ldg.
Memphis
Holly Springs
Corinth
Tupelo
Okolona
Saltville
Danville
NORTH CAROLINA
Durham Station
Raleigh
Goldsboro
Bentonville
Fayetteville
Salisbury
Charlotte
Asheville
Albemarle Sd.
Roanoke Island
New Bern
Wilmington
Fort Fisher
SOUTH CAROLINA
Columbia
Charleston
Fort Sumter
Fort Royal harbor
Hilton Head Island
PUBLIC LAND STRIP
INDIAN TERRITORY
Elkhorn Tavern
ARKANSAS
Fort Smith
Little Rock
Arkadelphia
Santa Fe
Glorieta Pass
Albuquerque
Valverde
NEW MEXICO TERR.
El Paso
TEXAS
Fort Worth
Austin
San Antonio
BALCONES FAULT
Houston
Galveston
Sabine Pass
Corpus Christi
Brownsville
Matamoros
Bagdad
Rio Grande
MEXICO
Jefferson
Marshall
Tyler
Shreveport
Lake Bisteneau
Mansfield
Alexandria
Red River
LA.
Baton Rouge
Port Hudson
New Orleans
Fort St. Philip
Fort Jackson
Natchez
MISS.
Chickasaw Bluffs
Vicksburg
Edward's Depot
Jackson
Champion's Hill
Brierfield
Meridian
Selma
Montgomery
ALABAMA
Five Points
Opelika
Mobile
Pensacola
Fort Pickens
Fayetteville
Atlanta
Augusta
Macon
Columbus
GEORGIA
Savannah
Irwinsville
Okefenokee Swamp
Lake City
Ocean Pond
Fernandina
Jacksonville
St. Augustine
FLORIDA
Gulf of Mexico
Atlantic Ocean
Bahama Islands
New Providence
Nassau
Havana
CUBA
Bahama Channel
N
0 50 100 200 300
Miles

# PART I

# Fort Sumter
## April 12, 1861

Major Robert Anderson could not sleep, even with the calming sound of waves crashing against the rocky breakwall. Repeated attempts from the newly formed Confederate States of America to convince him to surrender the Federal garrison in Charleston Harbor had met with his honor-bound refusal.

Confederate Brigadier General Pierre Gustave Toutant Beauregard was probably out there even now, thought Anderson, deciding what course of action to take. The major sat up on the edge of his bed and gazed out of his window at the dark clouds floating in front of the moon. His eyes squinted into the night as he sought out signs of Rebel activity on the faraway Charleston shore.

Major Anderson was entirely correct. Confederate gunners were manning the heavy cannons and batteries on the shores of Charleston Harbor, and they were nearly ready to fire. Horses strained hard in their creaking leather traces as they pulled limbers of gunpowder and cannonballs to positions behind the huge guns of the Confederate army.

At four in the morning, General Beauregard gave the signal, and an earsplitting roar rolled across the waters. Red-orange flames of thundering artillery and bursting shells turned the darkness of night into an eerie semblance of day. Confederate cannons rained their deadly hail of exploding iron onto the isolated and undermanned Federal garrison of Fort Sumter. Fifty-pound cannonballs slammed against the walls of the fort, causing brick to explode into dust and come avalanching down. Union soldiers sought cover from the terrible onslaught.

The great Civil War between North and South had begun.

## BEAR HUNTERS

### MORGAN SPRINGS, TENNESSEE

### APRIL OF 1861

The huge black bear reared up on his hind legs and tested the air, first with his nose and then with his ears. He detected no scent, but was able to pick up the distinct sounds of trouble coming in the far distance. The sounds were new to him, but something in his instinct told the bear he was in great danger, even though these hills and woods were his domain. And in this domain, he was king.

The bear made a guttural sound, getting back down on all fours and moving a few paces to his left. Then he stood up again and cocked his ears in the direction of the foreign sound. His thick black fur bristled and stood out straight, having the strange effect of making the bear appear even larger than he already was.

The bear's ears worked in different directions in an attempt to identify the noise he had heard. The noise was definitely nearer now than when he first detected it. Finally, he knew.

Dogs! Coming hard on his trail with howls and sharp staccato barks.

The huge bear turned quickly, and bolted into the thick cedar swamp with a speed that belied his bulk of over five hundred pounds. A speed that could outrun a horse for a short distance, and enable the bear to do to the horse exactly what this pack of dogs intended to do to him.

Tear him apart and kill him.

"Goddamn, Frank, I'm about give in," panted my friend, Jodie Pickett, all red in the face. "Let's take a little rest and listen to the dogs run. What do you say?"

"Well, Jodie," I told him. "You go ahead and lay yer lazy ass down and let your hound get ripped to shreds. But I aim to be there to lend a hand once that bear turns and makes a stand."

"I'm with ya, Frank," said my ole buddy, Owen, who was lopin' along minus his long Kentucky rifle, which was an unusual thing for Owen to be minus of.

We were all running and stumbling through the dark oak woods, about a mile west of the Tennessee River, attempting to keep up with our four baying bear hounds. Two of the dogs were redbone females, one a male blue tick and the other one was a female black and tan, with torn and ragged ears.

I was totin' a .44 caliber Kentucky rifle, as did Jodie Pickett. The third boy, Owen Horton, did not carry a rifle, only leashes for the dogs and a cotton sack with some venison jerky in it. Us three boys had grown up together in these mountains, and had even gone to school with one another, whenever we went.

We were set up to hunt bear and we shore had one goin' now. Judgin' by the size of the tracks, this was a mighty sizable critter, and he would not run much further before he turned on the dogs. I wanted to be there when he did.

"Hold on!" I hollered. "Listen."

We all stopped in our tracks and tried our best to silence our wheezin'.

"What is it?" asked Owen.

"Listen to them dogs," said Jodie, grinning happily.

"They've got that bear at bay or else he's treed!" I said.

"Damn! Let's get on up there!" Jodie whined.

We all lit out at a fast trot toward the rocky mountainside where the mournful howls and the sounds of a fracas was comin' from. It took us about ten minutes to get to that thick stand of oaks, alongside of a rocky spot, but we ran out of the woods just in time to see my male blue tick go flyin' through the air and slam against a rock ledge.

That big black bear was roarin' and swattin' at them dogs like he was the devil himself and they were a swarm of skeeters. His claws were long, black, and curved, and his teeth showed big and white. Slobber was flyin' all over the place while this bear tore at our dogs, his roars hurting my ears.

"Shoot that son of a bitch!" I yelled.

Jodie raised his rifle and I did the same.

His gun spoke first. Fire and smoke roared out the barrel as a black powder cloud filled the air.

The bear was hit in the chest and rocked back. Then, he spotted us and figured that these three human critters must be the cause of all his misery. Before we knew it, that bear went down on all fours and came roarin' straight for us, fire in his little pig eyes and murder in his heart.

I leveled my long rifle and caught him in my sights when he got about thirty feet away. Squeezing the trigger gently,

I heard the thunder and felt the full kick of the brass plate stock against my shoulder.

The .44 caliber lead ball caught that big bear in the corner of his right eye and traveled into his skull, spellin' the end of his days on this earth. He tumbled over and damn near took my legs out from under me as he came rollin' my way. Then, the bear lay still except for the jerkin' of all four legs. I had seen this many times, and knew they meant that death would come quickly.

It did.

"Jesus Christ!" said Owen, falling to his knees. "That like to scared the hell outta me."

Jodie just sat down against a tree and caught his breath.

Jodie Pickett was not very tall. He was thin and had short red hair, which seemed to me to be standin' straight up, maybe out of pure fright.

I plopped down too 'cause I thought I was gonna have me a heart stoppage right here on this very spot. The dogs were worryin' the carcass of that big bear, and my blue tick male was just regainin' his wits from bein' tossed against that ledge.

"C'mon over here, Drum," I called to the poor dog, who was now walkin' kind of sideways, shakin' his big head. Drum staggered over to me and whined.

"Drum, you don't seem to set much value on your life," I laughed.

The dog just looked up at me with his sad ole eyes and laid his head on my lap. By now the rest of the hounds were finally gettin' tired of worryin' the bear, so me, Jodie, and Owen went over to it and commenced runnin' our fingers through his thick black fur.

"I reckon this is the biggest bear kilt in these parts since ole Dan'l Boone was through here," said Jodie.

"I reckon I'd put this bear up agin' anything Mr. Boone ever kilt," Owen fired back.

I knew that once these two got to arguin' over such a thing, the disagreement could go on for hours. I also knew that there was no way in hell to prove or disprove how big of a bear Daniel Boone ever kilt, so I changed the nature of this bear argument.

"Now, boys," I said. "How in the hell are we gonna git this varmint out of here and back home?" I leaned against a tree and gave them time to ponder on this question. The dogs seemed to be watchin' us and waitin' for an answer themselves.

"If'n I had a pair of wings, I reckon I'd fly him out," said Owen. He had a big grin on his face, as if he had just solved some puzzle.

"I reckon if we had us a couple of fat women back here, we could get 'em to drag this big bastard out to the road," said Jodie, feeling the need to top Owen's wings story.

I just hung my head, knowin' that these two fools would be firin' nonsense back and forth once they got started. But I was fooled when Jodie offered up a good idea.

"How about if we draw straws?" he said. "And the loser goes and gets a couple of horses and brings 'em back here to cart this bear out?"

"Sounds fair to me," said Owen.

I got a stick and broke it into three pieces, one shorter than the other two, and offered 'em out to Owen and then to Jodie.

Jodie pulled the short stick and headed out fer home grumblin', while me and Owen set to work guttin' this big bear out. It wasn't long before we had a heap of steamin' guts layin' in a bloody pile next to the carcass. Then we was able to get a rope around the bear's head and hoist him up a bit onto a stout tree limb so's the blood would drain out onto the ground.

"Well, that was shore a messy job," said Owen, wiping his arms with dirt and leaves. "But at least we're through. Poor ole Jodie has to traipse all the way back home and bring out the horses."

"I reckon it serves him right," I said. "It was his idea in the first place to draw for the short stick."

"It shore was," Owen said. "I ain't got no pity for him at all."

After restin' for a bit, we set to strainin' and heavin' and finally was able to get the bear up off of the ground where it could drain proper. Now there was nothin' to do but to wait for Jodie and the horses.

It was a long wait, and it was near late afternoon before we heard Jodie whistlin'. I whistled back and in about fifteen minutes, here came Jodie, leadin' two horses through the trees. When them horses smelled and seen that bear, their eyes got real big and the whites was showin'. They tried to turn and run, but we all three took ahold of them and held on fer dear life.

Once the horses settled down and seen that this bear was not gonna harm them, we was all right. I tied a rope around the bear's neck and tied the other end around the saddle horn of one of the horses and we set to draggin' it on out. That was quite a chore, for we kept gettin' hung up on rocks and trees, plus that bear still weighed about four hundred pounds, even without his guts and blood.

We changed horses several times, back and forth, but it was well after dark when we pulled the bear up to the house, followed by three dead-tired boys and four dogs who were in the same sad shape as we was. My ma and pa, along with four little brothers and sisters came out of the house to see what the ruckus was about that our watchdog was makin'.

"Good God Almighty!" said Pa.

"Will you look at that," offered Ma, holdin' a towel up to her mouth.

The rest of the young'uns just stood there with their mouths hangin' open. Everybody had seen plenty of dead bears, but never one to match the size of this one.

"Whatcha aim to do with it, son?" said Pa, as he came off the porch and walked our way.

"Reckon we'll hoist it up in the barn fer tonight, then Jodie and Owen will come back over tomorrow mornin' and help skin it out. We aim to split the meat amongst the three of us."

"Owen, you git homelier every time I set eyes on you," said Pa.

That was what Pa had always told Owen, ever since I knowed him. Fact is though, Owen was a fairly good-lookin' feller. He was tall and lanky, with dark brown hair and a constant grin on his face. The gals, they was always after Owen, but he never paid 'em much mind.

"I know that fer shore, Mr. Morgan," Owen grinned. "But the gals don't know it yet and they's just wild about me. Even widder women won't leave me be."

"Well, make shore them widders is widders and don't have no husband back home, or we'll be hangin' you up just like this old bear is about to get hung up"

"Yes sir, I'll watch out fer shore."

We set to work, hoistin' that varmint up high in the barn, with the help of a rope and pulley in the peak of the barn roof and a good tug from one of the horses. Now that the bear was safe from ground varmints, Jodie and Owen struck out fer home and it was not very long before I was in bed myself. I had nightmares all night of huge critters chasin' me and of my rifle misfirin' every time I needed it.

Next mornin' early, I headed fer the barn with a meat saw and some sharp knives. Just about the time I got out there, here came Owen and Jodie, drivin' a buckboard pulled by a single horse who looked like he might not have enough strength to cart himself around, let alone those two fools and a couple hundred pounds of bear meat.

We set to work on that bear, who was now hangin' by his back feet. We made cuts around both ankles and then slit the skin up the inside of both legs to the base of his tail. That, of course, bein' the asshole.

"Dang, Frank. How'd you like somebody to run a knife in yer asshole?" asked Owen.

"I don't reckon I'd take much enjoyment from that, but Jodie probably would."

"Like hell I would! I'd never let myself get into such a position in the first place."

"You keep sniffin' around little Becky, and one of her brothers will most likely fold you into such a position, whether you allow it or not," said Owen.

Jodie never said nothin' to that, he just skinned a little faster.

"This bear shore is stuck tight to his skin," I said. "Most bears, ya kin just peel the hide off, but this feller holds on so's ya have to cut every inch of it away."

"He's a fat one too. . . I reckon he's fatter'n a New York banker," said Owen.

"You ain't never even seen no New York banker," shot back Jodie. "So how would you ever know about such a thing?"

"I did so," said Owen. "There was a New York banker that came up on the mountain to soak in the mineral spring just last spring. I seen him, and he was fatter than a hog."

Talkin' of such tomfoolery made the time pass faster, and by now we had worked the hide off all the way over the front shoulders and was up to the neck. Jodie stood back and looked at the work we'd done.

"Sweet Jesus, Frank," he said. "Take a look at this."

I stepped back and looked at the skinned bear. "What is it?"

"With the hide and fat off of him, this bear looks just like a man. Look at that, he's got arm muscles, stomach muscles, leg muscles, everything, just like me."

"Holy shit!" exclaimed Owen. "He *does* look just like Jodie!"

"How is that?" asked Jodie.

"He ain't got no pecker."

I laughed, Jodie frowned, and we went back to work at skinnin' the head out. Finally we worked up to the nose, and once we finished at that spot, the heavy black hide dropped to the barn floor.

Jodie and Owen took the hide outside, stretched and nailed it to the barn wall with the wet side out. I set to sawin' off the arms, neck, rib cage, back sections and finally the back legs, pilin' all of that meat onto the back of the buckboard, which was backed up into the barn. That horse looked like he was either asleep or dead, and I couldn't tell which. I would have thought that the smell of bear and blood would scare the hell out of any horse, but it shore didn't have no effect on this lazy gray horse of Jodie's.

# War
## April of 1861

We split the meat up fair, into three piles. My two younger brothers, Wed and Billie, finally helped us out by carryin' our family's stack of meat up to the house in a wash-tub.

Then we heard hoofbeats comin' down the little road, hell bent fer election. We could see the dust flyin' even before we spotted the rider. All of us stood watchin' the little bend in the road to see who would abuse a horse in such a manner.

Finally, the horse came into sight, all lathered up, and bein' rid by one of the useless young fools who hung around the general store in the little town of Dayton, hopin' to catch the eye of a purty gal. His name was Hubert Ashford, but Owen always referred to him as Hubert Ass-fart. Ole Hubert rode his poor horse damn near right over Jodie before he could haul that critter to a jerkin' stop.

"War! War!" shouted Hubert.

Pa come runnin' out of the house. "What in the world are you squawkin' about, young feller?"

"They's gonna be a war," panted Hubert, near 'bout as out of breath as his horse, which stirred and kicked up dust as Hubert held tight on the reins. "Our boys done fired on the Yankees in Fort Sumter. Blasted them boys all to hell. Ole Abe Lincoln is gonna git the war that he is itchin' so hard for."

"Where's Fort Sumter?" I asked.

"Where the hell you been, Frank?" said Hubert, frowning down at me and wiping his brow. "It's over in North or South Carolina, although I don't recall which."

"Then you ain't so goddamn smart yerself, Hubert," I retorted.

"Well, I'm smarter than you. I knew there is a war. And you never woulda knowed nothin' if'n I hadn't come up here and warned ya'll."

"Who is the Yankees, Hubert?" asked Jodie. Everybody stopped their talking and just looked at poor Jodie like he'd growed another head.

"Yankees is the people up north that wants to tell us folks down here how to run our lives, son," said my pa.

"That's right, Mr. Morgan," said Hubert, hopin' he'd finally found an ally amongst us.

Hubert's horse was havin' a hard time standin' still, and he damn near tromped on my foot.

"Watch out fer that horse, Frank," offered Owen. "Ole Hubert Ass-fart ain't got him much under control."

I could tell by the look on Hubert's face that he had put up with just about enough of our nonsense, and that he was fixin' to light out up the road, warnin' everybody like Paul Revere had done when the British was comin'.

"Ya'll take care," Hubert yelled. "Fer the whole damn Yankee army is likely headin' right this way."

"What would the Yankees be lookin' for up here in the Cumberlands?" asked Owen, who was now beginning to take an interest in this conversation.

"They'd be lookin' to wipe out dumb-ass hillbillies like you, Owen Horton, and make the world a less ignorant place," shot back Hubert.

With that prophesy, Hubert Ass-Fart turned his over-heated horse sharply, causing him to rear up, and damn near tip Hubert out of the saddle. But Hubert was able to hang on, and he gave that horse a good kick in the rib cage, and away they went in a cloud of dust, up the mountain road. My little rabbit hound Myrt was hot on his tail, tryin' to take a bite out of that poor tired horse.

Now we turned to my pa, who was always a good source of information. Even Ma had come out and gathered in on this palaver.

"You reckon he knows what he's talkin' about, Mr. Morgan?" Owen asked.

"Don't know why he'd come up here and lie on such a thing," said Pa. "Everybody knows trouble's been brewin' ever since Abe Lincoln got to be president."

"But what's Lincoln got against Tennessee?" asked Owen.

"He wants to free the slaves," said Pa.

"Well, heckfire, that wouldn't bother us none," Owen said. "We ain't got no slaves noway."

I looked over at Owen, who wasn't the brightest mind I had ever seen, but he seemed to have a good point. Hell, I hadn't never even seen a slave, never mind ownin' one. I reckoned I could do my own work, and didn't need no slave doin' it for me. In fact, I'd just as soon have a good coon dog as to have a slave.

## Church

The next day bein' Sunday, we all got on our best duds, which was the same thing we wore to church each and every Sunday. Little Wed was twelve years old, and growin' like a weed, so his sleeves and pant legs was gettin' a little bit too short. Purty soon Wed would graduate into my old Sunday-go-to-meetin' suit, and then his clothes would be too big.

My two sisters came out of the house and climbed up into the back of the wagon that we was all gonna ride in to church. Ellie was fifteen and little Marilee was seven. Marilee was the foil for all three of us boys, and we took pleasure in aggravatin' her as often as we possibly could.

Today, it was Billie's turn. He had a field mouse in a little jar, and when Marilee settled, Billie set that little mouse free in the wagon. It took off seekin' cover, right in the general direction of Marilee Morgan. She squalled in a high-pitched shriek and jumped straight up in the air. I swear, her feet never touched the floor of that wagon before she was over the side, layin' right on her ass in her clean dress.

With Ellie, it was a delayed reaction. She had not yet seen the mouse, but she had damn near been scared to death with Marilee's shriekin' and jumpin' so fast out of the wagon. Once Marilee had vacated her position, that mouse was dang near right on Ellie, and probably intent on hidin' under her skirt.

I had thought that Marilee's shriek was loud, but it weren't nothin' to compare with the scream that Ellie let out. Ellie came flyin' out of the wagon, and Ma came flyin' out of the house.

"What in the name of the Lord is happenin' out here?" Ma hollered.

"Billie let a mouse loose on us, the little son of a bitch!" yelled Ellie.

Ellie promptly got whopped on the side of her head by Ma. I knew it was comin' and could have told Ellie that if'n she was gonna call Ma a bitch, she probably should not do it to her face.

That whop on the head caused Ellie to squall some more. Then Ma caught Billie when he wasn't bein' on the alert, and whopped him a good one for causin' that fracas with the mouse. That, of course caused Billie to squall.

I looked around me and the only young'uns who weren't squallin' was me and Wed. We was real happy that we hadn't got whopped ourselves.

Now Pa came out of the house, pullin' on his black jacket.

"What's happenin' out here? You folks'll wake up the preacher."

Ma just glared at Billie. "It's all taken care of, Justin. Let's git on to church before services are over."

Everybody climbed back into the wagon. Ellie and Marilee looked frightful from cryin', and their hair was all wild. Me and Wed thought it was all kind of funny, but we dared not laugh too hard, only kinda smiled to each other.

The wagon ride to the little log Baptist Church was about two miles, and took fifteen minutes. I was admirin' the scenery along the way, for it was springtime in the mountains, and the flowers was bloomin' and the grass was green. There was a little waterfall comin' out the side of a rocky ridge, and it was real purty with the mornin' sun hittin' it. I was takin' it all in when a fox ran across the road, causin' the horse to rear back and whinney. I wish't I had my rifle in the wagon so I could take a crack at him, but Ma didn't hold with totin' a firearm on the Sabbath.

Pa tied the horse and wagon under a big oak tree and we walked up to the front of the church, which was purty much back in the woods. There sure was a whole bunch of new faces at the church, and everybody was gathered into groups and jawin' about the war startin' up. I reckoned that a lot of people who didn't see fit to come to church every Sunday came today just for the war news.

The rest of us Morgans moved forth like a covey of quail. As we strolled up to the people millin' about, I seen Alberta Rivers and headed her way. I called her Bird instead of Alberta, which she seemed to like. Bird was about three-quarters Cherokee Indian but she looked full-blooded to me. She was tall and thin, with long black hair, dark eyes, and high cheekbones.

I'd known Bird for over ten years, as she'd gone to school with the rest of us from time to time. She was a year younger than me, and I'd never paid her much mind until lately. Bird was startin' to look kind of purty to me and I'd got into the habit of thinkin' about her more than was normal. She was good friends with Ellie and came over to our house now and again.

"Howdy, Bird," I said.

"Hello, Frank."

"Ready fer a good fire-and-brimstone blast from Preacher Reed?"

"I reckon you can use it more than me, Frank." She flashed her big black eyes up at me, kinda playful-like.

"Did ya hear of me, Owen, and Jodie killin' that big ole black bear?"

"Yes, I did, and you should be ashamed." Them eyes looked a little cross now.

"Why on earth would I be ashamed of killin' a big bear?" I was truly confused.

"Did you bother to throw tobacco into the wind as an offering to the spirit of the bear?" Bird asked, standing with her hands on her hips.

"Hell no," I said. "I blasted black powder smoke into the air and that is all." This set me to grinnin' like a coon for comin' up with such a fine answer to her fool question.

"Then the spirit of that bear will wander forever in the woods and he will never be at peace. And you should not swear on the Sabbath, and especially in front of the church. You are such a jackass, Frank Morgan."

Before I could give my retort, Bird turned on her heel and strode into the church. I wish't I could've at least told her to watch her own language on this here Sabbath, but she fooled me.

I walked in and got me a seat next to Owen Horton, right behind Bird and her ma. I commenced to smell something that did not set right in this holy building. In fact, it stunk like hell.

"Howdy, Frank."

"Same to ya, Owen."

"Where's yer sister?"

"Who, Marilee?"

"No, you idiot," said Owen. "Ellie."

"How the hell should I know. I reckon she's mopin' around here somewhere."

"Why would Ellie be mopin' on the Sabbath?" asked Owen, lookin' over at me.

"'Cause Billie set a titmouse on her, and Ma had to whop her across the head due to her poor choice of words, and now her eyes are all red and her hair looks a damn fright."

"Oh," said Owen, as he pondered on all of the information that I had just given out with.

Bird turned around and glared at me due to my swearin' in this holy buildin', and so did a couple of other folks. I let on like I was innocent of whatever they were thinkin' about me, and they all turned back toward the podium.

"Owen, what the hell is that smell?"

"I think somebody stepped in dog shit, Frank."

I turned up the soles of my well-worn brogans, but they were clean. I also noticed a couple of other people doin' the same thing.

"Owen," I said. "Check yer shoes."

"What fer?"

"Fer dog shit, what do ya think, you imbecile."

Owen bent over and looked at the bottoms of his boots.

"Well?"

"Yep, it's me."

At just that exact time, Preacher Reed strolled to the podium, leaned over it, and looked everybody square in the eye. Ever since I was a toddler, Preacher Reed had scared the hell out of me. I reckoned he looked just like Moses or Noah must have looked when they was alive on this earth. He had a red face, wild gray hair, and little spectacles that he peered over when he was tryin' to scare a feller.

Preacher Reed started right off into hollerin'.

"Who in this church of God is a sinner?"

Everybody except Owen and me hollered that they was.

"Then bow your sinful heads, and pray to Almighty God to set you and your brother on the path of righteousness!"

"Yes sir!" hollered the congregation.

"Trouble is in the air!"

"Amen, preacher," came a strong voice from the back of the church. I turned around, but could not identify who had testified.

"Who will take up the sword, and defend your loved ones from the demons with the love of mongrelization in their hearts?"

"I will!" everybody shouted.

"Who will carry the rifle of the Lord into the wilderness to meet the evil patrons of Satan?"

"I will!"

"Who will stand before the devil himself in defense of southern womanhood?"

"I will!"

By now several men had jumped to their feet, and I could see the fury in their eyes. Eyes which burned a hole in yer very soul if'n ya was brave enough to look into 'em. Even Owen rose up and started shakin' his fist. Of course, his movin' about got that smell of dog shit flowin' real fast, even drownin' out the smell of armpits.

"Who will man the cannons of the angels and make their stand against the Yankees when they come to our land to rape and plunder?"

"I will!"

Now I became took up in all of this high spirited yellin', and I bounced up to my feet and even got up and stood atop of my pew seat. There were not many men inside of that little church who were not doin' the same, hollerin' and wishin' that he had a knife in his hand and a Yankee in front of him, just so's he could do the bloody work of the Lord.

## MORGAN SPRINGS

After church let out, everybody was near about soppin' wet from sweat. That buildin' had got mighty hot from cramped quarters. All of the congregation was thankin' Preacher Reed for gettin' us all stirred up against Yankees and the devil. Me and Owen walked out back of the church where there was a rock ledge overlookin' a big wooded valley with a creek runnin' through it. We'd just sat down on the rock when we were surprised to be joined by my sister, Ellie, and Bird.

From the look in his eye, I could tell Owen reckoned Ellie was just about the most beautiful gal he'd ever seen. She had long blonde hair and blue eyes. A feller'd never know that Ellie was about a third Cherokee herself, for it shore never showed. I was tall and dark myself, and many folks wondered how me and Ellie could be brother and sister.

But as for the beauty of Ellie, Owen had never seen her in the early mornin' like I had. It was my own feelin' that Ellie sometimes looked like a witch from the graveyard.

"Frank, I'm gonna do it," said Owen, lookin' out across the valley.

"Do what?" I asked.

"Join the army."

"The Yankee army?"

"Hell no, you dumb ass!" he said." The Confederate army."

Nobody said anything, but I caught Bird lookin' at me. Then we all just gazed down over that beautiful wooded valley, thinkin' about what Owen had said.

Morgan Springs, Tennessee, in the Cumberland Mountains, had been named for my family. My great-grandfather, Lewis Morgan, had came here from Wales with his mother and two brothers, settling here in Cherokee country in 1798. Purty soon, Lewis had married a Cherokee gal, aged twelve, and they'd started a little farm on some rough mountain land.

When President Andrew Jackson had removed all of the Cherokees out to Oklahoma along the road that they called the 'Trail of Tears,' Lewis and them ended up with a whole bunch of mountain land. The Morgan brothers commenced breedin' like rabbits, and now there was a passel of Morgans spread all over this mountain and some as far away as Nashville.

Amongst this land was a flowin' wellspring that the Indians said had healing powers. To drink that water spelled the end of a whole bunch of diseases, and to soak in it meant you could heal wounds like gout, aches and pains, and the ague. The name of the spring became Morgan Springs instead of Indian Springs and that name stuck.

Some of the Cherokees had hid out and had avoided walkin' the death trail out West, and I was glad of it, for otherwise, Bird would not be sittin' beside me right now, with the wind blowin' her dark hair across her purty face.

I changed my position on the rock a bit, so's I could 'accidentally' end up rubbin' shoulders with Bird. At first, she pulled away, but then I was surprised when she came back my way, and I could feel the heat of our touchin' shoulders. Then our hands touched, and she looked over at me. I just left my hand right there, and I'll be danged if'n little Alberta Rivers wasn't so bold as to put her hand right on top of mine and leave it there.

This action caused my breath to almost leave me and caused a big lump to jump up into my chest. It also set Bird to grinnin' as she gazed out across that beautiful valley.

Right then, I heard a noise come up from behind and turned around just in time to see Jodie Pickett dismountin' his big black horse and come walkin' over to where we all was sittin'. Bird had moved her hand and shoulder away, so Jodie had spoiled my moment.

"Hey, ya'll."

"Hey, Jodie."

"They's a man just rode up to the front of the church. He's sayin' that Tennessee has seceded from the Union, and that Lincoln is callin' fer volunteers."

Owen looked over at me and didn't say nothin' and neither did I.

"What does that all mean, Jodie?" asked Ellie.

"It means that the Union is gonna wage war on all of the states that have broke away from it."

"Why don't they just let us be?" said Ellie.

"'Cause I reckon them fellers in Washington want to preserve the Union," answered Jodie, who had picked up a stick and commenced whittling at it.

"Like hell," said Owen. "They want to do just like the British did and tell us how to run our lives." He picked up a stone and threw it down into the valley. "And I reckon them Yankees is gonna git just what them English fellers got."

"And what's that, Owen?" I asked.

"Their asses handed to 'em in a bushel basket, that's what."

I laughed at that, but Ellie, Bird, and Jodie didn't.

"Is ole Jeff Davis gonna call fer volunteers himself?" I asked.

"I reckon he'll have to, or else he'll just cave in," offered Owen. "Anyway, when he makes the call, I'm answerin' it. How's about you, Frank?"

I didn't say nothin', and everybody looked at me. I reckoned that I would have to think this whole matter over a bit and maybe talk to Pa about it. Us Morgans was fighters and wasn't never shy about joinin' into a fracas. I had relatives who had fought and died at Yorktown, Bunker Hill, Texas, and even down in Mexico. We was a rough crowd and soldierin' came to us naturally.

Even Pa had joined up with a group in fightin' against the Creek Indians here in Tennessee and down in Georgia. He never talked of it, but I reckoned that he knew what fightin' and killin' was all about, and he wasn't shy about gettin' into a scrap.

Now, my little brother Wed came on down through the trees and stepped out to the end of the rock ledge that we was sittin' on.

"Wed, this here rock will only hold so many people you know," said Owen. "If you stand yer fat ass out on the end of it like that, we are all likely to go tumblin' down to our death."

"Horseshit," said Wed, as he gazed down to the rocky floor below and spit.

Spittin' down into that purty valley spoiled this nice scene that we had goin' on, so we all got up and started walkin' back toward the church.

"Where's everybody goin'?" hollered Wed.

"We aim to leave you standin' on the edge of that rock, and we're all gonna go up to the church and pray that you jump off," said Owen. We walked off with Wed just starin' at us.

When we got back to the church, we noticed that everybody was coveyed up and jabberin' about the war that was comin'.

"Who wants to go into the caves tomorrow?" asked Owen.

We all looked at one another fer a minute. Then I spoke up and said it sounded like a good idea to me. That caused Ellie, Bird, and Jodie to reckon it to be all right with them too. So we decided to meet near the Devil Rock Cave around noon tomorrow.

# CAVE OF THE BLOOD OATH 1861

Next mornin', I was up early and finished my chores. We had some cows, horses, hogs, chickens, and such on our farm, but our main crop was three fields of corn. Tobacco was our next most important crop, for that was sold for cash money down in Chattanooga. We was just now commencin' to set out some tobacco plants.

I struck out down the road which led near the cave, and it wasn't long before Ellie caught up with me, and then Owen. Once't we got there, Jodie and Bird was waitin' for us. Jodie had brought a pile of torch material, and we decided to go on into a new cave which we had never been in before. Everyone called it the 'Mouth of the Devil' cave, 'cause it had a big rock stickin' out above it that looked like a nose.

Us three boys each carried a lit torch, and we went on into the dark cave, which started out about seven feet high and was wide enough for two people to stand side by side. We walked in for about a hundred yards and came to a spot where you had to get down on all fours and crawl along. Nobody liked this much, but we kept goin', as no one wanted to be the first to say he'd like to get the hell out of this damp, dark place.

The further we crawled along, the more Ellie began to gripe, wonderin' what would become of us if'n the roof caved in. Jodie was concerned what we'd do if we came to the end of the cave and had to crawl backwards without bein' able to see what was behind us.

Purty soon, the cave got bigger, and we was able to walk upright just like a human being would be walkin'. We went along for a ways, when Jodie said, "Whooa, look here."

"What?" I whispered, tryin' to spot what Jodie was lookin' at.

"It's a pile of rocks over a flat piece of shale. Frank, this here looks like a door to somethin'."

We all walked back to where Jodie was and, sure enough, there was a bunch of rocks piled up, and it looked to be a man-made pile. We started pullin' them rocks out and finally came to a big heavy piece of slate that stood against the wall. It was all that me, Jodie, and Owen could do, but we finally horsed it aside.

"Well, I'll be danged," said Owen. "Another cave that someone saw fit to hide with them rocks."

"What do you reckon is in there?" said Jodie.

"Well, how the hell would I know?" I said. "Why don't we take a look?"

"What if there's snakes in there or somethin'?" Ellie asked.

"Then maybe we'll be lucky and they'll bite Jodie," I answered.

With that, we all hunkered down and went into that dark hole, which went down at a purty good angle, then got narrower and lower. Purty soon, we was crawlin' along, and it was startin' to get damp. Our oil-soakedtorches was smokin' the place up so bad that we could hardly breathe.

I reckon we all had seen enough of this mess, when I thought I heard something ahead.

"Hold on there," I said.

"What is it, Frank?"

"Shhhhhh," said Bird.

"Dang," I said.

"What?" asked Owen.

"Listen," I said. "Sounds like a waterfall."

Now we was all curious and crawled forward, even though it entered my mind that we might be drowned somehow, if'n this was really water. Purty soon though, we got to a place where you could stand up. There was a curve to the cave, and we could now hear water flowin' like all getout. I was first to go around that curve, and I'll be damned if that cave didn't lead into a big ole room with a waterfall comin' out of a crack in the rocky wall. That water tumbled about twenty feet and hit right into an underground river that went flowin' out through a big dark tunnel.

"Will you look at this?" I said.

"It's just like a big room," said Bird.

"Lookit over there," said Jodie. "They's two holes in the wall to hold torches."

Shore enough, somebody had chiseled two holes into that smooth and shiny rock wall. It was over forty feet up to the ceiling; but for some reason the smoke from our oil-soaked torches didn't linger, and got sucked right up through a crack near the top of this cave room.

We commenced to explore around the walls, and Bird found where somebody had scratched some pictures that looked like animals into the smooth rock.

"What's them things?" asked Bird.

"They look like buffalo," said Owen. "Maybe that there one is a dog."

"Over here looks like a man or somethin' and he's carryin' a long stick," I said.

"Where?" inquired Jodie.

"Over here," I said.

"That ain't no stick, it's a spear," said Owen. "Who in the world do ya reckon was in this cave?"

"Maybe it was ole Hubert Ass-Fart and the Stubbleton brothers," I said.

"No," said Jodie. "They'd be too lazy to stack up them stones."

"Then I reckon it was a caveman or some Injuns that done it," offered Jodie. "Prob'ly a million years ago."

Nobody cracked no jokes about that, and we just kept starin' at them pictures that had been scratched into the wall.

"Hey, here looks like a picture of a woman with a big pair of tits, standin' on a snake," said Owen.

"Dang, Owen," I said. "You ain't supposed to say such a word in front of Bird."

"What word?"

"Well, I shore ain't about to repeat it and get myself slapped for bein' so bold, but it was the word about what that woman has."

"Well," said Owen. "The word yer lookin' for is 'tits,' Frank, and everybody's got 'em. Even Bird, in case ya haven't noticed."

I snuck a sideways look at Bird and she was tryin' to keep from smilin', but wasn't doin' a very good job of it. Ellie was rollin' her eyes toward the ceiling, and I felt like my head was on fire, so I changed the subject. "Let's take a look into this little river."

We all walked over to the river that flowed out of the wall hole, and shined our torches down into the water. There was a pool at the base of this little waterfall, and it was about five feet across, and maybe two feet deep. Then it narrowed down, and a little river about a foot deep and two feet wide flowed out the far end and disappeared into a small tunnel which went right into the wall.

"Dang," said Owen. "There's some fish in this pool of water."

"No such of a thing," said Jodie. "How could a fish live in this dark cave."

"Well," shot back Owen. "I don't reckon I would know about how he lives, but if you will just look down in there, you'll see that there is a fish. In fact, there's two more of 'em."

"Them fish don't have no eyes," said Bird.

Shore enough, them fish had no eyes that I could see. They looked just like little catfish, and they was about eight inches long and almost pure white. I reached in the water, and had no trouble grabbin' one of them fish and flippin' it onto the rock floor. Just like I had thought, it was some kind of catfish, and it had the stingers stickin' out of its sides and on top of its back to prove it. I held the fish up real careful-like, and we all studied it. Where there should have been two eyes there was only pale spots, causin' me to reckon they once't had eyes, but now they was plumb blind from livin' in this dark surrounding.

"That's a blind fish," said Ellie.

"Throw it back in, Frank," begged Bird. The way she was lookin' up at me, all hurt like, I didn't have no choice but to throw him back. He swam off after his own bizness.

We commenced explorin' around the inside of that cave room again, and Bird found some rocks in a little circle where there had once probably been a fire. There was also some sharp pieces of stone that had been broken off, maybe for arrowheads or somethin'.

"I reckon we're the only ones to have set foot in this cave for a thousand years," said Jodie.

"We should keep this here cave a secret that just the five of us know about," said Owen.

"And anyone who reveals the secret of this cave should burn in a fiery furnace," offered up Ellie, who had got caught up in the feelin' that was runnin' high at this moment.

"Let's take a vote on keepin' this place a secret," Jodie said.

We all gathered around that little circle of stones and Owen laid his torch down in the middle. Our faces was all lighted up by the golden glow, and we just remained quiet for a minute. I was the first to speak up.

"Who all in this room is willin' to keep the secret of this cave's bein' here just between the five of us, and swears to do it in the name of the Lord?"

"I do," said Owen.

"Me too," shouted Jodie.

Bird and Ellie both nodded and so did I.

"We need to make it a blood oath," said Bird, and I was shore surprised at this gal bein' so eager to spill her blood, for she knew what that meant we had to go through now. We all looked around at each other and agreed that a blood oath, it had to be.

I reached into my pocket and brought out my foldin' clasp pocketknife, which was sharp as a razor and could shave whiskers off'n a billy goat. Since I supplied the knife, I decided that it was me that was gonna be cut first and that I was gonna do the cuttin'. I didn't want to have to watch everybody else gettin' slit open, and have to dread my turn comin', so I laid the knife on the outside part of the middle joint of my left pointin' finger and moved the knife enough to slit the skin and start blood flowin'.

"Oh, my God," said Bird.

"I'm gonna be sick," Ellie cried.

"Cut me, Frank," said Owen. "And make it deep."

I grinned and did as Owen asked, thinkin' he was smart too fer wantin' to get it over with quick. I looked at Bird and Ellie and noticed that they was gettin' kind of pale, for both me and Owen was drippin' blood onto that stone floor. That's why I was surprised that Bird stuck her finger in front of me and looked into my eyes. I thought that Bird had the same look in her eyes that I had once seen in the eyes of a wounded deer that I had to shoot a second time and put out of its misery.

I took Bird's hand in mine and noticed that it was real hot. I laid the knife blade on her little finger and looked at her. She was lookin' at me instead of the knife, and she had tears in her eyes.

"I cain't do this," I said.

"Cut it, Frank," said Bird.

"Dang, I'd just as soon whack off my leg as to make a cut on you, Bird," I said. "Owen, you do it."

"Hell, I ain't shy, give me the knife," said Owen.

With that, Bird grabbed the knife and made one hell of a slice on her own finger, causin' the blood to commence to flow freely. She held the cut finger up, and blood was drippin' onto the floor.

Next came Jodie, and I didn't have no trouble cuttin' his finger at all, except fer the fact that he hollered like hell.

Ellie was last, and she wanted Owen to cut her instead of me, for I reckon she thought Owen would have more consideration that I would. Owen split her finger, and I thought Ellie was gonna pass right out, even though she had the smallest wound of any of us.

Now we was all bleedin', but we was still alive.

"Everybody join our fingers together right over this torch, so that our blood mixes," I said. So we all five put our bloody fingers together and looked around at one another.

"Repeat what I say. I swear in the name of our Lord and on the eyesight of our mothers and on the souls of our ancestors that I will never reveal the location of this cave to anybody, no matter if they torture me to death or do worse."

Everybody repeated it finally, even though I had to coach Owen a bit, for he couldn't recall my whole oath. Once't we had all swore the blood oath, we was all quiet and just looked around at each other, and we all knew that we would keep this secret until the day came when we would cross over into the glory land.

We took a long last look at this secret waterfall cave, grabbed our torches, and commenced to leave this place.

Owen took the lead this time, and I brought up the rear as we worked our way back out the same way that we had come in. Bringin' up the rear, I could feel the darkness behind me, and it was a little scary 'cause my imagination started to run away on me, and I could visualize all sorts of demons and ghosts runnin' through the cave and tryin' to catch up with me before we made it out into the sunshine.

"Goddamn it, hurry along up there," I yelled.

Owen responded to my plea by letting a loud fart.

"Excuse me folks," he laughed. "That one just slipped out."

"Oh my God," whined Ellie. "That stinks!"

"Then somebody else farted too," said Owen, stopping and looking back into the torch light. "'Cause my farts don't stink."

"I think I'm gonna throw up," said Bird.

I just shook my head, wonderin' how Owen could be so bold as to let a fart into a crowd of purty gals. Especially when they were crawlin' on all fours behind him, and the fart would just hang there at face level.

It seemed like forever, but we finally came out of that secret entrance where the rock pile had been found. We pulled that big piece of slate back across the hole and piled them stones back as best we could. Then we worked our way out the long cave tunnel that took us out into the bright sunshine and the entrance to the Mouth of the Devil Cave.

## The Decision

It was the afternoon now, and we all said our good byes and headed fer our homes. As me and Owen was walkin' together, just the two of us, Owen asked what I thought about joinin' up with the army.

"Hell, I reckon we might as well go ahead and do it," I told him. "There ain't nothin' goin' on around here. I wonder if'n ya git paid fer fightin' with the army."

"I heard once that soldiers get paid purty good money," said Owen.

"Well, I should think so, what with the fact that they got fellers firin' guns at 'em all day long."

"I'm gonna talk to my pa tonight, Frank. You need to do the same thing, and stand yer ground when yer ma goes to cryin' and carryin' on."

"My ma don't never cry."

"She shore is likely to do so once't she learns yer headin' to war."

This whole conversation was causin' my head to spin. We didn't say nothin' else until we split up and went our separate ways, plannin' on gettin' together tomorrow to talk about what happened with our folks. I heard Myrt barkin', and purty soon she came runnin' and tryin' to jump up on me. I rubbed her head and went on into the house.

"Where ya'll been, Frank?" asked Pa.

"We was explorin' the caves down at the Mouth of the Devil."

"You young'uns best stay out of them caves, less'n they fall in on ya and you never get found," said Ma.

"Did ya'll find anything interestin', son?" Pa asked.

"No sir, just a long walk, and a bunch of crawlin' and squeezin' through tunnels."

"I shore don't know what people see in crawlin' around in them dang dark caves," said Pa. "But there's a lot of folks that does it."

"Pa?"

"Yes son?"

"Me and Owen are thinkin' of joinin' up with the army, if'n there is a war with the Yankees."

Ma stopped her work at the stove, turned around, and her hands flew to her mouth. "Oh my Lord, Frank. No!"

"Why Frank," said Pa. "You 'n Owen is a mite young to be thinkin' of such things, ain't ya?"

"Well, sir, we're goin' on seventeen and I reckon a lot of fellers have left their homes a long time before they ever get to be that old."

Ma sat down at the table with us. "Frank, if you was ever killed, I couldn't bear to go on livin' myself."

"I'm sorry Ma, but I reckon no soldier's ma wants to see her boys go off to a war, but the fact is that somebody has got to go and do the fightin'."

Pa stood up from the table, walked over to the window and looked out toward the barn. "Frank, I can't stop you from leavin' but I shore would like for you boys to give this some hard thought. Fact is, I ain't heard of no one callin' yet fer volunteers."

"How's about if we take a ride down into Dayton tomorrow and see if there's any news of what's goin' on, sir?"

Pa thought about this for a minute, but Ma broke in. "Justin, talk him out of this fool thing."

"Molly, it won't hurt none fer us to just go to town and get the news on what's goin' on after "Fort Sumter" bein' fired on." This caused Ma to get up from the table, and stomp over to the stove and start stirrin' a pot of somethin'. I knew from the look on her face that she was mad at Pa and scared of what I was about to do.

I rode on over to Owen's house that evening, and he met me out on the front porch.

"How did it go with yer folks?" he asked.

"Not too good with my ma," I admitted. "But I think Pa's resigned himself to the fact that I've about made up my mind to light out, and there ain't much him or Ma kin do about it, short of tyin' me up in the barn. He wants to ride down into town tomorrow and see if Jeff Davis is askin' fer volunteers, and I reckon that's a good idea."

"I spect it is," said Owen. "Hell, maybe the war is already over for all we know up here atop of this mountain."

"How 'bout yer folks?"

"Ma's cryin' and Pa thinks it's a good idea."

"Well," I said. "I reckon we've got our foot in the door then."

"I reckon."

Next mornin' me, Pa, Owen, and his pa saddled up, and we all four began the eight-mile trek down the mountain and over to the dusty little town of Dayton. Owen's pa, Buster Horton, was a big man with a bushy gray beard and arms that was near as big around as my leg. Buster Horton built fireplaces, chimneys, and houses out of cut mountain stone, and he was as strong as a bear from cartin' around them big chunks of rock all of his life. Pa and Buster was good friends, just like me and Owen, and they liked to go huntin' and fishin' together whenever they could get away.

"Justin," said Mr. Horton. "Maybe you and me should go off to fight the Yankees and leave these two young'uns home to tend the farm."

"That might not be such a bad idea, Buster. I expect you could whip a whole regiment by yerself."

Just about this time, we spotted a deer standin' well off the road, and Buster pulled his Pennsylvania long rifle out of the saddle boot, raised it up, and pulled the trigger. That long gun roared and belched out a big cloud of black smoke, but he missed the deer clean, and it bounced off into the brush.

"Dang, boys, I shore thought that was one dead deer. I must be gettin' old. I reckon the Yankees would kill me off real quick if'n I cain't shoot no straighter'n that."

"Hell, Buster, that dern deer was two hunnert yards out there. Ain't no shame to miss such a shot," said Pa.

"It is fer me, pardner."

We set out ridin' again, and it was well before noon when we rode up to the front of the courthouse. There was a little stand of oaks and some benches underneath 'em, makin' a real nice place to gather and talk politics, which was somethin' that the folks around these parts had always seemed to enjoy. There was a farmer with a big black floppy hat who was talkin' real loud and wavin' his arms in the air. As we got closer, we realized that this feller was takin' up the Union side of an argument, and he was not alone in his sentiments.

"My granddaddy fought with George Washington to make a nation here, and I ain't one to see it washed away so easy. Hell, this war's gonna be to keep the slaves, and we ain't even got no slaves up in these hills."

"This goddamn war is for states' rights and has nothin' to do with wantin' to keep no slaves," said a long lanky feller with a dangerous look about him.

"Bullshit, Jeff Davis and his whole goddamn crowd is slave owners, and they just want to preserve that plantation way of life," said the bearded farmer.

"That's a fact fer shore, and old Jeff Davis is gonna use you fellers to fight and die just so's he can keep his slaves," said another man.

"I ain't dyin', but you is shore beatin' around that old bush of death," said a man who had a long bowie knife shoved down the front of his belt. I noted the position of this long weapon and reckoned that this feller was liable to cut off his own pecker with that sharp knife if'n he made a wrong move.

We could see that manners was frayin', and that this here argument was gettin' hotter and hotter. I was surprised that the people takin' sides on this issue of rebellion was just about divided equal. Pa moved away, and the rest of us followed him.

"Dang, Justin," said Mr. Horton. "There's just as many people sidin' with the Union as is sidin' with the Rebs. Don't *that* beat all?"

"It's a surprise to me. It sure is gonna be hard gettin' along with all of yer neighbors if'n a war really starts up."

Just then, we seen a big wagon, pulled by four horses and covered with a white canvas goin' by. We recognized the driver as Mr. McPherson, who lived across the valley on a little farm. The rest of his family was peekin' out from under that canvas. Pa waved and hollered. "Mac, where are ya headed with that loaded-down wagon?"

Mr. McPherson pulled his team to a halt and leaned over the side. "Howdy boys. Fancy meetin' ya'll here amongst all these town folks."

"Where ya headed?"

"Gettin' the hell out of Tennessee and headin' back to Ohio where there ain't no slavers wantin' to destroy this nation."

"Dern, Mac," said Buster Horton. "You and yer family have lived in these hills fer as long as I remember. I never even knowed you was an Ohio man."

"I ain't no Ohio man, but I shore consider myself loyal to these here United States, and I ain't never wantin' to be considered a Reb."

"Well, Mac, what are you gonna do back in Ohio?" asked Pa.

"Reckon I'll probably join up with the Twenty-fourth Ohio, along with my two brothers."

"You mean the Yankee Army?"

"That's the one."

Mr. Horton laughed a bit at this, but I noticed that Pa never cracked a smile. Pa and Mr. McPherson was purty good friends and hunted together at times.

"Let me shake yer hand Mac," said Mr. Horton. "I hate to see ya leave these hills, and I shore hope you never come back down here shootin' at us if'n ya join up with the Yankees."

Mr. McPherson extended his hand and all four of us shook it. The rest of the McPherson family never even came out from under that canvas, they just looked at us. It gave me the creeps, especially when the thought came to me that straight-shootin' Mac McPherson might someday be aimin' his long gun at me.

Without any further words, Mr. McPherson slapped the rear of his team with those long leather reins, and away our old neighbors went, headed north fer Ohio.

We all stood and watched that covered wagon creak on up the main street of Dayton and disappear onto a northbound side street. It was kind of sad to me that this fracas was costin' us a good neighbor. I had just took it for granted that everybody in these Tennessee hills was gonna side with the South if'n a war ever came, but it now became obvious to me that this was not the case.

We worked our way on over to where another little crowd was gatherin' around a tall young feller in a gray uniform of sorts. He was wearin' a brimmed butternut-colored hat and I reckoned that this must be what the new army of the South was gonna wear once't the fightin' starts.

Mr. Horton walked up to this young feller, who seemed to be the centerpiece of this gatherin'. "Sir, we are wonderin' if you might know if'n the South is askin' fer volunteers to fight."

The tall feller looked over at Mr. Horton and grinned a bit. "Yes sir, we sure are lookin' for volunteers, but ain't you a bit long in the tooth to join in the fight?"

Buster Horton's face turned beet red, and Pa started to grin and rolled his eyes up to heaven, for he knew what was comin' next.

"Ain't askin' fer myself, you snot-nosed little son of a bitch," said Mr. Horton. "I'm askin' on behalf of my boy and his friend here. However, if I was to take a notion to fight, I reckon I'd start with you."

Now it was the army feller's turn to get a red face, and the little crowd grew quiet and looked at him, wonderin' if there was gonna be a scrap.

"I meant no offense, sir. I was just funnin' you a little bit. I apologize and tell you straight out that we are indeed recruitin' volunteers to take up arms in defense of the South. I have a letter from Jefferson Davis himself authorizing me to sign up six hundred volunteers from the Cumberland. The pay is ten dollars a month and the length of service is for one year."

Ten dollars, I thought, I ain't never seen ten dollars in my life.

"What is the age limits?" Owen shouted out.

"Right now it's set at seventeen to forty years of age," said the uniformed man. "But we don't require no proof as to age."

"Then how do you know if'n a feller is seventeen or ain't but fifteen?" asked Pa.

"If there's milk stains on his bib, then he's too young. If he ain't got no teeth and cain't hardly walk, then he's too old," laughed the recruiter.

Now it was my turn to fire a question at this feller. "If'n a feller signs up, what does he need to bring with him and where does he go to?"

"You'd be best to bring along yer own rifle, powder, and shot, just to make sure yer armed, in case we haven't yet received our British Enfields. The guns are supposed to be here, but the Yankees will likely be blockading our ports. Same thing might be said fer our uniforms. My ole ma sewed me up two uniforms, one of which I'm wearin' right now. You'd be smart to do the same. Make it gray in color, and use wool cause it keeps ya warm and sheds the rain purty good."

"What in the world kind of an army is it that cain't even supply uniforms and guns?" asked a lanky farmer in the crowd.

That soldier boy just glared out at the farmer and did not shed any kind of a grin.

"The Army of the Confederate States of America, and it's a temporary setback."

"Then where do ya go once ya sign up?"

"Chattanooga," answered the soldier.

"How do ya git there?" asked the farmer.

"You either walk or ride a horse, and follow the Tennessee River to the South. I don't see how you could miss it."

"Where do ya sign up?"

This question made the recruiter happy, and he produced a long sheet of white paper which had some writin' at the top, and which had about seven names and five Xs scribbled on it.

"Right here," he said.

Me and Owen was ready to sign up right then, especially me, thinkin' of all that money and of the adventure of leavin' home. But Pa took us all off to the side.

"Boys, I cain't hold you back if'n this is somethin' ya'll want to do, but you should think on it long and hard. War ain't no picnic and I reckon that a lot of the boys who leave these mountains won't ever make it back."

"I heard somebody say that we will have the Yanks whipped within two months and be back home," said Owen.

"Who said that?" his father asked.

"I don't know who it was," answered Owen. "Only that he just had one ear and smelled like a billy goat."

Pa just shook his head, probably over the fear that this fool was gonna go out and fight a war. I knew that Owen wasn't doin' our cause any good, so I spoke up. "I'd shore like to have a crack at that ten dollars a month."

Pa just looked at me with a sad look for the longest time. This made me uncomfortable, for usually whenever Pa stared at me for over two seconds, it meant that I was about to get swatted with the nearest thing he could lay his hands on. Therefore, it damn near gave me death from mortification when Pa moved towards me and gave me a big hug.

"Do what you want to do, Frank," he said. I looked over at Owen while I was gettin' this hug, and his eyes was as big as pumpkins, probably out of the fear that his pa was gonna get caught up in this emotion and grab ahold of him. However, Buster Horton was able to restrain himself and Pa finally let go of me.

I looked up at him, and I'll be damned if'n he didn't have tears in his eyes. I couldn't stand no more of this, and me and Owen walked back to the army feller.

"Where do we sign?"

## Leaving the Mountains

And so the deed was done. Me and Owen Horton was signed up to go off and fight Yankees. We had papers which ordered us to be in Chattanooga in ten days, and to be ready to be shipped to who knows where.

Ma took the news hard, and she was cryin' and squawkin' around. I'll be damned if'n she didn't get so carried away, that she also set to givin' me a big bear hug too. I could smell cornmeal, bacon grease, smoke, and soap in her hair, and I could feel her tears flowin' down against my own cheeks. Of course, the whole damn house was full of people watchin', and I was mortified to tears myself.

Naturally, Ellie went down to the Rivers' place and told Bird. When they both came runnin' in, Bird grabbed me and even *she* commenced to huggin' me and cryin'. Of course this hug wasn't near as bad as those that I'd just got from Ma and Pa, seein's how little Alberta Rivers was squishin' some soft things into my chest. These things shore felt interestin' to me, so I wrapped my arms around Bird, gave her a hug right back, and held on fer dear life.

We both realized at the same time that we had an audience, so we was embarrassed enough to pull back from all of this chest rubbin'.

Bird stayed for dinner and kept eyeballin' me all through the meal. In fact, I even caught sight of her peerin' at me durin' the saying of grace, and I know that Alberta Rivers knew better than to blaspheme in such a way.

I was startin' to feel my own importance in this house, and wondered at what a change there was in everybody's attitude towards me. They was passin' me pork chops and applesauce like I was the King of Russia. This set me to wonderin' why I had ever waited so long to become a soldier.

After supper, the girls cleaned up and washed the dishes, while Ma took a little rest on the front porch in the rocker. Pa lit up his pipe while I read my army orders for the tenth time, and Wed whittled at a stick. Billie was aggravatin' Marilee, as usual.

It was almighty quiet out here on the porch as the shadows grew long, and the sun went down in a blaze of orange across the mountain. I had to look at it for a minute, and I reckon that this was the most beautiful sunset that I had ever seen.

Ellie came outside all gigglin' about somethin', and Bird was right behind her with a silly grin on her purty face. Bird had on a long blue dress with a frilly collar, and she looked just about as good as I had ever seen her. In fact, I couldn't keep my eyes off'n her, and I reckon she knew about it, for she caught my eye ever' now and then.

"Frank, I've got a sand thorn in my foot. Why don't you walk Alberta on home," said Ellie.

Everybody looked at me as I got to my feet, and I reckon they was studyin' how fast I'd swallow this bait. So I just got up real slow, like I wasn't at all too anxious to take this little stroll down the hill. Bird said her good-byes, and we took off walkin' down the road. By the time we got to the old Morgan cemetery, it was near about dark, but there was a big round moon risin' fast.

Bird reached over and took ahold of my hand. This set my head to spinnin', and caused me to reckon that she shore was a bold gal for bein' so forward. We kept walkin' and not sayin' nothin', but my hand was startin' to sweat, and so was my forehead. Just then, somethin' big and dark took off from the edge of the graveyard and made some crashin' sounds as it busted into the brush.

Bird grabbed me around the waist and held on, her eyes open wide.

"Frank, what was that?"

"Polecat, I reckon," I said. Then added, real casual-like, "Or the ghost of a murderer."

"What murderer?"

"Oh, it was before your time Bird," I told her. "But this old man from Preston Bend murdered his wife and shoved her down a well."

"Oh my God. What well?"

"The one over at your house, Bird."

With that, Bird gave me a good slap across the face, but it didn't hurt much and I commenced laughin'. She tried to give me another swat, but I grabbed both of her wrists and held on. Bird was strugglin' and callin' me some names, but finally she started laughin' too. We both plopped down and leaned back against a big gravestone marked with the name, EMERETTE RIDDLE.

We was kinda out of breath from our ghost-fight, so we sat quiet and caught our breath. Once we was breathin' proper, we still kept quiet, and I reckon we was both listenin' for any more sounds of whatever had gone runnin' out of the cemetery.

By now the moonlight was shinin' bright, and I looked down at Bird's face. Her eyes was glowin' with a little sparkle. There was also some tears in those dark Injun eyes and I wondered why. Then, she looked up at me and caught me in the act of my starin' down at her. I reckon it was just the natural thing to do, and I leaned her way a bit. She closed her eyes, and I took my chance to steal a kiss before she realized it was comin'. I touched my lips to hers and reckoned that she was gonna slap me a good one for bein' so forward and randy, but to my surprise, she kissed me right back.

Bird's lips were soft, warm, and moist and she tasted like wintergreen. I didn't know much about kissin' no gal, and I had never had no trainin' of any kind in the art of smoochin', but I tried to do the best I could.

Well, Miss Alberta Rivers was shore full of surprises tonight, for the next thing I knew, her little hand was slippin' inside of my shirt and wanderin' all over my bare belly and chest. We was still holdin' on to that good kiss and her lips was gettin' hotter and hotter. Then, I'll be damned if'n I didn't feel Bird's tongue come dartin' into my mouth just like a snake's. This didn't seem to be a natural thing, for a gal to be stickin' her hand in a man's shirt and her tongue into his mouth, so I thought I would give it a try and see how far I got before I got knocked silly.

I let my own tongue slide forward, and I'll be damned if'n that bold little Cherokee didn't start suckin' on it! This tongue move had went so well that I thought to myself, what the hell, I ain't gonna be around here much longer anyway, what with my goin' off to wage war, so I went ahead and gave it a try.

I slipped my hand between two buttons on Bird's dress and ended up with my hot hand right smack on Alberta Rivers' bare bosom. I had never felt no tit before, and I was surprised that it felt like a soft, warm pear, only with a hard nipple on the end of it.

Bird kinda froze up a little, but I just left my hand right where it was and hoped for the best.

The best lasted for only about one more second before Bird slapped me with a loud crack, usin' the same hand that had only recently been wanderin' all over my upper regions. Then, she was up and runnin' out of the graveyard and down the path to her house, leavin' me sittin' there like a fool with a near-broke jaw.

However, I felt like a king, what with gettin' my first feel of a live gal, somethin' I had recently been hankerin' for somethin' awful. In fact, I felt so good that I reckon if'n a regiment of Yankees appeared on the road, I would've killed 'em all.

I went on home with a happy heart and a sore jaw, and that night I dreamed of Alberta Rivers chasin' me with a big stick of wood down the streets of Dayton.

Next mornin', I was up before dawn, sittin' out on the front porch and aimin' to watch the sun rise over the mountains. Purty soon all of the rest of our crowd was up and racin' one another to the outhouse, and there was some people who was thankful that the seat was wide and had two holes in it. Ma fixed us a breakfast of duck eggs, taters, and corn bread. We washed it down with milk from our old gentle Jersey milk cow, and then us menfolk retired to the front porch to stretch and get ready for the mornin' chores.

Then, my serene mornin' was jolted and I seen a sight that damn near scared me half to death. Up the road, came old Jackson Rivers, Alberta's pa, and he was walkin' with a purpose too. I thought I saw his eyes blazin' as he strolled on right in my direction.

Jackson Rivers was mostly Cherokee, all six feet four and two hundred forty pounds of him, and he was well-known to people up here on the mountain. The reason Jackson was well-known was that he had kilt a riverboat man at a picnic down by the Tennessee River.

I had not seen the murder, but the story was that this here riverboat feller from Pennsylvania had drank too much of the whiskey that he was haulin', and got himself drunk. He then took a shine to the purty Mrs. Jackson Rivers and tried to give her a big hug from behind. She let out a squall and here came Jackson, barrelin' headlong into that huge riverboat man.

That set off an awful fracas and the riverman pulled out a bowie knife and laid Jackson Rivers open across the stomach. Jackson was lucky, and his guts did not spill out, for the cut was not quite deep enough. Now the riverman got Jackson wrapped up in his big arms and started squeezin' the life out of him.

Jackson Rivers was a kind and gentle man, and nobody never would have dreamed that he fought dirty. But he did. He drove his forehead smack into the riverman's face, bustin' that ole boy's nose. Blood flew all over the spectators, and they had to step back, as did the riverman, who had just about gone blind from pain.

However, the worst was yet to come. Jackson Rivers gave that Pennsylvania feller a kick in the crotch that caused him to let out a roar of pain and fall to the ground. Then, Mr. Rivers grabbed the river feller by the hair of the head, lifted him up and half drug him over to a split-rail fence post.

He got behind this feller and got ahold of the back of his head and set to slammin' his face into that fence post. Purty soon blood and snot was flyin' everywhere, women was screamin', and there was about five people, includin' Mrs. Rivers who was tryin' to put a stop to this action by pullin' Jackson off of the riverboat man.

But there was no stoppin' him. He just kept smashin' and smashin' till there wasn't much you could recognize as a face on that riverman. Finally, Jackson tired out and stood back, lettin' that poor wife-grabber fall limp to the ground, stone-cold dead.

The riverboat man had a partner, but he hightailed it out, and took off on their boat before Jackson Rivers might decide to kill him too.

As for the murder, there wasn't much sympathy for the dead feller, seein' how he'd taken unwanted liberties with another man's wife. Plus the fact that he was from up north anyway.

The dead man was covered up and the picnic resumed, but it wasn't as lively as before. Everyone wanted to buy Jackson Rivers a drink, or to drink a toast to the Cherokee Nation, most of whom was now out in Oklahoma in the Injun Territories.

They buried the riverboat man the next mornin', down by the river that he had probably admired. The burial detail couldn't dig too deep, for they hit some rock shale and had to stop. They rolled the big man into the shallow hole and put a little stick cross into the ground.

A couple of weeks later, somebody walked by the lonely grave, and found that some coons had dug up the corpse, and some varmints had ate everything cept'n the skull and one hand. The feller who found this gruesome sight had just kicked the remaining body parts into the river, and I reckon the catfish had made a good meal off of these left-overs.

So these was the thoughts runnin' through my mind as the dangerous murderin' Jackson Rivers came walkin' at me on the very day after I had taken terrible liberties with his very daughter.

"Mornin' Justin, Wed, Frank," Mr. Rivers began. Before we could respond, he threw in, "Is it true?"

I just about died, but Pa just said, "Mornin' Jack. Is what true?"

I never said nothin', just stood there froze, not knowin' if I was gonna live or die.

"That young Frank here is aimin' to leave the mountain to fight Yankees?"

"I'll let Frank tell you that, Jack, but let me get you a cup of coffee."

"Sounds fine, Justin," Mr. Rivers nodded. Then he turned to me. "Is it true, Frank?"

"Yes sir," I gulped out. "I reckon me and Owen Horton is gonna head on down to Chattanooga and join up."

"Well, young fella, I'm shore gonna miss you, and I know that Alberta will too, for she talks about you all the time."

Mr. Rivers stayed for coffee and Ma even forced a plate of duck eggs, taters, and corn bread on him. I reckon Mr. Rivers had more to say on this little occasion than I'd ever heard him speak in the eight years that I knowed him. He was shore a pleasant feller, for a murderer, and I stuck around for every word he had to say.

I gave out with a sigh of relief when he left though, and I was mighty glad to have escaped this close call without havin' my brains beat out against a fence post.

The next few days flew by fast, and I never laid eyes on the bold Alberta Rivers, even though I strolled past her house about ten times.

At the same time, I'd never seen so many friends and relatives in my life, and I had shore never got so many hugs and slobbery kisses from aunts, cousins, and such that was sad to see me leave these hills to wage war on the Yankees.

Two of my uncles gave me some weapons they said might come in handy in a fracas. Uncle Samuel Morgan gave me a long knife in a leather case which he said was sharp enough to cut farts with. And Uncle Verdie David gave me a little five-shot revolver which he had once't used to kill an injured panther that sprung on him up on Walden's Ridge.

Even my pa kicked in, givin' up his own polished .44 caliber Kentucky rifle. I know for a fact that he loved that rifle almost as much as he loved his wife. Maybe even better, for all I know.

Pa also gave me somethin' else . . . another hug.

Lord Almighty. Pa was givin' me more hugs than he had gave me in all my sixteen years. He was gettin' to be as bad as some of the fat widder women around here.

"Son," he said. "You use this gun only if it needs to be used. War is a rough time, and you might fall upon a chance to pick up a better gun than this here old Kentucky rifle. You go ahead and take the better gun, and just wrap this here rifle around a tree so's it won't be used by no damn Yankee agin' our boys. If'n you can sell it, go right on ahead, and use the money as best you need to. All I want to do is to see you come back down that road in one piece."

When I took that straight-shootin' gun, I had a choker fly up into my throat. Later Ma took to huggin' and blubberin' over me and beggin' me not to go, to just stay here on the farm with her and Pa. But she knew that I had signed my name and was committed to head for Chattanooga tomorrow.

We had three more days before we was due in Chattanooga. Pa and Mr. Horton had wanted to drive us down in a wagon or take some horses, but me and Owen was good walkers, and we wanted to make our way down to Dayton, and then take the two-day stroll to where we was due to meet up with a Major Reynolds in front of the main church.

Both me and Owen was near about worn out from all the good-byes, and we took off at the crack of daylight, loaded down with guns, knives, food, and sleepin' gear.

"Goddamn, Frank," said Owen. "We should have brought along a mule just to cart all of this gear."

I laughed, but deep in my heart there was an empty pit from leavin' this mountain home. That pit grew even bigger when we walked on by the dark and quiet home of the Rivers family.

We kept on walkin' and didn't say much. Owen did have some fun talkin' about all the fat women he'd smooched. He reckoned that this would be the last time he ever signed up for a war, just because of them kissin' widders. I laughed again, and didn't hear nothin' sneakin' up behind us. But then I heard a cry.

"Frank! Wait up, please!"

I looked around, and my heart jumped. Down that little road came the bold Alberta Rivers, barefoot, wearin' a familiar blue dress and runnin' like a deer. When she got closer, I could see tears streamin' down her purty face. I was also afeared that she was going to run right over me, 'cause she was goin' downhill too fast to be able to stop.

And that is just exactly what she did.

Down we went. Rifles, blankets, pots, and pans flyin' every which-a-way, and we ended up rollin' down that dusty road. Bird somehow ended up on top of me, and she was kissin' me, huggin' me, and tellin' me that she loved me, while Owen Horton stood there with eyes about as big as pie tins.

I got caught up in this action and was taken with sentimentality and I'll be damned if'n I didn't start tellin' Bird that I loved her too, but that me and Owen had to get on along to Chattanooga.

"Don't go, please," begged Bird. "I'll never see you again."

"I'm sorry, Bird. I'm done signed up. But don't you worry, I'll be back."

"No you won't."

"Yes I will."

"I'll wait for you."

"I'll wait for you too, Bird," I said, which sounded kind of stupid and caused Owen to grin.

"I love you, Frank Morgan."

"I feel just about the same way, Bird," I said while backing up. "And I want to apologize for bein' so randy the other night."

Bird didn't say nothin' to this fool statement, only her face got beet red. By now me and Owen was walkin' backwards, and Bird was standin' there with her hands on her hips, and her dark hair blowin' across her face while the orange sun rose behind her. I reckoned that was the purtiest sight that I had ever seen, and I would remember it for as long as I lived. But we had to turn around and go.

Owen aggravated me half to death about what I meant about bein' so randy. "Seems to me," he said, "that you must have pulled somethin' that you had to apologize for to Alberta."

"I don't know what yer talkin' about, and I don't want to say no more on that subject."

Owen just looked at me, studyin' my face for signs of a lie while we walked on.

It was a hot day, and by the time we walked into the town of Dayton, we had shed our coats and was now carryin' them along with the rest of our load. I was thankful that Pa had a leather strap on his rifle and I was able to carry it across my back.

We didn't take no time to stop in town, and just kept walkin' till we hit the Tennessee River. There was a ferry-boat which carried us across the wide river, and it was run by One-Eyed Washington Morgan, another of my relatives. The normal fare was ten cents but One-Eyed Wash wouldn't take no money and shook my hand. He wished us both good luck and said that he would say a prayer for us in church come Sunday.

On the other side of the river, there was a road that ran alongside of it. We turned south and headed for Chattanooga. We stopped once't and took us a little swim in the cool river and caught us a mess of crawdads for our supper. We put 'em into a sack, still alive, and headed on towards our destination.

Just before dark, we set up camp and spread out a piece of canvas to sleep on. Owen built up a big fire and set a pan full of river water on it to boil them crabs. It was gonna be a pleasant night, and the skeeters wasn't too bad, even though we was right beside of the river.

We had just got set to throw the crabs into the water when we heard a voice call out to us.

"Hello the camp, white cowboys comin' on in."

We stood up and Owen picked up his rifle just in case. Into the light of the fire came two smilin' young fellers wearin' leather boots, jeans, and long-sleeve shirts buttoned to the neck. They was also wearin' these big ole cowboy hats. They was much like me and Owen, in that they was both carryin' rifles and packs of possibles.

"Howdy, fellers," said the older lookin' of the two. "I'm Roy Grubbs and my partner here is Joe Buck."

"Howdy," Owen nodded. "I'm Owen Horton and this here is Frank Morgan. If'n yer of a mind, ya'll can share our campfire."

"Well," said Roy. "That's right neighborly of ya'll, and we bein' civilized fellers would ask you to lower that long gun if'n you'd like to."

Owen leaned his gun against a tree, and told the two boys to have a seat and make themselves at home.

"Where ya'll from?" I asked.

It was Joe Buck who answered with a grin. "We hail from Texas, and are headed fer Chattanooga to join up with the army."

"Texas! Goddamn," said Owen. "Ya'll shore are a long way from home. You boys walk all of the way?"

Them Texans was silent for a minute and just looked into the campfire. Then Joe Buck took a stick and poked at the red coals, makin' sparks crackle and fly.

"No sir," Joe Buck said. "We rode some good horses all the way up through Fort Smith and crost the Mississippi. I reckon we was makin' fair time and havin' good luck until we got into Tennessee."

"What happened then?" asked Owen.

"Some son of a bitch stole our horses while we was takin' a swim," Roy Grubbs butted in. "Right out from under the nose of young Joe Buck here."

"I don't know how you figure, Roy," fired back Joe. "You got eyes too."

"True enough," answered Roy. "But my eyes was underwater and you was supposed to be keepin' yours on the horses, as I recall."

I had noticed that both of these boys was wearin' mean-lookin' sidearms, and I didn't want this argument to turn into gunplay, as I might be the one to get hit by a stray bullet. So I decided to change the nature of this conversation.

"You boys ever ate crawdads?" I inquired.

They both turned and stared at me like I had growed another head.

"You mean crabs?" asked Roy.

"Yes sir."

"No," said Roy. "I ain't never got that hungry."

"Well you're shore in for a treat," said Owen, bringing forth his bag full of squirming crabs.

Roy and Joe's eyes got big as they stared at the lumps moving inside of that cloth sack. I took out four big potatoes that Ma had packed and stuck 'em in some of the glowing coals at the outside of the fire.

Roy got a sack and produced some coffee, sugar, a pot, and a big jar of peaches. "If'n me and Joe are invited to join in this meal, let us put forward somethin' towards the makin' of it."

Owen was starin' at them peaches, and I half expected him to start droolin' at any minute.

We got everything cookin' real good, and when the water came to a boil, Owen dumped the sack full of live crabs into the pot. Roy and Joe just stared, lookin' like *they* was the ones who was bein' boiled alive instead of them crawdads.

"Don't that hurt 'em?" said Joe.

Now it was me and Owen's turn to stare at Joe Buck.

"Well Joe, I don't reckon it feels none too good at first," said Owen, and we all started to laugh.

It didn't take very long before the crabs was bright red and no longer squirmin' or swimmin'. Owen dumped out the water and set the big pan of red crawdads within reach of all four of us. I got out the potatoes and some corn bread while Joe and Roy poured coffee and brought forth the jar of peaches along with a single spoon. Everybody was real hungry and dove in to this hot and strange meal. But I noticed right off that them cowboys was eatin' everything except the crawdads.

"Try one of these crabs, boys," I said. "You'll be glad ya did."

"Dang," said Roy. "I shore hate to eat such a thing."

"I feel just about the same," parroted Joe Buck.

Owen put a nice red crawdad on each of their tin plates and said to give it a try. He showed them cowboys how to break off the tail and suck out the meat. Them boys' hearts wasn't in it, I'm shore, but they wasn't no cowards, and they gave it a try just like Owen Horton had showed them.

Roy Grubbs' eyes lit up a bit. "I'll be goddamned, Joe. These little bugs is right tasty."

Joe Buck was eatin' a crab of his own, a little bit at a time. "I never thought I'd end up eatin' no crabs," he said.

"But then again we had us a cook down in Texas who got us caught up in eatin' frog meat."

"How did you like frogs?" asked Owen. "Me and Frank eat 'em by the hundreds."

"They was fair." said Joe.

"Fair, hell," said Roy. "You ate enough bullfrogs to fill our hats."

"Well," said Owen. "What do ya'll think of these crabs?"

"I reckon they're even better than frogs," said Joe, reachin' for another.

We finished our supper, told a few stories, and bedded down for the night. It was a pleasant evening, disturbed only by a few skeeters and a screechin' panther back in the hills.

Next mornin', we was up at dawn, and headin' south toward Chattanooga. Roy Grubbs and Joe Buck offered to part company with us, as they didn't want to intrude into our company. I had taken a likin' to both of these Texas cowboys and so had Owen, so we invited 'em to walk along with us. We was all headed to the same place, and there is safety in numbers anyway.

We had found that Joe Buck was the same age as me and Owen, and that Roy Grubbs was about twenty-five years old. He said that he felt like an old mother hen with three chicks. Roy was nearly six feet tall, lanky, and had short sandy-brown hair. He also had an enormous mustache that covered some of his mouth. I wondered how he ate food without swallowin' part of his mustache.

As for Joe Buck, he was about five foot ten and medium build. He had dark hair and big veins that stuck out of his arms. I reckoned he had been a hard worker, probl'y on some big ranch.

And, in fact, these boys *did* hail from a ranch, out near a town called Hondo, which I had never heard of. Roy said it was in Comanche country, three days ride from San Antone.

"How come you boys didn't join up with a Texas regiment?" asked Owen.

"That's just what we intended to do," said Roy. "We wanted to hook up with John B. Hood's Texas Cavalry, but he had already took off for Tennessee. So we grabbed us two good mounts and took off after him. Unfortunately, Joe let them get stole, and now we are on foot like a couple of Chinamen."

Joe Buck got red faced and started to say something, but I beat him to the punch and avoided another argument between these armed gunslingers.

"What ya aim to do now?"

"Well, since we ain't got no horses, I reckon we're just gonna join up with whoever'll have us. We just want to kill some Yankees before the war is over."

"You boys ever killed any men?" I asked.

"Joe Buck here hasn't killed no men yet, but he shore is a *Comanche*-killin' son of a bitch," said Roy. "I've kilt a few Injuns, and about four outlaws that needed killin', but never no civilized human."

Me and Owen never said nothin' about the fact that we hadn't killed nobody, but I reckoned that was just because Tennessee was a more civilized place than Hondo, Texas.

We kept up a good walkin' pace, and several times we was passed by people on horseback and in wagons. Once't four rough-lookin' fellers rode silently by us and gave us the once over. I was glad that we had four armed people, as that may have saved us some trouble.

## CHATTANOOGA

Shadows were growin' long when we saw the town of Chattanooga, which was on the far side of the river. We had to hire a ferry and re-cross. It cost ten cents, and the boat was pulled by a mule on the far side of the river, pullin' a long rope. There was also a mule on the side where we was now standin', and he was tied to a tree and eyeballin' us boys. I had always thought that mules were real smart. This mule was lookin' at me like he knew something that I didn't.

We were in some mountainous country, but I was in awe of a huge mountain near the town. It went straight up and disappeared into some low hangin' clouds. Joe Buck had some grandparents who lived here in Tennessee, and he told me that this was Lookout Mountain. He pointed out another rocky ledge nearby and said that was called Missionary Ridge, although he didn't know why. We all reckoned there must be some missionaries who lived up there.

There was a big curve in the river off to our left, and the ferryboat man said that was called Moccasin Bend. Owen asked him why, and the old feller just looked at him for a minute before he explained that if you jumped into the river right around there, you'd prob'ly get bit by a water moccasin.

That kind of scared Joe Buck for some reason, but I think that the old man was just pullin' our leg. At least I hoped he was.

I was surprised at all the people millin' around. We got into town and found the big church that we was lookin' for, but our Major Reynolds was not around, and we figured we'd look him up tomorrow.

Behind the church was a big hay field, and it was a strange sight what with all the white tents, campfires, and men walkin' around. I reckoned there must have been over two hundred men millin' around behind the church, and that did not even count those fellers who was in town and in the saloons.

We reckoned we'd stay together, and went back into the hay field and found a good place to camp. Firewood was gettin' fairly scarce, and me and the Texans went back into the woods to find some dead limbs, while Owen spread our bedrolls and started a little fire with some dead grass and twigs.

Once we returned with a pile of dead oak, Owen got a good fire goin', and we cooked up some corn bread and boiled some ear corn we'd stole out of a big cornfield. Roy said that stealin' was legal for soldiers, and that the farmers ought to be glad they can stay home and tend to the farm while the rest of us was gettin' shot at.

Some fellers commenced to stop by and get acquainted with us and let us know what was goin' on. They said this here was the main camp for signed-up soldiers and newcomers. And that tomorrow, we'd find out more.

Some music started up, and it sounded real nice out there under the stars. I reckon it was even kind of romantic, and I started pinin' for Alberta Rivers and rememberin' her good kiss along with that tongue sneakin' into my mouth.

Joe Buck was starin' into the fire and had a faraway look in his eyes. I soon found out that he had a gal he was smitten with back in Texas. Her name was Rosita Vega, and when he described her, I was surprised that she must have looked just like my Bird Rivers. His gal was Mexican and mine was Cherokee, and I commenced to reckon that me and Joe Buck had a lot in common, aside from the fact that he had done some killin' and I hadn't.

I learned some more about Joe Buck while we was talkin'. Both his ma and pa was from Tennessee, and they had bought a whole bunch of land for real cheap down in Texas, so they all headed out there. I also found out why Joe Buck turned pale when the ferryboat feller had mentioned water moccasins. It seems Joe had a little brother who got bit by a big moccasin in Texas and damn near died. Joe had been a witness to that big snake hangin' off of his screamin' little brother. His pa had jerked it off, and that snake was tryin' to bite Joe, before his pa could kill it.

It was well past midnight before we could finally get to sleep. I dreamed of a black bear chasin' me and Bird through our secret cave, but it seemed like I had just nodded off when I was rudely awakened by a bunch of horses and wagons runnin' past our camp.

It was just breakin' dawn, and I jumped up to see about seventy-five mounted soldiers and some more horses pullin' wagons and cannons. Them mounted fellers all had on gray uniform jackets, and was armed with long, curved swords and handguns. They had on a various assortment of hats, some of 'em with big feathers stickin' out, and they shore seemed to be happy. Roy said that these was cavalry and that if he had his horse, he would join up with 'em.

Everybody started stirrin', and some fellers was buildin' their fires back up from the banked coals, when I seen a bunch of uniformed soldiers with gold braids and fancy uniforms start to file in. Some of 'em was banterin' with a few of them Cavalry soldiers, and I wondered if'n one of these men was the Major Reynolds that I was supposed to seek out.

# TRAINING FOR WAR

That question was answered when a uniformed boy commenced blowin' a bugle, and a mounted cavalry soldier rode through the camp tellin' everybody to gather up by that big oak tree. We soon did as we was told, and an older feller with some gold braid on his fine uniform approached and began talkin' to the crowd.

"Men," he said. "My name is Major Reynolds, and I have to assume that many of you have been told to report to me. You all have signed up for a one-year tour of duty with the Army of the Confederate States of America. This unit will be the Third Tennessee, and at this time I will be your commanding officer."

This brought out a cheer from some of the men in camp, and a few fellers even threw their hats in the air. The major raised his hand for quiet.

"Your training will take place right here. I want to introduce Captain Barnes, Lieutenant Farnsworth, and Sergeants Halloran, O'Neil, and Johnson. Our duty is clear. We are to defend our Southern soil and our way of life from the enemy to the north. This is now our nation, and we must make sacrifices to keep it. I now wish to turn this regiment over to Captain Barnes, and thank you for volunteering."

We gave another cheer and Captain Barnes stepped forward. He had us get into a straight line and stand at attention. Some of the boys had trouble keepin' their faces forward, for they was used to lookin' around at what was goin' on.

Purty soon we were divided into three different companies, each with their own sergeant. We was lucky in that me, Roy, Joe, and Owen were still together, and our boss soldier was Sergeant Halloran. He was a great big red-headed feller with a beard and a big mustache, and spoke with an Irish accent. It didn't take very long for the sergeant to get mad at us clumsy recruits, and he broke into an Irish language that none of could understand.

None of us that is, cept'n Joe Buck who understood every cussword the sergeant was yellin'. Joe whispered to me that his ma was Irish, and she did the same thing when she was mad. Just as soon as Halloran took notice that Joe Buck could talk and understand that Irish language, I reckon Joe became his pet.

We was showed some ideas about marchin' and how to come and line up when a bugle blows and we was all about half-starved to death, for we had been interrupted before any of could get any breakfast. We kept on marchin' with the smell of bacon and coffee floatin' in the air. Finally the sergeants cut us loose to get somethin' to eat.

There was some darkies cookin' up flapjacks and bacon, and we all had to stand in line with a tin plate before we dug in at them vittles. There was a big washtub full of black coffee, and most everybody helped themselves to that except me and Joe Buck. We would have just as soon had a glass of milk, I reckon.

After breakfast, we cleaned up our campsite, picked up our rifles, and fell in with Sergeant Halloran when the bugle blew. He put us into lines, four abreast, and commenced makin' us march together. We was showed how to do a little skip so as to get back into step, if'n we ever was failin' to march proper. That was a good trick to know, as we was all fallin' out of step quite regular at that point.

There was a raggedy, barefoot black boy about ten years old who was marchin' alongside of us and beatin' a drum.

The beat of the drum was supposed to help us keep in step with our fellow recruits.

Sergeant Halloran should have been named Sergeant Hollerin' for he kept gettin' mad and yellin' at us.

"Jesus Christ," said a big-bearded feller marchin' behind me and Joe. "We came up here to kill Yankees, not to be walkin' around in the goddamn sun."

"You'll be walkin' in the sun till ye by Jesus get it right, me bucko," yelled the red-faced Sergeant Halloran.

After about two hours of marchin' around the streets of Chattanooga, our ragtag little company headed out to the far side of town and took some target practice with our rifles. At least those of us who had a rifle did. The sergeant had us shootin' at a pie tin against a sandy bank, about a hundred yards away. We shot one at a time, while the others watched, and you could tell when you hit the old pie tin, for it would jump and make a metal sound.

I was surprised. These raggedy old boys didn't look like much, but they could sure as hell hit that pie tin most every time. Even the sergeant was smilin' over this and was pattin' people on the back and talkin' in Irish.

We backed up to one hundred fifty yards, and the little group of Joe Buck, Roy Grubbs, Owen Horton, and me was right up there with the best shots. We could hit that tin, at least what was left of it, near every time.

Once the hot sun reached its peak, we was allowed to go back to our camp for a while and wait till the next bugle sounded. As for any lunch, we was on our own. Our group just had some beef jerky and cornpone, as we didn't feel like cookin' no meals. We found a shady spot and went to sleep for a while before the bugle woke us up.

We lined up and was given a speech by the captain on how we could be proud to be able to defend the Confederacy against them Yankee soldiers, who was probably headed our way right this very minute.

Then we split up and marched around with Sergeant Halloran hollerin'.

That's how it went for the next few weeks, and we commenced to get bored as hell. Up at the crack of dawn to the blowin' of bugles, marchin' around in the streets and fields, doin' some shootin' for practice, and gettin' speeches from just about everybody who happened by. We'd all thought we'd be killin' Yankees by now, but we had never even seen one. In fact, we hadn't even heard of no battles takin' place other that the one at Fort Sumter, and that had been a long time ago.

The boys who fired the cannons had a practice site set up outside of town. They were under the command of an officer by name of A. P. Alexander, and the sounds of cannons bein' fired was goin' on most every day. Them boys was doin' a lot of firin' across the Tennessee River at a target on the side of Lookout Mountain. People who lived on and around that mountain was mad as hell, cause the cannons had scared all of the game off, and caused their hens to stop layin' eggs, and their cows to dry up.

Sometimes we all got fed together by the army, but most of the time we had to get food for ourselves. We was fishin' in the Tennessee for our meals, raidin' cornfields, and killin' nearly every livin' wild animal within twenty miles of Chattanooga. Roy said that we'd ate so many possums that Owen was even startin' to resemble one.

The farmers in the area was beginnin' to complain to the major about their disappearin' crops and livestock, but the major stuck up for us.

Most everybody who was camped out here with us was good ole boys. They took to callin' us the 'Texas boys,' even though me and Owen was from right there in Tennessee. That was all right with me and Owen though, and we figured that the only difference between Texans and Tennessee boys was that they lived on flatter land, and their Indians were not as civilized as ours.

There was a crew of boys from Mississippi who camped together, and they seemed to be a purty rough crowd. They got drunk about three times a week, and liked to fight with one another over the most trivial of matters. Them boys seemed to be kind of ignorant, and I couldn't hardly understand a damn thing they said. One of 'em got drunk and started makin' fun of Roy Grubbs hat, and Roy knocked the shit out of him and broke a big tree limb over his ass.

The rest of the Mississippi boys got a big kick out of this fracas, and told Roy not to worry, that ole boy had asked for what he ended up gettin'.

We was marchin' one mornin', and all of a sudden we heard a bunch of drums beatin' and heard horses' hooves. Sergeant Halloran ordered us to stop and stand at ease. We shaded our eyes and looked down the road that led into town, and I saw the most beautiful sight that I had seen since Alberta Rivers stood there with her hands on her hips, holdin' her hair out of her dark eyes.

It looked to me like a long gray snake comin' through the mountains, with light flashin' and sparklin'.

"Holy by Jesus Christ," said Owen.

"What is it?" I asked, still shadin' my eyes.

"I don't rightly know," said Roy Grubbs. "But it looks like a bunch of soldiers, some walkin' and some ridin'."

"I hope they's on our side," said Joe Buck.

There was a lieutenant standin' nearby. "Don't worry boys," he laughed. "That's General P. G. T. Beauregard and the rest of the Third Tennessee, up from Memphis. We've been expectin' 'em."

We just stood there with our mouths open like a bunch of sharecroppers, gazin' at this grand sight. Out in front was about one hundred-fifty men on horseback, and they was dressed real fine. Many of 'em had on big hats with feathers stickin' out. They was the cavalry, and they came ridin' hard into town, wavin' their hats at everybody, especially the ladies.

Next came four high officers, ridin' abreast of one another. And on each side was fellows bearin' the flags of the Confederacy and the flag of Tennessee. Behind them was four drummer boys beatin' out a marchin' cadence, followed by soldiers for as far as I could see. They was marchin' real nice, and had good guns with fixed bayonets on their shoulders. About the only thing that marred this great entrance was some barkin' dogs tryin' to take a nip out of a couple of the marchin' soldiers.

When the band struck up 'Dixie,' many a dry eye commenced to fill with tears, and them soldier boys was grinnin' from ear to ear as they came marchin' into town.

Our officers had us fall in and stand at attention alongside the road. Lookin' down that line, I reckon we was a purty good sight to behold ourselves, except we didn't have no uniforms to speak of, and our guns was a hodgepodge of everything imaginable.

However, we was well-enough trained to present a fairly good spectacle.

When the officers rode by, they saluted us, and maybe it was my imagination, but I thought that General Beauregard was lookin' right at me when he saluted.

It took over an hour before the whole army got into town. We stood at attention all of that time, and only two fellers passed out. Nobody helped 'em out, and they just had to lay there in the dust with dogs sniffin' at 'em.

Once they was all in, someone yelled out for us to stand at ease and fall out. We was relieved, and we all gathered around General Beauregard, who was about to give a speech to us from horseback.

"You Chattanooga men. You soldiers of the Third Tennessee. Are you ready for a fight?"

"Yes Sirrrrrrr!" came a roar from everybody; and that was a true statement.

General Beauregard just sat there in his polished saddle and grinned fer a minute.

"Well boys," he said. "We're going to rest here for two days, and then head north. I cannot tell you our destination; only that we are not going north for the cool climate. We aim to attack the Yankee army. Are you with me boys?"

Such a roar arose that I could not tell what them boys was yellin', only that they was shore approvin' of any goddamn thing that this here general had in mind for us, up to and includin' gettin' kilt.

We waited two more days so that them soldiers could take a breather, for they had walked over two hundred miles. During them two days, there were even more soldiers who came pouring in, along with about thirty-five cannons, and the caisson wagons which accompanied each cannon with powder and shot.

There were soldiers from Alabama, Georgia, and Mississippi who mixed with us Tennessee boys, and of course our two Texas cowboys.

During the next two days, we did a lot of practice on loading and firing our guns as fast as we could. Most everybody had their own guns, and they were muzzle loaders.

To fire the gun, you first had to pour a measured amount of powder down the barrel, and then seat a round lead ball down on top of it with yer ramrod. Many fellers wrapped that ball in a piece of rag and spit on it so that it would slide down easier.

Once the ball was packed down onto the powder, you put a percussion cap onto the nipple, which was under the hammer, and you were ready to fire.

Most of the time the gun went off. If it didn't, you had to try it again with another percussion cap. If it still didn't go off, you might just as well try to find another rifle.

Finally, during this wait, we got in a good supply of equipment from off a train. There were rifles, uniforms, leather gear, bayonets, lead, powder, caps, and a bunch of food. Bags of flour, cornmeal, apples, salt, lard, some hogs, and a few head of cattle.

Us Texas boys was lucky enough to get up near the head of the line, and we all got us a genuine issue .58 caliber Enfield rifle with a brand new shiny bayonet. We also got a uniform jacket, leather gear, forage hats with flat tops, and little leather brims.

We made a rush back to our little tent and tried everything on. By God, we shore looked like soldiers now, instead of hog farmers goin' to market. Owen had his hat cocked off on the side of his head, and Roy got a big kick out of that.

"What the hell do you need a hat for Owen, if'n ya don't use it to keep the sun off'n yer head?" asked Roy.

"This is the way Tennessee fellers wear their hats, Roy," replied Owen, grinning.

"How come?" inquired Roy.

"I don't know," said Owen. "We just do, that's all."

Now, of course, that didn't make no sense at all, but shore enough, we all four took to cockin' our little hats off to the right side of our head a bit. It weren't long before half the damn regiment was wearin' their hats the same way, no matter if they was forage hats or not.

One day, we were called together and was surprised to find that a load of mail had caught up with us. We gathered around with high hopes while a sergeant called out the names from the letters, at least those names that he was able to read. All of us Texas boys except Roy Grubbs got a letter, and Joe Buck was lucky enough to get three of 'em.

We went off to the side and tore them letters open. Mine was from Ma, and I was shore glad to hear from home.

*Dearest Frank,*

*We all are fine and we hope that you are the same. Is everyone treating you all right, and are you eating proper?*

*Your pa kilt a wild hog, and we smoked it up. The crops are all in the ground and we are hoping for rain. Alma Parker died of the consumption and her husband is blue from the loss.*

*Bird has been coming down and asking about you. You should write her a letter and me too.*

*Little Wed was bit by something, but we do not know what it was. He took sick, but is fine now. We all miss you and hope to hear from you directly.*

*Your loving mother,*

*Millie Morgan*

I noticed that things had gotten quiet around here as everybody was readin' their mail from home, and those who had not got anything was feelin' bad, and mopin' around kickin' their toes in the dirt. I was especially sorry for Roy Grubbs, but he said that he didn't have nobody who might care about him that was able to write, so he wouldn't never get no letters.

Somethin' else I noticed. There was a hell of a bunch of people who was followin' this army around. Wagonloads of people who was in the business of sellin' everything from whiskey to clothing, to boots and food. There was also a bunch of slaves who followed us around on foot, most of 'em the property of some of the soldiers or the officers. However, some of them was freed slaves, and they was just lookin' for some work to do to make a little money.

## Wives, Whores, and The Paymaster

That was somethin' else that come our way. We got paid.

There was a feller called a paymaster, and on the first day of every month, he set up a table, and he had a box that was chockful of freshly minted Confederate money.

You would line up with your company, and when the paymaster called yer name, you would just march right up there, and he would give you some money. In my own case, it was the grand total of eleven dollars instead of the ten that we had been promised, and I was shore happy to have earned this much for the little bit of work that I had done. Hell, this was easier by far, than farmin' them rocky fields up on Walden's Ridge.

One more thing that followed the army around.

Women.

Now some of those women was wives of soldiers, and they did cookin', sewin', and other such things, and slept right in the tents with their husbands.

And there was some other women, who was not wives.

"Holy dogs," said Owen to Roy, pointin' out one of them fine-lookin' gals. "That there golden-haired gal is just about the purtiest thing I ever seen, next to Ellie Morgan."

"Don't be messin' around with such women, fellers, and you will be better off," said Roy Grubbs.

"How come, Roy?" I asked.

"'Cause them is whores, Frank. Where the hell you been?"

"What's a whore?" asked Owen.

Roy stopped what he was doing and just looked at Owen. So did Joe Buck, and, to our surprise, so did the blonde-headed gal, who gave a big smile to all of us Texas boys as she waved from across the street.

"A whore is a gal that takes yer money," said Roy. "And does for you what a wife usually does and maybe even more."

"What's wrong with that?" I asked.

"'Cause," replied Roy. "She sometimes gives you more than you paid for."

"Like what?" inquired Joe Buck, who was now gettin' interested in this risqué conversation.

"Like some ailments that make you go blind, and makes yer short leg dry up and blow away," said Roy.

"Yer short leg?" asked Owen.

"Yer *dick*, you ignorant hillbilly."

Us Texas boys all drew in a sharp breath and looked across the road at the purty gal, who was makin' motions for us to cross over to her side.

We all scattered.

## AN ARMY HEADS NORTH

At the crack of daybreak on the third day, we had struck our tents, gathered the gear that was absolutely necessary, and were lined up ready to march. I reckon that most everybody had some belongings that they did not need, but also did not want to lose, so we boxed them all up, put our names on the boxes and stored them in a building which would be safe.

Us Texas boys put all of our stuff into a long wooden crate and wrote our names on it. Inside was four rifles, some extra knives, our old hats, some pots and pans, and such stuff. I posted a letter to my pa askin' if he could come on down to Chattanooga one day and pick up our box for safekeeping. I knew that he would be glad to get his Kentucky rifle back, and that he would also be glad to do us this favor.

It was silent standin' at attention alongside of that road, with only our sergeants standin' and facin' us. Everybody was at attention, and fully loaded, ready to go.

I heard hoofbeats and seen a bunch of officers, headed by General P. G. T. Beauregard gallopin' our way, with mounted color-bearers ridin' hard behind them. It was a beautiful sight and them officers stopped damn near right in front of us Texas boys and whirled their horses.

General Beauregard stood up in his stirrups and gave out a yell. "North boys, north to meet the enemy! Let us take up this holy crusade in the name of the Confederate States of America!"

It was Major Vaughn's turn, and he yelled, "Left face!"

We all spun to our left and cheered.

"Columns of four!"

We went into that formation.

"Forwarrrrrd, MARCH!"

Thirteen hundred men moved forth in perfect order, and some drums started up a cadence beat as the local town band played 'Dixie.' I wish I had been able to break out of the ranks just to see this grand sight. I saw that nearly everybody in town was out linin' that road, and the tears were streamin' down their faces.

We was a long, wide, gray line movin' down the street like a freight train, and we was all spoilin' fer a fight. As we marched by the big hay field where most of us had been camped, I had to take a second look. What had once been a beautiful field, surrounded by trees, was now crushed and torn up. Every tree for a half mile had been cut down for firewood or for shelter, and the field was littered with lean-to's and soldier trash.

That field was shore a sad sight, and I hoped that the farmer who owned it would be able to get it back in order. I reckon that he was one feller who was glad to see us go.

The long column marched for nearly five miles and crossed the Tennessee River on a pontoon bridge, which was a bunch of heavy boards laid across some big wooden boats. Somebody was purty smart to have thought up them boats, 'cause they was on wheels like a wagon and could be pulled out of the water once we crossed.

Two horses got scared when they was crossin' and jumped into the water with their riders still in the saddle. Both of the riders got out, but one of the horses broke its leg and drowned in the river. Before it finally went under, that horse was screamin' like crazy and it was a pitiful sight to behold.

Once on the other side, we took a little rest and had some bacon and coffee. Then, we was on the move again, but we didn't have to march in step because nobody was watchin' us anymore. It was a steady movement of men, horses, cannons, and wagons and we was coverin' good ground in the hot sun. I looked back to the end of our column and sure enough, there was those wagonloads of businessmen, wives, and whores, just taggin' along, followed by about fifty or so darkies.

I reckon we made over fifteen miles that day, and camped alongside of a little creek at the base of a small mountain. We had our own rations and everybody had to fend for himself on this meal. Us Texas boys cooked up some cornmeal johnnycakes, coffee, and bacon. It shore wasn't as good as Ma's cookin', but it tasted good enough for us soldiers of the South.

A bugle blew before daylight, and we had the same thing for breakfast that we had for supper last night. Johnnycakes, coffee, and bacon.

By daybreak, we had struck camp and was walkin' northeast to who knows where. We walked all day long, and my feet was gettin' sore by the time we reached the spot where we was goin' to camp that night. There was a good surprise for us though, for cooks had went on ahead of our column and had rustled up one hell of a meal of stew and biscuits. They had killed and butchered two whole steers, and threw in over four hundred pounds of potatoes, carrots and onions. Them boys had three huge hog-scalding cauldrons on a wagon that they had hangin' over three different fires.

"Dang," said Joe Buck. "This is more like it. I'm shore gettin' tired of our own cookin'."

"We should get us a wife to do this stuff for us, like that old Alabama feller," offered Owen.

"How about that purty whore?"

"She'd do just fine," said Owen. "Frank here could be the lucky boy to jump over the broomstick with her."

"Yeah," said Joe Buck. "He'd probably furnish his own broomstick, I reckon."

We kept up with this tomfoolery until we had got a big pan full of stew and biscuits. Then we sat and ate like hogs, washin' it down with canteen water from that little creek. Some boys got a bit of music goin' with guitars and a fiddle, and we went on over to their fire and joined in a little sing-along. They was singin' 'Old Dan Tucker,' 'Dixie,' and 'Jack of Diamonds.' It was a real pleasant evening, what with the moon shining, the music, and the sounds of frogs in that little creek.

Many of the men sat around in the firelight and smoked on their pipes while gazin' into the fire. I reckon they wondered what was ahead for us at the end of this hard mountain road.

As for me, I was thinkin' of home and what everybody was doin' right now. I reckoned they might all be out on the front porch, drinkin' cold tea, and watchin' the moon over the ridge. Alberta Rivers might be there, spendin' the night with Ellie, and they would be wonderin' about me and Owen, just as we was wonderin' about them.

Next mornin' we was up and off just like before, marchin' as soon as it was light enough to see the road in front of us. It took almost three more days before we marched into Knoxville. There was a bunch of people linin' the road to get a look, and there was also about five hundred more soldiers waitin' to join up with us. They was from South Carolina, and they was shore a rough lookin' crowd of fellers. I was glad they was on our side and not the other.

There was no restin' or waitin' in this town though, and we walked out the very next morning, eighteen hundred men strong and headed northeast. On the second day out of Knoxville, we heard hoofbeats and saw dust stirrin' behind us. We had to leap off the road to keep from gettin' run over by about a hundred and fifty cavalry, followed by eight big cannons, headed hell bent fer election someplace ahead of us.

At the head of this cavalry was a big officer with fierce eyes and long black hair. He was a scary-lookin' feller to me, and the sergeant said that he was Nathan Bedford Forrest. I did not reckon that I'd want to cross swords with him, and I was glad that he, too, was on our side.

The following day, we was on Virginia soil and the rumor began to circulate that we was headed in the direction of Washington. Our spirits raised considerable, for we could picture ourselves takin' the capital and puttin' an end to this war. As for me, I didn't see how any army on earth could have matched up with our eighteen hundred grim-faced soldiers.

I had always reckoned that Tennessee had the biggest mountains of all, but we got into some bigger ones there in Virginia. Our roads cut through the hills like a snake, and you had to walk for ten miles just to make two as the crow flies. Supplies of food was good and our mail was catchin' up with us about every three days.

I finally got a letter from Bird and I snuck off under a rock bluff before I opened it up and read it.

*June 10, 1861*

*Dear Frank,*

*News has reached us that your regiment has left Tennessee and that you are headed north.*

*I do not know where you are going to, but wish that I did. We all are worried over you and Owen and hope that you will be all right.*

*Everybody in church said a prayer for you boys last Sunday. Your ma busted out crying and had to leave the service.*

*I doubt if you know this, but your friend Jodie Pickett joined up with the Yankee army. He rode on up to Kentucky to do it. His ma and pa still came to church, but no one would talk to them and there was no prayers sent forth on behalf of Jodie.*

*I just want you to know that I love you and think of you every day and night. I will wait for you until this war is over and hope that you do not find another girl along the way.*

*Love,*

*Alberta Rivers*

I laid back and read this letter over and over, and had to grin a little about Bird bein' worried over me findin' another gal. Hell, I hadn't seen hide nor hair of a decent gal who was not married, for a month. I don't know where all of the young gals had gone to, but they shore was scarce when the Third Tennessee came around.

Roy Grubbs seen me layin' over here in the shade and came on over.

"I see you was lucky enough to get yerself a letter, Frank."

"Yes sir," I said. "I shore did."

"Who's it from?"

"Alberta Rivers."

"Ain't that yer gal?"

"I reckon some folks think she is, and some think she ain't."

"And what do you think?" inquired the nosy Roy Grubbs.

"I think she is a right fine gal, fer bein' mostly Cherokee."

"I don't know what the world is comin' to," said Roy.

"What do you mean by that?"

"I just been thinkin', Joe Buck is walkin' around in a goddamn daze over a Mexican gal, and now you're all smitten with an Injun. Ain't you boys ever thought of chasin' after a white gal once't in a while?"

## RICHMOND

That damn fool conversation was cut short before I had a good chance to light into Roy 'cause a bugle blew for us to line up in the road. Once we were all here, we was ordered to commence movin' along. We pushed hard that day and made quite a few miles. It started to rain in the afternoon and got purty miserable by the time we pitched camp along side of a little pond.

We didn't get fed very well that night, only some turnip greens, boiled pork, and cornpone. Us Texas boys pitched our canvas tent, but it was too late, and we was soaked through to the bone. To make matters worse, that pond was a fine breedin' place fer skeeters, and they liked to ate us alive.

When we got up the next mornin', it was rainin' even harder, but we took off just the same. I had bite marks all over me, and was shore glad to be leavin' that skeeter pond behind. The road was gettin' muddy, and several times we had to pitch in and help the horses pull them heavy cannons out of a mud hole.

One of our good mules broke a leg while pullin' at a stuck cannon, and Sergeant Billie Hickey shot him in the head. The mule was hardheaded and the sergeant had to shoot him twice more before he gave up the ghost. After we passed by, the darkies set upon that mule with sharp knives, and I reckoned they would be eatin' mule steaks tonight.

"Goddamn," said Roy. "I never seen nobody eat a mule other than an Apache."

"What's an Apache?" asked Owen.

"That's a rough Injun with no morals at all," said Roy.

That night we had beans and corn bread for our supper, and I could smell steaks cookin' from the rear. I thought that maybe them darkies was smarter than we were. At least they was eatin' better on this rainy night.

Next mornin' it was still rainin' but not nearly as hard. We had a cold breakfast, and set to marchin' down that muddy-assed road. At least the general had enough sense to let the soldiers march ahead of them heavy cannons so we wouldn't be wadin' through their deep ruts. Even at that, we had to pull out the cannons every time we got down to the bottom of a hill and hit the really rough mud holes.

Next day, it had finally stopped rainin' and the sun was beatin' down hard on us. It shore felt a lot better than all of that rain though, and we was thankful. The wind kicked up a bit, and things was dryin' out fast. We picked up our pace, and the cannons stopped gettin' stuck as much.

Day after day we marched, always to the northeast. Rumor commenced to circulate that we was in country that was familiar to a couple of boys who had once lived in Virginia. They said we was bound for Richmond, which was the capital of the Confederacy, and just a stone's throw from Washington. And right up near Abe Lincoln's boys in blue.

Shore enough, in three more days, we got into a tight formation, unfurled the battle flag of the Third Tennessee and marched real smart into the outskirts of Richmond with our drums beatin' out a cadence. It made me real proud, to see a whole bunch of cheerin' people linin' the streets, and I even spied a few purty young gals. Some of us waved our hats back at the gals and gave out with a few hoorahs, which made the sergeants real mad. They had been tellin' us all along that we didn't have any discipline, and that we acted like a pack of coon hounds.

We rounded a curve in the streets and I damn near died on the spot when I seen a force of soldiers that put our eighteen hundred men to shame. They was standin' at attention, but some of 'em was crookin' their necks to see what was comin' around the corner. We marched down in front of 'em, and I seen the battle flags of Georgia, Alabama, Mississippi, and Louisiana, along with one hell of a bunch of Virginia flags. There was a bunch of cavalry officers and a covey of generals and colonels. I was walkin' next to sergeant Halloran, and he pointed out General Robert E. Lee and J.E.B. Stuart to me.

Once we got into town, we lined up with the other regiments, and was finally told to stand at ease. A couple of the generals gave a speech that made us think that we would soon be in a scrap, and that was fine with most every one of us.

Then, we broke out and set up camp behind a railroad yard. I had never dreamed that so many soldiers would ever be in one spot, but they shore was. It was like a beehive of armed men, all spoilin' fer a fight. We was given some supplies of cornmeal, boiled pork, salt, and lard, and then we was on our own for the rest of the afternoon and night.

Once we got a good campfire goin' and had put our tent up, there was a feller with a long beard who came over and introduced himself as Patterson Brown from someplace in Virginia. Patterson was a real nice feller, and he'd been there for ten days, so we commenced pumpin' him fer information.

"Do ya reckon we'll be in a fight purty quick?" asked Owen.

"Well boys," said Patterson. " Ole Jeff Davis ain't goin' to the expense of feedin' twenty-five thousand men for nothin'. I know that there is a big railroad junction to our north by the name of Manassas, and right beyond that is Washington. Some say we're goin' to head on up that way."

"Have ya'll seen any Yankees yet?" asked Roy Grubbs.

"No sir, not yet," said Patterson. "But I reckon that when we do, there'll be a bunch of 'em.'

We camped out there for two days, and spent a lot of time marchin', drillin', and practicin' shootin' our new muskets. As for my own gun, it shot just a little bit high and to the right, so I just did like my Grandpa Sam Morgan had told me, and aimed low and to the left.

Doin' that, I reckon I could hit a pumpkin at a hundred fifty yards nearly every time I pulled the trigger. We wasn't usin' round lead balls for shot like I always had at home. There was some new bullets, and they was long, and had three grooves around the bottom, and had hollowed out bases. They were called minie balls, and it was said that they was a whole lot more accurate than round balls. And after shootin' 'em for a while, I reckoned that they was right.

At the end of the second day, Sergeant Halloran came around and told us that we was goin' to strike camp and head out at first daylight tomorrow. He was dead right as usual, and we was marchin' north in the dawn, along with a good portion of the rest of the soldiers that was camped in Richmond. Roy reckoned that we must have over thirty thousand men. It took us two days before we spread out in a long line and camped on the south side of a river which had the strange name of Bull Run.

## THE BATTLE OF BULL RUN

We was told to dig in and get set for a possible battle here on this Virginia creek. Us Texas boys got us a little shovel, and dug a trench hole, and went even further than that by pilin' some logs in front of our trench. Two Georgia brothers, by the names of Jason and Jeffrey Gibson were laughin' at us and asked if we was Texans or groundhogs.

The cavalry boys had galloped off to the north, scoutin' for Yankees and possible troublemakers who may be headin' our way. It wasn't very long before they came ridin' hard back in and headed straight fer General Beauregard and his crew.

Then all hell broke loose. Captains and lieutenants came gallopin' up and down our lines, yellin' at the sergeants. Of course, that set the sergeants in motion, and purty soon they was yellin' at us soldiers to form up into the battle lines just like we had been taught. I'd be lyin' if I said I wasn't scared, but I reckon everybody else was just about as afraid as I was.

All four of us Texas boys was standin' together, side by side. We was in a group of about ninety men, shoulder to shoulder, three lines deep. Sergeant Halloran, a lieutenant, and a colonel was standin' behind us, I reckon to make sure that nobody amongst our lines took off for the woods.

The place on the river where we was standin' was called Blackburn's Ford, due to it bein' a shallow place in the river where you could get equipment across without drownin'. We reckoned that the Yankees would like to have this spot to themselves, along with another shallow place off to our left called Sudley Springs.

"What's goin' on, Roy?" asked Joe Buck.

"How the hell would I know," said Roy. "I've been standin' here with you the past hour, not scoutin' across the river."

"How come we're formin' up into battle lines?" asked Joe, with his voice goin' all squeaky.

"'Cause I reckon there's goin' to be a battle, Joe. Ain't that why we walked a thousand miles and got our good horses stole?" said Roy, looking at Joe Buck when he said it.

Me, Owen, and Joe just gulped at this thought and turned our attention across the Bull Run River. I saw some movement comin' over a hill on the far bank, and my eyes was fixed on that. It was five men on horseback, and once't they got to the top of that hill, they just sat there and gazed across the river at our gray-clad army, just the same as we was gazin' at them. One of them riders turned his horse and galloped back out of sight, but the other four just sat in their saddle and looked at us in a bold fashion.

Within three minutes that missing rider reappeared with another feller who was carryin' a big flag that used to make me proud to be around: the Stars and Stripes flag of the United States of America.

I heard a horse gallopin' behind me and turned around to see one of our fellers ridin' hard to a little hill just to our left. He was carryin' the battle flag of the Confederacy, and we all let out a cheer when he faced off across the river against the Stars and Stripes.

Then I seen some more movement on the other side of the river, and shore enough, here came some horses pullin' cannons and caissons. The horses were unhitched and them cannons was turned around in quick order, and

I'll be goddamned if they wasn't aimed in our general direction. I was scared shitless, but my spirits rose considerable when horses came gallopin' behind us, pullin' our own cannons. In fact, the cannon which was nearest to me I recognized as being one that I had helped pull out of two mud holes.

I had been cussin' that cannon at the time, but now I was shore glad that we had went to the trouble of tuggin' it out.

I heard drums begin to roll and looked around. There was three young drummer boys beatin' the hell out of their drums in perfect harmony. Had it not been for the fact that I was about to die of fright, I reckon I would have enjoyed hearin' them drums bein' played so good.

Now I seen a whole hell of a bunch of motion across the river, and was horrified to see about a thousand blue-clad soldiers in perfect ranks come marchin' over the hill and take a stand in front of their cannons. Only they was on a lower level near the bottom of the hill. Them Yankees had their own drummers, and they was beatin' on their little drums till hell won't have it.

If I stopped to think about it, I reckon that would have made a purty picture, what with all of them blue soldiers with long rifles tipped with shiny bayonets starin' across the river at us. The sky behind them was blue, and the slope they was on was a dark green. As for the river, it was brown, and that would have been the only thing that spoiled the beauty of the scene before me.

I think that Roy Grubbs might have sensed that I was startin' to think nonsense, and may have been well on the way to takin' leave of my wits, for he began to talk and try to calm us boys down.

"Don't worry boys," he said. "Them Yankees is just as scared at what they're lookin' at as we are. Just remember that if the shootin' starts, them city boys cain't hit a bull in the ass with a broom handle. The same cain't be said against you fine riflemen."

We stood in our ranks and watched the activity across Bull Run with great interest. Men, cannons, and horses was movin' into place, and we just stood our ground. I reckon it took about a half-hour before they had everything in place and finally slowed down in all of that activity. Them Yankees was standin' in plain sight, and so was we. It crossed my mind that maybe we should fire a volley at them before they did it to us, but I wasn't in charge of nothin' so I just kept still about it.

At that exact time, a cannon on the Yankee side of the river roared, and belched fire and smoke. Then another one went off, and another, and another.

Our boys opened up with several of our cannons, and the loudness set my ears to ringin'. Explosions started up behind us where the Yankee cannon shots was landin'. One of them explosions was real close, and I heard some screamin' and felt somethin' wet splash against the side of my face. I wiped it with my hand and found that I had been splashed with somebody's blood. That in turn made me a little sick, but I didn't have long to think about it, for Sergeant Halloran ordered our front line to fire a volley at the Yankees.

Thirty rifles went off at the same time, and damn near broke my eardrums. The stink of the black powder was terrible to smell, but our line was next to be ordered to aim and fire, and we damn shore did. As for me, I took careful aim at a big Yankee across the river and pulled the trigger. My gun roared and bucked back against my shoulder. Once the smoke cleared, I was mortified to see that my Yankee target was still standin' there, and in fact, he was firin' right back. My line bent down, and the line behind us stepped forward to fire while we was rammin' powder and lead down our muskets.

I heard some splattin' sounds and heard a groan from behind me. One of them Mississippi boys had got hit in the stomach, and he was sittin' on his ass, holdin' his hands over his belly. I got my musket ready to fire again, and at that time a cannonball hit at the end of our line. I heard some screams and seen pieces of soldiers flyin' through the air. A goddamn human arm landed out in front of our ranks, and it shore wasn't none too pleasant to be lookin' at. My line was given the order to fire again. I took careful aim at my fat Yankee counterpart and remembered this time to shoot low and to the left, and squeezed my trigger. This time things was different, and my target went over backwards, screamin' and holdin' his chest.

It came to me like a thunderbolt that I had just killed a man. I recollected the holy Bible, and realized that I had just broken the very first commandment of the Lord, which was 'Thou Shalt Not Kill.' That thought gave me no pleasure, but I didn't have time to ponder on it, for we had to duck down and reload again. We had a color bearer who was standin' out in front of us wavin' our Tennessee battle flag. He got hit twice and went down to the ground. Another soldier ran out and picked up the banner, but he was hit too. Finally a third feller went out and grabbed it and he was not hit, so the flag was saved from layin' on the bloody ground.

I was drenched in sweat, both from the blazin' sun and the fact that I was scared half out of my wits, but I kept up my turn at firin' at that passel of Yankees across the river, and they kept on firin' back. My gun was gettin' hot and the barrel was so fouled that it was startin' to be hard to ram the lead down.

Now, I heard some more drums beatin' behind me and off to my left. I looked over there and seen the brigade of General Longstreet's Georgians double-timin' it towards the river. It was a grand sight for me to see them boys come trottin' up and givin' out with the rebel yell. They stopped, formed a line, and fired a quick volley across the Bull Run. About a dozen Yankees dropped to the ground, and Longstreet's boys moved forward and gave out with another round of shot.

The Yankees stepped back again, and this caused Sergeant Halloran to give our company the order to charge. We did as we was told, and I shore felt a lot safer runnin' down towards the banks of that river than to just be standin' there hearin' them horrible splattin' sounds and hearin' the screams of soldiers that I had just been eatin' breakfast with.

When Longstreet's men saw us Tennessee boys chargin' and howlin' like banshees, they did exactly the same thing. I reckon the Yankees probably shit their britches when they heard that Rebel yell, for it even scared me, and I was on the same side as the ones doin' it. The Yankees commenced to back up slowly at first, but then they just turned tail and ran over the hill from whence they had come. Some of 'em even dropped their rifles so that they could run a little faster.

We got down to the edge of Bull Run Creek just about the same time as Longstreet's brigade. Everybody was hollerin' for the Yankees to come on back for another go at it and some of the boys was even firin' shots at the top of the now empty hill. The Yankee cannon at Blackburn's Ford had also disappeared, pulled by soldiers who did not want to wait for the horses to be hooked up to it.

## Letters, Beans, and Tomfoolery

By now, the firing down our lines along the Bull Run River had stopped, and the Yankees had withdrawn out of sight or out of range. They were not very disciplined in their manner of retreat, and I could see some of them scamperin' through the woods like jackrabbits.

We was ordered back from the river, and when I turned around a great sadness overwhelmed me when I saw all of our dead and dyin' troops. They was scattered all over the ground on our side of the river, and their conditions was enough to make a body want to head fer home. I seen men with no arms, no heads, and missing a leg here and there. One poor feller was torn right in half and I couldn't bear to look at him to see if I might have known who he was. There was a whole bunch of wounded fellers, moanin', screamin', and beggin' for a drink of water.

Wagons were comin' across the battlefield, and they was pickin' up the worst of the wounded first and carryin' them back to a grove of oak trees to where there was a medical tent set up. I bent over and gave the last of my water to an Alabama feller who was hit in the crotch and beggin' fer a drink.

"Holy goddamn hell," said Owen. "That scared me half to death."

"Did ya'll see that feller who was in two pieces?" asked Joe Buck.

"Which one?" I asked.

"Well how many was there, Frank?"

"I counted about ten," I said. "If'n we're talkin' about losin' heads, arms, or legs."

"No," said Joe Buck. "I was just talkin' about havin' yer tits and arms on one hunk and everything else scattered somewhere's else."

"I reckon I only seen one of those," I said.

"Cain't you hillbillies find something else to talk about?" said Roy.

We got back into our formation and watched across the river for another attack, while a bunch of fellers was helpin' get the dead and dyin' out of our way. I was right pleased to see them poor fellers taken out of there and so was everyone else.

After about an hour of watchin', we were allowed to find us some shade trees and take a rest. A wagon came by and it had some bread and pork hunks on it, so we all dug in with our dirty hands. Another wagon came by and re-supplied us with powder and shot. Most of us took the opportunity to clean our rifles and get a little oil down into the barrel.

I guess that everybody was expectin' the Yankees to come back fer another fight, but they didn't, and that was fine with me.

There was a railroad line that ran up through here from Richmond, and while we was waitin' to see if the Yankees would come at us again, we could hear trains comin' and goin' and bringin' our troops out here by the thousands. We could see 'em comin' up to the edge of the battlefield and after dark we could see their campfires. Sergeant Halloran came by and told us that them was the divisions of General Joseph Johnston, and that Johnston was here also.

Us Texas boys was glad to see more Reb soldiers comin' in to help us out. We had some warmed-up beans and bread for supper, and I took the time to lean against a tree and write my first letter to the folks back home. I wasn't much of a letter writer, but I had seen firsthand just how quick life can leave a feller in this war, so I decided to write, just in case I crossed over the Jordan myself.

*Dear Ma, Pa, Ellie, Bird, and the rest of my famlie,*

*I was just in a rough fite and I am still alive. I hope you are fine and that Pa got his kintuky rifl. I hav a friend hear by named Roy Grubbs and he never gets no letters from nobody so mebbe Ellie or Bird could take time to write him a letter som day.*

*There is talk we mite be goin to take washington right quik and then this war will be ovur. I hop so and then i will be home.*

*Yor sun,*

*Franklin Morgan*
*3rd Tenessee*

It took me a long time to write this letter, and I was glad that I had went to school and learned my letters so well. I reckoned that Ma would cry over gettin' this mail in a month or two, and I also hoped somebody took time to write to Roy Grubbs.

"What did ya write there, Frank?" said Roy.

"I cain't tell ya, Roy."

"How come, is it full of love talk?"

"No sir, it's just personal business between me and my own ma."

"Did you tell her that you loved her?" asked Roy.

"Hell no," I said. This conversation was startin' to make me squirm.

"Why not?"

"That ain't such a thing that a feller could ever say to his ma, Roy. Is everybody from Texas as rude and dumb as you are?"

Roy Grubbs had to stop for a minute and contemplate on that one. He took his hat off and wiped the sweat off from the inside of his hatband.

"Well, I reckon they are, except maybe for Joe Buck's ma. She seems civilized."

"Joe's ma weren't born in Texas, was she?"

"No sir, I believe she was born in Tennessee."

"Well," I said. "That's just what I mean!"

This ignorant conversation was ended when Owen Horton's bean dinner hit bottom and he cut loose with a loud fart.

"Was that a cannon shot?" yelled a voice from a nearby campfire.

"No, but this is," said a voice from another campfire, followed by his own roaring fart.

Joe Buck joined in this cannonade of farts, and began laughin' like a fool. Owen had built up some more gas and he cut loose, but it was only a squeaker.

"Misfire!" cried out a voice from the night.

"Aim them guns over at the Yankees!" yelled another and I heard a bunch of laughter.

And that is how we spent the next hour, fartin', laughin', and talkin' tomfoolery, and spoilin' the romantic moment of my writin' my first letter to the homefolks.

## FIRST MANASSAS

We finally got to sleep, and it seemed to me like I had just nodded off when bugles blew and woke us all up. It wasn't even daylight out yet, when we stoked our fires up and cooked up some kind of corn cakes in lard and heated up some coffee. By dawn, we was already lined up in companies and regiments and spoilin' for a fight.

However, that fight never came, even though we could spot Yankee troop movement, and could also see dust risin' on the other side of the river. It had been real hot, and the dust was terrible. There was no way for a large body of men to move without raisin' a cloud of dirt and giving away their position. All through this day and the next, trainloads of Southern troops kept coming into Manassas Junction to bolster our strength.

Two days after our scrap at the Bull Run, it was July twenty-first, and we had thirty thousand men in the area. We was not even out of bed yet, when cannons started roaring from the far side of Bull Run Creek, and all hell broke loose. Everybody jumped up and stumbled around in the dark to find his rifle and other gear. We finally got into our battle groups and squinted out into the dark.

Explosions was goin' off all around me, and I could hear screamin' and moanin' from our side of the river. We was able to make our way down to our little trench hole and bolster up our part of the mile long line of Confederate soldiers who were spread along the creek.

"I cain't see a goddamn thing, Roy," I shouted.

"Me neither, Frank," said Roy. "But I reckon the Yankees is in the same fix."

Dawn was just breakin' and we lay in fear, watchin' across the river at the sheets of red and yellow flame bellowin' out of those deadly Yankee cannons. I reckon that this sight might have been kind of purty if you stopped to think about it for a minute. But by now, our own cannon boys was shootin' back, firin' at the flames on the other side of the river and hopin' that no poor Rebel soldier had the misfortune to be standin' in front of our own cannons.

Once it was light enough for us to see across the river, I shore wish't I hadn't seen what I saw. There was a whole brigade of Yankee soldiers comin' over that hill, and headin' down to the river near Blackburn's Ford. They stopped, aimed, and commenced firin', and I could hear lead flyin' past my head and hear them terrible splats. We returned the fire, dropped to our knees, and reloaded while the ranks behind us took their turn at firin' their own guns. By God, we stood our ground, and we was givin' back just as good as we was gettin'. Them Yankees must have thought twice about crossin' to our side of the river, for they stopped short of the banks.

Just about that time, I heard a fracas far to our left, and heard a hell of a bunch of firin' from down by Sudley's Church. A rider came down our line abusing the tar out of his horse, and yellin' that the Yankees had crossed the river above our lines, and that they was flankin' us to our left. We reckoned that the move which had been made at us from across the river had just been a diversion, and the main trouble was comin' from our far left. However, there wasn't nothing that we could do about that, for we was still caught up in this skirmish on the other side of Bull Run Creek.

It wasn't long though, before that firing to our left got closer, and we could see that our boys was movin' backwards towards us, bein' fired on by a bunch of cannons and infantry. Our fellers were catchin' hell, and tryin' to adjust our lines. I could see the whole battle strategy just as plain as day. We started backin' up also, and the only thing that kept us from being overrun by blue-coated Yankees was a damn fool charge by five hundred of our Louisiana Tigers.

They gave out a yell and tore right into them Yankees, some of 'em waving bowie knives over their heads.

That brave charge gave us a little breathing room, but it soon fizzled out, and the Yankees was comin' at us once again. We was in a retreat towards a place called Matthews Hill, and I seen that the Fourth Alabama and the Second Mississippi was dug in and was goin' to make a stand there. Us Texas boys were together, and even though we was backin' up, it was an orderly retreat, and we was not runnin' like jackrabbits, the way them Yankees had done two days before.

Lead was flyin' like hailstones, and all of a sudden Roy Grubbs got rocked and fell right on his ass, holding his hands across his belly.

"Are you hit, Roy?" I yelled.

"I think so, Frank," he muttered. "It shore don't feel too damn good."

I got down on my knees while the rest of our boys just stumbled back towards Matthews Hill, and I raised up Roy's shirt, expecting his guts to come plopping out of him.

"Is it bad?" said Roy, laying down on his back and gazin' up at the sky.

"Hell, no," I said. "It's just a long red welt, and it ain't hardly bleedin'. Get up and get back into the fracas."

Roy looked down at his hairy belly and a look of relief crossed his face. He jumped to his feet and grabbed his rifle. Then me and him commenced our orderly retreat just as fast as our legs would carry us.

I did see one strange thing on this retreat though. There was some hungry Georgia boys who took time out to climb an apple tree to try and shake out some apples for themselves in the middle of this fierce battle. A cannon shot hit near the bottom of that apple tree, and them Georgia boys came plopping out of that tree like a bunch of monkeys.

Our stand on Matthews Hill lasted only about an hour, and then we was so badly outnumbered that we had to begin our orderly retreat once again. We was losin' men fast and furious, and I was amazed that I had not yet been killed, what with all of the minie balls that I heard zingin' past my head.

By noon, we had crossed the Warrenton Turnpike and a shallow creek named Young's Branch, and was almost at the bottom of a slope which led up to a farmhouse that was known to us as the Henry place. This was referred to as Henry House Hill, and there was a widder woman by the name of Judith Hill who refused to leave her house and was still inside.

I was running low on powder and lead, and was beginnin' to see this as a lost cause even though I reckoned that I had shot down about five Yankees and maybe more. All of the Texas boys was still alive, and Sergeant Hollerin' Halloran was about to lose his voice from shouting out so many orders at us, most of which we couldn't even hear.

If there is a hell, I reckon we was in it. The air was so full of white cannon smoke that you could barely see what you was shootin' at. Men and horses was screamin', and the sounds of guns and cannons had just about rendered me deaf. By now we had backed up to the top of Henry House Hill, and there was some high officers behind us, including General Bee, who was about to pull their hair out over our retreatin', and they wanted to put a stop to it right here.

Them officers was real close to me, and all of a sudden I saw General Bee point over to a ridge which was bein' held by a bunch of Confederates. "There stands Jackson like a stone wall!" he yelled. "Rally, men! Rally behind the Virginians!"

I took heart at this and also took a closer look. Sure enough, there was General Thomas Jackson and he wasn't doing no retreating. His boys was dug in and fightin' hard.

We decided to do the same, and to make our stand right here on Henry House Hill. It was kill or be killed, and we set to killin' just as fast as we could load and fire. Thank God, some more powder and shot arrived, and it was just in the nick of time, for I was down to my last three lead minie balls. Something else arrived, Colonel J. E. B. Stuart's First Virginia Cavalry and the Fourth Alabama.

Word also arrived that Jefferson Davis himself had arrived by horseback from Richmond, and he was watchin' this battle. As for me, I didn't want to do anything that might make Mr. Davis reckon that the Third Tennessee did not come to fight, so fight I did.

"Lookit that Frank," said Roy. "What the hell are them boys dressed up like?"

I looked over to where he was pointin' and seen a bunch of Yankees with big red bloomer britches and clown hats.

Even Sergeant Halloran had to stop fightin' fer a minute to gaze over at them odd fellers.

"Them boys are the New York Zouaves," he said.

"Are they dressed up for a costume party?" asked Roy.

"I don't know what they're dressed for, boys," yelled the sergeant. "Get back to fightin', fer the love of God."

"Look out, Frank!" hollered Roy.

At that, Roy Grubbs tackled me and knocked me for a loop. From behind me, an unexploded cannon ball come bouncin' right over where I had been standin', and hit Sergeant Halloran in the stomach. He let out a groan, and went flying backwards about twenty feet, landing in a patch of weeds.

"Jesus Christ!" yelled Owen.

"Get back to fightin'!" said Roy.

"What about the sergeant?" I said.

"He's done for," said Roy. "And so are we if'n we don't set to shootin'."

"Let's fire on them boys in the red bloomers," I said. And we all did.

The battle continued on Henry House Hill with neither side givin' an inch. Finally, a bunch of Yankees, which included them Zouave fellers, made a charge up Henry House Hill, and right into the guns of General Jackson's Virginians. They was met with a fearsome volley of rifle fire, which I reckon they was not expectin', for they stopped in their tracks and one hell of a bunch of 'em fell down. Then they backed up.

And then they turned and ran.

General Jackson's men came out of their position and charged after them retreatin' Zouaves, who were runnin' hard back from whence they had come. The Fourth Alabama joined in the pursuit, then J. E. B. Stuart's cavalry, and finally us Texas boys and what was left of our company, which was not much.

We gave out with the Rebel yell and was loadin' and firin' just as fast as we could. Them Zouaves was droppin' their rifles, and was runnin' through fresh brigades of Yankees who had just arrived at the battle. The fear took hold, and in short order, damn near every one of them Yankees was caught in an embarrassin' retreat, runnin' just as hard as they could go.

I seen some of their officers on horseback try to stop their flight, but purty soon even them officers was hightailin' it right past their own men, on their faster horses. We kept up the chase, and when we crossed over a hill from where the Yankees had come from, I seen another strange sight. It seems as how a whole bunch of civilians had brought their lady friends and picnic baskets out to watch the battle. There was fine little horse and buggy rigs all over the far hill, but they was all gettin' into motion and tryin' to hightail it out with the rest of the Yankee army.

Our boys got some cannons up on top of our hill and commenced firin' into that retreatin' mess of people. One shot blew up a stone bridge over Cub Creek, and that really set them Yankees into a panic. Soldiers was knockin' high-hatted fellers off'n their buggy rigs, and were usin' them rigs to get the hell out of here and back to Washington.

I cain't speak for no one else, but as for me, I was dead tired. I reckon we should have ran after them Yankees and taken Washington, but I never could've made it. We kept up rifle and cannon fire from the hill until there was no one left in sight for us to shoot at. Roy, Owen, and Joe Buck came over, and we just sat down in the weeds and hung our heads in exhaustion.

Finally, we got up and went back to see about Sergeant Halloran. He was layin' there, still alive, but his guts was hangin' out, and I could see two rib bones stickin' out of his back. As to how he could live in such a shape, I do not know, but he did, and he could even talk.

"And how did it go, me buckos?" Sergeant Halloran whispered.

"We whupped 'em good, Sergeant," I said.

"Ahhh, and I'm wishin' I could've been there with ya, boys. I've just been layin' here thinkin' that I left Ireland to get away from the fightin', and will ya be lookin' at how I meet my end."

Roy removed his hat, and I could see tears rollin' down his smoky cheeks.

"Shed no tears for me, buckos, for I'll soon be home with me dear old mother." Blood started to trickle from the side of his mouth.

We all looked at Sergeant Hollerin' Halloran, who I reckon was a purty good old boy.

"Make me a promise, buckos."

"Yes sir, anything you want," said Joe Buck.

"Promise me that you boys will see this war through to the end, no matter what."

We was all silent and looked at each other.

"Well boys, won't ya be givin' a promise to a dyin' Irishman?" whispered the sergeant.

Each and every one of us Texas boys gave our word to the old sergeant, and he gave out with a sigh as his spirit soared out of his body, bound for heaven or Ireland. I'm not sure which.

## Aftermath of Battle

We did not even bother to build a campfire that night and our only meal was some jerky and a drink of water from the Bull Run Creek. I didn't think of it at the time, but later we wondered just how many dead men was layin' in that creek that we was drinking from. Roy was becoming kind of a philosopher, and he reckoned that it might not be healthy to drink from rivers with dead bodies stacked up in 'em, and none of us bothered to argue the point.

We also spent some time ponderin' over the solemn promise we had given to the dyin' Irishman. Due to the fact that he had died right after we had made that solemn vow, we all reckoned that we were pinned down on this promise, and had to keep our word, or else we would never see the purly gates of heaven.

That night along the Bull Run Creek, I slept so hard that I doubt if'n a cannon shot could have woke me. The skeeters buzzed around in great feasting swarms, but even those varmints couldn't beat us Texas boys out of our well-earned rest.

Next morning, we was in control of the battlefield and there was not a Yankee in sight. A spy had rode back to our lines and reported that soldiers was sneakin' into the town of Washington like a bunch of whipped dogs, and that a good many of 'em had left their rifles behind. We was put on a detail with a bunch of other men to take wagons across the battlefield and collect guns and anything else that the Yankees had left behind. It was a windfall.

By the end of the day, we'd picked up nearly thirteen hundred rifles, sidearms, a slew of cannons, rations, powder, shot, and forty live horses. Other wagons, manned by darkies, was pickin' up our dead soldiers and gettin' set to bury them poor fellers in the Virginia soil.

A company of Yankees showed up under a white flag and begged to be able to pick up their wounded and dead. General Beauregard allowed them to go ahead, and we were workin' out in the battlefield with the very same Yankees which had just been firin' lead at us yesterday. After a while, there was some banterin' goin' on between us and those Yankees, and I thought to myself that these boys was not really so bad after all. In fact, the ones I talked to was farmboys just like me, Owen, and Joe Buck. They was with the Twenty-fourth Michigan and were one hell of a long ways from their homes. Them Michigan boys shore talked funny and I had a hard time understandin' what they was sayin'. However, there was one Yankee from New York and none of us could make out what the hell he was talkin' about, so we just ignored him and kept talkin' with them Michiganders.

"How much pay do you'uns draw?" asked Owen.

"What is a 'you'uns'?" asked one of the Yankees, with a puzzled look on his face.

"A you'uns is ya'll."

"You mean *us*?"

"Yes. Goddamn, no wonder you'uns is losin' this fracas."

"What's a 'fracas'?"

"Never mind. How much money do you Yankees get paid for gettin' shot at and pickin' up corpses in the hot sun?"

"Thirteen dollars a month," said the Yankee.

"Jesus Christ!" yelled Owen. "We only get eleven dollars."

"Maybe that's because of your bad vocabulary," said the Michigander.

"My bad what?" hollered Owen, and that got us all to laughing. We was all Americans, I reckon, but we shore didn't talk exactly the same language, especially them New Yorkers.

One of 'em was a farmboy named Johnie Empey, who said he came from a place called Davisburg, Michigan. Owen laughed at that and asked him if that town was named after Jefferson Davis. Johnie got a big kick out of that too, and when we parted company, he told us to come on up to Davisburg after the war and he would take us fishin' for suckers in the Kearsley Creek.

Now I knew what a sucker fish was, and it shore wasn't much. "What do you do with them trash fish after ya catch 'em, Johnie Yank?" I asked.

"We eat 'em," said Johnie.

"Dang, ya'll shore must be hungry up there in Davisburg," I replied.

"About that time a Reb lieutenant came gallopin' up on a big black horse and gave us hell for talkin' to the enemy. He told them Michigan boys to get back to work or he would blast 'em off of them wagons. Johnie Empey glared at the lieutenant in a bold way, slapped the reins across his horse's ass. "Be seeing you'uns in Richmond, Johnie Rebs," he yelled as he rode off.

I don't think that set very well in the lieutenant's craw, and I dang near expected him to pull his iron and go to fightin'. But he was able to restrain himself.

## Battle of Ball's Bluff

And so we won both of them battles, and the war was on for sure. Poor Mrs. Henry died in that fracas after having her foot shot off. Everybody reckoned that she was the first civilian to die in this war, and we all felt bad that a woman had to suffer so.

Word was that Jeff Davis was mad as hell that we hadn't pursued the Yankees into Washington, but General Johnston said we were more disorganized by victory than the Yankees was in defeat. I reckon he was right on that.

Our army purty much stayed in this area and waited for the Yankees to make another try either at us or on the city of Richmond, but they never did. All summer long we waited, and we was runnin' short on supplies and food. There was so many soldiers crowded into this area it got to where you couldn't walk into the woods without steppin' in shit piles.

We spent quite a bit of time drillin', and was gettin' better service on the delivery of mail. As to mail, a miracle had happened. Roy Grubbs started getting letters.

He was gettin' more letters than any of the rest of us, mostly from Bird and Ellie, along with a few from Marilee and even my ma, for God's sake. Roy wouldn't let none of us look at his letters, and he liked to lay around readin' 'em and smilin' like a coon. Owen tried to steal Roy's pile of letters from his leather pouch, but Roy caught him and threatened to cut his fingers off.

We was gettin' restless to get out of here and into another fracas, when the Yankees did us a favor and livened things up a bit.

In October, the Yankees under Generals McClellan and Stone tried to sneak their army across the Potomac at a place called Ball's Bluff. They had some bad luck, in that our spies told us ahead of time that they would be comin', so we moved our army down to head them off. To make matters even worse for the Yankees, there was sixty-foot-high bluffs on the far side of the river where they tried to cross.

There was a battle, but as far as we was concerned, it was more like a turkey shoot. It was just a matter of us Rebs pourin' fire into them poor Federals, who were tryin' to get across the river and scale the bluff on the far side. They didn't really stand a chance in hell of doin' it, but they gave it a good try.

The word that we got later was that the Yankees suffered fifty percent casualties and headed back to Washington once again. I reckon that ole Abe Lincoln was fit to be tied, and some of us wondered if the Yankees might just about be ready to give up on this war.

## Back to Tenessee

The fall season was in full swing in northern Virginia and winter was coming fast. The Confederacy was having a hard time supplying all of those troops north of Richmond, so two things happened.

Thirty-day furloughs were bein' given out to some troops, and soldiers were being reassigned further south, due to Yankee activity in Kentucky and Tennessee.

Me, Owen, Joe Buck, and Roy Grubbs volunteered to be detached back to Tennessee if the opportunity arose, and we also asked for leaves of absence so we could visit home. We were surprised when all four of us were granted our request. By November first, we were on a troop train headed south. Our orders were to be in Nashville by December first for reassignment.

There was no way that Roy and Joe could return all of the way home to Texas, but they had heard so much about me and Owen's home in Tennessee, that they agreed to come with us. I know that Roy was wantin' to meet up with all the gals who had been writin' to him, and I also know that Owen was wonderin' what Ellie had been sayin' in her letters to Roy.

It only took us a week to get back to Dayton, what with ridin' the train aways and farmers givin' us a ride on their wagons whenever they passed us on a road. Everybody was real friendly towards us Rebel soldiers, feedin' us and allowin' us to sleep in their barns.

Old One-Eyed Wash gave us a free ferry ride across the Tennessee and even gave us a bag of apples. We was walkin' out of Dayton, headed up the mountain fer Morgan Springs, when an old boy with a wagonload of corn came up behind us.

"Jump in back, boys. Where you'uns headed?"

"On up to Morgan Springs, sir."

We all four clamored into the back of the big wagon, the bearded farmer swatted his mules on the ass, and away we went. He spit some tobacco juice off to the side, and said that his name was John B. Dean. We gave up our own names and he reckoned that them was all fine southern names.

"Where ya'll been, boys?" asked the farmer, turning around on his seat.

"We was up in Virginia at a place called Manassas Junction," I said.

The farmer turned even more in his seat, and looked back at us, his mouth hanging open. "Well, I'll be damned. Was you boys in the fight?"

"Yes sir," said Owen. "We shore was."

"Were it as terrible as we heard?" asked John B. Dean.

"It was rough," said Owen. "Though I reckon it was more terrible for the Yankees than it was for us."

All the way up the mountain, the farmer pumped us for information about the war. We answered all of his questions and was glad to do so, in order not to have to be walkin' up this high hill. That farmer even went past his cutoff and carried us right up to where I asked him to stop.

Right in front of Alberta Rivers' little farm . . .

The Rivers' dogs was barkin' up a storm and I seen Mrs. Rivers come out on the porch and shade her eyes and try to make out who them four dirty-uniformed soldiers was, and what they was doin' standin' out in the road. Then Mr. Rivers came out, followed by Bird, who was wearing a man's shirt and an old pair of britches. She was barefoot and her long black hair was pulled back and tied in something that resembled a horse's tail.

I waved and Bird let out a shriek that would have put a panther to shame. Then she came runnin' across that yard like a deer and screamin' every step of the way.

This was kind of embarrassin' for me, but I walked off towards Bird and held my arms out. When she got about ten feet from me, Bird somehow became airborne.

It like to scared the shit out of me to see her flyin' through the air like that, and I knew I was gonna get a jolt, but I was obliged to catch her. Well sir, I did manage to catch that flyin' gal, and it knocked the breath out of both of us, and down on the ground we went, just like before.

"Frank! Frank! You've come home. Are you all right?" cried Bird.

"Well Bird," I gasped. "I was fine before you laid me out in this road. I think my chest might be broken."

"Oh my God, Frank Morgan, you stink worse'n a billy goat," said Bird, holding her nose while still astraddle of me. From my vantage point, laying on my back in this road, I could see that we were drawing a crowd. Owen, Joe Buck, and Roy was just standin' there with wide eyes and open mouths, but now they was joined by Bird's ma and pa.

"Howdy, Frank," said the murderin' Jackson Rivers. "Bird, get off'n Frank ere you squish him."

"Yes sir," said Bird, gettin' up with a smile, and finally taking notice of Owen and them gawkin' Texans. "Howdy, Owen. Who are these soldier boys?"

I got to my feet and dusted myself off. That little struggle had stirred me up, and I suddenly noticed what Bird had been talking about in such a bold way. I did stink worse than a billy goat. "Howdy Mr. and Miz Rivers," I said. "These two boys is Joe Buck and Roy Grubbs. They're from Texas and been fightin' Yankees along with me and Owen here. Roy and Joe, this here is Mr. and Miz Rivers and their daughter, Alberta."

Hands was shook all around and I thought I noticed a twinkle in Roy's eye when he took the hand of Miss Alberta Rivers.

"I just want to thank ya'll for writin' them letters," said Roy, holding his hat in both hands and lookin' down at the ground. I ain't got nobody, as Injuns kilt my ma and pa and carried off my little sister. Ya'll shore made war a lot more pleasant, and I appreciate it."

Now this grand speech brung a tear into the eye of Miz Rivers and she went over and gave Roy Grubbs a big hug. I guess I should have warned Roy that the last man other than Jackson Rivers who had hugged this woman ended up gettin' murdered and ate by varmints.

The Rivers family wanted us to come on in fer dinner, but me and Owen wanted to get along to our own homes. We tipped our hats and said good-bye, then commenced walkin' up that dusty road. Roy Grubbs walked backwards, wavin' his hat in the air.

"Miss Alberta, I shore want to apologize for us not takin' a hot bath before we came by. Next time ya'll see us, we'll smell like a load of roses."

Bird picked up a rock and sent it in our direction, causin' us Texas boys to scatter and duck.

Owen veered off at the two tracks which led to his own farm and we agreed to stop by later and meet his folks unless they came over to our place. Me, Joe, and Roy continued walkin' up the road and it wasn't long before I saw the smoke from our chimney risin' above a little stand of trees. At just about this same time, the hounds set to barkin' and Myrt come sailin' around the corner, intent on eatin' us all alive. Luckily, she spied me and cooled off on her murderous intentions and set to lickin' my face and jumpin' all over me with her dirty feet. But I was glad to see her and took to rubbin' her head and tryin' to duck her wet tongue.

Ma come runnin' out, followed by Ellie, Marilee and Billie, all makin' a big fuss over me and tryin' to kiss me just the same as my old dog Myrt had done. Then Pa come out and I was surprised to see that he was limpin' along with a big stick crutch under an arm.

"Howdy, son," he said. "We shore are proud to see you home again."

"Oh Frank," said Ma. "You shore need a bath."

Marilee had been givin' me a hug, but she backed off real quick and had a funny look on her face. I was somewhat embarrassed to be in such a shape, so I backed off and introduced Joe Buck and Roy Grubbs to the family.

"I'm shore happy to meet ya'll," said Roy. "And I'd like to thank you ladies for the fine letters that you sent along to me. I'm much obliged to ya."

Joe Buck shook hands all around and seemed to be shy about this whole deal. "I shore hope we ain't puttin' ya'll out by comin' home with Frank," he said.

"We're proud to have ya stay here with us for as long as you can," said Pa. "And we've got your hats and clothes that you'uns boxed up in Chattanooga."

"Did you get yer rifle back?" I asked.

"I shore did, Frank, and I'd like to be puttin' it to use, except a horse pitched me on a rock and broke my goddamn leg."

"Justin!" said Ma.

"Sorry, Millie."

Ma got tired of this roadside conversation and made us all come into the house for a bowl of hot stew. Roy and Joe didn't want to come inside, sayin' they smelled too bad and they'd rather just wait outside. But Ma wouldn't hear of it.

After our stew meal, there was still some daylight left, and it was a warm evening so Ma gave us the clothes that we'd sent back from Chattanooga. She also gave us a bar of lye soap and aimed us down to the spring to take a bath. Roy and Joe Buck was interested in them springs, as I had told them of the healin' powers that the water held. There was two spring holes, one for drinkin' and another one farther down, dammed up with stones into a nice deep pool for soaking.

And soak we did, naked as jaybirds and latherin' ourselves up with that lye soap. Roy still had a red welt across his stomach from the Manassas fracas, and he hoped the spring would heal it up.

"Why didn't you ever go up to the medical tent and have one of them doctors take a look at that gouge?" said Joe Buck.

"Well, Joe, it's like this. Everybody that I seen visit that doctors' tent either died or got something cut off'n 'em. Did you boys ever see that big pile of legs and arms that was stacked outside of that tent?"

"Ain't no way they could have cut off yer stomach," said Joe.

"All the same, Joe. I didn't have any hankerin' to test that theory."

We was all ponderin' on that pile of extremities while we washed up, even soaping up our long, greasy hair. Ma had washed out them clothes that we had sent back and it felt good to get clean duds on and get out of them filthy uniforms. The best thing as far as Joe and Roy was concerned was in puttin' on their beat-up old cowboy hats. I couldn't help but notice they was wearin' them hats cocked off to the side a bit, Tennessee style.

"Goddamn, son of a bitch!" yelled Joe Buck, jumping back away from the big log that he had laid his boots on.

He near 'bout scared the shit out of me and Roy both, causing us to jump back.

"Snake!" cried Joe."Look at that big bastard!"

"Where?" inquired Roy.

"Right there under that dern log!"

Me and Roy peered over to the other side of that rotten oak log and shore enough, there lay a five-foot-long, brownish-gray evil-looking snake. It was curled up like a rattler and was watchin' us with its beady eyes while flickin' out a red tongue.

"Get a stick and whop that varmint," said Joe Buck.

"No, wait a minute there," I said.

"What?"

"He's only a king snake?"

"King o' what?" asked a white-faced Joe Buck.

"He ain't king of nothin', but he eats other snakes and rats. We don't never kill no king snakes."

"Dang, Frank. I don't like to take a bath with a long snake layin' around. I'll probably never take another bath as long as I live," said Roy Grubbs.

I finally was able to talk them Texas boys out of murderin' that poor little king snake, but it was quite a chore. I reckoned that them boys had never left a live snake in their wake during all of their travels, and it shore galled them to start now.

We finished gettin' dressed and made our way up the tree-covered hill and headed for the house.

It weren't till a long time later that I found out Ellie, Marilee, and Alberta Rivers was hidin' behind a big rock, gigglin' like fools over the fine show that they had just seen.

## THE HORSE BUSINESS

Once we got back to the house, Ma took our filthy uniforms and threw 'em into a hot tub of soapy water to soak. Pa and us menfolk went out onto the front porch to watch the sun set over the mountains. Pa lit his pipe and began to explain about his broke leg. It seems he'd sold all but one of his good horses to an old boy buyin' them for the cavalry.

"I don't think I had much choice, boys. If'n I didn't sell 'em, I reckon the army would have just came and *took* 'em. Anyway, this feller paid me fifty dollars apiece for the eight horses I had. He left me one horse that he was pullin' along, and gave me that stallion for free. Said he'd be glad to be shed of the critter, for it was always tryin' to bite a hunk out of him."

"So how'd ya come by yer broke leg, Mr. Morgan?" asked Joe Buck.

"I thought I could break that stallion and sell him, once he was rideable, but it didn't work out that way. That damn horse bucked so hard he broke the cinch strap and sent me and the saddle skyward. I came down on a rock and had to crawl all the way back to the house, while that goddamn horse just stood there starin' at me."

"How long ago was that?" asked Roy.

"That was three weeks ago and that dang horse still watches me. Ellie and Wed had one hell of a time just gettin' the bridle off'n him."

"What do ya aim to do with him now?" asked Roy, who seemed to be takin' a strange interest in this bad horse.

"Probably shoot the son of a bitch, or just let him loose. I've broke many a horse, but I do believe that critter is unbreakable."

Roy and Joe Buck glanced at each other and had a funny look in their eye. "Sir," Roy Grubbs began. "I'll give you thirty dollars for that horse and any old saddle you can dig up. I'd shore like to take a crack at ridin' him."

"Are you crazy, Roy? I'd shore hate to see you in the same fix I'm in, broke leg and all."

"Mister, me and Joe here have broke a few horses in our day, and it would help pass the time and go a little way towards payin' for our grub while we're here."

Pa just took a pull on his pipe and looked to the side of the house. Here came Bird, Marilee, and Ellie with a bunch of flowers.

"Where in the world have you gals been?" asked Pa. "Yer ma's been lookin' for ya."

"Oh, we've just been pickin' flowers and lookin' around," said Ellie. Them gals shore had a mysterious look on their faces and I knowed that somethin' was going on. But Pa missed it, and went back to his horse talk. As for me, I kept watch at them gals and wondered what the hell they was up to now.

"Roy," said Pa. "I've got an old saddle that's worth about ten dollars, and that horse is free to you. That's my final offer and I hope you don't take me up on it, for that horse would probably kill you if you try to break him."

"Deal!" said Roy, standin' up and takin' a ten-dollar bill out of his pant's pocket.

Ma come out on the porch and said she had two beds already made in Wed and Billie's room for Joe and Roy, but they would not hear of displacin' my little brothers, and stood their ground, wantin' to sleep out in the barn.

"Damn," said Pa. "There's snakes and rats prowlin' around that barn and who knows what else."

"Is there any chiggers or Comanches around here?" asked Joe Buck.

"Well, no sir," said Pa. "I reckon there ain't."

"Then it will be a great improvement over what we've become used to, Mr. Morgan."

We spent the next hour tryin' to convince Joe and Roy to sleep inside, but they was set in their ways, and I could see that further arguments were of no use on this matter. So after a while they trudged on off to sleep in the barn.

Next morning, we was up at daylight and found them Texas boys leanin' against the corral rails watchin' that big black stallion, who was watchin' right back. Ma fixed us a breakfast of eggs, biscuits, and potatoes, after which we menfolk headed out to the barn. Pa showed them boys the saddle, a bridle, blanket, and two horsehair ropes. Joe grabbed the saddle and Roy brought out the rest of the stuff, and everybody in the family, including Bird, who had spent the night sleepin' with Ellie, gathered 'round for the show.

Roy and Joe each had a rope, and Joe also had a blanket as they entered the corral. That big black horse laid his ears back, and came runnin' at Roy, makin' one hell of a horse-snort racket. Joe threw the blanket across the horse's eyes and blocked his vision, while Roy sidestepped and twirled the rope over his head. The horse got rid of the blanket and went after Joe while the girls screamed and Roy threw his lariat around both front ankles of the snorting horse.

And down the horse went, so hard we could all hear the wind get knocked out of him.

Joe Buck twirled and threw his rope, which gently settled over both rear ankles of the horse. The men pulled hard and hung on while the stallion tried to regain his footin' and continue the attack, but he was quick to find that gettin' up off the ground was a hell of a lot harder than gettin' down onto it. The stallion commenced to twistin' and tryin' to bite whatever had wrapped itself around his legs, only succeedin' in bitin' himself. That, of course, made the horse madder than hell, and he commenced screamin' and blowin' snot all over the place.

One big snot gob landed on Ellie's arm which set all of them gals to screaming too. It also set little Billie to grinnin' as he was always glad of anything that caused misery for the gals.

Anyway, that dang horse was thrashin' all over the place, and I thought he might kill himself in the effort he was puttin' forth. Joe and Roy hung on for dear life, and after about ten minutes, the mean stallion just laid his head down on the ground and quivered all over.

Roy called to me to bring him a burlap bag, and I did. Joe pulled the bag over the horse's head and had me hold on to his rope while he somehow got another length of rope under that horse and tied it around the upper chest and behind the shoulders. Then Roy tied the left front leg of the horse to the rope which was around his chest, and to a point where the foot could not touch the ground when the horse got up.

That horse was just about gave in from exhaustion, and Joe removed the hobbles off from his feet. At first, the horse just laid there, but then he realized he was partially free and he somehow stood up.

On three feet.

Joe and Roy swung into action, puttin' a blanket and saddle on that mean ole horse before he even knew what hit him. A rope was put around his neck and the burlap bag was taken off. Quick as could be, Roy and Joe forced the steel bridle bit into the stallion's mouth, and pulled the leather bridle up over his ears. By now, the horse was startin' to realize what was taking place, and he started hoppin' around sideways, tryin' to bite anything in sight.

But due to the fact that he was totterin' on three legs, he couldn't maneuver very well, and the bridle bit meant that he was unable to bite anybody very easily.

Back over his head went the burlap bag, and it stayed there until the horse settled down a little. After a while, he finally got the where he was standin' still.

"Ready, cowboy?" said Joe Buck, looking at Roy.

Without further adieu, Roy Grubbs jumped into the saddle. Joe Buck cut the foot hobble and pulled the bag off'n that mean horse's head at the same instant.

Well, that horse might've been tired, but he was now free on the earth. His first move was to jump straight up into the air with all four feet, twist to the left, and then to the right, before he hit the ground. Roy had them leather reins held tight in his left hand and had his right hand up in the air and stretched out behind him. Why he did that, I don't know, for I would have been holding onto the saddle horn with my free hand if I was the one up there.

Next move was for the horse to start a series of serious bucks while kickin' both feet out behind him. I reckoned that critter would have been real happy to feel a back foot crunchin' into somebody's head.

Another succession of twistin' bucks didn't do no good either, so the horse figured he would fall down onto his side and get back up real quick. I couldn't believe my eyes at what I had just seen, and wondered how it was that Roy's leg was not crushed.

The horse-fall caused all of the womenfolk to scream, and caused my pa to curse and use the name of the Lord in vain. Ma heard that and stalked into the house while the rest of us cheered Roy on.

The tired horse was still able to buck hard for over four minutes, but then he started to tucker out and commenced to run around the corral with his ears back.

"Open that gate, Joe!" yelled Roy.

None of us could believe that Roy was gonna take a chance on gettin' bucked off outside of the corral, but shore enough, Joe opened the gate, and Roy sailed out of the pen and into an open hay field. The horse had one more buckin' session and then he just started trottin' around, plumb tuckered out. However, Roy wasn't about to give him a rest, and started neck-reining the horse around. I was surprised that the mean horse was purty much going wherever Roy wanted him to go.

After a few more minutes, Roy trotted the horse up to Joe Buck, who held the bridle so's Roy could get off. Roy took the bridle back once't he got down. Joe swung up into the saddle and away he went. The horse tried his best to buck Joe off for a couple of minutes, but he had no success with this rider either. Joe began teaching the horse how to respond to neck-reining and even had him to where he would back up when Joe pulled back on both reins at once.

"Roy," I asked. "How come you turned your horse over to Joe?"

"Cause he's better with horses than me. Besides, my dang leg hurts."

Ellie and Alberta sidled over to Roy Grubbs and told him how scared they had been for him, and wondered if there was anything they could do for his leg.

"My dang leg's just fine gals," said Roy. "I hurt it worse once when I fell off a bar stool in San Antone." That got the girls over their being scared and set them to gigglin' like fools.

Joe rode the horse around for over an hour and finally brought him back into the corral, soakin' wet, stiff-legged and not trying to bite anybody any more. Pa hobbled over to where Joe and Roy was foolin' around with the tired horse.

"Boys, that was some grand horseridin'," he said. "Where'd ya'll learn to stay in the saddle like that?"

"Well, sir," said Roy. "Down in the part of Texas where we came from, if'n ya fall off'n your horse, an Injun will most likely cut off yer scalp. That gives us extra reason to stay in the saddle."

So now our family had two fairly dependable horses, and we all decided to try to round up some more to break while us boys was home on leave. Me and Roy rode around to neighborin' farms, seekin' out bad horses that their owners had purty much gave up on tryin' to break. Roy referred to these horses as a 'rough string,' and we was able to buy eight horses for a grand total of eighty-five dollars.

Them horses was mostly mean as hell, but not nearly as rough as the one that Roy had bought from Pa and broke. I took my turn in the saddle, along with Roy and Joe, and we set to breakin' horses, hopin' to make a profit by sellin' them later in a more gentle state. We didn't work fulltime at this, only usin' it as an excuse to get some exercise and sharpen our wits.

## WIDDERS

One night, we went coon hunting with Owen and Buster Horton and kilt five big coons. Ma and Mrs. Horton baked up three of them critters the next afternoon and we had a real good supper of coon, dumplings, and sweet taters.

The next day was Sunday and we all went to church. Ma made me, Roy, and Joe wear our army uniforms, and Owen Horton did the same. Everybody in church was makin' a big fuss over us, and the single women, along with the widders, was all comin' around us Morgans, hopin' to meet them two Texas soldiers of the Confederacy. In short order, Joe and Roy was kickin' their toes in the dirt, while bein' surrounded by admirers.

"Ohhh, you boys are so brave to come all the way up here from that godforsaken state of Texas just to fight to save us from them Yankees," said Mrs. Eunie McCracken, a fat widder woman of over sixty years who got so emotional she planted a big wet kiss on an embarrassed ole Roy. Mrs. McCracken then turned and looked hard for Joe Buck, but he was smart and had headed for the safety of the church.

During the service, I sat by the bold Alberta Rivers. I could feel the heat of her shoulder against mine and several times, I thought I felt the heat of the preacher's eyes burning into my soul.

I was glad to hear Mrs. McCracken start bangin' away on the old church piano and the congregation start up singing 'Amazing Grace.'

The pleasantry, however, did not last for long before the preacher commenced to yellin' and hollerin'. He gave a real fire-and-brimstone sermon and railed at anyone and everyone north of the Mason-Dixon line. Once again, by the end of the sermon, every able-bodied man in that buildin' was fit to be tied and just aching to kill a few Yanks in the name of the Almighty.

When church let out, Roy and Joe had to run a gauntlet of fawning women and girls. I led 'em down onto the big rock that jutted out over the valley, and they was real glad to get to this peaceful place which was only accessible to young people and billy goats.

"Dern, Frank," said Roy. "Don't you boys ever show any attention to these women up here?"

"Why?"

"'Cause it shows that they's starvin' for affection."

"What're you talkin' about?"

"I was scared that I was gonna get jumped and straddled right during the service, and not just by one gal, but dang near the whole congregation."

We was rescued from this blasphemous conversation against the women of Morgan Springs by the appearance of Bird, Owen, Ellie, Marilee, and Sadie Throckington, a friend of Ellie's who I reckon was about eighteen or so.

"What are you soldiers doing hidin' down here?" asked Ellie.

"Roy is a-scared that the widder women intend to cart him before the preacher and ask him fer his hand in marriage," I said.

All of the gals looked at Roy fer a second, wonderin' if that could be true, but then they laughed at the notion.

"You're just too handsome, Roy," said Ellie, drawing a dark look from her admirer, Owen Horton.

"I don't think it has nothin' to be with handsomeness at all," said Roy. "There's a feller I know down in Uvalde that got his nose cut off by a Comanche. Now I'll tell you, that old boy looks right *rough* without no nose. But I don't think even *he* would be safe from these Tennessee widders."

"What does that feller look like without no nose?" asked Owen.

"He looks like a dern hog," said Roy. "And on top of that, you can near 'bout see right into his brainpan."

"Oh, my God," said Sadie, and we all looked at her for usin' the Lord's name on the Sabbath.

"Is he pullin' our leg, Joe?" asked Bird.

"No, ma'am, he sure ain't," replied Joe. "However, there's a feller down in Hondo that got run over in a cattle stampede, and he looks a hell of a lot worse than ole Nosey Smades does."

"I don't think so," said Roy.

"Well, *I* do," said Joe Buck. "It scares me just to look at that feller. He ain't got but one eye, and looks like a dern cyclops."

"Ohhh," moaned Sadie.

It was at that time that Ellie remembered her manners and introduced Sadie to Roy and Joe. They jumped to their feet and took their hats into their hands and began bowin' and sayin' "Howdy ma'am" like a couple of lovesick fools. Sadie was dang near as goodlookin' as Bird. She was tall and thin, had brown hair, and a pointed nose. She also sported a huge set of bosoms, which I caught Roy glancing at when he thought no one was lookin'.

Then we all got set back down and was all quiet for a bit, admirin' the mountain view on a fine sunny Sunday morning. Bird sat down by me once again and she laid her hand on mine and looked over into my eyes. It was at this moment that I wish't that I never had to go back to the war again, and that I could just stay here forever on this peaceful mountain. However, I knew that this was not possible as I was signed up for a year, and had given my solemn promise to a dyin' soldier to see this thing through to the end of the war.

After that, the time went by real fast. Me and Bird was able to get off alone a couple of times, and I got to steal more than one kiss off'n her, but I didn't try to steal nothing else, fearin' on gettin' my ears boxed again. Besides that, it was the Sabbath. Miss Alberta told me that she loved me somethin' fearful, and that she thought about me all of the time. I, in turn, told her that I was feelin' them Cupid arrows tearin' into my heart also, but I held back on tellin' Bird that I loved her, though I'd sorta let it slip out before I left the first time. But now that I'd tasted battle a bit, I held off sayin' it again for fear of my never coming back from the war.

Roy later took to courtin' Miss Sadie a bit, and they went horseback riding down to Dayton and over to Walden's Ridge. Once I caught her and Roy smoochin' down by the spring, and it sure was a good thing the preacher didn't see 'em, or he would have give a sermon against Texans in general and all loose women in particular.

Time flew by, and soon the day came when me, Roy, Joe, and Owen was obliged to leave and head back to war. The weather had turned downright cool and we took along some extra blankets and heavy clothes. We was lucky this time, in that Pa borrowed a big wagon to haul us to Nashville.

Pa had wanted us to take four of the horses that we had broken, but Roy told him to try and sell 'em, and we would split up the money, minus his costs for feed and such.

# Bad Manners

We said our good-byes, kissed our gals, and headed off down that mountain once again. The weather was clear, but downright cool. Pa had his team of good work horses hitched up, and they set to trottin' along the downhill grade. It got cold in that wagon, what with the air whippin' by.

Once we got to the bottom of the mountain, the horses slowed down to a fast walk, and the air was quite a bit warmer than up on the mountain. All of us except Roy and Pa had on uniforms, and the people along the way waved at us and cheered us on in our efforts. However, I did notice that there was some people along the way who might have been Yankee sympathizers, for we did not get no cheers from them, only dark looks.

We did not stop for anything in town, and soon hit the road for Nashville. Once we was hailed down by a feller in a one-horse buggy rig and he seemed to have word that somebody had spotted a division of Yankees in southern Kentucky, headed south at a trot. We thanked him for the information, but laughed about this rumor later, figurin' the Yankees had all they could do just to keep us out of Washington.

We drove all day, and my ass was sore as hell, but I reckon everybody else's was in the same condition. That evening, we stopped and camped alongside of a little creek. Ma had made up a big kettle of beans and we just heated them up over a fire and ate 'em along with some bread that she had sent along. About an hour later, it was the same old deal that we had run into up at Manassas. Gas swole up our innards and bean farts commenced rollin' out like thunder. Owen, as usual, was the first one to cut loose.

Brrrraahhttt!

"Goddamn, Owen, ain't you had no lessons in manners from yer ma?" said Roy.

"My ma don't like to lecture on farts," laughed Owen, just as he slid out another.

Not to be outdone, Joe Buck busted out a long loud one.

Now, I was never one to fart out loud right after dinner, but my belly was hard as a rock, so I tried to ease one out and attempt to mix it in and maybe blame the smell on Owen. However, I was mortified in that the fart gave itself away with a whistlin' squeak, followed by a horrible smell.

"Holy shit, Frank," whined Owen. "It's a dang good thing yer ma ain't here right now, she'd skin you alive."

"Frank," said Roy Grubbs. "I do believe somethin' crawled up inside you and died. Mr. Morgan, I reckon you ought to cut a limb and take it to yer young'un here, for his rudeness."

In fact, that fart was so rough that everybody jumped to their feet and left me alone in that foggy-fart area of the campfire. I just sat there grinnin' like a coon, knowin' that I had won this great battle.

That night was kind of miserable, now that I think back on it. Not so much because of the ruggedness of them smelly farts, but due to the fact that it started to rain. We left the fire, which was just smolderin' anyway, and tried to hide under the wagon. Of course, the wagon was not big enough to shelter all five of us, so we all ended up gettin' soaked to the skin.

It was still rainin' when dawn started to crack, so we just skipped a breakfast fire, hitched up the team, and rolled out onto the soggy road. It was a cold day, even once the rain stopped. We all wrapped up in blankets, and was quiet when the wagon bounced along on our cold and windy ride to Nashville.

That ride took the rest of this day and over half of the next before we pulled into the outskirts of the big town of Nashville, Tennessee. Like Chattanooga, there was a huge army encampment on the edge of town, and that is where we headed for.

The headquarters was marked by a big sign on the front of a rough wooden building. Me, Owen, Joe, and Roy walked into the buildin' while Pa stayed outside with the horses. We met up with a Lieutenant Newton, who sat behind a big cluttered desk and sported an overworked look. Once he saw our papers, the lieutenant called in a sergeant and told him to take us out to the campground and get us set up. I went outside to say good-bye to my pa.

"Well, sir," I said. "This is the right place. These boys are gonna set us up with new rifles and a tent, so we'll be just fine."

"Frank, you take good care of yourself," said Pa. "Keep yer head down and don't forget to write home to yer ma and tell her how things are goin' for ya'll."

"Yes sir."

"Say yer prayers, boy, and watch those cusswords."

"Yes sir, I shore will."

"I reckon ya'll should keep yer word to that dead sergeant and stick this out to the end."

"I aim to, Pa."

"Crawl up here and give me a hug good-bye. My leg aches too bad to get down."

I thought that was a strange thing for my pa to be sayin' to me, for he had never gave me many hugs in my life, which I could recall. I felt kind of silly, climbing up in the wagon, and it was my feelin' that every soldier in Nashville was most likely watchin' this show of affection. Even the horses turned their heads around and was watchin'.

"I love you, son."

"Yes sir," I said. "I feel just about the same way."

With that, Pa slapped the reins on the horses' rear ends and I jumped down off of the moving wagon. Pa turned and waved, and I did the same, as he disappeared down the road.

I would never see him again. . .

## Nashville
## 1862

All of us Texas boys were reissued .58 caliber Enfield rifles, some food, and two canvas tents. Then we were taken out into the big campground and turned over to a gray-clad, bearded sergeant and assigned to the Fourth Georgia. It was kind of surprisin' to us boys that we were no longer members of a Tennessee regiment, but that was the price we had to pay for our leave of absence. The Third Tennessee was still in Virginia.

"It don't make no sense to me," said Roy. "The Army of Tennessee is in Virginia and the Army of Georgia is stationed in Tennessee."

"I reckon that as long as we are in the Confederate army, it don't matter anyway," said Owen.

We found a fair spot to pitch our tents, and was happy to find that we did not have to go out and scavenge our own firewood. There was several wagons full of dried and cut firewood which had been picked up by some black fellers who were called the fire brigade."

We managed to get settled in just in time to greet Old Man Winter in earnest. The weather turned real cold and it even snowed and stuck. Our whole army was bogged in, so we just hunkered down and tried to keep from freezin'.

The food supply was not very good and we had our rations cut three times. Poor Roy and Joe was not used to seein' snow that didn't melt away and this winter was really hard on them. As for drills, we would get out about two or three times a week to march around and fire our rifles a bit, just to make sure that they worked.

During that long fall and winter, me and Owen both reached our seventeenth birthdays, but there were no parties to be had for us. The cold days turned into weeks, and the weeks flew quickly by. Boredom and sickness spread among the troops like wildfire. There was something goin' around that caused a feller to run a high fever, vomit, and have the diarrhea at the same time. Several boys died and was buried in the city cemetery. All four of us Texas boys caught the malady, which lasted about five days, but we were fortunate to live through it.

In the month of March, the weather broke, and it got downright balmy. The Fourth Georgia broke camp and began marchin' south. Ten thousand men, glad to be leavin' Nashville and on the move again, were spoilin' for a fight and were about to get it.

Rumor began to circulate that the Yankees were no longer huddled up and hidin' in Washington, but that they had actually entered Tennessee. I could not believe that this was possible, but a letter that I got from Alberta Rivers verified it.

*Dearest Frank,*

*I have not heard from you for some time and hope that you are all right. Everyone around here is healthy. Your pa is getting around good now and threw away his crutch. He killed a deer and two turkeys last week.*

*Frank, I am sorry to report that a detachment of Yankee cavalry came right down our road two days ago. They did not stop for anything and just seemed to be looking around. Mose Green fired a shot at them and they returned the fire and killed old Mose in a hail of gunfire.*

*I still love you and hope that you will write to me.*

*Love,*

*Alberta Rivers*

I had to read this letter twice to make sure that I get it right. Then I just held it against my chest and leaned back against a tree. Joe Buck saw me lookin' so strange and came on over.

"What's the matter, Frank?"

"Bad news from home," I said.

"Nobody didn't die or nothing, did they?" asked Joe Buck.

"Not yet, Joe," I said. "But the Yankees are in Tennessee and they was even bold enough to ride right by my house."

"Was they shootin' and stealin'?"

"No sir. Bird says they was just lookin' around, but I reckon they'll be back."

"Dang, Frank. That distresses me to no end."

"It don't set too goddamn well with me neither, Joe."

But I knew that there was nothin' that I could do about it. It was all in the capable hands of my pa, and the Almighty.

We commenced marchin' again and seemed to be turnin' to the west, judging by the sun. We were not being told where we were headed, so that opened us to all sorts of rumors. Roy Grubbs even swore that we were headin' for Texas and that he shore as hell hated to walk nearly all the way to Tennessee, due to Joe's lettin' his horse get stole, only to have to turn around and march back to where he came from.

It took five more days of marchin' before we finally came to our destination and set up a fairly permanent camp. It turned out to be Jackson, Tennessee, and we were soon reattached to our old General, P. G. T. Beauregard, who had been sent out here from Virginia. Our sergeant, who was another Irishman by the name of O'Neil seemed to be real smart when it came to geography. He said that this place was just west of the Tennessee River, south of Fort Henry, and northwest of a little place called Shiloh.

There were some more soldiers who came up from Mississippi, and I'll be damned if they didn't have a bear in a cage. Them fools said that this bear was their mascot and that if things got rough for us, they would set him loose on the Yankees, and that would spell the difference in a close battle. That bear cage was on a wagon, and the horses which were pullin' it around shore seemed skittish. They were constantly lookin' back at that big black bear and showin' the whites of their eyes.

The bear shore drew a crowd, and I enjoyed standin' around myself, and lookin' into his little pig eyes. One damn fool stuck his hand into the cage, and tried to hand the bear an apple. That goddamn bear moved as fast as the eye could see and got not only the apple, but three fingers off'n that man's hand. Blood was spurtin' all over the place, and the feller who had just lost his fingers was screamin' like a woman. As for the bear, he just sat back and swallowed the fingers, along with the apple.

That scared the hell out of everybody, and they was goin' to shoot the bear for nippin' off them fingers. However, cooler heads prevailed, and the bear was spared, though nobody else offered him another apple

We settled down in Jackson and were glad to be able to rest up a bit. There seemed to be a hell of a lot of commotion goin' on, what with cavalry boys gallopin' around and pullin' in a bunch of cannons. It wasn't long before we got word that a Yankee general by the name of U. S. Grant had captured both Fort Henry on the Tennessee, and Fort Donelson, up the Cumberland River. Further rumor had it that Grant was headed south.

I reckon that the rumor must have been true, for it was not very long before high officers were scurryin' around like rats, givin' orders and gallopin' to and fro. In short order, word came down that we were to break camp and start marchin'. A chill went down my spine, and it was evident to everybody that somethin' big was goin' on and that we was soon goin' to be in the middle of it.

## BLOODY SHILOH
## APRIL OF 1862

Our boys moved out. Cavalry, cannons, ten thousand troops, and that finger-eatin' bear, who was growlin' and scarin' the hell out of them poor horses. We was pointed southeast and movin' at a fairly fast pace. As we went along that well-worn road, we picked up some more companies of Reb soldiers. Where they came from, nobody seemed to know, but we were always glad to have more boys to throw at the Yanks once the fracas began.

"Dern, Frank," said Roy Grubbs. "Look over at that ole boy and tell me what you see."

I looked to where Roy's finger was pointin' and I seen one strange-lookin' Confederate soldier, if that was what he was. He looked to be about twenty years old and about five foot ten, with no beard or mustache. He was lean and mean lookin' and had long, silky black hair that dang near reached his belt in back. That old boy was dressed kind of funny, in that he had on deerskin britches and moccasins, for the love of God!

He sported a gray Confederate jacket and a floppy hat that came down dang near over his blazin' black eyes, along with a long bladed knife in a buckskin sheath, and a long barreled Brown Bess flintlock rifle.

"What in the world is that ole boy?" I said.

"That's what I asked you, if'n ya recall," said Roy.

By now, Owen and Joe Buck had walked up near to us and joined in at starin' at the dangerous-lookin' feller.

"Looks like an Injun, to me," said Joe Buck.

"Comanche?" asked Roy.

"If'n he was a Comanche, I reckon he'd be ridin' a horse, Roy, don't you?" said Joe, firin' an exasperated look at Roy.

"Well, Joe, that all depends. Maybe he fell in with a poor horse-watcher like yourself, and got his goddamn horse stole."

Joe Buck just shook his head and looked down at his well-worn boots.

Now it was Owen's turn to put in his two cents. "Looks kinda like a rough version of Alberta Rivers to me. Only his hair is prettier."

That caused me to fire a black look over at Owen.

"He might even be a Mexican," said Roy.

"What in the hell would a Mexican be doing fighting Yanks in America?" said Joe.

"I reckon a Mex's got just about as much business killin' Union sympathizers as an Injun," offered Roy.

At just about this time, I reckon that strange feller realized that we was gawkin' at him and he looked over at us in a bold manner. He held our gaze till all of us Texas boys turned our eyes away and looked elsewhere. Everybody, that is except for Roy Grubbs, who was caught up in a stare-down with that long-haired feller.

Then ole Roy, he done a mighty bold thing. He walked sideways over to where he was strollin' alongside of that strange feller, and commenced to quizin' him. Me, Owen, and Joe could hear the conversation, so we didn't have to move any closer and take the chance on gettin' kilt.

"Son," we heard Roy say. "Just what in the world are you?"

"What you?" came the reply.

"Why, I'm a Reb soldier and a Texan by the nature of my birth," said Roy. "Now what about you?"

"Me Ojibwa."

"Oh-jib, what?"

"Ojibwa," replied the dangerous-lookin' feller, starin' right straight back at Roy.

"Is that an Injun?"

"Me Injun. Ojibwa."

"Where's yer horse?"

"Ojibwa no like horse. Ojibwa eat horse."

"Dang, why would a man eat somethin' he could just as well be ridin'?" asked Roy, tiltin' his hat back and scratchin' at his forehead.

"Horse taste good. Ojibwa have legs just as strong as horse."

"What's yer name?" inquired Roy.

"What yours?" fired back the Injun.

Roy just looked at this rude feller fer a minute, and I half expected him to pull his iron and shoot the Injun, but he finally gave in. "Name's Roy Grubbs, late of Bandera, Texas."

"Ojibwa name be Sash-a-baw."

"What in the hell kind of a name is that?"

"Ojibwa."

"What's it stand fer?"

"Means Walks-by-Still-Waters. Injun know what Grub means. Grub means white fly-worm."

Now that seemed to strike Joe, Owen, and myself as downright humorous, and set us to slappin' our knees like fools. It apparently did not seem so amusin' to Roy, who just stopped marchin' and caused a bunch of soldiers to bump into one another and slow down the march to battle.

In short order, Roy regained his wits and quick stepped his way back into the ranks alongside of the rest of us Texas boys. I reckoned that he'd gave up on questionin' that Injun, even though he kept looking over at him, and Sash-a-baw occasionally glanced over at Roy.

"Where's that ole boy from, Roy?" asked Owen.

"I don't recall that he ever said."

"Well go on over there and ask him."

"You go on over," growled Roy. "I ain't talkin' no more to no goddamn uncivilized Ojibwa, with his hair damn near draggin' the ground. My next words to him just might be said over his grave plot."

I looked over at Sash-a-baw and I reckon he must have heard Roy, for he started to grin a little bit, and adjusted his old relic of a rifle to his other arm.

It took us three days of hard marching, but we finally met up with the main army of the Confederacy. They was camped in a big valley, and it was the most soldiers that I'd ever seen in one spot. They was hurrahin' us boys and a little band met us near the camp and struck up 'Dixie.' Of course, that raised our spirits considerable, and caused our division to march in order, and present a fine sight to those hat-wavin' Rebs.

It was mid afternoon and the clouds was movin' in. Rain was in the air, so we set to pitchin' our tents in a hurry and gettin' a campfire started. The rain held off and we met some of the other soldiers who was camped here. Word was that there was about forty thousand soldiers here now, countin' our division. We were under the command of General Albert Sidney Johnston, who everyone thought was a good ole boy. Other generals here was Hardee, Polk, and Braxton Bragg, who was known to be cantankerous as hell.

J. E. B. Stuart's cavalry was also here, and could be spotted gallopin' around to and fro, stirrin' up a lot of dust.

The sun went down, and that little band drew a fair crowd when they commenced to playin' tunes. One of the band boys had a fiddle down by his side while he was pluckin' a guitar, and Roy Grubbs asked that young feller if he minded if ole Roy sawed that fiddle a while along with the band. The musician give a look which said he won't too crazy about no stranger usin' his fiddle, but he caved in, and Roy quickly had that shiny fiddle up under his chin. He commenced to sawin' out a sad tune called 'Lorena,' which was right popular at this time.

I never knew that Roy Grubbs was musical, but he could shore as hell play that fiddle. All of the other band boys just quit playin' and listened to those sad notes rollin' across the valley. Purty soon, we was drawin' more and more soldiers, and they were real quiet while listenin' to that song. Some of the boys set to wipin' their eyes on their sleeve and blowin' their noses, either out of sadness or colds that they had suddenly developed.

Somethin' caused me to look out to the edge of the campfire light and shore enough, there squatted Sash-a-baw, watchin' the white men makin' sad music and sportin' what some might have construed as a grin.

After about an hour of music, the skies opened up and rain started to pour down and scatter all of us musical fans. We scurried for the tents, and was fairly wet by the time we got under the canvas cover. Me and Owen was in one little tent and Roy teamed up with Joe Buck in another. We sat under the canvas lookin' out for a bit, and had just decided to turn in, when me and Owen spotted somethin' strange out under a big oak tree.

It was a sad sight to behold, but sittin' out there in the rain was Sash-a-baw, with the rain pourin' off the brim of his floppy hat.

"Dang, Owen, don't he have no cover?" I asked.

"Now how the hell would I know , Frank?"

"He must not have any cover, or else he wouldn't be sittin' out there in such a storm."

"I reckon not," said Owen.

"Call him in."

"I ain't callin' in such a wild-lookin' Injun. Hell, he might scalp both of us."

I just looked over at Owen fer a minute and then I made up my mind. "Hey there, Sash-a-baw!" I yelled.

He looked over at me through the driving rain.

"Come on in here, out of the weather!" I hollered.

"Me stay here," he said.

"Get on in here, Injun!" I shouted. "You'll drown out there in that rain!"

Sash-a-baw did not say anything and proceeded to tuck his chin down into his gray flannel jacket and go to sleep in all of that wet weather.

I thought to myself that he was a dang fool and proceeded to turn in for the night. However, I kept raisin' up and lookin' out the front of our tent and there he sat, lookin' like he was dead and froze in a sittin' position. Purty soon, I couldn't stand it no more. I got up and found a little square of canvas that had been cut out from a worn-out tent. Running out into the rainstorm, I threw that piece of cover over the top of Sash-a-baw. I'll be damned if'n that Injun didn't just sit there and never move or say thank you for my consideration. So I ran back into the tent and went to sleep.

Next mornin', I woke up and was glad to hear that the rain had stopped. Although it was not yet daylight, I could smell wood smoke and somethin' good cookin' in our area. Stickin' my head out the tent, I seen Sash-a-baw pokin' at a good fire which sported a nice rabbit cookin' on a spit above the flames. Where he had got the dry wood, I don't know and didn't ask. I did, however, pull my pants on and go out by the fire.

"Mornin', Injun," I said.

"Ugghh," was his only reply, and I figured that must be good mornin' in the tongue of the Ojibwa.

"Where'd ya come across the rabbit?"

"Injun snare rabbit."

"Dang, I never knew rabbits was dumb enough to hop around in such a rainstorm."

With that, Sash-a-baw just looked up at me for a minute. Then he tore off a big back leg of rabbit and handed it to me. "Soldier eat," he said. So, I did. Well, it shore was good rabbit, even had some salt and seasoning on it.

"Dang," I said. "This shore is tasty."

"Ugghh," was the reply.

It weren't long before Joe, Owen, and Roy Grubbs came out of their tents, but by that time all of the rabbit was ate up. Sash-a-baw let them use his fire and he took off walkin' for parts unknown, carryin' that big ole relic of a rifle.

When I went lookin' for him later, I found that Injun squattin' once again, lookin' into the bear cage. The bear was starin' right back at Sash-a-baw and if'n I did not know any better, I would swear that they had come to some kind of understandin'. I walked over to the cage, but the bear did not even look my way. He just kept starin' at Sash-a-baw, who was starin' back. I knew enough about animals to know that they do not like to stare for very long at anything, figurin' it to be rude, I reckon. However, Sash-a-baw and this black bear was engaged in a regular stare down.

At about that time a bugle blew, signallin' that we was to fall into our own companies so that the sergeants could yell at us some. Me and Sash-a-baw walked over to our gatherin' spot, and purty soon we was joined by the rest of the Texas boys, who were kind enough to bring my rifle along with them.

We were ordered to eat and to fall into marchin' columns in exactly a half hour. Some boys got breakfast and some did not, however, in one-half hour, all of the tents were struck, and we were marchin' to the northeast. Us Texas boys had been assigned, along with the Fourth Georgia, to the cantankerous Braxton Bragg's division. We were on one road, along with General Breckenridge and his division, while Polk's and Hardee's crowd were on another road. Some of the boys did not walk on the road, but fell off to the side and were walkin' through fields and woods.

All day long we marched, and camped out once again, that evenin'. Word was that we were in an area called Shiloh and that there were some Yankees up ahead at Pittsburgh landing, on the Tennessee River. They had not bothered to dig in defensively and we were gonna surprise 'em the next morning.

And surprise 'em we did . . .

Up before daylight, and doin' without any breakfast or campfires, we had spread out into three battle lines, each one bein' about a mile long. Without drums or fanfare we commenced walkin' that slow death walk towards the flames and smoke of the Yankee campfires ahead. By the time they spotted us comin' and started firin', we were dang near on top of 'em. It was six A.M. and still early enough so that some of them Yanks were not yet up and armed.

Our buglers blew charge, and all hell broke loose. We came bustin' out of the trees and I reckon that about ten thousand Reb muskets went off at exactly the same time. Our cannons had also opened up and I could see explosions ahead of us. Our columns did not stay intact and soon there was Reb soldiers runnin' like banshees through the Yankee encampment, firin', reloadin', and givin' out with the Rebel yell.

By then, the Yankees knew that they were in deep trouble, and they were startin' to fire back and retreat. Their cannons opened up also, and I could see their deadly orange-red flames lickin' in our direction. I could hear furious gunfire on both sides of me, some loud and some very far away. There was terrible fightin' goin' on fer the full mile-length of our battle lines. However, as for me, I only knew what was goin' on in my general vicinity, and it was gettin' bloodier by the minute. Our division stormed through a campground, and I'll be damned if'n some of our boys didn't stop to take advantage of the breakfasts that the Yankees had left behind when they were so rudely interrupted. How a body could think of his stomach under these conditions, I did not know, but some Reb soldiers was runnin' along munchin' on strips of bacon and bread.

We pushed forward and past an old white wood building that was purty much back in the woods. There was a sign out front that said, SHILOH CHURCH, and it reminded me of our little Baptist church in Morgan Springs. One of our boys ran into the church to see if'n anybody was there and he took his hat off before goin' inside. I reckon that he was a churchgoer himself and did not want the Lord to see him wearin' his hat into that holy building no matter what the circumstances were.

Up ahead of us was a stand of trees and I was gettin' tired of runnin'. All of a sudden, one hell of a bunch of rifles spat flame and lead balls from out of them trees and a bunch of our boys fell. One of 'em, a young feller from Mississippi who I had once gone fishin' with, had his arm blew right off at the elbow. He was screamin' and floppin' around on the ground, blood spurtin' all over the place. I was shocked by the sight and stopped to help him out, but the sergeant gave me a kick in my ass and yelled to keep goin'. So I did.

By this time, we had lost all thought of tryin' to stay in dressed battle lines, and it was every man for himself. I was not the only one who was lookin' for cover. Gettin' down behind a big fallen tree, I was joined by Roy Grubbs on one side and Sash-a-baw on the other. The Injun raised up his old Brown Bess rifle, aimed and squeezed the trigger. There were two explosions. First came a little one from the primer pan, and the second one followed shortly thereafter from the powder at the bottom of the barrel. Fire and smoke belched out of that old smooth bore with black smoke fillin' the air.

Roy started to laugh.

"Goddamn, Sash," he said. "That gun makes a noise like a horse fart."

"Gun shoot straight."

"Did ya hit anything?"

"Mebbe."

Roy and Sash-a-baw was reloadin' while I stuck my head up over that big log, and noticed four Yankees hidin' in some brush and lookin' off to our left. They did not see us boys and was intent on murderin' some of our comrades. I laid my rifle across the log and took careful aim at a blue-clad soldier's rib cage. Squeezing the trigger slowly, the gun roared and flame came burstin' out the end of the barrel. The soldier that I was aimin' at flew sideways, and I seen a spray of pinkish blood splatter the Yank who was next to him. Now, that feller who got hit started shriekin', but I couldn't make out what he was sayin'.

"Shoot that son of a bitch again, Frank, and shut him up!" yelled Roy.

At about this time, the other three Yanks turned their guns on us and fired. I ducked down and heard lead balls hissin' right over the top of my head.

"You goddamn sesesh' bastard, you kilt our Willie," yelled one of them Yanks. Then, he came runnin' out of the brush, across the openin' and straight at us boys. Roy raised up, fired his rifle at that mad Yankee and missed. The Yank was bearin' down on us fast with his bayoneted rifle, and I was startin' to fear for my life. Sash-a-baw stood straight up and cut loose with his gun that sounded like a horse fart, and hit the Yankee right in the mouth. Teeth and big chunks of the Yankee's head went flyin' through the air, and he fell flat on his back, legs kickin' out and quivering.

We reloaded, and had to roll to the side to avoid bein' trampled by a bunch of chargin' Rebs, who urged us to join 'em. We got to our feet and ran straight for the place where them four Yanks had been. When we got there, the feller who I had shot was the only one left and he was in sad shape. He looked up into my eyes and begged me to shoot him, for he could not stand the pain. I am sad to say that he looked to me to be about fifteen years old and really not a very dangerous feller.

"I cain't shoot ya in cold blood, Yank," I said.

Roy and Sash-a-baw had stopped also and had heard what we had said.

"Sash," said Roy. "Why don't you go ahead and shoot this poor feller?"

"You shoot 'em," said Sash-a-baw.

"Don't ya want to lift his scalp?" asked Roy.

I decided to end this conversation with a blast from my Endfield and end the misery that this pitiful young Yankee was feeling. Misery and pain that I had caused in the first place.

"Forgive me, Lord," I said. Raising my rifle, I sighted down of the forehead of the injured Yank. The feller squeezed his eyes tight shut and commenced mumbling a prayer, while Roy covered his ears with his hands. Both Roy and Sash-a-baw turned as white as a ghost, although Roy was the whitest.

I tried my very best, but was not able to pull the trigger. The Yank finally opened one eye.

"I'm sorry, Yank," I said, lowering my log gun. "I reckon you'll have to find somebody else to murder you. I can't do it. I'm sorry that I shot you in the first place."

With that, the Yank started mumbling something. Either a curse or a thanks, I don't know which. Me, Roy, and

Sash-a-baw left this scene at a trot and took off after our division, which was now well ahead of us. It didn't take very long to catch up with our boys, for the Yankees had stopped runnin' for the moment, and was makin' another stand behind a sunken road. A cannon shot exploded fairly close to us and it blew one of our boy's feet clean off. Another feller stood up holdin' his eyes and screamin' that he was blind. He stumbled forward and was hit with two minie balls, spellin' the end of his misery.

We laid low behind a stone fence, firin' at will and duckin' down to reload. I had fired about six shots, when the Yankees pulled back from the sunken road and started retreatin' in a hurry. We moved forward for a couple of hundred yards and was stopped once again by heavy fire from in front of us. Lucky for us boys, we were now in a cemetery, and the gravestones provided good cover to hide behind. I, personally, was behind a big white marker which I took note of while pouring powder down into my hot barrel.

*JOSIAH SNYDER*
*Rest in the Arms of the Lord*
*1782 - 1843*
*61 years 219 days*

"Mr. Snyder," I said. "I want to thank you for the use of your gravestone." Some gunfire went off, and I heard three thumps against Josiah's stone, which caused chunks of rock to go flying through the air.

I caught my breath, when the dumb thought came flyin' into my head, wonderin' why it was that people went to the trouble of figurin' out the leftover number of days that some people such as Josiah Snyder had lived. It seemed to be a lot of trouble to me, not mentioning the expense of havin' those numbers carved into a stone.

At about that time, a bunch of Reb gunfire commenced from my left. Lead minie balls rained down on the Yanks who was takin' target practice at Josiah's headstone. I heard some groanin' and cries coming from the Yankee position and raised my head up once again. All I could see were blue coats scamperin' away from our boys, and presentin' a damn-interesting target for yours truly.

Raising my rifle, I took aim at the slowest Yank and pulled the trigger slowly. *Pop!* went the rifle and a little puff of smoke whisped out from under the hammer.

"Misfire! Goddamn it," I muttered.

I got another percussion cap and replaced the bad one on top of the steel nipple of my rifle. Taking aim once again, I had only a split second before my slow Yankee target disappeared over the hill. I squeezed the trigger again and my Enfield roared.

The Yank dropped his rifle and fell face first onto the ground. He never moved once't he hit the dirt.

Our boys burst forth, and I quit Josiah Snyder's grave and ran after the Yanks. Sash-a-baw was runnin' on my right and I'll be damned if'n he weren't givin' out Injun war whoops. I was also glad to see Joe Buck, Roy, and Owen runnin' along with us, still alive and full of fight.

The fightin' went on all morning, with the Yanks retreatin', making stands, and then retreating once again back towards the Tennessee. Dead Rebs and Yanks were everywhere, along with hundreds of wounded soldiers from both sides. Nobody was doin' anything for the wounded, and I hoped that none of us Texas boys would join their ranks on this day.

We reached a big open field with a fence and a peach orchard on the far side. When our boys started movin' across that field, Yankee cannon and rifle fire took a terrible toll on us, and we were forced back to the cover of a heavy woods.

General Johnston came gallopin' up with a flag bearer and some officers. He took a look out across that field with his glasses.

"Boys!" he yelled. "That appears to be a regular hornet's nest up ahead. Are you game to take it?"

A big cheer went up, and the sergeants set to formin' battle lines out of the men who had made it this far. We waited for about a half-hour, and was joined by General Polk's division. All of this time, we could see that the Yanks were buildin' strength on the far side of the field.

Finally, we had enough men to make a fight of it and we marched smartly out of the cover, led by General Albert Sidney Johnston himself. Our cannons opened up and so did the Yanks'. We in the ranks would fire, kneel, and reload while the line of soldiers behind us would advance and do the same. Then, we would go forward and do the same thing once again. Fire from the Yanks was terrible and I felt like I was in a lead hailstorm. Boys was fallin' all around me, when our bugler finally blew retreat.

To say that we got out of that hornet's nest faster than we had gotten into it would have been a great understatement. I reckon that the Yanks got some great pleasure out of seein' our asses and pumping elbows. Once't we got back into cover, we caught a breather and reloaded. By now, my rifle was so fouled with black powder residue that I had to clean it out a bit with a rag. I kept lookin' out across the battlefield and hopin' to high heaven that the Yanks would not come pourin' across it, for they would have had me in a bad fix, what with me havin' an oily rag down my gun.

General Johnston kept ridin' his horse up and down our line, cheerin' us on, so I knew that another charge was comin' soon. Shore enough, in less than twenty minutes, we reformed and came streamin' out of the woods when the bugler blew charge. I seen J. E. B. Stuart's cavalry come chargin' on my left, and a grand sight it was.

As for my line, we were catchin' hell once again from the peach orchard, and the word was that the Yankees had dug in here for a fight, and that they had been reinforced with boatloads of troops from the Tennessee River.

Anyway, by late afternoon, we had made a dozen charges at the Yanks, and they had held their ground. The field that we had labeled the hornet's nest was so covered with dead men, Yanks, and Rebs, that I could have walked across that field on bodies and never once set foot on the ground.

General Johnston came ridin' back with us from about the seventh charge, and I noticed that he had a leg wound and was bleedin' down into his high leather boot.

"General!" I yelled. "You've been hit, Sir!"

"Where?" he yelled back, and I was surprised that he had not noticed the hole in his leg.

"In your leg, Sir!"

The general looked down and got kind of whitefaced when he seen that his blood had filled the boot to near 'bout overflowin'. I don't know if it was the shock of what he saw or not, but General Albert Sidney Johnston, the top officer of the Confederacy, suddenly fell from his saddle.

Within one hour, he was dead.

# RETREAT
## APRIL 7, 1861

By late afternoon, we were exhausted, hungry, and thirsty. The officers had finally given up on takin' that bloody battlefield, and I thanked God for that. A stalemate had been reached at this spot, and even though our boys had routed the Yanks at first, we were saddened by the loss of General Johnston and thousands of our men.

This great and terrible battle had ground to a halt, and we camped for the night. All of the Texas boys and Sash-a-baw had made it through alive, and that was a wonder. Beans and corn bread was the fare for tonight and none of us got much sleep, what with the screams of sufferin' comin' from the battlefield.

Everybody was up well before daybreak. We had a quick breakfast, and fell into battle lines, dreadin' the comin' of the day. Light came early, and it was not brought by the sun, but by cannons. Exploding shells lit up the night and I could see everything clear. It was evident that the Yankees had brought in reinforcements during the break in battle, and that those fresh troops were ready to fight.

Sheets of gunfire went off, and lead balls filled the air. We fired back, and the fracas was on once again. At least we were allowed to seek cover instead of standing side by side like a bunch of goddamn fools.

General Beauregard had taken command due to the death of Johnston, and it did not take long for him to figure out that we had better back away from this battle and swallow our losses. Orders were given to retreat, and we was glad to do so.

Reb cannons on both flanks covered our backup, and the Yanks were loathe to make much of a pursuit. I reckon that they had enough of our hospitality to suit them, so they just watched us pull out of there.

We took the same roads away from the battlefield that we had come in on, and the word was that we were headed for Corinth, Mississippi, just over the state line, which was several days walk from here. Our retreat was orderly, and there was a hell of a bunch of walkin' wounded Reb soldiers. We also had a bunch of wounded fellers in wagons, but no dead.

We had left our dead on the battlefield . . .

Judging from our present numbers, there must have been one hell of a bunch of 'em.

## MISSISSIPPI

It took us ten days to reach the Reb fortifications at Corinth, due to our slow pace, and the fact that we had to stop several times along the way to bury the poor fellers who were dyin' of their wounds. We kept expectin' an attack from the Yanks to our rear, but it never came.

We did not have to pitch our tents here, for there were regular barracks for those of us who were fortunate to get here first, and that included us Texas boys and Sash-a-baw. However, Sash did not want to sleep inside of a buildin', so he just stayed outside, and declined the use of a tent.

A headcount was taken and we were horrified to learn that we had lost over ten thousand men at that terrible battle of Shiloh. It did make us feel better to learn that the Yankees had lost over thirteen thousand themselves, and that is probably the reason that they did not pursue us. The second night in Corinth, us five comrades gathered around a campfire that Sash-a-baw had goin'. Roy was still interested in this Injun, and he set to finding out the information that he was missing on the Ojibwa.

"Sash," said Roy. "Just where do you come from?"

"Far north, land of big lakes, much snow, moose, and beaver. Git-che-gu-me."

"Canada?"

"White man call it Mish-e-gun."

"What are ya doin' down here?"

"Injun fight Yank soldiers."

"How come ya decided to head down here and join the fracas?"

"Sash-a-baw kill-um Ottawa medicine man over squaw. Ojibwa and Ottawa chase Injun all the way to big river. Injun steal canoe, and follow current down big river and join up with gray soldiers. Injun need food and dollar pay."

"Damn," said Roy, stirring the hot coals.

"Do you take much pleasure out of killin' Yanks?" asked Joe Buck.

Sash-a-baw didn't answer this question, but it caused him to break into one of his little grins.

"How did ya happen to hook up with the Reb army instead of the Yanks?" asked Owen.

"Yanks shoot long rifles at Injun, gray soldiers don't."

With that, I reckon Sash-a-baw had enough of all this talk, as he got to his feet and stretched. "Where bear?" he asked.

"Just follow yer nose in the direction of that stand of oak trees yonder," said Roy. "I heard him growlin' about somethin'."

Sash-a-baw took off in the direction which Roy had aimed him at, carryin' his old Brown Bess as usual.

"Frank," asked Roy. "How come that Injun likes to study the bear all the time?"

"I reckon it's for the same reason that you set so much stock in studyin' the Injun."

"Did he kill any Yanks with that old blunderbuss?" asked Joe Buck.

"Well," I replied. "I know he kilt one in particular, and saved my ass from gettin' bayoneted. Shot a Yank right in the mouth."

"Why'd he shoot a man in the mouth?" inquired Owen.

"Reckon it was because that feller's mouth was open so wide, cussin' us Texas boys over killin' his pal."

"Dang," said Roy. "I never in my life seen so many dead men in one spot, and I hope to hell that I never do again."

However, he would. Twice . . .

Joe and Owen took off to find the bear and his Injun friend, while I sat down on a stump and commenced to write a letter to Bird. I had not written in quite some time and figured this was a good time to do it. Takin' a quill and a little bottle of ink, I started to write down my thoughts.

*Dear Bird,*

*I am now in a place called Corinth, Mississippi. I hope I spelt that rite. We was in a rough scrape at a place called Shiloh, on the Tennessee. 10,000 of our boys was kilt or wunded, but I am all right, as are Roy, Owen, and Joe.*

*It is my thought that we won the battle, but we backed out of it just the same when the Yankees brought in a few boatloads of solders bent on killin us.*

*We made friends with an Ojibwa Injun who likes to studie a bear that we have in camp. I hope Roy does not kill this Injun, for I know that he has done so in Texas more than once. (Kill Injuns)*

*I hope that you are fine and that you think of me once in a while. Pray for us Texas boys and that Injun, for we sometimes get into tite fixes.*

*Sincerly yers,*

*Franklin Morgan*

# PART II

# FORAGERS

## May of 1861

Justin Morgan made his way out to the barn, sidestepping piles of horse manure as he went along. Myrt followed closely behind him doing the same thing. Bringing up the rear was Billie Morgan, who was not so adept at avoiding the piles of round dung balls, stepping right into a fresh pile.

"Damn it!" moaned Billie, causing his father to stop and grin at the brown-stained bare feet of his son.

"Better watch your language son. Yer ma'll tan yer hide."

"Yes sir."

"And you best watch your step, too," Justin added with a smile.

The trio went into the barn, where Justin filled two pails with oats, walked back into the warm sunshine, and approached the horse corral. Seven fine horses were penned up, and the rest were grazing in the field. The horses trotted over to the edge of the pole fence with their ears pointed at Mr. Morgan, praying for oats.

Justin threw the oats in a large circle on the ground inside of the corral, and the horses moved instantly and started picking at the grain. It amazed Justin that the horses could manage to pick up little grains of oats with their lips, but they did.

Hoofbeats sounded along the road, causing Justin and Billie to stop watching the horses and look down at the direction of all the racket. Soon, twelve blue-clad riders thundered into sight, and turned off the road, and up to the Morgan barn.

"Who is it, Pa?" asked Billie.

"It's Yankees, son. Run and tell yer ma to stay inside with the young'uns."

"Yes sir," said Billie, running hard for the house.

Three dogs made their way for the strange horses and set to nipping at them and barking loudly.

"Better call off your dogs, mister," said one of the Yankee soldiers.

"Them dogs is just doin' what they're supposed to be doin'. What kin I do for ya'll boys."

A soldier with sergeant's stripes rode out from his fellow soldiers. "We are here for your horses and other animals, sir."

"My animals ain't fer sale."

With that the sergeant turned to two soldiers behind him. They all laughed.

"Sir," laughed the sergeant. "Maybe you don't understand. We aren't here to *buy*; we're here to *confiscate* what we need on behalf of the Union army."

"That sounds like thievery to me," said Justin.

"It ain't thievery to take what we need from no goddamn secessionist scum like yerself, you son of a bitch," growled the sergeant.

Justin Morgan's face turned beet red, for he was not accustomed to having his dear departed mother referred to in such a way. He walked over to a fence pole and picked up an eight-tined pitchfork which was leaning against it.

Four Yankee soldiers pulled their sidearms.

"I wouldn't be so handy with that shit-fork, hayseed. My boys are kind of jumpy," laughed the sergeant.

"I reckon you and your boys had just better pull on out of here, and look to do your stealin' someplace else," said Justin, balancing the pitchfork in one hand.

At that point, the door of the house opened. Mrs. Morgan and Ellie stepped out onto the porch.

"Whoooeee, will ya look at that," said a soldier.

"Sergeant, do ya reckon we should take *them* animals along with us too?" said another, pointing at the Morgan women.

Justin, now holding the pitchfork in both hands, with the business end pointed towards the blue-clad foragers, stepped towards the mounted soldiers.

Four shots rang out almost instantaneously, as a number of soldiers pulled their guns. Powder, lead, curses, and smoke filled the air, and Justin Morgan was rocked backwards with three holes in his chest. He dropped the fork and fell to his hands and knees. With each weakening beat of his heart, dark streams of blood spurted out of two holes, staining the ground.

Ellie screamed and Justin raised his head and looked over at his wife and daughter. Two more shots exploded, knocking the already mortally wounded man onto his side. His legs kicked twice, and quivered.

Justin Morgan was dead.

The Yankee soldiers split up, three of them going into the house, and the rest commencing to round up horses, cows, chickens, and whatever they could lay their hands on. Two big wagons were brought forward and quickly filled with grain, saddles, and everything that may be useful to the Union army.

Mrs. Morgan had run screaming to her husband, and was lying on the ground with her arms around him, moaning out her grief. Ellie, Wed, Billie, and Marilee also ran out and joined their mother on the dusty ground.

Once the soldiers had rounded up everything they could carry or drive off, they started to leave. The sergeant urged his horse forward, took his hat off and addressed what was left of the Morgan family.

"Ma'am," he said. "I'm right sorry for what happened here, but your man should not have taken up that pitchfork. We left you a milk cow and a horse to work your garden with."

No one bothered to thank him, and the soldiers rode out onto the road with their stolen contraband. Dust filled the air as the foragers disappeared, followed by two barking hounds, still nipping at the horses.

## THE LETTER

We had word that the Yankee army from the Shiloh battle was indeed headin' our way, but they shore as hell were slow. We dug in and waited, but after over three weeks, they had not showed, so General Beauregard just decided to head to the north and avoid these boys. If'n they was really spoilin' fer a fight, we would be easy to find. This time though, there was not so much walkin' involved and we made great use of the railroad. A long string of traincars took us first to Atlanta, Georgia. Then, it took us right back to where we had started.

Chattanooga.

Roy said that our makin' our way around the whole Union army was the equal of sneakin' the sun past a rooster.

Our mail had been chasing us across the country, and it finally caught up with us here. Roy had six letters, Joe Buck had three, Owen had two and I had three. The first one was from my ma and I opened that up first.

*Dearest Frank,*

*It is with a heavy heart that I tell you of the loss of your dear father. He was shot down and killed by Yankees who were bent on stealing our stock.*

*My only wish is that you continue to wage war and that you kill as many Yankee soldiers as you are able to.*

*We are making out just fine. Mr. Horton is a great help to us and Wed is able to supply all of the meat that we require by hunting.*

*Your dear father was buried in the old family cemetery, next to his father. God bless you and keep you well. I hope this letter finds you in due time.*

*Your loving mother,*

*M. Morgan*

Tears started to roll down my cheeks and I had to read the letter again to make sure that I had really read what I had. I reckon Roy noticed me, for he scooted on over to where I was sittin'.

"Frank, are you all right?" asked Roy, putting his hand on my arm.

"No sir, I'm not."

"What is it?"

"Roy, it's my pa."

His face went an ashen color. "What about yer pa?" he asked, squatting down beside of me.

By now, the rest of the boys had stopped readin' and had their attention turned to me. Even Sash-a-baw was lookin' my way.

"He's dead, Roy. Yankees kilt him and stole our stock." With that the tears really commenced to roll. Roy sat down by my side and put his arm around my shoulders while I sobbed over the loss of my dear pa.

"Dang, Frank," said Joe Buck. "Your pa was a good feller and I'm shore sad to hear that he's gone."

Owen Horton made his way over too. "I cain't believe that, Frank. Yer pa is just like my own kin." He took the letter and read it. His eyes filled with tears too as he passed the letter around. I looked off to the side and noticed that Sash-a-baw was watchin' me. I reckon he knew what was goin' on, but he was not saying anything. He just stood there, watchin' all of these grown white men cryin' like babies.

## Mountain Home

It was General Beauregard's idea to rest us boys in Chattanooga for a bit. Somehow, Roy borrowed two horses and tack, while me and Owen obtained a one-week leave of absence, intent on headin' back home, due to death in the family. Just as soon as we got our papers, we hit the saddles and said good-bye to Roy, Joe, and Sash-a-baw. We took off at a trot, and I turned in my saddle to wave good-bye. Sash-a-baw was already walkin' in the direction of the bear cage and his new-found friend.

Them horses was good mounts, and we kept up a steady pace on the road alongside of the Tennessee River. We stopped and made camp just before dark at a place that showed signs of prior camp activity. There was a circle of stones around some burned logs, and a little pile of dried wood layin' close by. We threw a fishin' line out into the river, baited with a long night crawler. Within ten minutes, Owen was hand linin' in a big catfish, which we fried for our supper.

"Where do ya reckon Roy got ahold of them horses?" Owen asked that night, as we was sittin' around the fire, swatting skeeters, and listenin' to the critters of the night.

"I reckon he borrowed 'em from the cavalry boys or else he rented 'em from the livery stable."

"I'm glad he did," said Owen. "For I shore as hell would have hated to walk all the way home and back in one week."

"Me too. Especially since it's mostly uphill."

With that, a panther screamed on the far side of the river and scared the hell out of both of us.

"Was that a cat, or what?" asked Owen.

"Sounded like a woman to me," I lied. " . . . Or a ghost."

"Ghost, hell. Don't start that shit."

"What shit?"

"Tryin' to throw a scare into me so that I cain't sleep."

"I didn't know you was so nervous about ghosts."

"Goddamnit, Frank. Quit talkin about ghosts."

I could have had a lot of fun with Owen over this, but I was not my usual happy self, over the death of my pa, so I just let this good opportunity go by and proceeded to go to sleep. Last time I looked at Owen, he was sittin' beside the fire with his eyes wide open and shiny, lookin' around at every little sound.

Next mornin', we was up and ridin' before daylight. Breakfast was a chunk of cornpone taken in the saddle.

Owen was bitchin' cause he had not gotten no sleep and that caused him to be grouchy. We caught old One-Eyed Wash's ferry across the river, and he pumped us for information on the war during our ride.

"I heard you boys kilt thirteen thousand Yankees down at Shiloh."

"I know we kilt a hell of a bunch of 'em," said Owen. "And I know they kilt more than a few of our boys."

"Well, I'm shore glad you two boys is all right," said One-Eyed Wash.

Once again, Wash would not take no money for our ride, and he gave us his lunch of side pork and bread to eat along the way. I hated to take the man's meal, but he would not hear of us refusin' it. He even got so carried away as to start huggin' us boys and embarrassin' the hell out of us in front of four witnesses who were watchin' all of this while waitin' to ride the ferry back across the river.

We jumped into the saddle, waved our hats, and trotted off towards the town of Dayton. By late afternoon, our tired horses had made the hard climb up to Walden's Ridge. Owen broke off for his house, and I headed on to mine.

Our dogs met me down the road, and I think Myrt was the only one to recognize me, for she was dang near goin' crazy. I reined up in front of the house, and my whole dern family came runnin' at me, each one from a different direction. They was all huggin' me, kissin' me, and showin' even more emotion than the widder women at church.

Ma was cryin', dang near drownin' me with her tears, in spite of the fact that I probably stunk like hell. The bold Alberta Rivers came runnin' up to me, having appeared from who knows where. She was huggin' me too, but could not get all of me, for Ma would not loosen her hold, and I ended up gettin' pushed around in different directions by these two gals.

Everybody finally came to their senses, and I was allowed to go into the house and sit down at the table like a normal person. The only thing that was different, was the fact that Ma made me sit at the end of the table in my pa's chair. That was hard for me to do, and I did not feel comfortable sittin' there.

Ma served coffee, and some little cookies, and told me the sad story of Pa gettin' murdered by thievin' Yankees. My ma was a Christian woman and never one to say anything bad about anybody or to hold a grudge. For that reason, I was fascinated by the hatred that came spillin' out of her about the Yanks. She wanted every one of 'em dead and everybody at the table, including myself, felt exactly the same way.

Everyone was glad to see me, and they each had something they wanted to tell or show me. I was being tugged from six different directions at once.

Things finally cooled off, and Ma set to makin' supper while me and Bird got a chance to take a walk down to the spring to fetch a pail of water. When we got to the spring, I commenced to look around for snakes and such, when suddenly Bird surprised me from behind. Her arms came around me and locked me into a big squeeze.

"Dang, Bird," I said. "You're as strong as a bear."

"Turn around," she said. And I did. Now, Bird began to squeeze me from the front side, and stood up onto her tiptoes, and gave me a big wet kiss. She tasted like terryberry leaves, and I could feel her breasts crushin' themselves into my chest.

That kiss wasn't like nothin' I'd ever got from my ma, or any of my aunts. It was also a lot wetter than anything I ever got from the widders, who was known to slobber a bit when smoochin' young boys. I opened my eyes and took a look at Alberta. She had her own eyes closed tight and seemed to be enjoyin' this smooch a great deal, so I just held with it.

We finally broke apart, and Bird professed her love for me, and her strong hope that the war would soon be over, and we would meet the future together, whatever that meant.

"I've been so lonesome for you, Frank, I thought I'd just dry up and die," she said.

"I reckon that I felt just about the same way, Bird," I answered, kickin' my toe in the dirt.

"You didn't take up with no other gals while you was gone, did you?"

"No, ma'am," I said. "The only company I've had was eight thousand Reb fellers. I'd forgot what a purty gal looks like."

"Do you think I'm purty, Frank?" asked Bird, puttin' her hand on my chest.

"You're the purtiest gal in Morgan Springs. I know that."

"Well," she said. "I don't reckon that says much, since there ain't many girls around here."

I wasn't shore just what she was fishin' for, so I just kept quiet on that note, and Bird still rewarded me with another hot kiss.

Bird and me made our way back up the steep slope, and was surprised to find a bunch of company at our house. Mr. and Mrs. Rivers was there, along with Owen Horton and his pa. Everybody sat out on the front porch and listened to me and Owen tell stories of what we had seen, firin' a number of questions at us.

"Owen says you've got an Injun fightin' with ya'll," said Mr. Horton.

"Yes sir," I said. "His name is Sash-a-baw, and he claims to be from way up North. He seems like a purty good ole boy, and he shore ain't afraid to kill Yankees."

It was good to sleep in a bed once again, and it was well past daybreak before I woke up. Me and Ma walked down to the cemetery and visited the grave of my dear old pa.

"It shore don't seem natural, not havin' him around any more," I said.

"I know," said Ma. "I miss him every minute that I'm awake."

"Are you gonna get by all right Ma, or should I slip away and come on back home?"

"What'd you say?"

"I just asked if'n you wanted me to come on home and quit the army."

"Frank, don't you ever say such a thing, or even think it. Your poor old pa would roll over in his grave if'n you didn't see this thing through. I want you to kill every goddamn Yankee you see!"

I was shocked to hear my ma blaspheme in such a manner. "Let's get on home, Ma," I said.

We quit that lonesome graveyard, and walked quietly back up the hill. I was worried about Ma, for she was shore quiet and had not even given me hell one time since I had gotten home. However, I reckoned that was the natural way with things, once't you lose yer husband or a wife.

Back home, I split a bunch of firewood and hoed at the garden for a spell. Then, I decided to trot on down to Owen's and see how he was makin' out.

Owen came out onto the porch wearin' his army pants and a gray shirt, and we decided to take a stroll down towards the cave.

"Seems mighty dang quiet around here, don't it?" said Owen.

"It shore does. In fact, it's downright spooky and unnatural."

"Maybe we've just got too used to bein' around several thousand swearin' men all the time, along with the gunfire that goes with it," said Owen.

"I reckon."

We had neared the mouth of the cave, where we had once sworn out our holy oath of secrecy. All at once, a rifle shot rang out and a lead ball hit just to my left, spatterin' me with rock fragments.

"What the hell!" I yelped.

"Yankees!" said Owen, pointing up the hill. Shore enough, there was about ten mounted riders, dressed in Union blue. Several more shots roared, and lead balls was rainin' down in our area.

Me and Owen lit out like a bat outta hell, runnin' and stumblin' through the trees and rocks. Thunderin' hooves behind us spelled the facts that the Yankees was hot after us with murder in their hearts.

In short order, we reached the mouth of the cave and headed on in. We didn't have no lights, but was lucky in that the sun was purty much shinin' right into the cave mouth, and givin' off enough light to help us out. We was lucky too, in that we knew the cave like the back of our hand, and once't the light ran out, we stumbled on in the dark, knowin' what was ahead of us.

We reached the tough spots and just kept on goin' in the dark until we finally reached the blocked-off entrance into our secret waterfall cavern. It was pitch black by now, but we could feel the stack of rocks.

Taking the rocks down as best as we could, we finally made it into the secret place, and started blocking the entrance up behind us.

By now, we could hear voices comin' behind us, and I could see a light flickerin' back down the cave. We got into the secret cave just in the nick of time, and closed off the hole. We just sat with our backs to the cold rock wall, scared half out of our wits.

"Dang, Frank. I think I pissed my pants," said Owen.

"Quiet," I whispered. "They's right outside."

"What if there's a snake in here?"

"Better a snake than a Yankee noose."

"You don't reckon they'd hang us, do ya, Frank?"

"How the hell would I know, Owen? But if'n you don't shut up, we'll soon find out."

We heard voices just the other side of our stone doorway, and held our breath in the cold, pitch-dark cave. The voices stopped movin', and we knew that whoever was chasin' us was just about two arm's lengths away from the very spot where we were sittin'. My chest hurt, and I thought for a minute that my heart had stopped because of my tryin' to be so quiet.

## A Fairly Dangerous Man

Roy Grubbs sat on a firelog and gazed out across the campground of General Beauregard's divisions. He began thinking of home and wondering what everyone might be doing at this very moment in Bandera, Texas. He reckoned that his boss, Luke Buck, and his right-hand man, Pedro Vega, might be breaking horses, and he wondered if they missed him.

Luke's wife, Bridey, was most likely cooking supper and fighting her never-ending battle with trying to keep a wisp of light brown hair out of her eyes. Roy admired Bridey Buck more than any woman he had ever come across, but he could never let it be known, for she belonged to another man.

At that very moment, Bridey's oldest son, Joe came up behind Roy and laid his hand on Roy's shoulder.

"Jesus Christ, Joe, you scared the hell out of me."

"Well, you ain't much of a soldier then, Roy, if'n I could sneak up on you so easy. What if I had been an Apache?"

"What the hell do you know about Apaches?" asked Roy.

"I know that they ain't civilized, and that they'll bash your brains out if'n you're so easily snuck up on," laughed Joe.

"Joe, let's walk on into town a ways. I'm gettin' bored out here."

And so the two soldiers strolled the short distance into the poor portion of Chattanooga, avoiding horse droppings in the road. As they walked along, a black mongrel dog with one eye fell into step alongside of them.

"Joe," said Roy. "Is this one of your coon hounds?"

"Looks like a Texas dog to me, Roy. And also he shore looks like he's had a hard life. Just look at them raggedy ears and that scarred up nose."

With that, Roy stopped and squatted down, lying his hand on the old dog's head. The dog looked down at the ground and allowed himself to have his ears scratched. Then he looked up at Roy and seemed to have a tear in his eye.

"What if this dog is not what he appears to be, Joe. What if he's actually a Yankee spy?"

"Well, if he is a spy, he shore as hell ain't gonna learn anything from a couple of dumb-assed hillbillies like us. We're the last ones to know anything," said Joe Buck.

Roy walked into the first saloon that they came to, followed by the big dog, who now seemed to have a grin on his face, and then Joe Buck, in that order. They walked by a couple of young toughs, who seemed intent on aggravating an old man, and took a place at the far end of the dusty saloon. The dog lay down in the corner and kept his eyes glued on Roy.

"Barkeep," said Roy. "I'll have a beer. Colonel Buck here will have a sarsaparilla, and my friend on the floor will try one of those little sausages that you've got hangin' there."

"No dogs are allowed in here, boys," said the bartender, a sad-faced man with a huge handlebar mustache.

"This dog belongs to J. E. B. Stuart, barkeep, and we are in charge of him. I'll take it as a personal favor if'n he's allowed to stay, and so will General Stuart."

At that instant, the bartender was distracted by the two young toughs, who had just poured beer on the old man's head. He was obliged to forget about the dog and tend to the disturbance at the other end of the bar. But first, he delivered the beer, sausage, and sarsaparilla. Roy cut the sausage into three sections, and gave a piece to Joe and another to the grateful dog, who wolfed the tasty morsel down hungrily.

Joe took a sip of his drink, watching the action at the end of the bar. Angry words were flying, but Joe could not tell what was being said. The bartender turned around and walked back to the bar. One of the young ruffians, a civilian of about eighteen years, with a black floppy hat pinned up in the front, and wearing a Colt .44 revolver, shoved the pitiful old man in the face.

Joe noted that Roy seemed to be ignoring this fracas, and was messing around with the dog. The floppy-hat youth now took notice of the two new potential victims, and came swaggering their way, followed by another young man with a wispy mustache and a huge knife scar across his forehead. The scarred youth was missing his front teeth, and sported a handgun stuck down the front of his trousers, along with a sneering grin.

"Who in the hell brought that goddamn mangy dog into this bar?" shouted Floppy-hat, loudly.

Joe said nothing and Roy did not even look up, but proceeded to feed the hungry dog his own piece of sausage.

"Are you soldier boys deaf?" yelled Floppy-hat, his face growing beet red.

Roy now turned his attention to this red-faced bully, who had a youthful scrubby growth of what might someday become a beard, given a couple of years.

"Are you addressing me, Sir, or the dog?" asked Roy, tilting his hat back on his head a bit. Joe, who was on the safe side of Roy, noted that Roy also tugged at his belt buckle, which had the effect of moving his revolver from his ass cheek, to his hip. He also noticed that Roy dropped his hand and pulled the leather thong off of the hammer of his gun. This was all done from such a position, that it could not have been seen by Floppy-hat. Whether Scarface saw it or not, Joe could not tell.

"I'm hell on earth!" bellowed Floppy-hat, which caused Roy to grin.

"Barkeep," said Roy. "I'll buy Mr. Hell-on-Earth and his sorry-assed friend a drink, if'n you can keep them from disturbin' my peace of mind."

"Who the goddamn hell are you callin' sorry assed?" screamed Scar-face. However, his question went unanswered, when Floppy-hat made the bizarre announcement, "I'm known as a fairly dangerous man in these parts."

"Well," said Roy. "I reckon I'm proud to meet up with such a dangerous bastard as the likes of you. I don't think I am near as dangerous, so maybe you should just move on and let me drink my beer in peace. You can go back to pushin' around that poor old feller with no gun."

"I'll be a son of a bitch," said Floppy-hat, his eyes looking like they were going to explode. "I aim to kill you and send yer black soul to purgatory, you bastard!"

Roy moved away from the bar and faced the two bullies. There were two other men in the saloon besides the old man, and they moved to a position where they would be out of the line of fire.

"Young fellers," said Roy. "I've offered to buy you a drink, and to tell you the truth, I'd just as soon not die here on this spit-covered floor, and I know that you boys feel the same way. There is a way out of this tight spot for both of you rascals."

"And just what the hell might that be?" snarled Floppy-hat.

"Apologize to the dog?"

"What!" yelped Scar-face.

"You have hurt the feelings of this dog," said Roy. "And if you will just apologize, bygones will be bygones and you two scalawags can return to your farms and your mothers' tits."

That did it.

Floppy-hat reached quickly for his Colt, and his scar-faced friend clumsily tried to draw his own weapon from the front of his belt.

Joe Buck had no weapon, but he did reach for his sarsaparilla bottle to give it a throw. However, his aid was not needed.

In one smooth motion, Roy Grubbs crouched, and his hand went flying down to his revolver. Grasping the handle, he lifted his right leg a bit and pulled the gun out of the leather holster, cocking the blue-steel hammer back and putting his forefinger on the trigger in the same motion. At the very instant the end of the gun barrel had risen above the leather, Roy cocked his wrist upward and raised the revolver, aiming it at a point in the middle of Floppy-hat's chest.

The fairly dangerous man had not even cleared leather, when the explosion of Roy's Walker Colt .44 shook the walls of the saloon and caused dust to fall from every crack and crevice. A deadly bolt of orange flame flew from Roy's revolver, to the front of Floppy-hat's dirty cotton shirt, catching it on fire all around the little round hole that appeared. Floppy-hat seemed to have been kicked by an invisible horse, and he rocked backwards against a wall, mouth agape, and eyes taking on a glassy look.

Scar-face had done a fair job of getting his own weapon out of his belt, but he was so unnerved by what transpired before him, that he dropped the gun on the floor. Roy aimed his smoking revolver at Scar-face's forehead and cocked the hammer again.

"Are you ready to meet your maker, sorry ass?" said Roy.

"Ohhhh, please, sir. I ain't a part of this," said Scar-face, as the snot began to run out of his nose and down to his lips. He wiped his nose with his shirtsleeve and began to sob. "Please don't kill me."

"There's only one way out of this scrape for you, boy." said Roy.

"What's that, sir?"

"Apologize to this dog."

Scar-face almost balked at this insult. He looked down at the one-eyed dog, who had been half scared out of his wits by the blast of the revolver, and studied him for a minute. Then, Scar-face looked slowly up into the eyes of Roy Grubbs. Those eyes belied the grin on Roy's face, for they projected impending death.

The bully got down on one knee and looked at the frightened dog, who looked right back.

"Dog," he said. "I want you to know I am sorry for any trouble that me or Josephus might have caused you. The fact that he is kilt, may make you feel better."

With that, Scar-face looked pleadingly up at Roy Grubbs.

"Get the hell out of here," said Roy. "If I ever lay eyes on you again, I'll put a smokin' hole in the front of your shirt, same as your friend here."

With that, Scar-face ran gratefully toward the door, but made the bad mistake of trying to retrieve his handgun on the way out. Joe Buck stomped on his fingers, causing a crunching sound, and a scream.

Once Scar-face had made his cowardly exit, Roy Grubbs walked over to where Floppy-hat had slid down the wall, and threw some beer on the smoldering shirt, putting out the little fire.

Floppy-hat slowly raised his eyes up to look at Roy's face. He tried to talk, but at first could only emit a wheeze and some frothy red foam. Finally, a hoarse whisper came out.

"You've kilt me, you bastard."

"It would appear that way, young feller," said Roy. Floppy-hat then fell over onto his side, busting his head on a spittoon in the process and making a mess on the hardwood floor.

Roy and Joe were soon taken down to the local jail and questioned along with the bartender and the three witnesses. All stories seemed to support the fact that the ruffian had gotten what he had asked for, and that he had drawn first. The only thing people seemed to be sad about, was the fact that Roy had not shot the other bully.

## DARK AS A DUNGEON

"Are they gone, Frank?" whispered Owen.

*"Shhhh!"* I said. "Listen." The two Yanks was on the other side of the rock wall.

"I'm telling you, this is the only place them Rebs could have gone, without us seeing 'em."

"That might be so, but I ain't crawlin' back into that dark hole just to get at two no-account Confederates."

"Hey, what the hell is this little pile of stones doin' along here?"

"What kinda accent is that?" Owen asked.

"Yankee," I told him. "New England or something."

"Forget about piles of stones,"said one of the Yankees. "Let's get the hell out of this spooky place. We can lay for 'em outside and pick 'em off when they pop out."

"I'm game for that. Let's head for the sunshine, boys."

"But what about this pile of rocks?"

"You stay here and pluck away at them if you want to, Walter. We're gonna get our asses out of here."

A forbiddin' silence followed. However, another noise started from the other side of the stone wall. Sounds of rocks bein' removed from the door and thrown off to the side. I could feel Owen stiffen and start shivering against my arm. The stone removal went on for about a minute, when a muffled voice was heard, ordering the rock mover out of the cave. This was followed by shuffling feet and silence.

We remained quiet for over twenty minutes, before Owen inquired in a whisper. "Do ya reckon, they're gone."

"I hope so."

"I reckon we should stay in here for a bit, just to make sure. Don't you, Frank?"

"No, let's go runnin' on out there and strangle the whole bunch," I answered.

We sat there in the silence, listenin' as hard as we could. Finally, I had to say something.

"I wonder if there's any bodies buried in this cave," I said.

"Goddamnit, Frank. I knew you was gonna start up on that stuff."

"What stuff?"

"Tryin' to throw a scare into me, as usual. It's bad enough sittin' here in the dark, without you makin' it worse."

"I'm sorry." I told Owen, near 'bout meanin' it. We got quiet again, before I finally said, "Owen?"

"What?"

"Which snake is the most poisonous. A copperhead or a cottonmouth?"

"I'm gonna beat your ass, Frank. I mean it. Cut that shit out."

After that, there was very little talking. Time crept slowly by, until we'd both lost track of it.

After what seemed like a lifetime, the decision was made to make our exit. The rocks which covered the door were removed and an openin' was made into the darkness of the other side. We made no attempt to close the doorway again, figuring to send someone else in to do it. Someone with a torchlight.

Workin' our way out towards the mouth of the cave, we moved as silently as we could, what with not being able to see. It was dark outside, but we stopped short of the cave mouth and listened for voices. There were none, so we decided to run out as fast as we could.

Straight for home.

## THE GETAWAY

Me and Owen travelled through the woods as much as we could, stayin' off the road and keepin' silent. We was jumpin' at every little sound, expectin' Yankees to start firin' at us from behind every rock and shrub.

We made it safely home, and our decision had been made to light out tonight, and get the hell out of here while we could. Ma agreed and packed me up some food to take along, while Wed saddled my borrowed horse. Without sayin' good-bye to Bird and several others, I hugged my old ma, swung up into the saddle, waved adieu, and headed down the dark road.

Owen was ready and waitin' for me, his horse doin' a little dance in the road. We set off at a trot, but I had to stop once to heave a rock at my dog, Myrt, who had decided to come along with us. The rock missed, but Myrt was no fool and she caught on quick, tuckin' her tail between her bowed legs and scamperin' fer home.

Once't, when we passed the Miller's place, a horse whinnied and liked to scared us to death. We thought the Yanks had bushwhacked us for shore. When we reached the Tennessee River, we just bedded down for the night without no campfire, waitin' for One-Eyed Wash to show up in the mornin' and carry us across the river.

Wash showed up early and was glad to see us again, but sad to hear that Yankees was chasin' around up on the mountain.

"I seen them very same rascals," said Wash. "They made me ferry 'em across the river. Them sons of bitches never paid their toll and even stole a ham off'n me!"

Once't we got to the far side of the river, we bid goodbye to ole Wash, who took his hat off and put it over his heart. Then, he stood watching us as we rode away in the direction of Chattanooga.

I reckon we abused them horses a bit and made 'em trot along a little faster than we should have, but just after dark, we rode into camp. It didn't take us too long to find Roy Grubbs, but there was no sign of Joe Buck or Sash-a-baw. Roy said that they was around somewhere, and he proceeded to take our sweaty horses off our hands and lead 'em back to the livery stable, where he had rented 'em. I wanted to go along with him, but Roy said me and Owen had better get on over to headquarters, and report seein' Yankee cavalry up on the mountain.

We walked on over and gave that information to a young lieutenant, who thanked us for the report. Then, we made it back to our tents, where Joe Buck had a nice campfire goin' along with a big pan of beans simmerin' over the fire.

"I'm surprised to see you boys back so early, said Joe. Didn't ya'll have two more days leave?"

"We shore did," said Owen. "But it wasn't too healthy for us up on the mountain."

"Fever?"

"Yankees. Swarmin' all over the place and lacin' us with rifle balls," answered Owen.

"What the hell is Yankees doin' up there?"

"Well," said Owen. "For a while, they was bent on puttin' holes in me and Frank here, even though we had not disturbed them in any manner. What's been goin' around here?"

"It's quiet, as far as the army goes. There's a rumor goin' round that we might head down to Vicksburg, but I ain't seen no signs of movin' out."

"You boys been havin' any fun?" I asked.

"Sash's been studyin' that bear as often as he can. I caught some fish in the river and sold 'em for ten cents, and Roy kilt a no-account feller in a rough saloon."

"What?" yelped Owen. "How'd ole Roy kill the feller?"

"By heapin' scorn on his head, then shootin' him in the chest and settin' his shirt on fire," answered Joe Buck.

"Why in the world did Roy see fit to shoot the feller?" I asked.

"Nearest I can figure out," Joe Buck said, with a face just as straight as you can walk. "It was on account of the feller would not apologize to a one-eyed dog."

# SUMMER 1862

The rumor of our headin' to Vicksburg never came true, and that was fine with me. We languished around Chattanooga for over a month and finally pulled out heading north. Some strange things was happenin' and most of 'em were not good. First of all, our Confederate money was beginnin' to be worth less and less. In fact, it got to such a point that a feller could not hardly get rid of it.

Second of all, the food that we were receivin' was comin' in smaller portions and further between handouts. Owen said that somebody must think that C.S.A. must stand for 'corn, salt, and apples,' for that was about all we were gettin' around here. Roy didn't agree with that at all, sayin' that we lived mostly on beans and pone, with a smatterin' of fatback thrown in.

"I reckon we could slip back to Texas," said Roy. "And come back here with enough beef to feed this whole damn Reb army, if'n the Injuns didn't kill us."

"I don't know how you would ever swim 'em across the Mississippi," said Joe Buck.

Sash-a-baw was listenin' to this foolish conversation, and figured that he came up with an idea which would solve the river problem.

"Kill cow, cut up. Bring across water in canoe."

"Jesus Christ, Sash, you'd need ten thousand canoes," said Roy. Sash-a-baw merely poked at the fire with a long stick and pretended that he had not heard what Roy said.

"What Injuns kill white soldier?" asked Sash-a-baw.

"Comanche, Kiowa, Washita, Cheyenne, Sioux. Hell, you name it," said Roy.

"No Iroquois?" asked Sash-a-baw.

"What the hell is an Iroquois?"

"Heap bad Injun. Iroquois no take scalp. Take whole head."

We all just looked at Sash-a-baw, and wondered where in the hell these Iroquois were located, but nobody ever asked.

In our travels, we had a couple of minor fracases, but due to the large size of our division, the Yankees could not match up with us, so they always withdrew. We marched up to a railhead, but I don't know what town it was. Here, General Beauregard had orders to split his army, and send part of it east to hook up with a general from Georgia, by name of James Longstreet. Once again, us Texas boys was sent away to join up with a bunch of strangers.

Roy snuck that one-eyed black dog onto the troop train, and Sash-a-baw came along sadly, for I don't think he wanted to part company with the bear.

In short order, we was rumblin' along through the night to who knows where. It was hot and crowded on that train, and we was glad to finally get to where we was goin', even though we had no idea of just where we were.

It was just crackin' daylight, when the train groaned to a stop. The door was pulled open and we all piled out. Within sight was a large encampment of Reb soldiers. It didn't take long for us to find out that we were now a part of the Army of Northern Virginia, which was headed up by a feller by name of Robert E. Lee.

# SECOND MANASSAS

A sergeant led us out to an open spot on the campground and told us where to line up the next day with our new regiment. It didn't take too long before it started rainin' like hell and we just stayed inside of our leaky tents. As usual, Sash-a-baw stayed outside.

"I don't know what's wrong with that Injun," said Roy. "Hell, even this one-eyed dog has got enough sense to get in out of the weather."

I reckon the dog understood that he was bein' talked about, for he looked up at Roy with his one good eye and wagged his tail a bit. Later on, we got fed, and it was low off the hog, as usual.

Next mornin', the bugle blew and we fell into our lines. Our new sergeant, for a change, was not an Irishman. He was a big, bearded feller from Florida, and he struck me as the kind of feller that you did not want to cross or get on the wrong side of. His name was Sergeant Smith, which was a good American name. We was surprised when General Longstreet himself came out to greet us new troops. Longstreet, was also a big bearded man and he did not seem to be the excitable type, nor was he fancy in his dress.

"Boys," he said. "I want to welcome you all to the Army of Northern Virginia. If you are spoilin' for a fight, I reckon you're in the right place for it. We aim to head north and create a little stir among the Union army."

A half-hearted cheer went up to make the general feel good. Whether it worked or not, I could not tell.

It took two days, but shore enough, there started to be a lot of activity and rumors flew like ducks. Gallopin' horses, cannons movin', and officers sportin' worried looks signaled that we was about to move out.

And we did . . .

I reckon that it was a secret as to where we was headed, but we knew it to be northeast, by the sun. We mostly marched, but sometimes we would hop a troop train for a bit, and that was a good chance to rest and see the country. After three long days, I'll be damned if'n I didn't find myself right back where all of my fightin' had started.

Manassas.

It was late August, and it was apparent that another fight was about to take place here. I recognized a lot of spots, and they had not changed very much. First thing next mornin', we spread out into battle lines and was promptly attacked on our left. The sounds of cannons on both sides damn near busted my eardrums, but the thing that I was really worried about was those deadly minie balls whistlin' over my head.

A gaunt, bearded feller next to me got hit right in the side of the throat and was spewin' blood all over the place. He commenced screamin' and gurglin' and floppin' around in all of that wet blood. Another feller put a dirty rag over that terrible wound, but it soaked through in about one second, and the poor throat-shot feller died in short order. He was from Tennessee, just like me.

At just about the time that feller met his maker, we was attacked on our right flank. Our boys held, only to be hit from across the Warrenton Turnpike by a hell of a bunch of Federals, who struck at the middle of our lines. I was goddamn glad to just be able to hold onto my life, for there were a bunch of our boys who had got kilt or wounded, when I'll be dang if'n General Longstreet didn't give the order to attack.

"Did I hear that right?" yelled Roy. "We're about to make a run at them Yanks?"

"I reckon!" I yelled back.

"Well, I guess that makes sense. They've only got us outnumbered three to one!"

But, we did as we were told, for I am sure that our sergeant would probably have plugged anyone who refused to make this crazy charge. Our objective was a high spot named Bald Hill, and we fought our way up to the top and I'll be dogged if'n we didn't capture it. Right quick, we pulled some cannon up there and it now became apparent why we had been ordered to take this spot. From here, we could block any retreat by the Yanks, if'n they saw fit to do so.

And they did. . .

I reckon it was just the sight of our cannons starin' down at 'em, and more on the way up the hill that set the Federals to want to get the hell out of there and let well enough alone. They commenced to retreat, while we blew the hell out of 'em with the three cannons that we had pulled up on Bald Hill. It was good target practice, and a fun time was had by all of us who had the good fortune to still be alive.

## ANTIETAM
## SEPTEMBER 17, 1862
## THE BLOODIEST DAY

Nobody could argue the fact that we had won the second battle of Manassas, and the fact that us boys under General Longstreet had a lot to do with it. Even General Lee sought us out and congratulated us. He was quite a sight, sittin' ramrod straight on that gray horse of his, which matched the color of his hair. It seemed that everybody thought highly of Lee, for a lot of 'em took their hats off when he rode by, and placed them over their hearts.

We took off once again, for parts unknown, and was all surprised when the lot of us crossed the Potomac River into Maryland. We had now left Virginia soil and were in Yankee territory.

Our army had split up into four different parts and us Texas boys was stickin' with the First Corps, under Longstreet. We marched fast and within short order found ourselves in a little town named Sharpsburg. The citizens was watchin' us Confederate soldiers like we had two heads or somethin', but some of 'em gave us a little cheer. In fact, one purty young gal brought me out a glass of water, and that made my heart flutter in my chest. Roy Grubbs soon took advantage of this opportunity to redden my face, when he hollered up, "Ask her fer her hand in marriage, Frank."

That, of course, caused the purty gal's face to color up and she headed back to her house.

First Corps kept on marchin' through town and soon spread out on some ground with a little creek named Antietam to our front. Behind us some three miles lay the Potomac and to our immediate rear was Sharpsburg. One thing that made us happy, though, was the fact that we were not ordered to dig trenches, although we would later wish that we had.

We had no more than arrived, when we commenced to see dust comin' from the far side of Antietam Creek.

"Holy Jesus!" yelled Owen. "Will you take a look yonder."

"What is it?" asked Joe Buck.

"Yankees," said Owen. "Appears to be about ten million of the bastards."

We all stood on tiptoes and shore enough, lookin' like a long blue snake makin' its way down a windin' dirt road, came the whole goddamn Federal army. Bayonets reflected sunlight and looked like a sparklin' river. Had it not been so scary, it might have looked like somethin' a feller might paint a picture of. Some of our boys commenced to scurry around, lookin' for rocks and logs to pile up in front of 'em, but us Texas boys figured that was a waste of time, for we would likely not be stayin' put at this very spot.

Through the long night, our army was gettin' bigger all of the time, and so was the Yankees'. Campfires glowed on both sides of the Antietam and everybody wondered what the morning would bring.

Sergeant Smith rolled us out well before daybreak. We got just a mouthful of breakfast, and was spread out in a double line, which was supposed to be two miles long. Yankee artillery broke the peace and our boys thundered back from their high positions. That cannon duel went on until it was light enough for us to see to the other side of the creek. All I could see was blue coats and gleaming bayonets.

Off to our left was a white church and there was a big cornfield out in front of it. We had a good view of a regiment of Yankees chargin' into that cornfield from their side and workin' their way through corn and rifle balls, toward the church. The Rebs gave 'em what for, and the Yankees had to retreat out of the corn. Now, the order was given for some of us to move up and defend a bridge across the Antietam River, so we did.

"Why'd anybody need to cross a bridge?" said Joe Buck. "Hell, you could probably wade across that creek and not get yer shoes wet."

"I reckon maybe Yankees don't like to get their shoes wet," said a grizzled Georgian.

We reached a good spot overlookin' that bridge, and we got there just in time, for here came a whole damn division of Yanks, whoopin' and hollerin', intent on takin' that crossing. We did not even wait for an order to fire, but just started cuttin' loose with our rifles on the Union troops. Our cannons were also brought to bear on them poor fellers, and they were fallin' like flies and gettin' blown to bits by exploding cannon shot.

It was such a slaughter, that the Yankees had to pull back. We reloaded and waited, all the time watching that terrible battle which was taking place in the cornfield. It was the devil's own work, for sure, for the Yankees would finally make it to the end of that cornfield, only to be driven back out of it by our boys, who would come stormin' back to the far side, accompanied by the Rebel yell.

Then, the Yanks would come chargin' back, and the Rebs would quick step it backwards. It was downright fascinating to watch, but we were brought back to our own rough fix, when the Yanks came stormin' at the bridge again. We blasted 'em just as fast as we could pull the triggers and reload our hot rifles.

Yankee cannons was now concentrated on our position and the sounds of our screamin' wounded split the air and gave me a headache. We held though, and drove them Yanks back to their own side of the river.

There was another place, up closer to the river, called Sunken Road, and our boys down there was shore catchin' hell from Yankees who had decided to go ahead and get their feet wet in the Antietam. Sergeant Smith said that General D. H. Hill's boys was defending that sunken road, and that the Yankees would need divine intervention to run ole D. H. out of there.

All mornin' long, we defended that little bridge with only two Georgia regiments. I reckon the Yankees must have thrown two divisions at that bridge, and I could see a general on the other side, with a big tall floppy hat and funny lookin' whiskers on the side of his face. He looked like he was fit to be tied, for his boys could not take that little old bridge.

However, all good things must come to an end, and so did our gallant defense of the position that we were charged with. Yankee artillery and rifle fire had taken a heavy toll on us and we were runnin' low on ammunition. At the very moment we were given the order to pull back, the feller beside of me was hit in the right shoulder by a minie ball. That lead ball went right through him and came out the other shoulder, splashin' blood, flesh and bits of bone all over Sash-a-baw.

What was left of our two regiments stood up and began backin' away from where we had made our stand, firin' and reloadin' as we made our retreat. I reckon it was around one o'clock and we were exhausted. However, us retreaters was one hell of a lot better off than many of our fellow Rebs, who was dead or wounded, for we just left 'em behind.

The Yankees stormed across that little bridge, and we expected 'em to come hot after us, but for some reason, they stopped to regroup. That was fine with me, for it meant that a lot of us would live to see another day.

By now, the Union boys had taken the cornfield and Joe Buck remarked that not a single cornstalk was left standin'. They had also taken the Dunkard Church and the sunken road, not to mention our little bridge across the Antietam. A good many of us Rebs pulled all the way back to the outskirts of Sharpsburg, and the Yanks was now after us hot and heavy.

At around four P.M., General McLaw's division arrived on the battlefield to strengthen us. Shortly thereafter, A. P. Hill's division arrived from Harper's Ferry. They had marched a good many miles, and were probably dog tired, but they shore seemed to have some fight left in 'em. We started fightin' back from out of Sharpsburg, and by evening, we had pushed the Federals back across the river.

It was a stalemate.

We just laid down and did not pay much attention to the snipin' that was now goin' on from both directions. Everywhere I looked, there was dead and wounded soldiers. It was even worse than Shiloh, and I never reckoned I would ever see the likes of that battle, but here it was. One poor feller was standin' up and leanin' against a fence pole. He had been hit in the face with a cannonball and was missin' most of his jaw and his left cheek. The eye on that side was hangin' out of its socket and he was shore one sorry sight. How he was still alive and able to stand up, was beyond me.

"Do you know who that old boy is?" asked Roy, pointing to that wounded Reb.

"I don't reckon I do," I answered.

"That's the feller who helped me get them two horses for you and Owen. His name's Baker, and he is from Alabama."

"Shouldn't we go down and help him out?" asked Joe Buck.

"I'd like to," said Roy. "But I cain't stand to look close at such a sight as that. Anyway, I ain't no doctor, and couldn't do nothin' for him anyway."

Our problem was solved at that very moment, when a medical feller commenced to help out the man with most of his head blown off.

"Did ya'll hear about Preacher Somers?" asked Owen.

Preacher Somers was our chaplain, and nobody had heard anything about him, so this opened things up for an Owen Horton story.

"That chaplain kilt two Yankees with a rifle and cut another one's throat with a knife," said Owen.

"Horseshit!" said Roy.

"It's true," said Owen. "Brody saw it. And that ain't all."

"What else, then?" asked Joe.

"After doin' murder, ole Preacher Somers took off runnin' after them retreatin' Yankees, callin' 'em a bunch of goddamn cowards and yeller dogs," exclaimed Owen.

"A preacher said the word 'goddamn'?" said Joe.

"Just as big as ya please," said Owen.

"Don't that beat all. I shore hope my ma don't get wind of that," said Joe Buck.

Some rations was given out and us boys got a bit, and just went to sleep right where we lay. Next mornin', we was put into defensive formations and expected the Yankees to come at us once again, for they had us outnumbered two to one, but they never came. I reckon that they had just about enough of this battle to suit 'em, same as we did. Word was that many officers had wanted to pull back across the Potomac last night, but General Lee did not want 'em to think that they had beaten us.

At the end of this second day, we did pull back under the cover of darkness, fordin' that wide river into the safe arms of Virginia. There was a great sadness on our boys, for we had left all of our dead and most of our wounded soldiers behind on the battlefield.

As for us Texas boys, we had lived through another terrible battle. Joe Buck had been grazed on the arm with a minie ball, but he just wrapped a rag around it, and reckoned he would live to fight another day.

General Lee and the Army of Northern Virginia pulled back south of Leesburg, Virginia, to lick our wounds and re-supply. During our stay there, we learned that our casualties at Antietam were over ten thousand, and that the Yankees had suffered around fifteen thousand. It was the bloodiest single day of this crazy war.

We also learned that our old division under Braxton Bragg had been in a big battle over in Perryville, Kentucky. Our boys won that fracas, and everybody was proud as roosters.

Sash-a baw had a hard time gettin' the blood washed out of his uniform jacket, but he got out as much as he could. Then, he took the time to lean back against a tree, stare at the little brook, and reflect back on what had brought him here.

## The Ojibwa

White men were spreading across the land of the Ojibwa, like waters from a great rain. Some people referred to the Ojibwa as Chippewa, and the tribes were of the same people. Attempts at fighting against the incursion of the whites slowed them down a bit, but not much.

Still they came, like a never-ending flood.

The French had referred to the Ojibwa as the band with 'high hair.' This was due to the fact that the hair on top of the men's heads was cut and trained to stand straight up, bristling like a porcupine. Ears and noses of both men and women were pierced and adorned with anything from feathers to sea shells.

Sash-a-baw had been born and raised near the fort where Chief Pontiac had overwhelmed the British garrison of Mackinac. The hunting grounds of the Ojibwa extended from Canada to Detroit. Hunting was a good life, fish and game were plentiful when Sash-a-baw was young, but when more white men came into the land of the Ojibwa, game became scarcer and scarcer.

In the spring of the year, tribes of the Potawatomie, Huron, Ojibwa, and Ottawa put aside all differences and gathered together at the fast moving, shallow waters that whites called the Rapids of Saint Mary's. The French referred to this prime fishing spot as Le Sault Du Sainte Marie.

Even this place was being overrun with white men, who had torn a gaping hole through the rock and built what they called locks to bypass the rapids.

The only tribe which was not welcome to share in the bounty of this place of many fish was the Iroquois. These fierce warriors were the hated enemy of all the Great Lakes tribes, and their differences could never be put aside.

Young Sash-a-baw became the pride of his parents, and of the entire Massasauga band of the Ojibwa, for not only did he turn out to be a feared warrior, he was one of the best hunters in the tribe. A master with the bow and snare, Sash-a-baw supplied more than enough beaver, rabbit, deer, and moose meat for his own family, along with some tribal members who were not so well suited to the rigors of the hunt.

Sash-a-baw's specialty was snaring beaver in their underwater runs, sometimes swimming under a lodge, and up inside of it to set a snare. He also had great luck in tearing a hole in beaver dams, and laying in wait for beaver who would respond to the sound of rushing water, in order to make repairs. Using a long spear, Sash-a-baw would surprise the beaver and kill it. He was, however, very careful in avoiding killing off every beaver in a lodge. Sash-a-baw would always leave enough breeding stock to produce offspring for the next year, and he did this by moving from one hunting ground to another, all the way from Saginaw to Mackinac.

Spring was the time of the spawning whitefish, and all of the tribes came to the age-old camping grounds of Le Sault Du Sainte Marie to gather and smoke the fish for their winter food supply. Warriors braved the swift, turbulent waters in canoes, and hoisted great nets full of fish with long, stout poles.

It was at this gathering that the warrior Sash-a-baw's troubles began. Troubles that would cause him to flee for his life from his own people.

During the gathering, Sash-a-baw noticed a beautiful Ottawa maiden smiling shyly at him, turning away once she saw him notice her. Sash-a-baw tried to start up a conversation with this mysterious woman, only to have her turn and run away from him. Knowing that she was with the Ottawa tribe, Sash-a-baw pointed the maiden out to a friendly Ottawa warrior and asked her name.

The warrior looked stonily at Sash-a-baw. "She Potanka, wife of Massaugi, medicine man. Why do you ask?"

"No reason," replied Sash-a-baw. "Ojibwa thought that he had seen this woman before."

The Ottawa warrior studied Sash-a-baw for a moment, and then changed the subject to the spawning whitefish.

From that moment on, Sash-a-baw paid no more attention to the beautiful wife of the Ottawa medicine man, even though he still sometimes caught her looking his way.

Four suns later, there was a council meeting of the elders of the Huron, Ojibwa, Pottawatomie, and Ottawa tribes, all of whom were now present at Le Sault Du Sainte Marie. Not being an elder, Sash-a-baw retired to his pole-and-bark lodge and fell asleep on his soft bed of beaver pelts. He had fallen into a deep, dream-filled sleep, which was known to be a good omen to the Ojibwa.

A willow stick, threaded with lengths of leather thongs, hung over the bed of Sash-a-baw. This was a dreamcatcher, made to trap the good dreams of the Ojibwa as they floated by, and allow the bad dreams to pass through the webbing, only to perish in the light of the day.

Sash-a-baw was awakened by a movement behind him, accompanied by a soft, warm body fitting itself against his bare skin. Crying out, Sash-a-baw jumped up, and looked down at the face of the intruder, which was illuminated by moonlight filtering through a crack in his lodge.

It was the shyly smiling face of Potanka, wife of the Ottawa medicine man, looking boldly at his naked body. Potanka was also without clothes.

At first, Sash-a-baw thought that this was only a good dream that had been trapped by the dream catcher, but that notion was dispelled when Potanka reached out and ran her hand up the inside of his muscular thigh, not stopping until she had touched his uncovered parts. His response was immediate, and he fell down into the forbidden arms of the beautiful Potanka.

Their lovemaking was like the furious battle of wolves. Rolling over and over on the soft pelts, Potanka cried out in pleasure, locked her long legs around Sash-a-baw, and raked her nails across his back. He could not get enough of her, and at the very moment he cried out with release, the door of Sash-a-baw's shelter came crashing in.

Sash-a-baw, who was on the bottom, looked up into the blazing, hate-filled eyes of Massaugi, husband of Potanka, and blood relative of Chief Pontiac himself. . .

Massaugi raised a gleaming tomahawk and brought it down with a mighty stroke, into the skull of his wife. Blood flew across the walls, and onto Sash-a-baw, who looked up into the horrified eyes of Potanka. She gave out a groan and fell sideways, onto the dirt floor of the lodge, dead. Howling with hatred, Massaugi tried to remove his tomahawk from the skull of Potanka, but it did not come out easily. This gave time for Sash-a-baw to roll over and grab the spear that he used for slaying beaver. By now, Massaugi had managed to work his weapon free, and he raised it against the Ojibwa warrior.

He was too late.

Raging with anger, Sash-a-baw drove the spear through the Ottawa medicine man, and crashed through the bark wall with his forward momentum.

The sound of the fury of battle was drawing tribal members from all bands, who looked in horror at the naked, blood-spattered Sash-a-baw, standing over the dead medicine man of the Ottawa.

Knowing that what he had just done meant death, Sash-a-baw ran back into his now-unholy shelter, and retrieved some clothing, a knife, a bow, and some arrows. Then he ran out through the startled throng of onlookers, and into the woods. He did not know where he was headed, but Sash-a-baw found a moonlit trail which led to the north and to the south.

Sash-a-baw took the southbound trail and ran for his life, never looking back. He ran all night and well into the next day, a ground-consuming lope of the Ojibwa hunter-warrior. Finally, Sash-a-baw could run no more and he fell exhausted along a bubbling stream. His racing mind slowed down enough to allow him to see his predicament. He had violated all tribal hospitality customs, taking the wife of an honored guest of the Ojibwa, and bringing shame on the whole tribe. That, in itself, was enough to warrant his death, but Sash-a-baw had sealed his doom by murdering a revered member of the Ottawa nation.

Every member of every band of the Great Lakes tribes, and even the Iroquois themselves would be seeking the renegade Ojibwa. His severed head would assure great honor for anyone who could produce it to the chiefs of the Ojibwa and the Ottawa.

His legs aching with pain, Sash-a-baw raised his tired body and began his lope down the southbound Indian trail, to an unknown destination. He ran for two days and nights before he finally stopped to rest and eat some brook trout that he had managed to catch with his bare hands. This was rocky country, and there was no way for even the finest tracker to follow the tracks of the Ojibwa in this terrain.

During this rest, Sash-a-baw was startled by four well-armed runners of the Huron nation. Hiding in a vine-choked ravine, Sash-a-baw watched the warriors trot by, knowing that they were looking for him.

It was dark when the Ojibwa burst out of the woods and onto the shore of the Great Lake, with Mackinac looming across the waters, and the island of the Great Turtle to his left. Waiting until morning, Sash-a-baw approached a Frenchman who was about to canoe across the waters with a load of furs. The Frenchman was happy to have an extra hand aboard with an oar, and gladly carried the fleeing warrior away from the little village of Sainte Ignace, across to the other side.

Sash-a-baw was happy that the Frenchman had not yet heard the tale of his shame, for it may well have spelled his doom. Once on the south side of the straits, the Ojibwa did not linger, but began once again, his lope to the south. He ran all night, and rested in a stand of giant pines during the following day.

Waiting till dark, Sash-a-baw abandoned the well-worn trail for the woods and made his way to the west, hoping to avoid the warriors who were not only behind him, but were also now in front of him. He lost track of days and nights, and ran as hard as his body could endure.

Many days and nights went by, when Sash-a-baw came to a river known as the Muskegun, and in short order, he came to a band of camped Indians of an unknown tribe. Waiting until late night, Sash-a-baw crept up to the riverbank and stole a canoe. With a barking dog at his back, the Ojibwa slipped into the dark river and paddled silently, as hard as he could.

Six suns later, Sash-a-baw came to the end of the big river, a great lake of high waves and ice-cold water. He began to run along the sandy shore, still heading south.

A beaver dam along a small stream allowed Sash-a-baw to try his hand at his old practice of tearing a hole in the dam and waylaying the first beaver who showed up to repair the damage. The meat was sweet and fresh, even though it was raw, and it would sustain the Ojibwa hunter-warrior for several days to come.

In the following days, Sash-a-baw had to swim across several wide rivers, but he stuck to the shore of the huge lake until he came to a great river which flowed to the south. Breaking away from the shore of the lake, Sash-a-baw decided to follow the river shore and try to steal another canoe.

The chance to do so came two days later, when he found an overturned canoe hidden in some bushes along the riverbank. Stealing for only the second time in his life, Sash-a-baw slid the birch-bark canoe into the muddy water and began a two-week float down the river. Surprisingly, the big river which he was traveling on, emptied into an even bigger river, still flowing to the south.

On and on he floated, having no idea of where he was.

The day came when Sash-a-baw noticed several blue-coated soldiers camping on the shore. He was surprised when the soldiers fired several shots at him across the wide muddy river. Sash-a-baw was not hit, but his canoe was sunk.

He began, once again, to travel by foot, always to the south.

Finally, not knowing where he was, exhausted and starving, Sash-a-baw was surprised by twelve well-armed soldiers of the Confederacy.

Surprisingly, these men were friendly, and offered to share their food and their campfire. Feeling that he may now be safe, not only from the Great Lakes Indian nations, but from the blue-coated soldiers, Sash-a-baw joined up with the twelve Rebel soldiers. He later put his X on a piece of paper, pledging to wage war on the white man, and to actually be paid for doing something he had always dreamed of.

A good dream, perhaps captured by the dream catcher.

## THE BORDELLO

After that terrible day at Antietam Creek, we settled down for a bit, and tried to gain strength for whatever lay ahead. We were drillin' and marchin' every day, and most of us was gettin' tired of that stuff. I reckon that most of us was an undisciplined lot, for we were not really soldiers, only farmers, cowboys, clerks, and such, who had been given a gun and told to go to killin' Yankees.

Some of our boys, especially those fellers from Mississippi, hated like hell to take orders, and I think that their officers were about ready to start shootin' them. At the present, there seemed to be an uneasy truce between the Second Mississippi and their officers, but I did not know how long it would last.

The division that I was in was now camped on the outskirts of Richmond, Virginia. Me, Joe Buck, and Owen was sittin' on a log and grousin' at everything we could think of.

"I shore hate this sittin' around," said Owen. "I'd rather be fightin'."

"Well, count me out on them thoughts," said Joe. "I take no enjoyment over seein' all that blood and gore."

"I wonder if'n there's anything to do in town?" I asked.

"Might be . . . There's supposedly about a dozen whorehouses in Richmond," said Owen.

Joe and I looked over at him.

"And how would you know that?" Joe asked.

"Elijah Pitts told me so. He said that he'd been over there and had him a high old time."

"Doin' what?" I asked.

"Ridin' them whores, Frank. What the hell do you think a feller would do inside of a whorehouse," said Owen, grinnin' like a rat.

"And what would you know about ridin' a whore?" I asked. "You ain't never partaken of such goin's on that I'm aware of."

"I think it's somethin' that comes natural," said Owen. "How about you, Joe, have you ever seen the elephant?"

"What elephant?"

"Dang, Joe. That's just a figure of speech. Have you ever had the pleasure of dallyin' with the female species."

"I ain't never rode one, if that's what yer askin'," answered Joe Buck. "But I've stole me a kiss or two, and had a nice dance with a gal."

"Well, that ain't nothin'. Hell, even Frank Morgan here has probably went that far. But I know that Frank ain't never seen the elephant or rode no woman," said Owen.

"Well," I grinned. "I guess us three Rebs are all in the same boat. We ain't never broke that particular commandment, as of yet."

We were all quiet for a minute, studyin' a Georgian who was tryin' to get a bridle on a mule. The mule was a mean one and he was tryin' to bite the poor feller, who finally bashed the mule across the head with a pole.

"Boys," said Owen. "Let's do it."

"Do what?" inquired Joe Buck.

"Get after them whores," answered Owen.

"What if Roy Grubbs finds out," I said. "He told us to step wide of whores."

"Hell," said Joe, surprisin' me. "Roy ain't exactly our boss. Besides that, I think he's probably the biggest whoremonger of all. He keeps disappearin' from sight and comin' back with a silly look on his face."

"Let's take a vote on gettin' horizontal with some whores," said Owen.

It wasn't a very close vote, for we all three raised our hands, grinnin' like coons.

That evening, armed with directions and advice from Elijah Pitts, us three jackasses approached the Injun, Sash-a-baw, and asked him if he would like to join us in our adventure. To our great surprise, ole Sash agreed to come along and try his luck at gettin' after a white woman.

It didn't take us long to find the bordello which we were seeking. It was a shabby abode which butted up to the back of a hardware shop. A big black-haired feller with a scraggly beard and an ax handle met us at the door. He thought himself to be in charge of this whorehouse, and he did not want to allow Sash-a-baw inside, for he was an Injun. We tried to back him down, hinting of death and of the fact that we were bad hombres, but that feller would not budge.

However, a dollar caused him to change his mind, open the door with a grin, and wish us luck. Once inside, we were met with a well-worn fat lady in a tattered robe.

"Dang, Frank," whispered Owen. "I hope this ain't our prize."

"Me too," I whispered back. "But she shore looks like a whore."

Our fears were answered when the fat lady said that she had three fine girls, and that it would set us back four dollars apiece for the privilege of having at them.

"Bring 'em out," said Joe Buck. "We'll take a look at 'em."

The fat lady smiled at young Joe bein' so savvy, and she disappeared back through a blanket-covered door. In short order, the fat lady reappeared with three gals.

One of 'em was skinny and had a bad complexion. Her hair was all wild, and so were her eyes. She looked like she was about fourteen years old, and she was claimed by the love-starved Owen Horton.

The second gal was about thirty years old, and did not look too beat up or ugly. Her hair was red, and it was her that made the claim on her chosen suitor. She chose Sash-a-baw, sayin' she did not want to deflower any young'uns. Ole Sash grinned and followed her off into a side room, with his four dollars clutched tightly in his hand.

Me and Joe Buck looked at the third and final object of our lewd ideas. I'll be goddamned if'n that gal did not look just exactly like my grandma. She was about sixty years old and sported a full head of gray hair. At least, though, she had a fairly nice smile and big bosoms.

I thought of backin' right on out of this whorehouse, but Joe Buck outsmarted me and blocked my exit.

"Frank," he said. "You go ahead, and I'll take whichever gal finishes up first."

"Now Joe," I said. "I don't want to be a hog. You go on first, and I'll wait."

Granny solved this problem by grabbing me by the hand and leading me upstairs to a candlelit room, with a cornshuck bed and a little table with a pan of water and some soap.

"What's your name, soldier," asked Granny, and I'll be hanged if'n she didn't even *sound* like my ole grandma.

"Elijah Pitts," I lied.

"Well, Mr. Pitts, get them clothes off, and let me have a look."

"A look at what, ma'am," I choked out.

"At yer frog."

"Ma'am, I didn't bring in no frogs," I squeaked.

"Yes you did, son. He's in yer pants, and you use it to make water with."

Now, it came to me what this old lady was referring to. This was unexpected to me, in that she was wantin' me to actually take off all my clothes. To make matters even more clear, Granny went first, droppin' her dress off'n her shoulders and lettin' it fall to the floor.

I damn near had a heart failure right on the spot, for ole Granny did not have on a single stitch of clothes beneath that dress. There she was—nekkid as the day she was born.

Granny's breasts were not up in the same area where Bird's had been, and they kind of sloped down towards her stomach area. Below that was a patch of fur that I had spent many an hour wonderin' about, ever since I had spied on the widder Mason takin' a bath in the crick behind her house.

"Go ahead, Elijah," she said. "Get them clothes off, and quit staring at my crotch."

I reckoned that we had gone too far for me to back out now, due to the fact that I had already looked at ole Granny in her birthday suit. I pulled my shirt over my head, kicked off my boots and dropped my pants.

Granny commenced to chuckle, and I was mortified to tears, when I realized what she was lookin' at.

I had big holes in my long johns, and my socks was about as raggedy as they could be. I felt my neck get hot, and went ahead and jerked off them socks and long johns just as fast as I could.

Embarrassed to the hilt, there I stood, just as nekkid as Granny, with my frog in full view.

Granny smiled and took me by the hand, leadin' me over to the pan of water.

"Ma'am," I said. "What are you aimin' to do?"

"I'm gonna wash you up and check out your weapon."

"I didn't bring no weapons, ma'am, and I just had a nice bath last week."

"This *here* weapon," she said, taking ahold of my frog, which dang near caused the death of me. Then, Granny commenced to wash my little frog with a soapy, wet rag. I was now resigned to my fate, but I still could not help closin' my eyes and groanin' when Granny was so bold as to get right down there and take a close look at my frog.

"Lay down on the bed," Granny ordered, and I did as I was told.

"Not on your stomach, Elijah. Have you never done this before?"

I could tell from the tone of her voice that she was gettin' exasperated over my bein' such a fool at the art of love.

"No ma'am," I whispered. "I ain't never had the pleasure."

"Well, roll over," Granny said. I did as I was told, closing my eyes, so as not to have to look at this old woman who looked and sounded like my grandmother.

Within seconds, my eyes flew open as big as pie tins. My frog had suddenly gotten very warm, for some reason. I tilted my head and looked down into the frog area, but all I could see was a bunch of gray hair, bobbin' up and down.

Granny or no Granny, that shore felt good, whatever it was that was takin' place down there. I just closed my eyes again and daydreamed that it was not an old Granny that was takin' advantage of my innocence, but that it was the young gal who had given me that drink of water when we was marchin' through Sharpsburg.

It started to get downright hot in that little room, and all of a sudden, I could hear a bed thumpin' somewhere's near by. Then, I heard Sash-a-baw moanin', and fer a minute I thought that maybe someone had bashed him over the head, but I couldn't worry about that Injun right now. He would just have to fend fer himself.

My frog suddenly cooled off and I opened my eyes, only to behold Granny movin' up and straddlin' me. Her bosoms was hangin' right into my face, and she lowered herself down on top of me.

My frog got warm again.

Granny suddenly started to movin' up and down on me, and I'll be danged if'n that did not feel almost as good as what she had been doin' when I was lookin' at the top of her gray head. I started to concentrate on them two big tits swingin' back and forth under my nose.

That other bed began bangin' against a wall, and I swore I heard Sash-a-baw let out a war whoop. Granny laughed and really went to work on my frog.

I just closed my eyes and let nature take its course, while listenin' to all of the moanin' and thumpin' that was goin' on in this building. I reckon it was about two more minutes, when I sewed my wild oats into ole Granny.

## FREDERICKSBURG
## DECEMBER OF 1862

Next day, us four womanizers got away from Roy Grubbs, and compared stories. I reckoned that my four dollars was well spent, and that I should not hold it against a whore for bein' old and lookin' like my grandma.

Sash-a-baw was well pleased with his whore, and so was Joe Buck, who had took his turn at the same woman that Sash-a-baw had dallied with.

Joe reckoned that the experience was such as to change his whole thought process as to females in general. He reckoned that this whole thing was a blessin', even though it was a sin, for he would now be knowledgeable of what was expected of a feller on his wedding night.

Owen Horton was not so boisterous, and it took us an hour to get it out of him that he had not sewed his oats.

"That dang gal would not stop jabberin', and she stunk worse than a barrel of old fish," he said.

"I don't reckon you smell like no load of roses yerself, Owen," said Joe Buck.

"That may be so, but she wasn't the one payin' the money. I was," replied Owen. "Why a young gal like that would already have so much to talk about beats the hell out of me!"

We did not return to the whorehouse, but I thought of it often. Roy Grubbs finally got wind of it, and tried to dampen our spirits, sayin' that we had better keep a keen eye on our frogs for signs of wear and tear. If'n our frogs took on an unnatural look, we had better hightail it fer a doctor.

That ole one-eyed dog was still hangin' around and followed Roy damn near everywhere he went. By now, everybody in the corps knew the story of Roy's gunfight, and it became a regular joke for a great many Reb soldiers to commence apologizin' to that dog, whenever him and Roy strolled by.

As for Sash-a-baw, his attitude had taken a great step forward pursuant to his dallyin' with that white whore. On top of that, Sash had found him two friends to take the place of that smelly old bear. They was Cherokee Indians from Tennessee, just about the same age as Sash-a-baw. Of course, Sash did not speak Cherokee, and the Cherokees did not know any Ojibwa, so they was forced to speak English to one another, which was sometimes a laugh and sometimes a wonderment.

Them three Injuns loved to gamble at somethin' which entailed rollin' some shells around in a wooden bowl and droppin' 'em on the ground. The shells was painted white on one side and black on the other, and apparently meant somethin' to the Injuns. They would yell and laugh like hell over the way them shells had fell.

We just loafed around in between marchin' and drillin' fer a few days and a rumor started flyin' that we was about to pull out and head north.

Shore enough, gallopin' horses and rollin' cannons gave the signal, and two days later, Longstreet's corps was marchin' north.

In short order, we were joined by General Robert E. Lee himself, who could often be seen ridin' alongside General Longstreet. Them fellers seemed to get along purty well and General Lee sometimes referred to Longstreet as 'My Old Warhorse.'

We stopped at a crossroads with a sign that pointed north and said Fredericksburg. Our divisions camped here, and within two days, we were joined by the divisions of Generals Pickett and John B. Hood.

Then, we started marchin' to the north once again, only our pace had picked up considerable. The next day, we arrived at Fredericksburg, Virginia. It was November twenty-second, and we were surprised that on the far side of the Rappahannock River stood what appeared to be the whole damn Yankee army. They were in the process of buildin' pontoon bridges across the river, for the regular bridges had all been destroyed. We soon found out that there were some Yankees over on our side, occupying and tearing the hell out of the little town of Fredericksburg.

Stuart's division arrived and some of us proceeded to dig in behind a long stone wall overlookin' Fredericksburg, while some of our boys stormed into the town and drove those Yanks back across the river. For a time, there was a good gun battle goin' on, but the Union boys decided it might be safer for 'em on the other side of the Rappahannock.

Once we got dug in good, and stretched out in a long defensive position, me, Roy, Owen, and Joe Buck snuck down into the town, and joined up with a bunch of gawkin' Rebs by the river. Those fools were sittin' on what had once been bridge beams, and was yellin' across the river to some Union boys. The banterin' was mostly friendly, with a lot of leg-pullin' goin' on.

"We'll be over soon to have dinner with you boys!" yelled a blue-coated soldier.

"If'n ya do, you blue bellies will have a long street to walk down!" shouted back a Georgia feller.

"We don't mind walkin' down streets," said the Yank. "What's fer dinner?"

"Ya'll better bring along yer own vittles," laughed an Alabama feller. "Less'n you boys like dried corn and possum."

"Possum! Goddamn, all we get is beef and biscuits!" yelled the Yank.

"Bring it on over with ya!" hollered the Reb. "We'll trade you some lead balls fer it."

"Hey!" came a voice from the Yankee side. "Have any of you boys heard of a couple of fellers by name of Frank Morgan or Owen Horton?"

Several Rebs looked at me, and Owen, includin' Roy Grubbs.

"Who the hell is that?" asked Roy.

"I don't reckon I know," said Owen, moving forward and shading his eyes across the river.

"I'm Frank Morgan," I yelled. "Who's doin' the askin'?" Everybody on both sides of the Rappahannock got quiet.

"Frank! You son of a bitch. It's me, Jodie!"

Me and Owen just looked at each other. Then, it was Owen who shouted back across the river. "Jodie Pickett?"

"One and the same!" hollered Jodie. "How're you boys makin' out?"

I'll be hanged if'n ole Jodie Pickett did not come walkin' down through them blue bellies just as big as you please.

"Goddamn you, Jodie," yelled Owen. "What the hell do you mean sneakin' off and joinin' up with them no-account Yankee scums?"

Those words brought forth a few curses from the Union side of the river, but finally Jodie got the floor again.

"Sorry boys. I couldn't fight against my own country, and I knew ya'll would never understand."

"Goddamn right!" hollered a voice from the Union side. "He ain't gonna fight for no shittin' Reb bastards the likes of you."

"Better'n gettin' his ass kicked every time he goes to fightin'," yelled another voice from the Rebel side of the Rappahannock.

A general grumblin' noise ground out from both sides of the river, until Jodie drowned them out again. "How's yer folks and the rest of yer family, fellers?" he yelled, grinnin' and leanin' on his rifle.

I looked at Owen, and we was quiet fer a minute. Owen took the opportunity to yell back across the swift river. "My folks is just fine, Jodie, but Frank's ain't!"

"What's wrong?" hollered Jodie.

"Yankee thieves shot Frank's pa down like a dog. Unarmed, and before the eyes of his whole dang family!" yelled back Owen, standing up before the hushed blue-coated army.

I did not say nothin', just watched this confrontation unfurl.

There was a rumble of voices goin' on both sides of the river, for everyone seemed to be listenin' to the conversation of old friends, who had become enemies in this terrible war. Thunderin' hooves caused us all to look to the road on the Yankee side of the Rappahannock, where a Union officer came ridin' up to his boys, madder'n hell.

"Here now!" he hollered. "You men quit fraternizing with the Rebs, and get back to your regiments."

A bunch of our boys started hoorahin' that mad officer, and he took his sword out and shook it at us, swearin' like hell. One of our Georgia boys fired a round at the officer, and the Yanks commenced scurryin' for cover. However, our boys gave that feller who had fired on the officer a piece of their mind, for peace was hard to come by. No one saw any use in startin' a battle with the Yankees unless one of our generals ordered it. Anything else was simply murder.

"Mighty sorry about that, Billy Yanks," yelled a tall, bearded Reb, wavin' his hat. "Ya'll kin shoot a round over our way if'n it'll make ya feel better!"

A couple of Yanks just waved their hats at us, and seemed to be grinnin'. They had probably hated that officer anyway, and if the truth was known, no tears would have been shed if'n he had been blasted out of the saddle.

Jodie Pickett approached the river and yelled across. "I'm shore sorry about yer pa, Frank. I reckon there's gonna be a scrap, so if you boys see me comin', I'd appreciate it if'n ya'll did not shoot me down, for I'd hate to be kilt by my own people."

Me and Owen just raised up and looked at ole Jodie fer one last time, waved, and walked away from the Rappahannock.

"Frank!" hollered Jodie.

We stopped and looked back at Jodie Pickett.

"I'm gonna wear a turkey feather in my hat!" Jodie yelled. "So if you boys spot it, fire at somebody else."

I think Jodie was just joshin' us, but I ain't sure. Me and Owen just looked at each other and smiled. Then, we turned and commenced walkin' once more.

It was a sad departing for me. Ole Jodie was sometimes a pain in the hind end, but he was always a friend to me, and I took no pleasure in the thought of tryin' to kill Jodie Pickett.

We returned to our camp, which was near a long stone wall, bearing the queer name of Marye's Heights.

## Marye's Heights

During the following ten days or so, it was a strange scene. There was no fightin' goin' on yet, but the armies on both sides of the Rappahannock were growin' by leaps and bounds. The Yanks were buildin' pontoon bridges, and they thought that they were bein' sly about it, but every one of us Rebs knew just exactly what was goin' on. We had spies, just the same as them.

Me and Joe Buck liked to spend time on top of a big hill, watchin' incoming columns of Reb soldiers movin' through a ravine. They were a welcome sight, and Joe thought it was real purty to see them regiments headin' our way. I thought it looked like a long, gray snake, with shiny scales, slitherin' through the hills.

One night, the damnedest thing happened, something I know I'll remember fer the rest of my life. All us Texas boys, along with our adopted Injun, Sash-a-baw, were sittin' by a campfire. It was just after dark, and we were alongside of a little dirt road, which came by the stone wall at Marye's Heights.

Hoofbeats signaled riders comin', and we thought nothin' about it. Roy Grubbs was fiddlin' out a mournful song on a borrowed fiddle, and this set all of us—cept'n Sash-a-baw—to longin' fer home and the loved ones we had left behind. As fer Sash, who knew what the hell he was thinkin'.

The horses finally came into the light of our fire, and I'll be danged if'n it weren't General Robert E. Lee himself, along with General Longstreet. All of us, except Sash-a-baw, jumped to our feet like a bunch of fools and saluted. Owen Horton saluted so hard that he knocked his hat sideways on his head, causin' him to be the picture of ignorance, and causin' me to be mortified for him.

"Stand at ease boys," said General Longstreet, and with a nod to Roy added, "That was a beautiful piece of music, soldier."

With that, both generals swung down off'n their horses.

General Lee spoke first, and I had the feelin' that I was in the presence of somethin' holy, which I can't explain and will not try.

"Where are you boys from?" asked General Lee.

I reckon we were all dumbstruck and at a loss for words, but Roy Grubbs finally saved us, speakin' out in his slow Texas drawl.

"Sir, me and Joe Buck here are from south Texas. Frank and Owen hail from Tennessee, while this Injun ran down here from Michigan."

This caused General Longstreet to break into a big grin, and bein' that he looked like he might be part Injun himself, he gave Sash-a-baw a good look over. Longstreet was a big man, with a huge black beard and laughin' eyes.

"Thank God for Texas, General Lee," said Longstreet. He had a Georgia twang to his voice.

"Texans always move them, Pete," said Robert E. Lee. "And thank God for the boys that Tennessee is able to send us."

I looked at the white-haired General Lee, and was surprised to see that his dark eyes seemed to be blazing. Maybe it was just the glow of the campfire, but I suddenly felt like either gettin' down on my knees for this man, or gladly givin' up my young life.

Maybe General Lee read my mind, and this would not have surprised me, for he was lookin' right back at me.

"How is your family faring at home, son? Is it Frank?"

"Yes sir," I answered. "My name is Frank Morgan, and my family is gettin' by I reckon. Yankee cavalry kilt my pa."

Robert E. Lee seemed to be very taken aback by this, and his mouth dropped open a little bit. "Was your father a soldier?" he asked.

"No sir," I answered. "He was just a farmer, tryin' to keep the Yankees from takin' off all of our stock. Pa had a hay fork in his hand, so the Yanks gunned him down, right in front of my ma and the young'uns."

General Lee looked at me for a minute, then took a step in my direction and rested his gloved hands on my shoulders.

"Frank," he said. "You will never know how sorry I am over this. I pray every day that this terrible war will be over soon, and we can all go home."

I'll be hanged if'n tears did not start to run down my cheeks, and I reckoned I looked like a big baby to them generals. "Thank you sir," I blubbered.

General Lee raised his hand. "No boys. Do not thank me, for it is I who thank you."

We were interrupted by a gallopin' horse, and a lieutenant came ridin' up and said somethin' to General Lee. Both generals got back on their horses, looked at us Texas boys and rode off without another word.

"Don't that beat all?" said Owen. He took his hat off and slapped his leg, causin' a cloud of dust to fly.

"Them generals talked to us boys just like we was human bein's," said Joe Buck. That caused Roy to look over at Joe and smile.

"Joe," said Roy. "I don't know how you could live so long around me, and still be so dumb. Last I knew, we *were* human bein's, except'n maybe for Sash-a-baw. I ain't too sure about him."

## Across the Rappahannock

The days went by, and we watched the pontoon boats bein' put together by the Union boys, and could not help but notice that the Yankee army was gettin' mighty sizeable. The days were gettin' downright cold, and it seemed that we never had enough blankets or food. Many of our Reb soldiers were bare-footed, and I reckon the cold Virginia soil did not feel so good on their feet. Especially those rowdy Mississippi fellers, who were used to warm ground squishin' between their toes.

Us Texas boys were still shod, although Owen's shoes had one sole hangin' down, and it flapped when he walked. As fer Sash-a-baw, he had on some moccasins that he had sewn together himself. He had stopped after the battle of Shiloh and cut a big piece of hide off'n a dead horse. Everybody was laughin' at him, but Sash paid them no mind, and later commenced to work on that piece of hide.

He scraped both sides and soaked it in a hollowed-out willow stump full of water. Then, he smoked the hide, soaked it again, and stretched it. By now, Sash was drawin' a little crowd of gawkers, especially the barefoot boys. One big old boy from Alabama laughed at Sash-a-baw and called him a squaw. Sash-a-baw picked up a heavy log and busted it across the Alabama feller's head, and that was the last person who called the Ojibwa a squaw.

It wasn't long before Sash had cut that hide into pieces, and sewed them together with leather strips from the same horsehide. The end result was two mighty fine moccasins, which Sash-a-baw wore everywhere he went.

The town of Fredericksburg had been evacuated, and a great many civilians were now camped up here in the woods around Marye's Heights. Some Reb sharpshooters had been firin' across the river at the Yank engineers who were tryin' to build those pontoons so they could float across and kill us. The Yankee General, Burnside, had sent a note over, sayin' that if we did not stop firin' on his boys from the houses, he was aimin' to commence shellin' the town. Our boys kept snipin' and most of the residents figured that it was time to leave. It wasn't long before Burnside kept his promise, and the Yankee cannons commenced firin' into the town.

On the night of December eleventh, a Federal band came down to the edge of the Rappahannock, near the burned-out ruins of a railroad bridge. Both armies listened with great interest, as the blue-clad band members started playin' 'Yankee Doodle,' 'The Star Spangled Banner,' 'Hail Columbia,' and other such songs that the Yankees took enjoyment in hearin'. The band quit playin' for a bit, and I reckon that they wanted our band to play a tune for them, but nothin' happened.

I was amazed at what happened next, for the Yank band struck up 'Dixie.' Laughter and cheers from both armies rolled across the cold Rappahannock and, all in all, it was a right enjoyable evenin'. We went to our cold beds late that night, but we did not suffer long from the cold. At two o'clock that mornin' Yankee cannons opened up with an earsplitting barrage. Within short order, the Reb artillery on Marye's Heights belched out their fiery answer. The terrible battle of Fredericksburg had begun.

## BARKSDALE'S STAND

Sash-a-baw was the first one to bounce up due to the rudeness of the early mornin' cannonade, but he was hollerin' in the Injun language, so none of us knew what he was sayin'.

"Thunderin' damnation!" hollered Roy as he jumped up, steppin' on Joe Buck's hand in the process.

"Shit!" squawked Joe, as he stood up rubbin' his hand. He was not payin' much attention to the cannonballs burstin' on our side of the river, but seemed more concerned with his hand.

Buglers were blowin', and our sergeant came runnin' up to us in his long johns, hollerin' for us to get to our positions. We were pullin' on our pants and boots just as fast as we could, and that old one-eyed dog of Roy's got so riled up, he took a little nip out of Owen Horton, and got himself a kick in the ass for his rude behavior. The reason that the kick connected was that it came in on the dog's blind side. Owen Horton was not a complete fool.

Us Texas boys made sure to gather up our little tents, blankets, and such for they were our most important possessions in this war. Then we ran to our spots behind the stone wall at Marye's Heights. The dog ran along with us, and Roy tied him to a bush behind the wall where he would not get hit with rifle balls. A well-placed cannon shot would get the dog, but nothin' less than that.

Once we got settled in, we looked down at the river. A bunch of commotion was comin' from the town, and word was that the Yanks had slipped their pontoons into the Rappahannock. General William Barksdale was down in the town, along with the Twenty-first Mississippi, the Eighteenth Mississippi, and a regiment from the Eighth Florida. These boys were mostly sharpshooters, and they were firin' on the Federals who were tryin' to cross the river.

There was no fightin' for us yet, but we could hear the sounds of a fracas in town and down at the edge of the river. At around noon, I reckon that every heavy gun the Yanks had opened up on the little town of Fredericksburg, Virginia. I knew that George Washington had spent a good part of his youth in Fredericksburg, and we just watched with a quiet silence as the old town was reduced to flames and rubble.

At around two thirty, Yankee soldiers commenced crossing the river in rowboats. They were takin' fire hot and heavy, but a good many of 'em made it to our side, and the battle for the town went on furiously. Towards evening, orders were given for General Barksdale and his men to pull out of Fredericksburg, and let the Yanks have it.

Every Reb soldier stood up when Barksdale's men came marchin' out of the burnin' town in perfect order. They were not in any hurry, and there was a proud steadiness in their orderly withdrawal. As they approached our lines, a great cheer went up from our boys behind Marye's Heights. I looked over at Joe Buck, and he must have had a tear in his eyes, for he was wipin' 'em with his coat sleeve.

Night finally fell, and the burnin' city lit up the whole sky. There was still a skirmish goin' on in the town, and our cannons were still firin' on the Yanks who were crossin' the river. We had not had a single thing to eat all day, and were damn near starved to death.

The next day was December 12, and the word that we got was that the Yanks were now busy lootin' what was left of the town. A Mississippi feller reported that there was a drunken Yankee with a bottle in one hand and a live goose in the other chasin' a small hog through the streets. We all reckoned that we would not mind havin' a hog, or a goose, or even that bottle, ourselves.

We did, at least, finally get somethin' to eat. It was some bacon, bread, and gruel, which seemed to be alive and crawlin'. Most of us gave up that movin' meal to the dog, who was not so choosy about his vittles.

By now, us Texas boys, who were becomin' famous for bouncin' around from regiment to regiment, were fightin' under the colors of the Twenty-fourth Georgia, and our commander was a feller by name of Colonel Robert McMillan. These boys in the Twenty-fourth were mostly Irishmen, and a good many of 'em were immigrants right straight off the boat. They were a good bunch of fellers, but half the time you couldn't understand what they was sayin'.

Those Irish fellers took a fond interest in Sash-a-baw, for I reckon that they had not encountered many Injuns. I understand that there are not any in Ireland, and most of the Injuns in Georgia had been sent out to Oklahoma by President Andrew Jackson. The Irishmen also took a likin' to the one-eyed dog, who had by now gotten a bath from Roy, and was cured of the mange. In fact, the dog was the only one of us who was not losin' weight, so I reckon the war agreed with him.

## IRISH KILLING IRISH
## DECEMBER 13, 1862

The early morning of December thirteenth came in cold and foggy. Reb cannons hailed the oncomin' day, by destroyin' our peace with a frightening barrage on the poor town of Fredericksburg. We assumed our positions, and could hear a bunch of activity from the Yankee army. Wagon wheels were creakin', and cold steel was clankin' from the valley down in front of us, and I'll be danged if a Federal band did not start playin' down across the valley. Them boys sure did seem to enjoy their music.

By ten o'clock in the morning the fog had lifted, and a grand sight presented itself to us boys perched behind that four-foot-high stone wall. Thousands of blue-clad Yankees were marchin' double quick, on the other side of the field in front of us, parallel to the river. Then they stopped and formed companies and regiments amidst the gallopin' officers and drummer boys. Once them boys got set, they turned towards our positions, and a quiet settled over the countryside that made my blood run cold.

"Ahh boys, a foul, black day it will be," said ole Paddy Conighan, an Irish feller who liked to sit at our campfire and study Sash-a-baw.

"It might be," said Roy. "But I'd damn shore rather be hidin' behind this rock pile than be gettin' set to stroll across that field."

"There shore is a hell of a bunch of Yanks out there," said Owen.

Sash-a-baw was workin' at slippin' a cap on the nipple of his rifle. We had finally gotten him to give up his old Brown Bess, and take up a fine .54 caliber Enfield that Joe had stolen off'n a dead Yank. Sash had been practicin' with this new gun, and could shoot purty straight for an Injun.

"Roy," I said. "Do you think we can stop 'em here?"

"I shore hope so, Frank," said Roy. "I don't like to think about the alternative."

Yankee drums started to roll, and their band was playin' a fine marchin' tune. Silver bayonets gleamed in the sun, as they commenced their slow death march towards us.

"Ain't they dressed fine?" said Owen.

"Owen," I said. "What the hell is bein' finely attired got to do with anything, anyway?"

Owen thought about that for a minute, as the Yankees continued their march to our position, then he came up with his best thought on the matter.

"I just mean that sometimes I get mortified by the sight of our raggedy-assed army, and wish't that we had somethin' decent to wear."

I just shook my head for this conversation, as usual, was not makin' much sense at this very moment.

Yank cannons commenced sweepin' the field in front of their advancing army, and our own cannons opened up on the Federals from the front and the sides. I pitied them poor soldiers a bit, when gaping holes were blown in their lines, causin' body parts to go flyin' through the cold morning air.

Down in front us was a sunken road, and the Twenty-fourth North Carolina were dug in there. When the Yanks got to within three hundred yards of the sunken road, Reb muskets opened up with a solid sheet of flame. Yanks were droppin' like raindrops off'n a roof, but still they came, and it began to look like they would go right through, and over us.

Once the boys down at the sunken road had done the best they could, they pulled back to our position at the stone wall. When what was left of the advancin' Yankees got to within a hundred and twenty-five yards of us, we were given the order to fire. The air exploded with an earsplitting shock, as hundreds of muskets roared at the same time. Black smoke filled the air, and the stink was dang near enough to make a feller gag.

I had picked out one particular Yank, who was out front and actin' like he didn't give a damn for his safety. When I fired, he went flyin' backwards, so I figure that I was the one who had shot him. In truth, there was probably over a hundred Reb rifles trained on this bold feller, and who knows which ball had spelled his doom.

Once we had fired, all of us boys knelt down and stepped backwards, reloadin' just as we had been trained. There was another line of troops who had been standin' behind us, and they moved up to the stone wall, took careful aim, and fired when the order came.

By then, I was reloaded, and I stepped forward to the wall, and rested my rifle across it. The Yanks were not so many, but they were now within eighty yards. Sash-a-baw could not restrain himself until the order to fire, and he just went ahead and cracked one off at a Yankee officer on a big black horse. Sash did not kill the officer, but he damn shore disabled the horse. It fell down, screamin' in pain, pinnin' the officer underneath. Our boys cheered for Sash-a-baw's good shot, but the sergeant was not so amused, and was hollerin' at the Injun.

Sash-a-baw gave the sergeant an evil look, and the sergeant decided to find somebody else to holler at. The Ojibwa was gettin' a reputation as a feller who you'd better step wide of.

The order came again to fire, and we did just that. Yankees was droppin' like flies, and were now close enough so that we could hear the minie balls thumpin' into their flesh. We could also hear their moans and screams, and I was not takin' any pleasure in this turkey shoot.

The worm turned a bit, when the advancin' Yanks stopped and dropped to one knee. They fired a volley at us, and a good many Irish-Georgians was hit, mostly, in the head, for that was the only parts of their anatomy which was stickin' above the stone wall.

As for us Texas boys, we had seen what was comin', so we ducked down, along with most everybody else. It was the most curious and dim-witted fellers who got their brains blown out in that volley.

Just as soon as the Yankees had fired on us, we stood up and returned the compliments. Our guns roared, and the Federals seemed to slow down in their advance, their lines breaking. By now, they were within forty yards of the stone wall, and some of us boys was gettin' jumpy, for this was too close for comfort. I reckon that a good many Reb prayers were bein' sent up, and they were answered when the Yankees turned and retreated back down the slope.

What a sight it was. Dead Yankees and horses littered the field in front of us. Wounded men were tryin' to crawl back to their lines, and I reckon they were half scared out of their wits that we would shoot 'em in the back, but our boys were not back shooters.

We were front shooters.

And it did not take long for us to get another chance at the art of front shootin', for even as the first wave of Yankees were makin' their way down the slope, another regiment was forming lines to take another crack at us.

"Here they come again, boys!" came a yell from down the lines.

"Hold yer fire, men," cautioned our sergeant.

"Dang!" said Owen. "I thought we had 'em whupped."

Those words of intelligence had barely escaped Owen Horton, when the second regiment of Federals came at us in double time. An officer on a big red horse was leadin' the charge, wavin' his sword and urgin' his men on to the stone wall.

"That officer on the red horse shore presents one hell of a good target," said Roy.

"And I'd shore like to have his horse," said Joe Buck.

Roy looked over at Joe, and smiled. "Now what would you do with a fine horse like that Joe? Let it get stolen while you wasn't payin' attention?"

"Goddammit, Roy. Won't you never stop talkin' about them horses?" said Joe.

"You men stop talking down there, and mind what you are up to!" hollered the sergeant.

Roy was sometimes not very good at followin' orders, and he ignored the sergeant and hollered down to Sash-a-baw.

"Hey Sash?"

"Huh?" said Sash-a-baw, lookin' down at Roy.

"Don't shoot that red horse!"

"FIRE!" yelled the sergeant, and our guns fired a solid sheet of fire and lead. The Yankees were a hundred and twenty-five yards out, and a good many of 'em fell to the ground. Our cannons were rakin' them Yanks with grapeshot and explosive balls, and it was a sad sight to see. The boys who were standin' behind our lines stepped forward and laid down a volley. Then, they stepped back, and we stepped forward and repeated the process. I was surprised to see the officer on his red horse still to be counted among the living.

I started to shoot him, but he was so brave that I didn't want to have him on my conscience, so I honed in on four men who were so close together that they presented a single target. I fired, and one of the fellers spun around and hit the ground.

By the time I had stepped back, reloaded, and stepped forward, it was a pitiful sight to behold. Most of the Yankees had been kilt or wounded, but a few fellers, along with the officer on the red horse, still came on. My line fired another volley, and that sent what was left of the Yanks headin' the other way. The red horse lay dead, and the officer, who was layin' on his back, must have had a number of bullet holes in him, for I could see three streams of blood shootin' up into the air with every beat of his heart.

Yankee sharpshooters had taken up positions somewhere, and they were bangin' away at us hot and heavy. Every now and then, one of our regiment would drop to the ground, most of the time bein' head shot.

We had all we could do, just to keep track of the Yanks who kept makin' a run at us from the front, so we could not be worryin' too much about snipers. However, it was always in the back of our minds, and brought to light every time one of our fellers got hit.

I lost track of how many assaults that the Yanks had made on the stone wall, but it was quite a few. My gun barrel was gettin' hot, and it needed cleanin' somethin' fierce, but the Yanks would not give us any time for such things. They just kept comin', and we just kept on mowin' 'em down.

"Oh no boys!" one of the Irish fellers exclaimed. "What a pity it is! Here comes Francis Meagher's fellows."

"Who is Francis Meagher?" asked Owen.

"The Irish Brigade," answered Paddy Conighan sadly.

With that, I stood up and looked down across the battlefield. The Yankees were in the act of formin' battle lines, to throw another regiment at us. These fellers were flyin' the Stars and Stripes, along with a big green flag. Most of the soldiers were wearin' little green sprigs in their hats, and a good many of 'em had green scarves around their necks.

"Sure'n it is a foul day for the Irish," said Paddy, as he shook his head. Then, like the rest of his countrymen, he laid his rifle across the pile of rocks, and waited for the charge to begin.

Paddy did not have to wait long, for here came that Irish Brigade, double-timin' it up the hill with fixed bayonets. Cannons and artillery raked 'em from the front and from both sides. The thought popped into my head that there was a good chance that these Irish fellers of the Twenty-fourth Georgia might not fire on their countrymen, and that I would get overrun with Yankees and Irishmen in general.

"FIRE!" yelled the sergeant, and my question was answered by the witherin' sheet of fire that was laid down onto the Irish Brigade.

"Holy mother of Jesus," said somebody. "Please forgive us."

"FIRE!"

And the other line of the Twenty-fourth Georgia pulled their triggers and did their murderous duty.

I had reloaded, and stepped forward to the wall. What was left of the Irish Brigade was still comin'. Many of these poor fellers were leanin' forward, with their forearms shieldin' their faces. They looked like they was leanin' into a blizzard, and indeed they were.

A blizzard of lead!

"FIRE!"

"FIRE!"

"FIRE!"

And finally they stopped. Their broken and shattered lines, or what was left of them, turned and walked back down the slope. Not a single shot was fired at the Irish Brigade as they retreated, and the damnedest thing happened. Most of our boys stood up and cheered! They was wavin' their hats and guns in a salute to those brave fellers. It was a fact that the Irish Brigade had come closer to the stone wall than any of the charging regiments of Yankees.

I was hopin' that this might spell the end of this madness, but that was not the case. I'll be damned if'n another line of Yankees were not formin' down at the base of the hill. All of a sudden, a Yankee cannonball exploded behind us, and a bunch of Irish-Georgians fell dead and wounded. I heard a bunch of strange yelpin', and was sad to see that Roy's one-eyed dog was layin' on his side. Most of his guts were hangin' out, and it was not a very pleasant sight. Roy jumped back to help the dog, and the sergeant was yellin' for him to get back in line. Roy told the sergeant to go to hell, and he held onto that mangled and dyin' dog until it had breathed its last.

"FIRE!" came the yell, and our guns roared again. All except for Roy Grubbs' gun, for he was still holdin' that dog.

And so it went, on into the afternoon, with charge after charge by the Yankees on our position. It was suicide, to say the least. And finally, thank God, it was over.

## Mine Eyes Have Seen The Glory

Yankee dead and wounded were heaped up to within forty feet of our wall. It was a fearsome sight, and at times the battlefield seemed to be movin' like a can of worms. Night was comin' and it was gettin' bitter cold out. I pulled on my jacket, and hunkered down behind the wall.

Some Yanks were comin' up the hill to see if there was anything they could do for the wounded, and we did not fire on 'em. Those efforts of mercy soon ended though, for there were just too many wounded, and it was too cold.

Night settled on us like a giant black blanket. Then, there was a sight such as I had never before seen. Lights started swirlin' across the sky, like the forms of ghosts. At first, I thought that there might be a big fire somewheres near, but that was not the case. Sash-a-baw was real scared, sayin' it was bad spirits. A good many of the Irish fellers was makin' the sign of the cross on their chest.

Me and Roy stood lookin' at the fire, and I asked him if he had ever seen anything like this in Texas. Closest thing he'd encountered was a prairie fire at night. This was no prairie fire, but it shore was a wonderment, and we could not take our eyes off of it.

Somethin' else also happened, and I am not too proud of it. Some of our boys ventured out onto the battlefield and commenced helpin' themselves to the belongings of dead Yankees. The biggest draw was boots, and I cannot blame our fellers, for many of them were barefoot and it was December. It was not long before our boys started to filter back in carryin' boots, jackets, blankets, guns, and even pants.

Us Texas boys were not interested in robbery of the dead, but to Sash-a-baw this was a natural thing which always occurred after winnin' a battle. So, over the wall he went, hopin' fer a pair of boots to replace his moccasins.

We lay there in the dark, with no campfire, and listened to the moans, groans, cries, and screams of the wounded Yankees. Purty soon, here came Sash-a-baw back over the wall. He had himself a shiny new pair of leather boots, and he had also lifted a pair for Owen.

"Dang!" said Owen. "I shore hate to wear a dead man's boots, even if mine *are* fallin' apart."

"Boots not come off dead soldier," said Sash-a-baw.

"Where did they come from then?" asked Owen, lookin' up from the boots.

"Live soldier!" grinned Sash-a-baw, headin' back over the wall.

"Jesus Christ Almighty!" moaned Joe Buck, as he lay back and stared up at the sky. "I shore hope my ma don't get wind of this."

Roy Grubbs got up and got himself a shovel, and I reckoned he aimed to go and bury that dog, so I went along with him to help. We got to a little spot under a tree, and Roy set to diggin'. The dead dog was already layin' there.

"Roy," I said as I watched him dig the hole. "I'm shore sorry that yer dog got kilt."

Roy stopped diggin' and looked at me.

"He wasn't my dog, Frank. He just liked to follow me around, and if you recall, he damn near got me kilt once."

"Well, how come you fed him and gave him a bath then?"

"'Cause he was hungry, and he stunk," said Roy, leanin' on the shovel and lookin' at the poor dog with its guts hangin' out between some shattered ribs.

"Then how come yer goin' to the trouble of buryin' him?"

"Frank," said Roy, lookin' up at me. "Get the hell away from me and this poor dog. I ain't never heard so many stupid-assed questions in my life. You said that you had been to school, but it shore as hell don't show!"

At that, I scattered and made my way back to the wall, where Owen and Joe had started a little fire. It was a long and cold night, and I did not sleep much, due to the pitiful sounds comin' from them poor wounded souls on the battlefield.

When the sun rose the next mornin', the Yankees appeared to be gettin' set to make another charge at Marye's Heights, but I reckon that they finally came to their senses, for the charge did not come. For the rest of this day, and the next, there were some minor skirmishes, but nothing to compare with the terrible battle of Marye's Heights.

We stood behind the stone wall, lookin' at the dead men and horses litterin' the battlefield. Something caught my attention, and I could not take my eyes off of it. It was about sixty yards out and to my left, and I studied it for the longest time, before I nudged Owen, who was standin' beside of me.

"Look over there, Owen," I said. "Tell me what you see."

"Where?" he inquired, shading his eyes.

"Just to the left of that dead horse. In front of them two dead soldiers piled up on top of each other."

"What is that?"

"I think it's a dang turkey feather," I croaked.

We both scrambled over the wall and ran out onto the battlefield. The sergeant was hollerin' for us to get back in line, but we paid him no mind. When we approached the object that had caught my attention, we slowed down, as if that thing might jump up and bite us.

I had hoped to God that I was wrong, and that my eyes had deceived me, but that was not the case. Layin' on his back, shot full of holes, and with a silent scream on his gray face, was my lifelong friend, Jodie Pickett.

"Oh God, Frank," said Owen. "Tell me that ain't our Jodie."

I dropped to my knees and lifted Jodie's head into my lap. I looked up at the sky, and then down the slope of the battlefield. There was a Yankee burial detail down a ways, and they just stood there starin' at what I reckon must have been a queer sight: two Rebs, cradlin' a dead Yank, with tears rollin' down their cheeks. Our own boys behind the wall were also starin' at us, and were silent as they watched.

I stood up and lifted Jodie Pickett in my arms. He was shot to pieces, and was as light as a feather. Three of our officers came gallopin' down the front of the wall, and were conferrin' with our sergeant, while watchin' me and Owen walkin' toward the Yankee burial detail.

When we reached the Yankees and their wagon, I went around to the back and laid Jodie down on the wooden floor of the ambulance. The three Yankees just stood starin' at me, and I thought I should give them an explanation.

"This here fellow is named Jodias Pickett. He is from Tennessee, and he is a good friend of mine."

I removed the feather from Jodie's cap and stuck it in my belt. One of the Yankees had a dumb look on his face, and that may have explained the stupid question that he asked of me.

"Did you shoot him?"

At first I could not believe what I was hearing. Then, I thought on it for a minute before I gave my answer.

"I shore hope not, Yank. But for two cents I'd shoot you!"

At the end of that second day after the battle, the Yankees withdrew across the Rappannahock in defeat. The Army of the Potomac had made fourteen separate attacks on the stone wall, and suffered losses of over twelve thousand men.

## THE HANGING

The Battle of Fredericksburg spelled the end of our fightin' for 1862. Both the Union and the Confederate armies needed to regroup and re-supply, and we could not hardly move cannons in the mud and snow of winter, so the Army of Northern Virginia went into what they call winter quarters. This meant that we aimed to sit it out for a spell, and many of the fellers got leave to go home.

Us Texas boys all got to do just that, but we went in different directions, with orders to be back in Richmond on March first of 1863.

Sash-a-baw struck off to who knows where, with his Cherokee friends. Roy and Joe headed for Joe Buck's grandparents' home up around Nashville, while me and Owen lit out for Morgan Springs.

The first leg of our trip was a long walk back to Richmond, and from there we were able to jump a troop train south to Knoxville. It took us five days just to get that far, and then we got hung up in Knoxville, for there were no trains runnin' in the direction we wanted to go. That bein' to Chattanooga.

There was somethin' interestin' goin' on in Knoxville, and it was to take place in two more days, so we stayed. It seems as how two men had kilt a farmer and his wife, and burned down their house. To top all of this off, the two scalawags had also cut up and mistreated the fourteen-year-old daughter of the murdered couple. It looked like this poor gal would likely end up in an asylum for the insane, for she was not actin' normal at all, and was screamin' all of the time.

There had been a trial, and the two accused fellers had been found guilty. They had been caught with some of the farmer's belongings, along with his horse, and that sealed their fate. It seems as how the young gal could not stop screamin' for long enough to identify the fellers, but those screams had so unnerved the jury, that they just went ahead and voted guilty.

"Frank," said Owen. "Why don't we just go ahead and get the hell out of here. Ain't we seen enough death for a while?"

"We ain't never seen nobody hung, though," I said. "This'll likely be somethin' we will remember fer a long time."

"That's just exactly what I'm talkin' about," said Owen.

I won out in the end, and we stayed in town long enough to be in attendance when some lawmen led the two scruffy-lookin' fellers up some wooded steps, and onto a freshly built wooden gallows. We were close enough to see that there was a preacher with them boys, and he was prayin' to the Lord and tryin' to weasel these bastards into heaven.

Those two boys were mean lookin', and I didn't see any way that they could not be guilty. There were two ropes hangin' down, and two lawmen looped the hangman's knot around each man's neck. The knot was placed on the right side of their neck, so that the rope would break their necks in the fall.

"Why do they want to break them boys' necks?" asked Owen.

"I reckon it's so they don't make a big fuss while tryin' to get a breath of air," I answered, even though I did not really know.

The crowd of onlookers, included a great many women and young'uns, and everybody sucked in their breath and got quiet when a big feller wearin' a black hood climbed the creaky steps. Both of the condemned men were lookin' at this scary-lookin' apparition comin' at 'em, and their eyeballs was about to pop right out of their sockets.

The younger of the two fellers commenced to bawlin' and the front of his dark trousers suddenly got even darker. The other outlaw was a great big feller, with wild hair and a full beard. He seemed to get mad, when his partner started cryin', and commenced cussin' out the hooded man who was headin' his way. Though I think if I'd been in this fix, I would not have wanted to anger that hooded hombre, but to each his own.

The executioner produced two more black hoods, and pulled them over the heads of the doomed men. That helped to stifle the cryin' and the cussin' a bit. However, the cryin' man's knees buckled, and a deputy had to hold him up to save the feller from chokin' himself.

Now, the crowd got so quiet you could have heard a pin drop. The sheriff read somethin', and then stood back.

He gave a hand signal to the hooded feller, who pulled back on a lever.

A trapdoor beneath each of the men opened out, and they plunged down toward the ground. Both ropes went taut at the same time, makin' a sickening *pop.* However, one of the pops made a different sound than the other one, and I'll be danged if'n that big feller's head didn't get jerked right off from his body when the neck gave way.

The head stayed inside of the black hood, which was held by the rope, while the headless body hit the ground with a thud. Now, it was my eyes' turn to pop out of their sockets, for that body commenced kickin' around in a circle. Then the knees would jerk up to the chest, and straighten back out. All of this time, blood was spurtin' out of what once had been a neck. I reckon that the feller's heart must have been still beatin', for that blood would pump and stop . . . pump and stop.

This action continued for about two minutes, and there were people screamin', gaggin', and pukin' all over the damn place.

Me and Owen got the hell out of there, not botherin' to wait no more for a train. We only wanted to put that town behind us, and walked without speakin' for most of the day, before Owen finally stopped.

"I don't never want to look at such a thing again, as long as I live," he said.

"I'm with ya, ole buddy," I said.

"And don't you be tryin' to get me to do it, neither."

"I shore won't," I said.

Owen stepped forward and looked at me even harder. "Goddamnit, Frank! I mean it!"

"Well, Owen, I can see that you're serious on this matter, and since you ain't gettin' no dang arguments from me, why don't we stop talkin' about it!" I said.

## WINTER
## 1862

It was startin' to get dark, and we came upon a fairly nice farm with a barn and some stock in a pen. I knocked on the door, hopin' to beg a little shelter from the cold. The thought was in the back of my mind that maybe the people inside would see fit to give us a bite to eat also. That notion was dispelled when the door came flyin' open and a wild-haired farmer stood with a shotgun pointed at me.

"What in hell do you want?" he shouted. A timid-lookin' lady stood behind him, wringing her hands.

"I reckon I'd like for you to point that scattergun in another direction, sir, if'n you don't mind," I said, removing my hat. "Me and my friend are on leave from the fightin', and are headed home fer a spell. We thought maybe we could bed down in your barn tonight, and get out of the weather."

"Well!" he hollered. "That's what you get from tryin' to break up the Union. You boys made yer bed, now go lie in it. But don't think yer goin' to lie in my barn. Now, skedaddle!"

The door slammed in our faces.

"Jesus Christ!" blasphemed Owen. "A goddamn Yankee sympathizer. We ought to burn his house down around his ears!"

"Let's just go," I said, and began walking away.

Owen followed, griping every step of the way. Finally, he stopped in his tracks.

"I can't just leave this behind, Frank. I can't live with it. Let's go back and steal his horse!"

"I ain't no horse thief!"

"Well, you just keep walkin' then. I'll catch up to you after dark."

"Owen, are you crazy?"

"Be ready to ride," was all Owen said as he turned and headed back toward the barn of the unfriendly farmer.

I could not believe my eyes or my ears. Owen Horton, a danged horse thief! Surely this war had made him crazy. Maybe it was the shock of seein' that feller's head gettin' pulled off.

I started trottin' down the little road, tryin' to put just as much distance between me and that wild-haired farmer as possible.

Darkness fell, and out of pure exhaustion, so did I. I just plopped down on the side of the road, and wondered if I would starve to death before I froze, or would it go the other way around. Not darin' to build a fire, I just took out my little wool blanket and pulled it over my head. Dogs were barking somewhere, probably at the thief from Morgan Springs.

Hearin' another noise, I stuck my head out from under the blanket. Hoofbeats. And they were comin' hard in my direction. I started to get up, but it was too late, and I damn near got kilt by a big black horse which liked to ran me over. The horse had a rope halter on him, a creaky old saddle, and a grinnin' Owen Horton.

"Climb aboard, Frank, and let's get the hell out of here!"

"Goddammit," I said. "You dang near ran me over!"

"We ain't got no time to debate this matter now, Frank. C'mon, and let's get movin'!"

"I hate to get into the business of stealin' horses," I whined.

"That son of a bitch had it comin', Frank. Imagine not lettin' two brave Rebs spend the night in his barn. Hell, he didn't even talk like he was from Tennessee! Sounded like he was from Ohio or somethin' to me."

"What if he comes hightailin' it after us with another horse and his scattergun?"

The black horse started to prance and spin around. He wanted to run, and so did Owen.

"He'll be hard pressed to get after us in the dark, Frank."

"How come?"

"Cause I let all of his stock loose, that's why. Git up here, Frank."

I grabbed Owen's outstretched hand and swung up behind him. The horse bolted, and I dang near fell off, but was able to hang on fer dear life. We galloped down the dark road, headin' southwest for Chattanooga.

It took us four days of hard ridin', but we finally rode up to ole One-Eyed Wash's ferryboat on the banks of the Tennessee River.

"Howdy boys," yelled Wash, as he made his way over to our side. "I'm shore powerful glad to see you fellers still alive. Dang, don't the army ever feed you'uns?"

"Not very reg'lar, Wash," I said. "And we're mighty pleased to set eyes on you."

"Where'd ya steal the horse?" asked Wash, and I just looked at Owen, who changed the subject.

"Any Yankees 'round here now?" asked Owen, as we pushed off for the other side.

"Oh, they come and they go, and aggravate me to death. I'd like it if you boys could get General Lee to set a cannon up on that ridge, and fire on them Yankees when I give the signal. Here, have some bread and cheese."

I reckon we must have acted half starved for Wash told us to slow down or we would choke. Then, he was quiet, and watched us eat with a sad look on his face.

When we got to the far side, Wash would not take no money, as usual, and we waved good-bye as we headed to Dayton.

Our stolen horse had been in good shape when he was first stole, but he was beginnin' to hang his head a bit from carryin' two people and not gettin' fed much. However, the same could also be said for me and Owen about not gettin' fed much, so we were all in the same boat.

Dayton appeared purty much the same as before, with the exception of a lack of people buyin' anything in the few stores that were open. Hubert Ass-fart was not to be seen hangin' around anymore, and that was an improvement. Goin' up the mountain made us feel better. We were on familiar ground and lookin' forward to bein' home.

"I shore am lookin' forward to seein' yer sister, Frank," said Owen.

"Who, Marilee?"

"Hell no, not Marilee. Ellie! Jesus Christ, Frank."

"What the hell do ya want to see her for?" I asked, befuddled by this conversation.

"Cause I like her," said Owen. "Me and her been exchangin' letters right along."

"What kind of letters?"

"Personal business," he finally said, after clammin' up a bit. "Things between a man and a woman."

"Well, Owen," I said. "I reckon some would consider you a man, due to all of the murderin' and the horse thievery that you've done. But as fer my little sister, she shore as hell ain't no woman."

"And just what do you consider a woman?"

"My ma is a woman," I said. "And your ma too. Them whores that we dallied with was also women, although I hate to mention them in the same breath as anybody's ma. Thinkin' back on them whores, Owen, I reckon you wouldn't know if yours was a woman or not, for you didn't have much luck with her."

"Goddamnit Frank! Don't be mentionin' them whores in the same breath as Ellie, or I'll box yer ears."

I commenced to laughin' and purty soon Owen was laughin' too. I kicked the tired horse in the slats and carried Owen right past his farm, over the hill, and into my yard. Myrt was creatin' a ruckus, and was tryin' to bite our stolen horse. When me and Owen slid off, she recognized me, and dang near went crazy.

The door to my house flew open, and here came Ma and the whole brood. I was surprised that Ellie headed for Owen instead of me, but I was gettin' so many hugs that I reckoned I could share my sister with anyone who had offered to box my ears over her.

My ma gave me a big hug, then stood back and looked at me. I reckon that I must have changed, for she put her hand over her mouth looked at me with tears in her eyes.

We were pulled inside, and folks commenced to wishin' us Merry Christmas! Me and Owen had not even realized it, but this just happened to be Christmas day of 1862.

# WEDDING ON THE MOUNTAIN 1863

I was a little shocked to see that my whole family, especially Ma, had lost weight, and did not look nearly as healthy as before. Ma must have had the same thoughts about me and Owen, for she went on and on about the fact that we looked like we never got fed. Of course, that set my ma on the mission of feedin' us, but I was surprised that this Christmas meal was corn bread and beans.

Ma looked embarrassed, and so did Ellie, but it was a feast for me and Owen. While we was eatin', I gave the sad news of Jodie Pickett, and that seemed to cast a pall over the whole family. I know that Ma and Ellie was always right fond of Jodie, and they often took his side against me and Owen when we pulled pranks on him.

The next few days proved to me that things were not goin' so good for the Morgan family. All of our stock was gone, 'cept for one milk cow, and I could see that my pa was sorely missed.

"What the Yankees don't take, the Confederacy does," said Ma. "In their ten-percent-of-everything taxes."

She went on to say that the prices in the stores were so high, that a body could not afford to buy anything. Even at that, the Confederate money was not worth nothin' anyway.

I finally got a chance to corner my brother, Wed. "What's the reason you can't hunt enough to keep meat on the table?" I asked.

Wed just looked up at me and I could see the hurt in his eyes. He wiped at his nose with a raggedy coat sleeve.

"Don't you think I try, Frank?" he said. "I go out dang near every mornin' and hunt till it's too dark to see. Everything is most nearly killed off, for we ain't the only family in these hills that's fightin' starvation 'cause of the war."

Those words hit me like a sledge hammer, for I had never dreamed that the time would come when game was scarce around here. I looked at my little brother, who had tears in his eyes, and it like to have broke my heart. I surprised the hell out of him by givin' him a big hug, and apologizin'.

Next mornin', me, Wed, and Billie took the horse down into some rough swampland that required a good deal of effort just to get into. Me and Wed took positions on some deer trails just inside of the swamp, while Billie rode the horse around to the far side with the dogs on leashes. The swamp was two miles across, and thick as hell. Billie tied up the horse, and set the hounds loose. Then he came through the dark swamp barkin' like a dog, which confused the hell out of ol' Myrt.

All of that racket and the smell of dogs spooked an old swamp buck, and he tried to sneak out the far side ahead of all the commotion. Wed heard the brush snappin' and then caught sight of that big twelve-point buck, sneakin' along his trail. He laid the sights of the old .44 caliber Kentucky rifle on the front shoulder of the deer and pulled the trigger.

I heard Wed's gun go off, and my heart started poundin' as I watched to see if anything might come runnin' my way. When nothin' came out, I walked over to where the shot came from. Ole Wed was grinnin' from ear to ear, his jacket off and his arms elbow deep in the hot guts of that big buck.

There was a hell of a lot of work to be done on the farm, and I set at it with vigor, for it was a hell of a lot more pleasant than wagin' war. However, it was not all work, for the bold Alberta Rivers spent quite a bit of time hangin' around and lettin' me spark her.

We took many walks down to the spring, and spent hours sittin' on a bearskin rug in front of my fireplace, where I told her all of the stories of the war that I could recall. Of course, I did not tell her the stories of our dalliance with whores, robbin' bodies on the battlefield, or of horse theft. I reckoned that those stories would be better kept under my hat. Bird was so entranced by my stories, that she allowed me to steal many a kiss from her. The only story which she hated to hear was the one about that hanged feller's head fallin' off. Both her and Ellie screamed and tried to cover their faces and ears, but it was too late. The tale had already been told.

Wed and Billie, however, just loved that story, and they kept askin' me for more details of what a feller looked like jumpin' around without a head. It was a good story, and I kept addin' a little bit more to it, so it kept gettin' better each time.

When we went to church, the menfolk liked to get me off to the side and have me tell the gory tale of the hangin'. I was dumbstruck when even the preacher came sidlin' up, wantin' to know everythin' I could tell him about this incident. He was sneaky about it, makin' it appear he was only interested for religious reasons.

I was not the only one on the mountain who was sparkin' a gal, for it did not take Owen Horton long to take a bath, change clothes, slick down his hair, shave off his beard, and come peckin' at my door. Of course, it was not me that he wanted to see, for I reckon he had seen enough of me for a while. It was my sister whom Owen was searchin' for. Ellie Morgan, who Owen now judged to be a full-growed woman, was probably fair game for whatever he had in mind.

It seemed to me that every time I turned around, here came Owen, with his face scrubbed and his hair in place. Him and Ellie would be jokin' around and playin' tricks on one another, then they would disappear to who knows where.

Ellie seemed to be settin' a lot of stock in combin' her hair, washin' her clothes, and even washin' herself. Bein' as we had to carry all of our water from the spring, that was no mean feat, and poor little Billie was dang near worn to a frazzle from totin' wash water.

Lookin' back on it, I reckon that I should've expected it to happen, but that was not the case. I was out at the barn, feedin' Owen's stole horse, when I was approached by the ole horse-thief himself.

"Frank," he started, wringin' his hat in his hands. "I've got to talk to ya."

"If'n you start flappin' your lips, Owen, talk'll just come flowin' out."

"I'm serious about this?"

"So am I," I answered.

"Frank?" he said, and then stopped, being at a loss for any more words. I decided to mock him.

"Owen?"

"Frank . . . I am here to ask you fer the hand of yer sister in marriage."

That seemed to drain Owen, and he sagged and turned white.

"Which sister?" I said.

"Ellie, goddamnit!"

"Owen, why in the hell would you want to marry Ellie? You've never seen her in the morning, and you should thank your lucky stars for that."

"I am sincere about this thing," said Owen. "I aim to make Ellie my wife."

"Why the hell are you askin' me?" I said. "I ain't Ellie's pa."

"I know that, but I asked yer ma, and she gave me the go-ahead, but she said that you are now the man of the house, and that the final say is up to you."

That bit of news caused me to sit down on a pail and study the floor of the barn. I did not see how any such a burden should fall on my shoulders.

"How do you intend to support my sister?" I asked, and I'll be damned if'n I didn't sound just like a Pa.

"The same way everybody else around here is supported. Plant a few crops, raise some hogs, horses, and cows, and count on the good Lord."

"What about the war?" I asked.

"I aim to stick it out till the end, and send Ellie most of my pay. Even though it ain't worth much."

"Where will Ellie be stayin'?" I inquired.

"With yer ma, at your house," answered Owen.

I stood up and kicked the dirt. "Don't you think that Ellie might be a bit too young for marriage?" I asked.

"Hell, Frank. Ellie's seventeen years old. My ma was married when she was twelve."

"Twelve! Jesus Christ Almighty!"

"Don't spread that around."

This tomfool conversation went on for about twenty more minutes, with the final result being that I would let him know of my decision after I spoke to my ma. Owen Horton pulled his well-wrung hat onto his head and stalked gratefully off.

I kept my word and spoke to Ma. She reckoned that it was time for Ellie to take a husband and that Owen Horton was a fair catch. I did not see fit to tell Ma that he was a whoremonger, a horse-thief, and that he was presently wearing a pair of boots stolen off'n a half-froze, wounded Yankee soldier.

I gave Owen the go-ahead, and he lit up like a firefly. The wedding was quickly set for February tenth. It would be held in the Baptist church, with a reception at the meetin' hall on Walden's Ridge.

The days leadin' up to the wedding flew by purty fast. Ellie like to have drove the whole family crazy, givin' orders like she was a general officer herself. She wanted everything to be perfect and I reckon that is a natural thing. A lack of money meant that the reception would be a potluck affair, and if'n anybody wanted to have a drink, they would have to tote in their own spirits. This caused Ma to despair to no end, for it was a shame on the family, in her mind, that we could not afford to throw a proper party. I tried to convince her that everybody on the mountain was in the same tight fix, but it did no good.

Bird seemed to change too. She was not her cheerful old self, and spent most of the time around me mopin' and gazin' off at the unknown.

However, this act did not fool me one bit, for I knew damn well that Bird would like for me to ask her for her hand in marriage also. It could be a double wedding, and everybody would fire out a passel of young'uns and live happily ever after. This was the dream of all young gals, but I was not ready to settle down, and would not be a part of this plot.

For that reason, Alberta Rivers was set on makin' my life just as miserable as she possibly could. She would not speak to me for long periods of time, and when she finally did speak, it was like she was talkin' to a dog, or an imbecile.

Bird even started talkin' about other fellers and tryin' to make me jealous. I warned her against gettin' me stirred up against anyone, for I was now a trained killer, well accomplished in the art of war.

She just laughed and pitched a little stone at me. I reckon that was just about the friendliest thing that Bird had done to me in quite a while.

## THE CEREMONY

The day of the wedding was on us in a quick hurry. Invitations had been mailed out, but the mail service was not very good, what with the war, and we did not have any idea of who got their letter and who didn't.

Two days before the wedding, Myrt started barkin' like crazy, and who should come walkin' up that little dusty road, but Joe Buck and Roy Grubbs. I did not hardly recognize them, for they were all cleaned up, as shiny as they could be.

"Dang, boys," I said. "I shore am glad to see ya'll. I reckon you got your invitations."

"What was left of it," said Joe Buck, pumping my hand. "The letter was torn all to hell, and we had to piece it together in some places."

"So ole Owen is goin' to jump over the broomstick," grinned Roy.

"I don't know nothin' about no broomsticks," I said. "But he is bound to get married to my sister. I tried to talk him out of it, but Owen is in love, and hangs around here all the time."

Ellie came runnin' out of the house, followed by Ma, and they gave Joe and Roy a big hug.

It was not long before Owen showed up, and he was shore glad to see our ole fightin' buddies.

"How did you boys get down here?" he asked.

"We was lucky enough to catch a train from Nashville to Chattanooga," said Roy. "We walked to the river, and caught us a ride to Dayton on a hay wagon."

Ma shooed everybody into the house for some bean soup as Myrt watched us with a cocked head. I reckon she was mad cause she did not get to bite a hunk out of anybody.

Two more days till the wedding, and counting. Our place was like a madhouse, so all of us menfolk took our leave for one day of serious huntin'. Returnin' to the heavy swamp which had produced the big buck, we set up shooter posts and had two drivers this time. Me and Wed.

I was stumblin' through that thick dark swamp, barkin' either like a dog or a fool, I do not know which, when three shots roared up ahead of me. Then another shot rang out, followed by another muffled round.

By the time I stumbled out of the swamp, Billie, Joe and Roy was halfway through the bloody act of guttin' out a black bear of considerable size and a small spike-horned buck deer.

"Who shot 'em?" I hollered, as I made my way to the surgery grounds.

"Joe Buck shot the buck," said Roy. "I reckon that's the way it should be, what with him havin' the same name as the deer. Little Billie here shot the bear. Three times, I believe."

Billie was grinnin' from ear to ear, and his ears was red as beets. This was his first bear and he was as proud as a rooster.

We later cut up the meat to be smoked, and tacked the hides on the barn wall. After that, Billie could most often be found sittin' out by the barn starin' at his bearskin.

Next day was Saturday, and this was to be the big day in which Owen Horton was to take his vows and later defile my sister. The wedding was at eleven in the morning. I reckon that everybody was invited, for any form of entertainment during this miserable war was a welcome respite.

Everybody got themselves a bath, even Billie and Wed. Us Morgans got on our best clothes, which were not much, and piled into the wagon. Ellie looked right purty, wearin' the same white lacy wedding dress in which my grandma and my ma had been married in.

I was the best man, and we hooked Roy into givin' away the bride. Standin' at the front of the church, and watchin' my sister comin' down the aisle, I had a chance to look out over the audience. I'll be danged if'n there were not at least two boys in attendance who I knew very well was presently Yankee soldiers. I glared at 'em, but they only grinned at me, and one of 'em, Beecher Goff, waved his hand and winked. At first I thought that this was a blasphemous act, to be winkin' in a holy church, especially for a Yank to be doin' it at a Reb. However, the more I thought about it, the more I just resigned myself to everybody havin' a good time and enjoyin' this wedding.

Owen Horton was shakin' like a leaf, and shore looked strange wearin' a borrowed black suit and a black string tie. He had on polished boots, and I couldn't take my eyes off'n 'em, wonderin' if they had been stolen off of a cadaver.

At the end of the ceremony, everybody got into lines, and shook hands with everybody else. When the Yankees, Beecher Goff and Carlysle Dildine, got up to me, I tried to squeeze their hands and bust 'em, but them boys had strong hands themselves, and held their own. I reckon it was a wash.

All the boys got to kiss the bride, and some of them kisses lasted longer than they should have. I could see that this was not settin' well with Ellie's new husband, who was gettin' red faced over this whole affair.

We made it through all of these ceremonies without anyone gettin' kilt or punched in the jaw, and then Owen and Ellie piled into a borrowed one-horse buggy and took off trottin' down the road. There was bunch of geegaws tied to the back of the buggy which set most of the dogs in attendance to barkin' and chasin' that outfit down the road. Ellie was turned around in her seat, wavin' at us all and headed into her new life as Mrs. Owen Horton.

## Yanks and Rebs

I shook the preacher's hand and slipped him three Confederate dollars for his services. Then we all piled into wagons, and headed for the reception party.

It took us over an hour to get to the big wooden meetin' house on Walden's Ridge, and most of the gals' hair was blown wild. I walked in the door with Joe and Roy, and was glad to see that our little band was tunin' up already. It was a three-piece affair, with a guitar, a fiddle, and a banjo, which had set me back another three dollars.

Ellie and Owen was already there. All of the gals was gathered around Ellie, gigglin' and screamin' and wishin' they had just gotten married also. Owen came moseyin' over to us Texas boys.

"Dang," he said. "Them gals shore create a lot of noise."

"Owen," said Roy Grubbs. "You and Ellie have stirred the fires of love in them gals, and it will not be safe at all around here for young Joe and Frank until they are married or gone. You could probably use a drink."

"What makes you think it will be safe around here for you, Roy?" asked Joe.

"Hell, I'm too old and worldly for these innocent mountain gals. They know to step wide of a raggedy-old heart breaker like myself," said Roy, as the music started.

"Roy, could I have this dance?" came the voice of what sounded like an angel.

We all turned around, and there stood Miss Sadie Throckington. Her hair was parted in the middle, and she had on a long pink dress, stretched tight over her bosom area.

Roy removed his hat and held it over his heart.

"Miss Sadie," he said. "Where in the world did you come from? I never seen you at the church."

"You didn't look very hard then, Roy, cause I was there," said Sadie. "C'mon, let's dance."

With that, Sadie guided Roy out onto the dance floor, and they commenced waltzin' along.

"Don't that beat all?" said Joe Buck. "Nothin' like that never happens to me."

At just about that exact same time, the widder Mason came up and grabbed young Joe Buck, and drug him out onto the dance floor.

The new Mrs. Horton came over, and escorted Owen onto the floor, leaving me standing out there alone, like a jackass.

I looked around for Alberta Rivers, and dang near had a heart failure, when I spotted her out on the floor dancin' with the Yankee Beecher Goff. My face got hot, my ears felt like they was gonna burst, and my chest hurt.

I could not imagine my gal dancin' with a goddamn Yankee, but here it was, right in front of my eyes. I had to step outside and sit down on the steps. A feller by the name of Jeff James came up and offered me a drink out of his jug. Ole Jeff James was a rough cob from across the mountain, and a good horse swapper. He was also alleged to have kilt a feller over a bad swap, but since the body was never found and many people reckoned that the missin' feller should have been kilt a long time ago, nothin' ever came of it.

Jeff James, who had managed to duck the war so far, wanted to drink a toast to General Robert E. Lee. I took me a big swallow, and it burned all the way down, and shut down my breathin' fer a minute.

"What the hell is that?" I choked, as he laughed.

"That is Tennessee corn-mash whiskey," Jeff smiled. "The best there is."

"Dang," I sputtered. "I'd shore hate to taste the worst there is."

Ole Jeff frowned, sputtered, turned on his heel, and stalked off, as I tried to catch my breath. Once my head stopped reelin', I took me a little walk around the building.

After a while, Roy and Joe tracked me down. We drank a toast to the happiness of Owen and Ellie, and they led me back inside.

By now, the meeting hall was purty well filled up, and us boys stood by the door. Owen Horton came over, and we snuck a drink, and toasted General J. E. B. Stuart, for he seemed like a good ole boy.

I commenced to survey the crowd, with my head startin' to buzz, and something struck me as strange.

"Boys." I said.

"What?"

"Look around you."

"What for?" said Owen.

"Owen," I said. "You should be able to see it, if'n no one else can."

"See what?"

"The makeup of this crowd," I answered.

Owen looked around for a minute. "I don't know what the hell you're talkin' about, Frank."

"Just this," I said. "This here crowd is split just about fifty fifty, with Reb citizens and Yank citizens. Reb soldiers and Yank soldiers. Reb spies and Yankee spies. Reb back shooters and Yank back shooters."

"Jesus Christ Almighty!" said Owen, lookin' around.

"What is it, Owen?" asked Roy.

"Frank is dead-assed right!"

## NIGHT SOUNDS

In spite of the makeup of our crowd, I reckon the dance was gonna go all right. Bird had taken a great chance by tryin' to make me jealous by dancin' with the enemy, and she could have well got one of us kilt over her idea of makin' me jealous. However, the end result, was that I could use this as an excuse to be free! No longer would I be obligated to stick with one gal, and I could shake the bushes all I wanted to, and even chase after whores without feelin' guilty.

It was strange, for I liked Alberta Rivers, and may have married her one day, but that day was not in the near future.

Yes sir, I was now free on the earth, feeling both a sadness and a gladness.

A young gal whose acquaintance I had never made, came up and asked me to dance, and I did so. She would have been real purty, except one of her eyes looked one way, and the other one looked in a different direction. After four drinks, I was gettin' downright bold, so after findin' out her name was Elizabeth Johnson, I just went ahead and asked the question which was on my mind.

"Miss Johnson?"

"Yes?"

"Do you see all right, ma'am?"

"What do you mean?" said Miss Johnson, lookin' either at me, or at the door.

"Ma'am, your eyes are aimin' in different directions, and I was just worried whether you see things in a clear light."

With that, Elizabeth Johnson stepped back and looked at me like I was a yellow possum. Then she stalked off in a huff, leavin' me standin' on the dance floor right by myself.

Roy and Joe noticed me standin' out on the dance floor without my partner, and they came and got me. We went outside, and Roy produced a little bottle of somethin'. We drank a toast to the Second Mississippi for they seemed to be purty good ole boys when they were not drinkin'.

Roy had tried to get Owen to come outside and have a little snort, but his new wife and his ma would not allow him out of their sight, now that he was a married man and all.

"I don't blame 'em at all," said Roy. "He has duties to perform tonight."

"What kind of duties?" I inquired.

"Husbandly duties, of which you know nothin' about, Frank," said Roy.

That caused Joe Buck to laugh. "I hope Owen knows about them duties," he said.

I began to get an idea of what them boys was talkin' about, and I thought maybe I should box their ears, but then it struck me as funny also. We was havin' a good laugh, and was about to drink a toast to Ole Abe Lincoln, when Bird and Sadie came strollin' out. The band was playin' a sad song, and Bird inquired as to whether she could have a dance with me.

"Dang, Bird," I said. "Did you run out of Yankees to dance with?"

Bird's face lit up to a bright red color, and she stomped back inside, followed by Sadie Throckington, who gave me a mad glare before she disappeared.

Roy stood lookin' at me like I was a horse turd, shook his head, and went back inside. The dance was not goin' very good as of yet, for most of the gals was on one side of the floor, and the fellers was on the other side. Each side was eyeballin' the other across the floor.

Roy took care of that . . .

Knowin' that Roy could play a bit, the fiddle player had offered for him to come up and give it a try. Roy got up on the little box stage and took the fiddle, while the band fiddler lit out to find Jeff James and his jug.

Roy admired the fiddle, and spoke to the guitar player fer a minute while I peeked in the door. Then ole Roy commenced sawin' away at an Irish reel. I thought I had heard some good fiddlin' of Irish jigs and reels, but this was the best ever. Most everybody in this buildin' had a little Irish in him, and it took only a few seconds before couples started takin' to the floor. Within' a half-minute, the floor was full, men on one side in a line and gals on the other. Their arms hung limp down to their sides, and appeared useless, but the feet were flyin' and stompin'. The whole building commenced shakin' to the beat of pounding shoes.

Hell, even Joe Buck got out there on the floor, and he was dancin' with my ma, no less. I reckon this signaled that Ma was no longer in mourning, for she was cloggin' right along with the best of 'em, as was young Joe Buck.

When the long reel finally ended, the men were sweatin' like hogs, and the women were beginnin' to glow. Little Alberta Rivers was right out there among them cloggers, only she was not dancin' with the Yankee Beecher Goff. She was stompin' with Sadie Throckington and Marilee.

All in all, it was a dang good party. Nobody got kilt, and there were only two minor fistfights. Beecher Goff had a horse step on his foot, and most everybody figured that it was broken. I reckoned that would spell the end of ole Beecher's dancin' for this evening.

Us Texas boys had a few drinks too many, and my ma was mortified to tears. She pouted all the way home, while Roy was apologizin' his ass off. Once at the house, Roy and Joe still refused to sleep anywhere but the barn. I had lost my bedroom to Owen and Ellie, and I was now relegated to the woodshed, which butted up to the back wall of my room.

I crawled into my makeshift bed, and it was not long before the newlyweds made their way into my old room. Our walls were not as thick as I would have liked, and purty soon my sleep was disturbed by some gigglin' goin' on from the other side. I reckon that I was about half-drunk, and I did not want to be hearin' any such noises.

Then, I'll be danged if'n I didn't hear a loud slap, and a little yelp. I wondered who got slapped, and what for. It got quiet for a while, and I thought that Owen and Ellie might now be asleep, but it became apparent that this was not the case. A thumpin' noise commenced to come from the far side of the wall, and it sounded like somebody churnin' butter. The thumpin' kept up, and soon I began to hear some moanin' and groanin'.

I could not stand any more of this disturbance, and pounded on the wall.

"What the hell is goin' on in there?" I hollered.

The noise stopped.

That was followed by another noise. That of my ma hollerin' at me to leave Ellie and Owen be.

"Frank," she yelled. "Stop beatin' on that wall, and quit that yellin'."

I resigned myself to my fate, and tried to go to sleep. Purty soon, that thumpin' started up again, and I thought that somebody was cryin'. Enough was enough, and I grabbed my blanket and headed out to the barn to be with Roy and Joe. I might freeze to death, and a rat might bite me, but there is just so much that a feller can stand when he is tryin' to get to sleep.

## On to Richmond

The time soon came for all of us Texas boys to leave, and head back for Richmond. We left that stolen horse for my ma and Ellie, in hopes that they could hide it from the Yankees, and get some work out of it. The Morgan larder was well stocked with smoked and canned meat, courtesy of us fine hunters. Joe Buck had shown Wed and Billie how to make snares and set them for bigger animals, such as deer, coons, fox, and such. Joe had learned this snare trick from Sash-a-baw, and he seemed to have good luck with it.

The snare was made out of wire, and was placed on animal trails with brush placed on both sides to guide the critter into the snare. The animal would run his head into the snare, and would end up gettin' choked when it struggled to get out of that tight fix.

Owen came along with us, but he had to drag a cryin' bride along with him for a spell, for she had ahold of his shirttail, and would not let go. It was a queer sight to see my poor sister gettin' drug down that dusty road by a determined Rebel soldier. In fact, the sight of it caused me, Joe, and Roy to laugh like hell. Ellie finally let go and chucked some rocks at us laughers, which set us to duckin' for our life. Ellie was a dang good rock thrower, and was not one to be trifled with.

It was the crack of dawn when we left, and when we went by the Rivers' house, there stood Alberta and Sadie Throckington. They was wavin' at us real sadly, and finally Sadie could not stand it no more. She came runnin' out to the road, and surprised Roy Grubbs by throwin' her arms around his neck and givin' him a big kiss.

"Drag her down the road aways," suggested Joe Buck, shakin' his head.

Alberta Rivers just stood her ground, but tears was rollin' down her face. That dance she had with the Yankee Beecher Goff had changed things between us, and they would probably never be the same again.

Myrt followed along with us until we got to the Horton place. I had to chuck a rock at her in order to get her to head back for home. Myrt had enough smarts to get out of range, then she just sat down and watched us with her head cocked.

Buster Horton had his wagon all hitched and ready to go. It had some straw and blankets in the back, so we just settled in and went back to sleep. We were carted to Chattanooga, and was able to hop a train headed north. It took six days of walkin', beggin' rides, and hoppin' trains, but we finally ended up where we had started from.

Fredericksburg, Virginia.

## Chancellorsville
## May of 1863

It was early March, and Robert E. Lee's Army of Northern Virginia was comin' back together and spoilin' for a fight. Up until this time, the war had been purty one sided, and we knew that the Yankees were no match for us Southern boys. They had outnumbered us in every battle, but we had still won dang near every fracas so far.

Frost had left the ground, but the roads were still muddy, so cannons could not be moved. The bigger parts of both armies were still on their respective sides of the Rappahanock River, just bidin' their time until the roads dried out.

Our supplies were mighty thin, and the food was poor. Salt pork and hardtack was the main fare, with beans for dessert. Many of the fellers were barefoot and our clothes was gettin' mighty raggedy. There was one cavalry feller who I had noted before, to have a big hole in his britches. I saw that same feller again when we got back from Tennessee and he had the whole seat of his pants out now. To top that off, this feller was not wearin' anything underneath his britches, and it was shore a pitiful sight to see him walkin' around with his bare ass stickin' out.

I was a little surprised when Sash-a-baw and his two Cherokee friends came into camp, for I thought them Injuns might just forget about this white man's war and disappear into the woods.

Sash seemed right pleased to see us Texas boys, even Roy Grubbs. He said that he had been studyin' the Cherokees during his stay, and that they were a polite and civilized tribe.

"Where was it that you ended up stayin', Sash?" I asked.

"With Cherokee," said Sash-a-baw, lookin' at me in a puzzled way.

"I know *who* you was stayin' with, but just exactly where did you boys end up at?"

"Mountains that smoke," he said.

"Why're they smokin'?"

"Mountains not smoke. Only look like smoke," said Sash-a-baw. With that, he apparently had enough of this conversation, for he walked off and left me standin' there.

It did not take very long for us Texas boys and Sash-a-baw to get assigned to a new division. We were now with Stonewall Jackson's brigade, camped out just south of Fredericksburg.

Time passed by slowly, and the weather commenced to get warmer and warmer. Word had it that a Yankee by the name of Fightin' Joe Hooker had taken command of the Federal army. They were holed up on the far side of the Rappahannock, waitin' for the mud to go out just the same as we were.

Owen Horton, who was now my kin, was feelin' homesick and not actin' like his normal self.

"It just stands to reason," philosophized Roy. "When a young feller like Owen gets his first taste of love, he can't think of nothin' else. Therefore, he is ruined for war, and Stonewall might just as well let him go on home."

I reckon the thought crossed Owen's mind to sneak on back home, but the fact that deserters were gettin' hung left and right, all over the South, caused him to rule that out.

Our winter rest ended in late April, when several divisions of Yankee soldiers forded the Rappahanock and commenced attacking our flanks. A lot of fightin' went on, but nothin' major as of yet. At ten in the mornin' on the second of May, we were ordered to move out, although none of us knew where we were headed. I knew that we were headed southwest, and we came out into an open place near a town called Catherine's Furnace.

I reckon we'd been tryin' to be sneaky, which is hard for twenty-five thousand men to do. However, a bunch of Yankees could be seen watching our movements, so the secret was out. We kept up our march to the double time, crossin' an unfinished railroad, several small rivers and a road called Orange Plank.

To our right was a forest which seemed so thick a snake couldn't slither through it. Our sergeant referred to this as 'The Wilderness,' and at around five o'clock in the evening, we began to form up into battle lines.

"Boys," said the sergeant. "The Yankees are just on the other side of them trees, and they do not know we are coming. Let's go amongst 'em and give 'em cold steel and shot."

"Dang," said Joe Buck. "That sounds fine, but how in the hell are we gonna get through that thick forest."

"That's just exactly why we've been on short rations, Joe," said Roy. "So's we could squeeze through them small openings."

At just about that time, General Stonewall Jackson himself came gallopin' down in front of our lines, wavin' his hat and wishin' us luck.

Some officers on foot got out in front of us and pointed their shiny swords at the thick forest.

"CHARGE!"

And charge we did. The division gave out with a Rebel yell that dang near curled my hair. Battle flags disappeared into the thickets, along with us raggedy soldiers, and the chase was on. Branches and vines were hittin' me in the face, and thorns were tearin' at my legs, but we never stopped. Animals could be seen runnin' ahead of us, and a skunk sprayed some of the boys as we went runnin' past.

Finally, we broke out of the woods, and I realized that we had surprised the Yankees, for their campfires and unfinished meals were in evidence. Deer, rabbits, and Yankees were runnin' for their life, and our boys opened up with rifle fire. Some of the Yanks tried to make a stand, but we overwhelmed them with twenty-five thousand men.

General Jackson himself rode amongst us, and I heard him yellin. "Press them! Press them!"

And press them we did! Runnin', stoppin' to fire and reload, then doin' the same thing over and over. This was not an organized battle such as we were used to. It was more like an Indian attack, for we would run from tree to tree and rock to rock, loadin' and firin', then runnin' like hell. The Yanks were doin' the same thing, only they were mostly runnin' in the other direction.

Several times, I lost sight of Joe, Owen, Sash-a-baw, and Roy, but they would always reappear. Sash-a-baw seemed to be enjoyin' this type of fracas, and he had substituted an Injun war whoop for the Rebel yell. One Yankee was runnin' away from the battle, when he heard that Injun yell. He stopped and looked back, and that spelled his doom, for he was hit in the face with a minie ball, which ended his fightin' career.

Not too long after that, I lost track of Sash-a-baw, and did not hear his war whoop no more. I figured he would show up sooner or later, for he always did.

Near dark, we were exhausted, and the Yankees had managed to form a secondary line. They set fire to a bunch of underbrush and the wind fanned the flames, and many a Reb soldier burned to death in the inferno. The smell of burning flesh was worse than the smell of skunk, and the screams of burning men was frightful.

"Damn," said Joe Buck. "I hate like to hell to hear such a thing as men screamin'."

The peaceful blanket of night fell, and the fighting broke off, allowin' us to regroup and take account of our losses.

However, the worst was yet to come . . .

Our great General Stonewall Jackson was returning to the Reb lines from takin' a look at the Yankee positions, when he was fired upon by our own sentries. I heard the shots myself, and me and Roy ran over there. It was a sad sight, for General Jackson was layin' on the ground bleedin' like hell. He had been shot twice in the left arm, and by May 11, General Jackson would be dead, strikin' grief into the heart of every Rebel soldier and citizen alike.

We met up with Owen and Joe near a stand of oak trees, and was glad to see 'em.

"Did any of you boys see Sash-a-baw?" asked Roy.

"I saw him about two hours ago," I said. "He seemed to be havin' a high ole time killin' Yanks and whoopin' it up."

"Is that what that whoopin' noise was?" asked Owen. "I thought I was havin' a bad dream."

"Maybe ole Sash is with his Cherokee pals," said Joe Buck. We all reckoned that was probably the case, but that was soon proved to be wrong. The two Cherokees came lookin' for Sash-a-baw too.

That kind of scared us, and we all fanned out and commenced lookin' for the Ojibwa. By midnight, we had not found him, and we returned to our campfire.

## The Burial
## May of 1863

By the next mornin', Sash-a-baw still had not showed up, but we could not look for him, due to resumption of hostilities. Now that we were out of the smolderin' woods, cannons were brought into play. The Yankees raked us with cannon fire. General Lee was attacking from the east, and we could hear the sounds of the battle raging.

It seemed to me that the battle was purty much even, so I was mighty surprised when the Yankees showed the white feather of cowardice, and commenced to retreat. General J. E. B. Stuart had taken over command from the wounded Stonewall Jackson, and he had us counterattackin' the Yanks. I reckon he was tryin' to destroy the Army of the Potomac before they could set up into a defensive position, or cross the Rappahannock River.

Nighttime fell again, and we set up camp. Sash-a-baw had not showed up yet, and we went from campfire to campfire, askin' if anyone had seen the Injun. No one had.

Next morning showed that the Yankees had crossed back to the far side of the Rappahannock. The battle of Chancellorsville was over, and we went huntin' for Sash-a-baw in earnest. Roy reckoned we should go back to the last place he had been spotted, and go from there.

We got to that spot, and it was a sad affair. Fire had worked its way through the woods, and everything was blackened. Burned corpses were everywhere, many of 'em curled around a tree, with a circle of cleared ground around 'em. We stopped and looked at one charred corpse, which had its mouth open in a silent scream.

"What are those little circles, Roy?" asked Joe Buck.

"Looks like these poor fellers tried to scoop back the leaves and twigs and make a safe place for themselves from the fire," said Roy.

"It didn't work out too well," said Owen.

"No, Owen, it didn't," answered Roy. "But I reckon that was their final hope. That shore ain't the way I'd like to die."

We spread out and worked our way through the grisly battlefield. In about twenty minutes, Joe Buck's voice broke the silence.

"Over here boys!" he yelled.

"What is it?" I hollered back, as I worked my way toward him.

"It's Sash-a-baw."

I was the last one to get to where Joe was hollerin' from, and by that time, Joe, Roy, and Owen were standin' in a half-circle, their hats in their hands, lookin' down at a charred and blackened corpse.

Sash-a-baw had that same little circle around him that many of the others had, and he seemed to be hugging a big oak tree. Most of his clothes were burned off, but his long bone-handled knife was still on his side and he still sported his bear-claw bracelet, and the tall black boots which he had stolen off'n a dead Yankee on Marye's Heights.

Ol' Sash was in a strange position, curled up against that tree, with his face lookin' up at the sky, and his mouth wide open.

"I shore hate to see ole Sash meet such an end as this," murmured Owen, with a tear in his eye.

"He shore traveled one hell of a long ways just to meet his fate in this fire," said Roy.

Roy had brought along a blanket, and I reckon he knew what he was goin' to find. We rolled the black corpse onto the blanket and folded it around our old friend. I got on one end and Roy took the other, and we carried the Ojibwa out of the smolderin' woods and onto a ridge which looked out across a little creek and a sloping field.

Joe had disappeared, but he showed up with a shovel, a wooden cross, and Sash-a-baw's two Cherokee friends. If'n them Cherokees were distraught, it did not show. They remained quiet, and watched as Joe and Owen set to diggin' in the soft Virginia soil. Many a Reb soldiers were buried in shallow graves, but this one was nice and deep, so no hogs would root it up.

I stood down in the bottom of the grave, and received the blanket and its contents. Laying Sash-a-baw lightly on the bottom of the hole, I made sure he was covered up good, and climbed up out of the grave. We all took turns spadin' dirt back into the hole, and even the Cherokees helped out a bit. We gathered around the grave, and it fell on Roy to say a few words. He moved forward with his hat in his hands.

"Dear Lord," said Roy. "We commit into your hands the soul of the Injun Sash-a-baw. I do not know if'n he ever was baptized, Lord, but he was a purty good ole boy, for an Injun. He was a good shot and a tough fighter, and this Reb army will sorely miss him."

We all nodded when he said that.

"I believe, Lord," Roy continued. "That Sash-a-baw did a murder up North somewhere, but from what I understand, the feller who got kilt had it comin'. For that reason, maybe you can see fit to forgive this Injun and receive him into the glory land."

"Amen."

## GETTYSBURG
## JULY OF 1863

Us Texas boys were saddened over the loss of our Injun friend, but everybody in the Reb army was mighty happy over havin' whipped the Yankees once again. Even at that, we had thirteen thousand men kilt or wounded in the battle of Chancellorsville.

It was said that the Federals lost nearly seventeen thousand.

We were joined by General Longstreet, and this swelled our numbers to nearly seventy thousand men. We were raggedy and hungry, but we were spoilin' for a fight, even though we had just finished a rough one.

The brigade which us Texas boys were assigned to were now attached to Longstreet's First Corps. In early June, we pulled out of the Fredericksburg/ Chancellorsville area and commenced marchin' north.

I took a minute to look back at the little ridge which sported the grave of Sash-a-baw, and took note of the white cross which Joe had carved on, and planted in the dirt. He had whittled some writin' on it, which said:

*SASH-A-BAW*
*Ojibwa Injun and Reb soldier*
1863

We marched at a quick pace, and I reckon we were all surprised when we marched into Maryland. It did not take too long before we were actually north of Washington, and it felt good not to be destroyin' Southern property. We were now livin' off'n the Yankees, and they were not at all happy to be furnishin' cows, horses, hogs, corn, and what have you, to the Confederate cause.

Days and miles fell behind us. We were makin' a deep thrust into the soft belly of the north, and were glad of it.

People lined the roads and watched us file past. A long serpent of gray and brown, with bayonets gleamin' in the sun. Leather squeaked, and wagon wheels groaned under their heavy load of death and destruction. I reckon that we looked like a lean and hungry bunch of wolves to them Yankee citizens, but we tried to be friendly. Every now and then a citizen would let out with a wave or a smile. But I saw one young gal get whopped by her ma after wavin' at us.

Our division had just gone through a town called Chambersburg when two officers came gallopin' up to General Longstreet. After a short, animated confab, word came down that we were to double quick it up the road, for there was a fracas brewin'.

It was July 1, 1863.

By the early afternoon, we began to hear the roar of cannon fire and thousands of rifle reports. A road sign signaled that we were bound for the town of Gettysburg.

"Where the hell is Gettysburg?" yelled Owen.

"According to the sign, Owen," answered Roy. "It's somewhere ahead of us."

"Well, what the hell kind of a name is that for a town, anyway."

"Probably a little burg, named after Mr. Getty," grinned Roy.

Just about that time, we heard some screamin' and hollerin' up ahead, and all of us were cranin' our necks to see what was goin' on. By the time we had got to the center of this excitement, we found that an old soldier from Alabama had slipped on a rock and fell down in front of the wagon wheel of a cannon. It had crushed his back in, and he was done for. However, the feller was still alive, even though he was squashed, and he was prayin' to the Lord to allow him into paradise.

"Dang," said Owen. "I never thought I'd see so many awful sights when I joined up with this army."

"Don't forget," I retorted. "This was all your idea."

"To see terrible sights?" said Owen, lookin' over at me.

"No sir. To join in on this war in the first place," I said.

It was now late afternoon, and the sounds of battle were getting louder and louder. Finally, our division came over a hill, and saw before us a terrible confrontation taking place between General Ewell's Second Corps, and a long battle line of dug-in Yankees. We had gotten there just in time to see that there was a little town in the vicinity of the battle, and a rider came in and reported that us Rebs were in control of that town, and it was Gettysburg.

Due to the coming darkness, the sounds of battle were waning. We were ordered over to a ridge, and to set up camp for the night. It was not a very peaceful setting, for we could hear axes strikin' trees in the area that the Yankees held. A Texas feller told us that this was called Cemetery Ridge, and that the Yanks were gettin' dug in tight. He was not too happy, and said that most people thought that Ewell could have taken the high ground of that ridge with a little more effort. Now, there would be hell to pay, if'n General Lee decided to try to move the Federals off'n this hill.

"Don't worry," said Joe. "Lee and Longstreet are smart enough not to send us on no suicide charges. They'll have somethin' up their sleeves."

I had started a little fire, and was in the process of cookin' some cornmeal mush. It was crawlin' with bugs, but Owen thought that the bugs were just our ration of meat for this month.

"Dang," said Roy. "These skeeters are as big as birds."

"I'm so dern hungry, I'm thinkin' about eatin' some of these Pennsylvania skeeters," said Owen. "At least they would be fresh meat."

Joe Buck lay back and pulled his hat over his face. "I miss that Injun," he said.

None of us said nothin', but ole Sash-a-baw dwelled in our thoughts. Whatever we were all thinkin' was forgotten, due to the explosions of two Reb cannons, firin' on those night workers on Cemetery Ridge. Orange flame lit up the dark, followed shortly by two explosions when the cannonballs struck the Yankee position. Loud screams signaled that the balls had done their deadly work.

"Jesus Christ!" said Roy. "It seems like those cannoneers could hold off shootin' them big guns at night and let a feller get some sleep."

"They don't give a hoot," said Owen. "They don't never have to do no fightin' anyway. All they ever do is to stand there and shoot them big guns at targets a mile away, and never have to look the enemy in the eye, like we do."

"When was the last time you gazed into a live Yankee's eye," laughed Roy.

"Every goddamn place I look anymore, Roy, there's Yankees watchin' me. I can see their eyes, and everything else about 'em," answered Owen.

Roy gave up this argument, and just lay down on his stomach and pulled his hat over the back of his head, tryin' to fend off the bloodthirsty skeeters.

## THE SECOND DAY
### JULY 2, 1863

We were rudely awakened by our sergeant the next mornin', even though it was still pitch black out. Everybody was runnin' to and fro, and we got pushed into marchin' lines, and quickly set to movin' to our right, through the dark night. My heart was poundin' like hell, and I had bad feelin's about this whole battle. Daylight finally started to break, and we had already been marchin' for over an hour. We finally stopped and stood at ease in some heavy woods, and watched the sunrise. There were two big hills off to the side of us, and the terrain was rocky and covered with trees.

Us Texas boys were now attached to the Twenty-sixth North Carolina, under Longstreet. They were a proud bunch of fighters, and we did not mind bein' a part of their division.

"Them hills are called Little Round Top, and Big Round Top," said the sergeant, almost in answer to my thoughts.

"It shore took a lot of imagination for some Yankee to come up with those fine names," mused Owen.

Although we had not been told what our objective was, it appeared to be either one of the Round Tops or the end of Cemetery Ridge. Furious fightin' could be heard from our far right, but that was soon drowned out by a great battle now takin' place on Little Round Top.

"Who's that bunch fightin' on the Round Top, Roy?" I asked.

"Texans and Alabama fellers, I believe," answered Roy. "Them Texans are John B. Hood's boys. The ones that me and Joe set out to join up with in the first place."

"Go on ahead and join 'em now," grinned Owen. "Sounds like they could use your help takin' Little Round Top."

Roy just looked at Owen and shook his head.

We just laid low most of the mornin', and a good part of the afternoon too, while the fighting raged nearby. It was around two when the officers came runnin' up and commenced yellin' to form battle lines. My heart was racin' and everybody was wonderin' what we were fixin' to do.

We marched out of the little woods that we had been in, drums rollin' and our battle flags lookin' mighty purty, whippin' in the wind. At that time, Captain Hardgrove galloped down the line and we were told that we were goin' to make our way through a peach orchard, and capture the far end of Cemetery Ridge.

We didn't have long to think about it, for the bugles blew, and away we went at a steady march. The Yankees had spotted us, and they directed cannon fire at our ranks. Once they found their distance, our boys began to fall. Arms and legs were flyin' through the air, and at one point, a human head came rollin' across the field, right in front of us Texas boys.

"Goddamnit!" hollered Owen. "That's just what I was talkin' about before. I hate to have to look at such a thing as that!"

I gulped, but nothin' went down, for my mouth was as dry as cotton.

"Charge!" yelled Sergeant Howard, and we broke ranks and commenced to run into the devastatin' fire that the Yankees were pourin' into us. That fire got so heavy, that we were obliged to take cover and work our way up the ridge as best we could. I began to see blue hats and wide eyes up ahead of us, and the thought came to me that the Yanks might be just as scared as I was.

I laid my rifle across a fallen tree that I was hid behind, and looked for a target to shoot at. Spottin' a Yankee hidin' behind a rock off to my right, I put my sights on him, took a deep breath, and fired. A black cloud appeared at the end of my rifle, and a red spray appeared where the Yankee's head had once been. Some chunks and a blue hat also went flyin' through the air.

As I reloaded, I wondered if'n that Yankee was not a human, just like me. Scared, hungry, and wishin' he was somewhere other than on this battlefield. I did not have too long to think about it, for the sergeant came along, yellin' for us to get movin' forward, or he would shoot us himself.

"Now that is a rude thing for the sergeant to say," yelled Joe Buck. "We have to worry about gettin' shot by our own officers, plus the Yanks."

"For two cents, I'd shoot that goddamn sergeant myself, and we would not have to worry," hollered back Owen.

It took us most of the afternoon to do it, but by evening, the Twenty-sixth North Carolina, along with a brigade of Texans, and some Mississippi boys stood atop of the far flank of Cemetery Ridge. We had won it fair and square, but at a high cost of Yankee and Reb lives.

Just about the time that we were congratulatin' each other, the word came that we were to move back down the ridge. None of us could believe our ears, but we did as we were told, bitchin' every step of the way, and bein' careful as to not step on any of our dead or wounded comrades.

The damn Yankees were even so bold as to fire a few shots at us, as we made our mournful way down the slope, right back to the place where we had started from.

## THE THIRD DAY
## JULY 3, 1863

That night, we were moved from the flank to the middle of our lines. When the sun rose the next morning, we were under the command of General Johnson Pettigrew. Many wounded men were a part of our division, and it seemed like a hornet's nest of activity, for men and officers were movin' everywhere at a fast pace. We were in a place that one feller called Spangler's Woods, when one hell of a bunch of Virginians under the command of General George Pickett came filterin' in and took their places alongside of us.

Morning came on too fast, and it seemed to me that I had not even gotten to sleep. As usual, hollerin' sergeants woke us up with yells and the toe of their boots.

July third was a mighty hot day, and the sun blazed down on us with a fury. Our biggest chore at this point was to find some shade. It appeared that a battle was going to take place, but not too much was happenin' as of right now. We waited and waited, and the morning slipped by.

"Maybe it's too hot to fight today," said Joe Buck.

Those words had no more that escaped his mouth, when such a roar of cannon went off, that it rendered me deaf for a minute. I reckon that every one of our one hundred fifty cannons went off at exactly the same time. Smoke and fire belched out, and I don't know what was worse: The sound, or the smell.

I don't know what the rest of the boys did at that moment, but as for me, I pressed my hands over my ears and buried my face in the grass. Within a few seconds, the Reb cannons commenced firin' at will, with no set pattern to their blasts. I finally raised my head, and I could see that our fire was concentrated on the Yankees who were positioned on Cemetery Ridge. There was a long stone wall along the crest of that ridge, and I had thought at one time that I was shore sorry for whoever had been obliged to tote all of them rocks off'n the fields and stack 'em up in piles.

I reckon the Yankees on Cemetery Ridge were thankful for them stone piles at this particular moment though.

After about ten minutes of this cannonade, the Yankees commenced to fire their own cannons back in our direction. Explosions began to go off all around me, and the screams of men mixed in with the cannon blasts. This form of warfare seemed to go on for over an hour, and finally it slowed down considerably. Then it halted altogether.

Officers came gallopin' down the line, orderin' the sergeants to assemble their men. Our sergeant came into the woods hollerin', and his face was white. I thought his eyeballs were going to bust right out of his face, and Owen reckoned that the sergeant was about to die of fright.

Us Texas boys stepped out of the woods as we were told, and began assemblin' into battle lines. Drummer boys were playin' real nice, and I knew that Roy always enjoyed the drum roll.

But when I looked down at Roy, I noticed he didn't seem to be gettin' any enjoyment out of this music at all. Roy Grubbs was starin' out across that mile-wide expanse of open field which led up to the stone wall. His face was just as white as our sergeant's.

The lines formed fast. Three lines of men, shoulder to shoulder, each line nearly a mile long. Pickett's division was to our right, and General Trimble's men were to our rear. I caught a glimpse of General Longstreet, and thought it strange that he was sittin' on a fence, lookin' unhappily across that same stretch of field that had made Roy's face get white.

General Pettigrew rode down the lines, sayin' that we were bound to take that ridge, and that our next stop would be Washington. Lieutenants, captains, and other high officers took positions out in front of us. One general took his hat off, put it on his sword, and held it up in the air.

"Now that is a brave feller," said Joe Buck. "Makin' such a target of himself."

The sergeant made his way to our front, and let us know that we were to march at the quick step across that field, and that our main objective was a little grove of trees, which stood just behind the stone wall. We were not to give the Rebel yell until we got over the wall, and the sergeant was obliged to shoot any of us who tried to turn back.

This set some of the boys to hollerin', sayin' that the Twenty-sixth North Carolina had never showed the white feather yet, and were not about to do so now.

General Pickett rode his lathered-up horse to where General Longstreet was sittin', and they seemed to have a short conversation.

Battle flags were unfurled and raised all at once, on a given signal. They looked beautiful, blowin' in the wind. I looked down the lines, and it was the finest sight that I had ever seen. Thousands of men, in perfect order, grim faced and waitin' for the order to take that hill.

General Pickett came gallopin' back to the front of his division, and he had his saber in his hand, wavin' it all about.

"Don't forget men, that you are from old Virginny!" he yelled.

This caused some of our boys to grouse that they were not from no place but the Carolinas, and were proud of that fact.

I thought about yellin' that I was from Tennessee, but did not have the chance.

"Forwarrrd. . .MARCH!"

The three battle lines began movin' out across that big field. With the exception of the drums beatin', it was deathly quiet in our ranks. The Yankees had not yet started firin' on us, and I reckon that they might be half scared to death themselves, just by the sight of this great body of men marchin' toward 'em.

I began to take hope that the Yanks might be on the run, when all of a sudden, cannon fire commenced poundin' our ranks from the Round Tops to our right. Grapeshot and cannonballs raked our lines, and men began fallin' to the ground. Federal infantry fire opened up on us from the far right, and the whole left side of our lines began to squeeze toward the center. There was a road ahead of us, along with a long split-rail fence.

Just before we got to that road, cannons opened up on us from atop of Cemetery Ridge. A cannon shot exploded just ahead of me, and I saw several of our men go down.

Roy Grubbs was one of 'em.

I tried to stop to help him, but the sergeant would not let me. He waved his sword in my face, and I have no doubt that he would have used that weapon on me if I did not continue forward.

Huge holes were being torn in our ranks from cannon and infantry fire, but the holes would be filled with men from the rear, and we would keep up this march, which now appeared to me to be one of suicide.

Our line was out in front, and once we got into range of the stone wall, we stopped and fired a volley. Screams comin' from behind the wall signaled that we had done damage. The Yankees answered that volley by standin' up and firin' a solid sheet of fire at us. Hundreds of men went down, and a minie ball clipped my left hand. I looked down at the numb hand, expectin' it to be gone, but it was only creased and bleedin'.

I was suddenly reminded of the never-ending divisions of Yankees who had made their way up Marye's Heights, leaning into the firestorm of lead with their arms over their faces to ward off the minie balls. Some of our boys were now doin' exactly the same thing. One feller picked up a big flat piece of slate rock and held it out in front of himself for protection.

On and on we went, in order, into the fiery flames of Yankee guns. A Rebel yell went up, which started a whole chorus of yellin', and inspired us to move forward at a trot. We were now within thirty yards of the wall, and I could see the fear-filled faces of Federal soldiers, peerin' at us as they tried to reload. Our yell turned to a roar, and over we went, claiming a number of cannons that were only recently blastin' us to bits.

The Yankees were backin' up, and I thought that this battle was just about won, when a whole dang regiment of fresh Yankee troops came stormin' our way with fixed bayonets. I gave up on my rifle, and pulled out the little pistol that I had been carryin' in my belt for all of this time, yet had never used. A big bearded Yankee was headed at me with his bayonet aimed at my innards. He had murder in his eye, and had singled me out as the one he intended to murder. Not having much time, I aimed my little pistol and pulled the trigger. I'll be danged if the pistol didn't go off with a loud bang. The Yankee stopped and looked down at his belly, which now had a little red hole in it.

"Goddamn you, you Reb son of a bitch," he exclaimed. "You've killed me!"

The Yank did not look too dead to me, for he then started comin' at me again. I shot him two more times, once in the leg, and once just over the left eye.

Now he *was* dead, and I was glad of it. More Yankees were comin' and I fired the rest of my pistol loads into the crowd. Then, I looked around, and noted that my division had not only halted, but were headin' back down the hill from whence we had just come.

"Fall back! Fall back!" came a yell, which sounded like the sergeant.

"Come on Frank. Let's get the hell out of here," hollered Joe Buck, who grabbed my arm and gave me a tug.

It had not been my intention to ever show the white feather, but I was now obliged to do so, what with the great number of mad Federals who were descending on us.

I walked backwards, out of ammunition, yet still takin' stock of the battle flags that were descendin' upon me and Joe Buck. I saw a green flag, and reckoned that was the Irish Brigade, gettin' even for their losses at Marye's Heights. I saw a Pennsylvania flag, and the battle colors of the Sixteenth Michigan. The Iron Brigade.

I heard a chant began to flow from the oncoming Yankees as Joe Buck tugged me down the slope.

"Fredericksburg! Fredericksburg! Fredericksburg!"

It got louder and louder, and we began to trot. Owen Horton came runnin' over to us, and I was glad that he was still alive. "Where in the hell is our support?" yelled Owen, who stopped and fired a round from his Enfield at the Yankees, who had stopped at the stone wall. The Yanks were still chanting, but took the time to fire a volley of about twenty shots at Owen.

Poor Owen was spun around and then blown backwards by the force of several .54 caliber minie balls strikin' him. A red spray flew through the air, and me and Joe ran over to him. Joe held up his hand, palm out, to the Yankees and begged them, "No more, boys. Please, don't shoot no more."

I bent over Owen and started to pick him up. He was bleedin' from the head, the chest, the arm, and who knows where else.

"No Frank," he pleaded. "I'm dead for shore. Just leave me here, for I don't want to be moved nor jostled."

I lifted Owen up across my shoulder anyway, surprised at how light he was, and began my march back down across the field, while Joe Buck walked behind us with both hands held out toward the Yankees.

"Fredericksburg! Fredericksburg! Fredericksburg!" they chanted, but, by God, they did not fire on us again.

We worked our way back to where Roy had went down, and were lucky enough to find him among the hundreds of dead and wounded Rebs. Roy was on his hands and knees, shakin' his head. Joe got down alongside of him and lifted Roy's head up. There was a big black bruise across his forehead, and he was bleedin' from out one ear.

"Joe," said Roy. "What the hell happened?"

"I think you got blasted with a cannonball explosion," said Joe. "C'mon, let's get off'n this field."

Joe put his arm around Roy's waist, and helped him hobble down the slope. Owen gave out with a big sigh, and went limp on my shoulder.

There was no doubt in my mind that my new brother-in-law and my best friend in the world had just crossed into the glory land.

"How's Owen?" said Roy, lookin' over our way.

"He's dead," I replied, the tears streamin' down my face.

## Robert E. Lee
## July 3, 1863

Men and wagons moved up to meet the survivors and the wounded soldiers who were streamin' back down the slope from Cemetery Ridge. In all of the battles I'd seen, never had I witnessed a slaughter such as this. Dead and wounded men, along with a great number of dead horses, covered the battlefield.

I still had Owen across my shoulder, when I noticed an officer on a gray horse gallopin' out to meet us. That rider turned out to be none other than General Robert E. Lee himself. When he got to me, I'm sure he recognized me, but he could not pinpoint where he knew me from. Jerking his horse to a halt, General Lee reached down and touched Owen Horton on the back.

"I'm so sorry boys," he said. "This is all my fault." General Lee looked over at Roy and Joe, who removed his hat and put it over his heart.

"It's all my fault," repeated the general. Then he urged his horse on, and rode out to meet the other survivors of what would later be called Pickett's Charge.

A wagon for the wounded pulled up, and I laid the body of my friend gently onto the bed. Joe helped Roy onto the wagon also, and I don't think Roy had all of his wits about him. The wagon pulled away, and I ran to catch up with it.

"That soldier who I put on your wagon is Owen Horton. He is from Tennessee, and is attached to the Twenty-sixth North Carolina."

The driver just nodded his head at me, and moved on to help a wounded feller up ahead of him.

We did not have much time to think about what had just happened, for officers came gallopin' down the line yellin' for us to regroup and prepare for a counterattack.

Me and Joe Buck were dog tired, and my whole arm was numb from gettin' hit in the hand, but we took up positions in the edge of Spangler's Woods, waitin' for the Yankee charge that never came.

By dark, it had started rainin' to beat the band. Wind and lightnin' hit, and made for a miserable night. We watched as lanterns moved out across the battlefield, as our boys tried to help out the wounded, even as the blood was being washed from the grass.

I could not stop thinkin' about Owen Horton. A blanket of sadness overwhelmed me, and I buried my face in the Pennsylvania grass and sobbed out my grief.

We held our positions all the next day, as the rain continued to pour. Roy Grubbs rejoined us, with his head all bandaged up.

"What happened down there, Roy?" asked Joe.

"I wish't you never asked, Joe," said Roy. "It was the worst thing I ever seen. I reckon I blacked out, for when I woke up, I was surrounded by a bunch of doctors and screamin' men. Them dang doctors were cuttin' off arms and legs just as fast as they could saw 'em. They was throwin' them body parts into a pile right beside me. I got a rag tied around my head, and got the hell out of there."

"Did you ever see what happened to Owen?" I asked.

"No sir, Frank, I didn't," said Roy. "I know that there was one hell of a long line of dead men stretched out on their backs, but I didn't go down that line at all. It was a gruesome sight."

Night fell, and the rain kept comin' down. The attack which everyone expected from the Federals never came to pass.

The Army of Northern Virginia pulled out of this dreadful place as lightnin' crashed about. Nine days later, on July 13, 1863, our tired, hungry, beaten army crossed the Potomac River, into the safe arms of Virginia.

I took the time to write a letter to Ellie, as to the death of her new husband. It was not an easy thing to do, and I reckon that I had been puttin' it off, but now, the time had come. I sat down on the ground and used a wooden crate for a desk. Roy had got me a piece of paper and an envelope. I stared at the paper for the longest time, searchin' for the right words.

*July 14, 1863*

*Dear Ellie Morgan,*

*This is yer bruther Franklin, writin to you of bad, bad news. Yer husband, Owen Horton, was kilt in a little town in Pensylvania, called Gettysberg. I was with Owen when he was kilt, and I carried him back down the hill to where our boys was collectin dead soldiers.*

*Owen died a fine death, with his face to the enemy. I was sad to see him go, as we had been friends fer a long spell and had kilt many coons together.*

*Where Owen is to be buried, I do not know, for we are now high tailin it out of Pensylvania, and left all of our kilt fellers back there.*

*Maybe we can find Owen later and dig him up and bring him on home.*

*I am still alive, and so is Roy and Joe. I hope you do not jump off a cliff over this piece of sad news.*

*Yer bruther,*

*Franklin Robert Morgan*

## LETTERS FROM HOME
### AUGUST OF 1863

Our army was camped south of Richmond, and I reckon we were tryin' to regain our strength. New recruits were comin' in, although not near as many as had come before. The same could be said for our food supply, for not much was to be had. Farmers all along our way were mad as hornets, for anytime we came near an orchard, garden, or cornfield, we stripped it bare. We were a sorry lot, I reckon, sometimes more like a plague of locusts than an army of righteousness.

Roy's head had healed up, and he was back to near normal. The delivery of mail had become mighty iffy. Sometimes we got a bit of mail, and sometimes we did not. One day, it all seemed to catch up with us at once, for there was one hell of a pile that came in, and many fellers got letters from mothers, wives, and sweethearts.

Even Roy got a letter from Miss Sadie Throckington. Joe Buck got a letter from his ma in Texas, and I received two letters. One was from Ma, and the other one was from Alberta Rivers. Both of them were dated a long time ago.

Finding a shade tree alongside of a little creek, I put my back up against the tree and commenced to read. Ma's letter was first.

*April 3, 1863*

*Dear Franklin Robert,*

*This letter is to let you know that we are getting by fine, and you should not worry about us. Spring is coming, and we will soon be planting a garden.*

*I still have the horse, but we always have to hide him when the patrols come through, or they will take him away.*

*We all miss you, and pray for you every day. Please write us a letter, and let us know how you are. Write one to Bird also, as she misses you greatly.*

*Your loving Mother,*
*Millie Morgan*

*p.s. One-Eyed Wash is dead. He was killed by some Yankees.*

I sat back against the tree and thought of One-Eyed Wash. He was always good to me, and the crossing of the Tennessee would never be the same. One by one, this war was takin' everyone that I loved or knew. Pa, Jodie, Sash-a-baw, Owen. All gone.

Since Ma had not mentioned the death of Owen Horton, I reckoned that she had not yet gotten my sad letter when she wrote me this one.

I sat for a spell, looking into the little creek. Then, I opened the wrinkled up letter from Bird.

*May 3, 1863*

*Dearest Frank,*

*You probably do not want a letter from me, but I am going to send one anyway. Frank, why do you see fit to treat me so badly. I only danced with Beecher Goff to make you take notice of me, and that is all.*

*You know that I love you and miss you. Please write me and tell me how you feel.*

*Tell Roy to write to Sadie also, if he can write. Your family is getting by, but miss you as much as I do. Wed is talking of joining up, but we are trying to hold him back from such doings. He is set on it, and it is all your ma can do to keep him from it.*

*Ellie misses Owen, and cries for him regularly. I hope he is healthy.*

*Love,*
*Alberta Rivers*

No, Bird, I thought, Owen is not healthy at all. In fact, Owen is dead! Just as dead as Pa and Jodie.

So Alberta Rivers misses me and is sorry. Maybe Beecher Goff can brighten her days when his foot heals up.

I felt some pangs of lost love, but put that out of my mind. I would not very likely live through this war anyway. I would have to write a letter home and try to persuade Wed not to go through with joinin' up. This war is not very pleasant, although I could not likely convince him of such.

## From Texas

Joe Buck sat down on a stump, slapped at a mosquito, and began opening up his own letter. Removing the yellow paper carefully, he began to read his mother's writing.

*Dear Joe,*

*You are always in our thoughts and in our hearts. We all hope that you are fine, and that Roy is the same. Your father has enlisted in the army, in spite of my protests and his age. Regulators travel the countryside regularly, and anyone between the ages of fifteen and fifty purty much have to join up. Failure to do so may end up in their losing their land, being arrested, or even worse, hung. There have been a number of shootings and hangings already.*

*Butterbean Love and Pedro Vega are still here, and they are very helpful. Luke sold most of the horses to the army. Rosita says to tell you hello, and that she thinks of you every day. She longs to walk with you along the Guadalupe, and hear of your adventures.*

*Please write to us when you have the chance, and be careful. Go to church if you are able.*

*Love,*

*Bridey Buck*
*Your Mother*
*5-2-63*

Joe Buck leaned forward, watching a troop of cavalry riding into camp and raising a dust cloud. He smiled when he thought of Rosita, and yearned for the day when they would walk along the river once again.

Joe was sad to hear of his father's enlistment, but he knew that if anyone could survive this war, it would be Luke Buck. Luke had outfought Comanches, Mexicans, outlaws, and the Texas frontier. A few Yankees would be of small matter.

Butterbean Love was a negro, and an ex-slave, so he would not have to worry about the regulators forcing him to join up. The regulators would not be interested in Pedro

Vega as of yet, for he was actually a citizen of Mexico, and had no argument for or against Americans.

Joe remembered his prankster of a little brother, Georgie, who had nearly died from snake bite in that same Guadalupe River that Rosita Vega wanted to walk beside. Georgie would now nearly be old enough to enlist himself, and that thought troubled Joe.

He stood up, vowed to write a letter home soon, and walked back to camp.

## The Copperhead
## 1863

I heard Roy Grubbs come walkin' along the creek where I'd just been readin' Bird's letter. Roy sat down on a rock, and said he noticed a strange smell in the air, almost seemed like the scent of cucumbers.

"I don't smell it myself," I told him. "What you got there?"

"Letter," was all Roy would allow, and I didn't pursue it, just let Roy open it up and read it himself. Purty soon, I saw Roy laugh and shake his head, then put the letter real careful back in the envelope.

"Miss Sadie," he said. "You'd better look elsewhere for a husband, as a wife does not fit my cowboy lifestyle."

I don't reckon ole Roy cared that I heard, but I didn't say nothing about it. "You sure you don't smell them cucumbers?" he asked.

"No, I don't, Roy."

He started to pick up a large, dry remnant of driftwood, which would put a fine start to tonight's campfire. He bent over and lifted the gray piece of timber and without warning, a copper-colored flash rustled the leaves, and smacked against Roy's right forearm. It stuck to him, the one-inch-long fangs buried in muscle and squirting deadly venom into the arm.

"Yaaahh!" yelped Roy, as he grabbed the snake and tugged at it, finally pulling it loose from his arm. "Goddamn! Shit!"

Roy drew his sidearm, and fired six shots at the serpent just as fast as he could pull the hammer back and jerk the trigger.

Two Rebel soldiers came running up.

"What in the world is all the shootin' about?" exclaimed one of the soldiers. "Is there a Yankee about?"

"What is it, Roy?" I asked.

"Copperhead. It got me real good," said Roy, sinking to his knees, holding tightly onto his forearm.

I stepped forward, and looked down near the water at a huge, squirmin' copperhead snake. The snake was over four feet long and as big around as a man's wrist. He was trying to bite himself in the two spots where slugs had torn into him.

I stepped forward two more steps and stomped on the snake's head, smashing it to a pulp.

"Let's have a look at where it hit ya, soldier," said one of the soldiers, a thin, bearded man of the Twenty-sixth North Carolina.

Roy pushed back his sleeve, showing two small puncture wounds, both trickling blood.

"Cut it, Frank," he said.

Without hesitation, I took his knife out of his belt, even as the bearded soldier wrapped his kerchief around Roy's arm above the wound, and twisted the cloth tight.

"Goddamn, Frank," said Roy. "Do you have to use such a big knife on me?"

I did not argue, but immediately laid the blade of Roy's bowie knife across the two red marks, pressed down, and drew the blade over the deadly bite.

"Shit!" exclaimed Roy, looking up at the sky. "That hurts like the blazes."

"Don't be such a baby, Roy," I said. "I could go get you a purty nurse, if you'd like to wait."

Roy ignored that comment. "I should have known from that cucumber smell that there was a copperhead around," said Roy. "I've only got myself to blame."

With that, Roy lifted his arm up to his mouth, and commenced suckin' the poison out of the cut. He would spit out the blood, suck the wound again, and spit once more. This continued for about five minutes, as the thin soldier kept the kerchief tight around the arm, trying to restrict the poison from entering the rest of Roy's body.

Then, the three of us helped Roy get to a medical tent, for the fervent attention of a half-drunk doctor. By the time he walked into the tent, Roy Grubbs was a pale gray color. He passed out onto a cot just before the doctor could ask him what was wrong.

## LIFE OR DEATH

I sat outside of the medical tent, worried over whether Roy was going to live through this or not. The copperhead that had bit Roy was the biggest one that I'd ever seen.

Joe Buck finally found out what'd happened, and he joined me in the vigil. Once the doctor finished with what he could do, he allowed me and Joe to look in on Roy. I was shocked to see that Roy was as white as his sheet, and that he was not conscious, and that his breathin' was raspy.

"I don't like this at all," said Joe. "I watched my little sister die of a fever, and she sounded just like Roy sounds."

"I know, Joe. It don't look good, but it is all in the hands of the Lord, right now. There ain't nothin' we can do about it," I replied.

The doctor came back in and ran us off. Me and Joe ended up in the Baptist tent, where we said a little prayer for Roy Grubbs to pull out of this bad fix.

The next day saw Roy in even worse shape, and he dang near choked to death on his own vomit. Roy was still unconscious, and he was shakin' like he was freezin' to death. My friend was goin' downhill fast as far as I could see, and I reckoned that Roy was bound to die.

On the following day, both me and Joe were sittin' beside of Roy's bed, and he was quiet and no longer shakin'. We reckoned Roy was about to make his way into the glory land at any time. We sat with our heads hung low, not sayin' nothing.

Roy scared the hell out of both of us, when, without openin' his eyes, he said, "Don't never kiss no whore, Joe."

Joe jumped up, wide eyed. "I ain't never kissed no whores yet, Roy. Why do you bring up such a thing?"

"Where's that dang Injun?" said Roy, his eyes still closed.

"Which one?" answered Joe Buck.

"Joe," said Roy. "I shore hated to bury ole Don out there in Comanche country. The buffaloes will likely trample over his grave."

"Roy, I don't know what the hell you're talkin' about!" hollered Joe Buck. "You ain't makin' no goddamn sense at all."

"SNAKE! SNAKE! Get it off'n me Frank!" screamed Roy Grubbs, flailin' at the air with his arms. Then, he laid back and was quiet. Me and Joe was scared half out of our wits, and Joe had turned a shade of white.

The doctor, hearin' all of that yellin', came rushin' over and asked what was goin' on. When I told him that Roy was talkin', but not makin' much sense, the doctor got a happy look on his face, and said that Roy was likely goin' to live. Then, he ran me and Joe off.

Next mornin', Roy was awake, although he ached all over. His arm was all swole up, and the place where I had sliced him with the bowie knife was all infected.

Within four more days, Roy was back on his feet, and he vowed to be more on the alert when he smelled cucumbers where there was no garden around.

## CHIKAMAUGA
## SEPTEMBER OF 1863

After the battle of Gettysburg, I reckon that the Yankees were feelin' bold. They split their armies, and sent a good many divisions down to Tennessee in order to split the Confederacy.

General Lee responded by sending Longstreet's division, with Generals Hood and McLaws, down toward Tennessee also. We commenced to march out in late August, and the weather was startin' to cool down a bit. People came out along the roads and lined the streets of towns when we went through, and gave us many a rousin' cheer.

We headed down through the Carolinas and into Georgia, livin' mostly off of the land, as it was harvest time. The farmers tried to get their crops in before we could get to 'em, but our foragers went out ahead of the troops and kept us supplied as best they could.

One farmer decided to defend his cornfield from the foragers, and he fired two shots at the boys. They fired back, and the farmer was mortally wounded. The farmer's wife and young'uns came runnin' out screamin', and created such a ruckus that the foragers just moved on, and left the cornfield be.

We later ran into a battle that was already started. General Braxton Bragg was fightin' a whole bunch of Yanks at a place called Chikamauga. It was on a creek, and by the time we got there, the battle was ragin' somethin' fierce. The main objective was a road, which was called the Lafayette, and it was the main supply line for the Yankees who were occupying Chattanooga.

General Bragg, I reckon, was shore glad to see us, and we got deployed and spread out immediately. In the center of the Rebel lines.

Next day, it was September 20, and we got involved in the fracas in a big way. I reckon that General Longstreet saw a gap in the Union lines, for we were ordered to charge, and did so. Five divisions went stormin' through the Yankee center, and swung right. That scared the hell out of them Yanks, and they showed the white feather once again, and retreated just as fast as they could retreat.

This charge turned out one hell of a lot better that the one at Gettysburg. When the smoke cleared, we had won the battle, and the Yanks were hightailin' it for Chattanooga. Me, Roy, and Joe lived through another battle, and none of us even got wounded. The same thing could not be said for eighteen thousand other Rebel soldiers.

General Longstreet wanted to pursue the Yanks, and try to destroy their army, but I reckon that General Braxton Bragg was happy with just being in control of the battlefield, and figured that was good enough. Word was that many of the general officers, including Longstreet, were madder'n hell over that.

Something new was takin' place. Reb soldiers had discovered that mule meat and horse meat tasted just fine. There was a whole bunch of horses who had met their maker on the battlefields of Chikamauga, and we started to work with our knives. That night, everyone went to sleep with a full belly. It was the first time in quite a spell that we had achieved that small feat.

## LOOKOUT MOUNTAIN
## MISSIONARY RIDGE
## NOVEMBER OF 1863

We went after the Yanks in Chattanooga, once we had resupplied, deployin' our division on top of Lookout Mountain, where we'd once ferried by, what seemed like so long ago.

We could see the city of Chattanooga from up there, and I did not see how any Yankee could ever make it up them rocky slopes alive. If'n he didn't fall to his death, the Yankee would get shot by a Reb for his trouble.

The rest of Bragg's army was at Missionary Ridge where they were attacked in late November. We heard that there was a new general for the Yanks, and his name was Ulysses S. Grant.

The Yankees outnumbered us, six men to our one, and it was not long before they had taken Missionary Ridge. Then, the Federal troops turned their attention on us.

They launched a full-scale assault on the slopes of Lookout Mountain, using ladders to get up the hill in some places. Sometimes we could not see what the Yankees were doing, for we were often above the clouds. Another problem for us was that our cannons could not be tilted far enough forward to shoot straight down. Two cannons were accidentally rolled over the ridge in their attempts at firin' on the Yankees.

The Yankees looked to me like a bunch of ants or spiders, clingin' to stone walls and climbin' up. They were brave boys though, I give 'em that, for our infantry poured hot lead down onto them every step of the way. One of our best weapons in this strange fight was to start a rock slide. Many a Yankee was swept to his doom by some Reb who just rolled a big stone down, startin' an avalanche of rocks.

As for me, I thought that we were holdin' our own, and the Yanks would be hard pressed to drive us from this mountain. For that reason, I was surprised when General Bragg ordered us to retreat.

Our morale dropped to a new low when we slipped off of Lookout Mountain by cover of darkness, and retreated into Georgia. The city of Chattanooga was now firmly in Yankee hands.

## Charge of the Schoolboys
## May of 1864

We were down in the dumps over havin' to give up the city of Chattanooga along with retreatin' from our solid positions atop of Lookout Mountain.

I heard that General Longstreet was madder'n a hornet over the order to retreat, and that Jeff Davis might be comin' out to replace Braxton Bragg.

What had started out as a gentlemens' war was now over. Instead of standin' in straight lines on the battlefield and shootin' at one another, we now commenced diggin' ditches, rifle pits, and parapets. A nice field could be transformed into a formidable fortification in forty-eight hours.

General Robert E. Lee had a new name. 'The King of Spades.'

Roy Grubbs said that these entrenchments looked like a prairie dog town, and he felt sorry for the poor farmers who owned these fields.

"Some ignorant farmer will get drunk and go to plow his field, fall into a trench, and never get out. He'll stand down in that pit hollerin' and'll starve to death. Just like we are now doin'."

As for mail delivery, it was mighty sorry. None of us Texas boys had received a single letter since I had written to Ellie about the death of Owen. I reckon that the fact that General Grant kept us movin' was one of the main problems.

It was now winter, and things slowed down a little, due to the fact that it was hard to move the heavy equipment that was needed to wage war.

A sickness had swept through the camp, claimin' hundreds of lives. It started out with a feller feeling dizzy, then it went to his stomach. The poor sick feller would commence vomitin' and would have a terrible case of the drizzly shits. Joe had caught it, but me and Roy did not, and we were glad of it. Doctors called it a form of the grippe, but I don't think that they really knew how to treat it. Within time, thank God, the sickness passed from our camp, and things got back to normal.

Roy, Joe, and myself were sittin' on some boxes in front of a little fire, musin' over our present state of affairs.

"I heard of a strange thing today from a feller," said Roy.

"What was that?" asked Joe, taking the bait.

"There was a Reb officer who got kilt from on top of his horse."

"What's strange about that?" I asked. "Thousands of officers have met the same sorry fate."

"It ain't that . . . The officer had three brothers who were kilt on top of that same horse at different times!"

This caused me and Joe to look up, and our eyes got wide.

"I don't know if'n I can believe such a thing," Joe said. "Who told you that?"

"A reliable feller from Texas," said Roy.

"Texas fellers are the most notorious liars in the world," groused Joe, stabbin' a stick into the fire. Sparks and flame flew.

"Well," I said. "Did they shoot the horse?"

Roy looked over at me. "Why would they shoot the horse?"

"'Cause it was bad luck," I answered.

Winter dragged on, and we had a few skirmishes with the Yankees. It seemed that this new General Grant was not goin' to let up on us just because of the bad weather.

In early spring, us Texas boys volunteered for a detail to accompany three wagonloads of rifles up to the Virginia Military Academy. The guns had been recovered from the Chikamauga battlefield, and were to be used to arm those VMI schoolboy cadets. We were all glad to be sittin' astride a horse once again, and took off in good spirits along with thirteen more volunteers and the creaking wagons.

Our trip was fairly cold for the most part, but we made it into Virginia without incident. When we turned the guns over to the commander of the school boys, he was mighty happy to get 'em.

Just as our detail was about to leave and head back for Georgia, we were pressed into the service of General John C. Breckinridge. There was one hell of a battle takin' place in the Shenandoah Valley between over four thousand Rebs and over six thousand Yankees. Breckenridge was raisin' as many men as he could, and he grabbed us, along with two hundred cadets from the Virginia Military Institute.

I don't know how proper it was for us to be grabbed up for a fight, but we did it anyhow, joining the bright and shiny cadets as they marched out toward the fight.

Them boys were dressed real fine, and all of their uniforms were exactly the same. They all had on the same type of hat, and were armed with Yankee rifles. I don't think that one of them schoolboys were over eighteen years of age, and I suspect that some of 'em were as young as fourteen.

A lot of the boys were left behind at the academy cause they were too young to wage war. Those youngsters were madder'n hell, wantin' to go along with us and kill Yankees. Roy grinned and called 'em milksops.

It made our havin' been pressed into battle a little easier, for we got to keep our horses, and were assigned two nice .44 caliber Walker Colt revolvers, along with a short rifle. To top this off, each one us were issued a saber and scabbard.

This would be our first opportunity to play at cavalry, somethin' that all of us had longed for. I was a fair horseman, but it looked to me that Roy and Joe had been born in the saddle. We all wondered how our horses would react to battle.

On Sunday, May 15, 1864, we would find out.

Our contingent of schoolboys, eager soldiers, and not-so-eager soldiers reached the battlefield at a place called New Market, Virginia.

The sounds of a skirmish was in our ears, as the schoolboys were put into battle lines. Many of 'em had gray faces, but not a single one tried to get out of this situation.

Us temporary cavalrymen were lined up behind the ranks of cadets, and we were to support the schoolboys if and when we were called upon to do so.

Those cadets were shore a fine sight, and they had the best drummer boys I had ever heard. They carried the flags of Virginia, the Institute, and the Confederate States of America, and they were a thing of beauty, standin' against the dark sky. On the order, we marched out onto the field, bein' led by the boys' commander, Lieutenant Colonel Scott Shipp. He was not a boy, but was twenty-four years old.

General Breckenridge galloped by, wavin' his hat in the air and cheerin' the schoolboys into battle.

One young feller was heard to say that the general looks 'like the Cyd.'

Drums were rollin', and them boys were marchin' in step better than any regiment I'd ever seen. It was a fine sight. Four schoolboys who had been left behind to guard the baggage, deserted their posts, and came runnin' up from the rear, joinin' the long battle line with their young comrades.

"How about these milksops, Frank?" yelled Roy. "Ain't they a sight to behold?"

The drumbeat seemed to grow louder, as the cadets passed by an artillery battery of Rebs. Some of the young soldiers manning the batteries recognized friends among the cadets as they marched past, and called out jibes.

"Here come the wagon dogs! Ho, bombproofs. Get out of them good clothes!"

Some of the cadets wanted to break out of their ranks and settle with their fellow Rebs on the spot, but they were stopped and herded on toward the awaitin' Yanks.

A black cloud loomed overhead, as the cadets of the Virginia Military joined the center of the Confederate battle line. To the history-conscious students, the center of a battle line meant only one thing. The place of honor.

Cresting a hill, the cadets passed one of their own batteries, already in action and engaged. Marching down the slope, the boy soldiers could hear the musket and cannon fire from the Yankee position. An artillery shell burst over their heads and five cadets fell to the ground.

"Close up men!" yelled Sergeant Cabell.

The line of cadets reached a ravine, and were within three hundred yards of the six heavy guns of the Thirtieth New York. The ravine offered good cover and shelter from the deadly cannons. Cedars, rocks, stumps, and scrubs filled the ravine. The advancing line slowed, but reappeared on the far side, with the cadets coming out before the older veterans of the Sixty-second Virginia.

Once, the cadets were forced to stop under heavy fire to straighten their lines. Then, the colorful march commenced again. A house split their lines, and the companies passed by on either side, restoring their lines on the other side.

Colonel Shipp stopped the line. "Fix bayonets!" he yelled. At that very moment, Shipp was struck and killed by a shell fragment, and several cadets were wounded. The line lay down. Someone yelled out an order to fall back, but another cadet rose and swore that he would shoot the first man who moved backward.

Captain Henry Wise rose to his feet and shouted out a charge on the guns. The cadets rose as one, and charged the batteries, still in near-perfect order.

Yankee gunners had changed from shrapnel to canister and then to double canisters. The air was filled with deadly iron missiles, but still the cadets came, never stopping and never faltering. Miraculously, the students found themselves among the Federal gunners, and they did their murderous work with rifle fire and bayonets.

Cheers arose when the flag of the Virginia Military Institute was hoisted on the hill among the Yankee guns. A rainstorm hailed the victory, but failed to drown out the cheers from the battlefield.*

## TOTAL WAR
### SUMMER OF 1864

As for us Texas boys, we were in a good position to bear witness to this grand charge. We dang near forgot that we were a part of the battle, for the fascination of the sight was such.

However, our captain yelled for us to charge also, at the same time the schoolboys did. By the time we got to the top of the hill, it was already in the hands of the cadets.

---

*Eight VMI cadets were killed, and forty-four were wounded in the New Market charge. Of the four disobedient baggage guards who had deserted their posts, one was killed, and two wounded.

An impressive ceremony still commemorates this battle every May 15th on the Lexington campus of the Virginia Military Institute. At roll call, selected students snap out their replies as the casualties of New Market are called. "Dead on the field of honor, sir," is the response to the roll call of the dead.

We did chase down some Yankees who were runnin' from the hill, and Joe Buck kilt one with his Walker Colt. Roy lost his horse, when it was kilt by a Yankee minie ball. Three of the fellow Rebs who had rode up here with us deliverin' the guns were also kilt and two more were wounded.

We left the Virginia Military Academy with a wave of our hats, leading two extra horses, but minus five men. Roy was worried what our sergeant was gonna to have to say when we got back to Georgia, but General Breckinridge gave us a signed letter praisin' our fightin' spirit, and sayin' that the losses were on his own orders.

Roy did not refer to the cadets as milksops no more.

When we finally rejoined our division, the news was not good. General J. E. B. Stuart had been kilt on May 11, at Yellow Tavern, which was just north of Richmond. To top that off, General Longstreet himself had been wounded by a volley from his own troops at dang near the same spot where Stonewall Jackson had suffered the same fate.

Longstreet's corps were now under the command of General Richard H. Anderson, and we did not know anything about him.

General Grant was keepin' up the pressure, and Roy said that he was worse than a dang bulldog. Our supply situation was terrible, and we were often reduced to only a single biscuit or a sweet potato for our dinner. Many a rat took his place on the dinner menu, and was said to have a fair taste, unless you were the poor soul who had been forced to skin him.

What was left of us Texas boys declared that we would not stoop to eatin' such a thing as a goddamn rat, but the day came when we joined in on this sorry meal ourselves.

We all screwed up our faces and took a little bite. My own thought was that I was going to puke it back out, but when Roy declared that it did not taste too bad, I finished my rodent like it was a Christmas ham. I would have ate another, but there was no more left at the time.

There was a new song out that was popular with the troops, even though the officers were dead set against it. Roy Grubbs was real good at playin' it on a fiddle as other sad Rebs sang out the chorus.

Hard times, hard times,
Come again no more,
Though we seek mirth and beauty,
And music light and gay,
There are pale forms slinking at the door.

Though their voices are silent,
Their pleading eyes implore,
Oh hard times, hard times,
Come again no more.

'Tis the song, the sighs of the weary,
Hard times, hard times,
Come again no more,
Many days you have lingered,
Outside my cabin door,
Oh hard times, hard times,
Come again no more.

At the start of this war, you would every so often see a fat Rebel soldier. That was no longer the case, as we all looked the same. Like raggedy scarecrows. Many of the boys looked and smelled like they had not had a bath in weeks, their hair was long and their clothes smelled to high heaven. Many a Reb looked like a skeleton with skin stretched over it.

Us Texas boys were lucky enough to have boots, even though some of 'em had been stolen off'n cadavers, and now had holes in the bottoms. A good many soldiers of the Confederacy would have liked to own our well-worn footgear, for they were barefoot, and their dirty feet often left bloody tracks.

No longer were the fresh recruits showin' up in enough numbers to make up for our losses. Our army was gettin' smaller and smaller, not only in girth, but also in numbers.

Another thing that affected our army was the fact that a good many of the fellers were down with diseases which were brought on from their dallyin' with whores. As for me, I had not dallied since my tryst with ole Granny, and maybe that was for the best, judgin' from the looks of some of our boys.

## PETERSBURG
### JULY OF 1864

In early June, our corps was sent north to help out in the defense of Richmond, the Confederate capital. Richmond was now a very well-fortified city, sporting over ten miles of trench works.

Petersburg, Virginia, was a railhead, and was the source of supplies for Richmond, and that is where Anderson's corps were sent, for it was rumored that General Grant was bound to attack this city first, and cut that supply line

Our division arrived in Petersburg in the nick of time, as General Beauregard's men were just about obliged to surrender to the Federals. We fought back, even as more and more Confederate soldiers arrived, and the city was saved.

The King of Spades would have been right proud of us, because we were diggin' holes just as fast as we could dig 'em.

At the very same time, the Yankees were also diggin' in and the long siege of Petersburg was on. The Federals would lob cannon shots into our lines and we would duck. Then, we did exactly the same thing to them.

One curious thing happened in July. The Yankees had gotten a regiment of Pennsylvania miners to dig a five-hundred-foot tunnel under the ground, to our positions. Then, they touched off eight thousand pounds of explosives, blowin' a huge crater among our boys and, killin' a number of Rebs and renderin' a good many deaf.

Once we regained our wits, a good many Reb soldiers, includin' us Texas boys were ordered up to the rim of the crater. Yankee soldiers, includin' somethin' that I had heard of, but had never seen yet, came pourin' into the crater through the tunnel. *Black* Yankee soldiers were amongst us, but they were havin' a hard time crawlin' out of that crater due to the steep walls. We just laid down and poured volley after volley of scalding and scorching fire into them poor fellers. We shot until our rifle barrels were sizzlin', and there was not a single Yankee movin'.

The Yankees who were able, fled from the tunnel and later on, our boys blew it up. Then, we set to work coverin' up them dead Yankee soldiers, black and white together, in a common grave.

Time wore on and the summer went by, as we tried to hold the Yanks off from their move to take Petersburg. We sometimes called a ceasefire, and soldiers on both sides traded news, coffee, and tobacco. At first, this made the officers mighty unhappy, but they were soon in on the informal fraternizin' with the enemy themselves.

Fall came, then winter, and the only thing that helped to liven things up was a cattle-stealing raid by some of our boys. They were successful, and for a spell, beef replaced rats as our main course.

By spring, we were nearly starved to death, but the siege still continued. General Lee decided to break out of here, and to try to hook up with General Johnston's army in North Carolina.

"I'll be mighty happy to get out of this dreary place," said Joe Buck. "I hope we get back to Tennessee, so we can sneak away and get some of Frank's ma's home cookin'."

"I'd like to get back to Tennessee myself," I said. "But I don't really care where it is. I just want to be somewhere where a feller can raid a garden, and walk around after dark without steppin' in shit."

General John B. Gordon struck into the Yankees' rear ranks as we made our getaway. It was April 1, 1865, and we had to fight nearly every step of the way. We started out with fifty-five thousand hungry, raggedy men, pursued by the bulldog General Ulysses S. Grant and one hundred twenty-five thousand well-equipped Federal troops.

General A.P. Hill was killed at Poplar Springs, and General Lee had tears in his eyes. Eyes that were no longer blazin'. Our retreat was blocked at Amelia Courthouse by Sheridan's cavalry, and we turned west, cuttin' across country. We turned to fight at Sailor's Creek, and were down to twenty thousand men. By the time our lines crumbled, we were down to thirteen thousand starved, wounded and exhausted men.

## Appomattox

We pushed on towards a place called Appomattox Courthouse, our trail strewn with the dead and wounded soldiers of the Confederacy, and with men who were just too tired to take another step. It was there we found our way blocked by Sheridan's cavalry once again, along with two corps of Yankee infantry.

I think General Lee knew that the game was over, and he met with his staff. We heard that some were suggestin' the army disperse and continue irregular warfare from camps in the mountains, but the sad General Robert E. Lee only shook his head.

"There is nothing left for me to do but to go and see General Grant, and I would rather die a thousand deaths," he said.

The white flag was lifted, and a meeting was set for Generals Lee and Grant to get together at a place belonging to a Wilbur McLean in the village of Appomattox Courthouse.

It was April 9, 1865.

We stood along the dusty road to the McLean house under a ceasefire. Yankees were ridin' in by the hundreds and finally by the thousands. This was our closest look at a Yankee in four years, without which we were tryin' to kill one another, and I reckon the same could be said for them.

"Will you just look at them fellers?" said Roy, noddin' toward the Federal troops. "They mostly look well fed, and everybody has on a matchin' uniform with boots. I'm mortified dang near to tears over the appearance that we must present."

At that exact same time, a bearded Yankee on a big red horse cantered by. He looked down at us Texas boys and laughed.

"What the hell is so amusin', you blue-bellied son of a bitch?" hollered Roy, movin' his hand to the handle of his Walker Colt.

"Easy Roy," said our sergeant. "Just let it go."

Roy's chin dropped, and he slowly removed his hand from his .44 as the Yankee rode on down the road, still laughin' at us sorry-assed Rebs.

We set up a vigil alongside of the road, and it was a few hours before we saw what we were lookin' for. General Robert E. Lee came ridin' down the road on his gray horse, lookin' real fine in his dress uniform. The horse was prancin' kind of sideways, and seemed to be proud of all the attention which was bein' rained down on him.

Tears were in my eyes as the general rode past where I was standin', for I knew what was in store. To my surprise, the general looked right at me, reached up and tipped his hat. "Hello, Frank," he said. "How is your mother?"

I was dumbstruck to think that he would remember my name, but I was finally able to blurt out, "She's still alive as far as I know, Sir."

"I'm glad to hear that son," said the general over his shoulder. After that, he was gone.

We stood our ground, along with some other boys from our division. About a half-hour later, General Ulysses S. Grant came riding by with some more officers. He sat comfortably in the saddle, wearin' a wrinkled uniform and dirty boots. I reckoned that this feller looked more like a dirt farmer than the bulldog general who had run our army into the ground. General Grant looked at me and Roy as he rode by, and I'll be danged if he didn't seem to wink at Roy.

"Did you see that, Frank?" he asked.

"I ain't sure," was my reply.

"I'll be hanged," said Roy, removing his battered hat and watching General Grant's black horse's ass sway down the road toward McLean house.

Two more hours of waiting, and it was over . . .

General Lee rode back down the road with a blank look on his face, and his back was not quite so rigid. We knew that the Army of the Confederacy was beaten. The only question that we had now, was whether we would be hung, shot, or put in a prison.

One thing that surprised me was that a good many of the Yankee soldiers linin' the road, removed their hats when General Lee rode by. A few of 'em said hello to the general, and not a single Yank had a harsh word to say.

One gaunt, ragged Reb soldier ran out into the road and removed his hat. "Are we surrendered, Sir?" he asked. General Lee did not answer, but his shoulders seemed to droop at the bold question.

Returning to camp, we waited with the color-bearers while all officers met with General Lee. Then the general came forward and we gathered around him.

"Men," he said. "We have fought through the war together. I have done the best I could for you. My heart is too full to say more."

A groan escaped, along with a few curses directed at the Yankees.

"What's gonna happen to us now, General?" came a voice from the rear.

"The Union army is are going to supply us with rations. However, the war is over and you are all free to go home whenever you wish, once you sign a form promising not to bear arms against the Union in the future. You must leave your rifles behind, but anyone who owns his own sidearms or horse will be allowed to take them home with you."

"What if we don't see fit to sign no form, Sir?" came the voice of a ragged one-armed soldier, who stepped out of the ranks.

"Then you are a prisoner of war."

I heard some whimperin' and sobbin' goin' on around me, and was mortified to see brave men cryin'. Then it struck me that my eyes were moist also.

The color-bearer stepped forward with the tattered old battle flag of our regiment. It was the same flag that had suffered through Manassas, Shiloh, Antietam, Gettysburg, Lookout Mountain, Petersburg, and a number of places in between. With tears in his eyes, the soldier commenced to roll the flag around the wooden pole. Another soldier brought forward a leather tube, and the ragged old flag was slid into the tube for the last time. It thumped when it hit bottom.

That was the last straw. Roy, Joe, me, and everybody who had witnessed this sad scene began weeping. Not so much for ourselves, but for all of the comrades that we had lost and for all of the misery that we had seen.

It was over. What had begun with an idea of a great adventure and a holy crusade had become a nightmare of death, pain, and destruction.

## THE AGONY OF A FORMAL SURRENDER

On April 10, General Robert E. Lee gave his decorous and moving farewell address to his men.

*"After four years of arduous service, marked by unsurpassed courage and fortitude, the Army of Northern Virginia has been compelled to yield to overwhelming numbers and resources.*

*"I need not tell the brave survivors of so many hard fought battles, who have remained steadfast to the last, that I have consented to this result from no distrust of them.*

*"But feeling that valor and devotion could accomplish nothing that could compensate for the loss that must have attended the continuance of contest, I determined to avoid the useless sacrifice of those whose past services have endeared them to their countrymen.*

*"By the terms of this agreement, officers and men can return to their homes. You will take with you the satisfaction that proceeds from the consciousness of duty faithfully performed, and I earnestly pray that a Merciful God will extend you His blessing and protection.*

*"With an increasing admiration of your constancy and devotion to your country, and a grateful remembrance of your kind and a generous consideration for myself, I bid you all an affectionate farewell."*

After this, only one thing remained to be done. A formal surrender, ordered by General Grant. Something that would remain burned into the Confederate memories forever.

April 12, 1865, loomed cold and gray, as the Army of Northern Virginia acquiesced to all of the demands which had been made by the six-man Federal Commission for the surrender.

Long lines of blue-clad Federal troops stood aligned and at attention on both sides of the road. There was no music, only the shuffling sounds of thousands of Confederate feet as they marched with that old swinging route step, battle flags swaying.

The sun broke through and glinted off muskets carried on the right shoulders of the gray-clad soldiers. On and on they came, ragged, starved images of their former selves. Proud, unbroken, but finally beaten.

General John Gordon led the long gray columns, followed what was left of the Stonewall Brigade, now reduced to barely two hundred men.

Crimson battle flags were so thick that the whole column seemed to be covered with a red cloud.

A Yankee bugle blew, and the Rebel soldiers were startled by the clattering sound of every Yankee raising their muskets onto their shoulders at the command of 'Shoulder arms!'

General Gordon turned in his saddle, shouted a command, and the advancing Confederates returned the salute of the Union troops by shifting their own guns from a right shoulder shift to shoulder arms.

Salute answering salute.

Soldier to soldier.

American to American.

Battle-hardened, war-weary veterans on both sides wept like girls, blinded by their tears. Not a sound was made, and a blanket of stillness fell over the soldiers of the North, as they held their breath. It was as if they were watching the passing of a ghost regiment.

At the end of the Confederate soldiers' march of agony, they stopped and turned towards Brigadier General Joshua Chamberlain's battle-hardened Twentieth Maine. The gray-clad soldiers of the former Army of Northern Virginia stacked and surrendered their muskets and cartridge belts, along with the battle-worn, blood-stained, torn, and bullet-riddled battle flags of the Confederate States of America.

## THE JOURNEY HOME
### APRIL OF 1865

Me, Joe, and Roy hung around Appomattox for two more days. Just long enough to see General Lee and his staff say their good-byes to the shattered remnants of a once-proud army, and to get six good meals. We also received parole passes from the Yankees, which we would be able to show as proof that we had served honorably and that we was now surrendered.

As to the surrender of our battle flags, we were proud to know a secret. The Yankees had not gotten our own regimental flag, for me, Roy, Frank, and some other boys had burned and buried it. We were not alone in this, for many other Rebel flags met the same fate rather than end up in Yankee hands.

I don't know where they was comin' from, but our army was growin' bigger and bigger, as stragglers, deserters, and wounded Rebs kept driftin' into camp. Most of 'em were comin' in to get some food, and their written parole passes which they would need to travel safely home.

We said many a tearful farewell to old comrades, and lit out in the early morning of April 13, headed for home, along with hundreds of others.

Ragged men were scattered along the roads, singly or in groups, some headed out across the hills, each with his own meager little sack of belongings, his parole pass tucked safely in a pocket.

Four days later, we received the strange and terrible news that President Abraham Lincoln had been shot down in a theater up North. Word was that it was a Southern sympathizer by name of John Wilkes Booth who had done the foul deed. We all wondered how the Yankees would settle this score, and reckoned that there was a good chance that they would most likely take it out on us somehow.

We finally made it to a railhead and commenced hoppin' trains, finally ending up in Atlanta, Georgia.

Dark clouds covered the sun, and spoke of rain, as a train commenced to pull out for Tennessee.

This would be my train, and it pained me deeply to say good-bye to Joe Buck and Roy Grubbs.

"Well pardner," said Roy. "I reckon we seen the elephant, shore enough, but here is where we part company, unless you see fit to come with us to Texas."

"What would I do in Texas, Roy?" I asked, amused that they would think of such a thing.

"Shoot Injuns, herd cattle, kill buffalo, dodge snakes, and have a drink with me in the Hondo Saloon," laughed Roy.

"Why don't you come along?" asked Joe Buck. "You could work on our spread for wages if you want. I know that my pa can use an extra hand, and Ma would feed you until you got as fat as a New York banker."

"Thanks for the invite, boys, and I may take you up on it one day. Right now though, I aim to head back to the mountain and see if my gal has married up with the Yankee

Beecher Goff. If she ain't, I just might beg for her forgiveness, and we'll walk on down to the spring," I said.

"Watch out for that big goddamn snake," laughed Joe Buck.

We shook hands all around, but Roy Grubbs said that would not do after what we had been through. I was mortified when he threw his arms around my neck and gave me a big hug. Now ole Joe Buck was usually a purty unemotional feller, but I'll be danged if'n he didn't do the same thing.

I jumped aboard the train that was bound for Chattanooga, and watched my two friends grow smaller and smaller as they waved their hats good-bye.

When I got to Chattanooga, I did not waste any time in lookin' over the destruction that this beautiful town had suffered, but walked out of the city, headin' for the crossin' point on the river.

One-Eyed Wash was no longer runnin' the ferry, for he was dead, and it was bein' run by Yankee soldiers. There were three of 'em who went across the river with me, and other than me havin' to show my pass, we did not say a word to each other. They looked at me and I looked at them. Whether they felt pity, hatred, or contempt, I do not know, and did not bother to ask.

I walked through the familiar countryside of the Tennessee hills, resting very little. My steps grew quicker and quicker, and I did not pause nor linger in Dayton. There were no wagon rides this time, and the sole on my left boot was flappin' like a duck's bill as I double-timed it up Walden's Mountain. I passed the Morgan graveyard, and paused to pay a respect to my pa. Then, I said a prayer and a thanks to the Almighty for lettin' me live through this terrible war.

Striking out on the road once again, my mind began to race, and I thought about Jodie Pickett, One-Eyed Wash, Sash-a-baw, Owen, and all of the others who would not be comin' home. I passed the Rivers' home, and thought about stoppin' and givin' Alberta a big hug, but I dispelled that idea due to the fact that I smelled so bad.

A sadness settled over me when I passed the Horton home, realizin' that I would never walk this mountain with Owen ever again. I quickened my pace and began to trot, placin' a great stress on my flappin' sole.

A muffled bark greeted me, as my old dog Myrt walked stiffly out to the road and warned me off of the Morgan property. When I reached down to pet her, I dang near got bit, for she did not recognize me at first. When she heard my voice, Myrt came to her senses and commenced twirlin' around and around in a circle, but not nearly as fast as she once did.

No one came out to greet me, and I burst in the front door, nearly scarin' the life out of Ma, Ellie, Billie, and Marilee. They did not recognize me any more than my dog had, and I reckon they figured me to be a robber or a barn burner.

"Dang," I said. "What kind of a greetin' is this for a son of the Old South?"

Everybody screamed at once, and jumped all over me, cryin', huggin', and kissin' on me, until they got a good whiff of what I smelled like.

The back door opened, and I reckon that I must have changed colors, for through that door strolled a smilin' ghost.

The ghost of Owen Horton was missin' his left arm, but grinnin' from ear to ear in spite of his condition.

"Frank!" hollered the ghost. "We've gave up on you and thought that you were dead."

He ran across the kitchen in my direction.

I backed up and stammered. "You're the one who's dead, Owen, not me!"

"No," said Owen."I ain't dead. Here, touch me!"

"Stay away from me!" I said. "I ain't aimin' to touch no dang ghost."

Owen started laughin' so hard he was barely able to catch his breath. He plopped down in a wooden chair. "I reckon it's a fact that the last time you laid eyes on me, I probably looked dead. The last thing I remember, was you pickin' me up off'n the Gettysburg battlefield, even though I told you I did not want to be moved. I woke up in a danged Yankee hospital, no less, with wounded Yanks and Rebs all around me. Them Yankee doctors cut enough slugs out of me to fill a milk pail, but I fooled 'em and survived all of their butchery. They cut off my arm just to spite me and sent me packin' home just as soon as I was able. Dang, Frank, didn't you ever get your mail?"

"Not for quite a spell," I said, now sittin' down myself.

"Can you folks excuse me and Frank, for just a bit, while we go outside and talk?" asked Owen

Everyone protested, but finally gave in when the one-armed feller presented such a sad face.

Owen and I walked over to the other side of the road, followed by my old dog Myrt, who was lookin' up at me with a happy look on her face. We stopped, and both of us looked down at the spring.

"Frank," said Owen. "You've got to make me a promise."

"What kind of a promise?"

Owen put his only arm around my shoulder and moved closer to me. I knew that this was goin' to be important.

"I want you to promise that you never, never, never tell Ellie or anyone else about them whores that we dallied with. No matter how mad you ever get at me. You must promise not to tell."

This struck me as funny, and I started to laugh. "Hell," I said. "As I recall, you didn't do anything to the whores anyhow."

"Goddamn you Frank. If I was not a cripple, I'd box your ears right now."

"Hold off there, Mr. Cripple," I laughed. "If it's so important to you, I swear on my mother's eyes that I will not tell of any whores dallyin' with the likes of Owen Horton."

"Good!" he said. "Now, I've got a good idea for us!"

For some unknown reason, this caused ole Myrt to let out with a bark.

"Owen!" I cried, lookin' down at that crazy dog, who seemed to know what we were talkin' about. "The last time I went along with your good idea, I ended up in a terrible war for four years, and damn near got myself kilt!"

"No, it ain't got nothin' to do with war," laughed Owen, as he looked at the darkening skies, with a reddish-gold sun setting across the ridge.

"What is it then?"

"Let's go on a bear hunt tomorrow. It'll do you good to get out in them hills again."

Those nonsensical words had no more than escaped Owen's mouth, when lightnin' flashed across the sky, and thunder rolled across the heavens like cannon fire.

Me and Owen ducked our heads out of instinct, and this scared Myrt, who tried to take a bite out of Owen.

At that very point in my life, I knew that there was a God, and that Myrt had more sense than Owen Horton.

The end

About the Author. . .

*Southern Thunder* is Ron Morgan's second novel. His first novel was *HORNS, A Story of the Old West.* A fan of the Old West and the Civil War, Morgan is currently writing *After the Storm,* a sequel to *Southern Thunder.*

Morgan is a retired police lieutenant. He lives in Holly, Michigan, with his wife Mary Ann and children, Ron Jr., Barbara, and Kathleen.